40-

W9-BGJ-595

The Man Who Shot Lewis Vance

Other Toby Peters mysteries not to be missed

Down for the Count
The Fala Factor
He Done Her Wrong
Catch a Falling Clown
High Midnight
Never Cross a Vampire
The Howard Hughes Affair
You Bet Your Life
Murder on the Yellow Brick Road
Bullet for a Star

Also by the author

Exercise in Terror
When the Dark Man Calls
Coop: The Life and Legend of Gary Cooper

The Man Who Shot Lewis Vance

A TOBY PETERS MYSTERY

Stuart M. Kaminsky

ST. MARTIN'S PRESS • NEW YORK

THE MAN WHO SHOT LEWIS VANCE. Copyright © 1986 by Stuart M. Kaminsky. All rights reserved. Printed in the United States of America. No part of this book may be used or reproduced in any manner whatsoever without written permission except in the case of brief quotations embodied in critical articles or reviews. For information, address St. Martin's Press, 175 Fifth Avenue, New York, N.Y. 10010.

Library of Congress Cataloging-in-Publication Data

Kaminsky, Stuart M.
The man who shot Lewis Vance.

I. Title.
PS3561.A43M3 1986 813′.54 85–25168
ISBN 0-312-51394-1

First Edition

10 9 8 7 6 5 4 3 2 1

To Joe, Carol, Scott, and Carter Schoenberg

"Pilgrim, forget what I said about buyin' a gun. You're a tenderfoot and Liberty Valance is the toughest man east or west of the Picketwire River. . . . Next to me that is."

—Tom Doniphan in *The Man Who Shot Liberty Valance*

The Man Who Shot Lewis Vance

1

When I opened my eyes, I saw John Wayne pointing a .38 at my chest. It was my .38. I closed my eyes.

The inside of my head seemed to be filled with strawberry cotton candy with little unnamed things crawling through its sickly melting strands. Nausea forced my eyes open again. John Wayne was still there. He was wearing trousers, a white shirt, and a lightweight tan windbreaker. He was lean, dark, and puzzled.

"Don't close your eyes again, Pilgrim," he said.

I didn't close them. He was standing over me and I was slumped in a badly sprung, cheap, understuffed hotel chair. I tried to sit up and speak but my tongue was an inflated, dry pebbly football. There was a flat half-full glass of brown Pepsi on the stained yellow table in front of me, but I didn't reach for it. That glass, and what had been in it, had put me out.

I wasn't sure of the day or the time. When I took those last few gulps of Pepsi, it had been a Sunday night in June of 1942. I had been sitting in a cheap Los Angeles hotel room with a guy who had identified himself as Lewis Vance.

Lewis Vance had left a message for me at my office, but I had been out of town filling in for a gate guard at an old people's home in Goleta. It had netted me $20 minus gas. The message on my desk, left in the uncertain hand of Sheldon Minck, the dentist I rent space from, had said I should call Lewis Vance in Room 303 of the Alhambra Arms over on

Broadway, that it had something to do with John Wayne, the actor. I'd called and Vance had told me to come right over. I didn't even have to drive. My office was on Hoover a few blocks away and I ambled over knowing I needed a shave and worrying about what was happening to the U.S. fleet off the island of Midway while I was in Goleta.

My gray seersucker was crumpled but reasonably clean—if you ignored the remnants of mustard stain on the sleeve. It was the best suit I had. The sky threatened rain but no one on the street seemed concerned. Soldiers, sailors, overly painted women laughing too hard to make a buck, and sour-faced visitors flowed with me. Before the war, tourists had been thick on Broadway on a Sunday, but tourists had stopped making their way to Los Angeles after the first threats of an invasion by the Japanese. Now Broadway was kids in uniform, waiting women, and girls and people who couldn't afford to or were too stubborn to leave. I was one of the latter.

Vance had said he had a job for me. Since I am a private investigator, I assumed it had something to do with my profession. At forty-eight with a bad back, pushed-in nose, and black graying hair, I was a reasonably formidable sight as a body guard. If I had been over five-nine, I'd probably have been busy nine or ten months a year with celebrities who wanted to show they could afford protection they usually didn't need. But there were plenty of muscle builders from the beaches—Santa Monica, Venice—who could be bought cheap and looked bigger and meaner than I did. They weren't meaner, but they were fine for show—as almost everything is in Los Angeles.

The people who hired me usually got my name from someone who had used me in the past. All they really wanted was protection or a grandmother found or a stern word or two to a former friend who owed them a few hundred bucks. Vance hadn't said what he wanted me for.

The lobby of the Alhambra Arms was wilting badly, had been since long before the war. There were four big wooden pots in the lobby that had once held small palm trees. The palms had sagged to the floor years before, and now the chipped green pots were used as ashtrays and garbage bins. It didn't look too bad because you couldn't see much of anything in the Alhambra lobby. There was a strict policy of not replacing light bulbs as they died. The ceiling was a cemetery of darkened bulbs with a few dusty die-hards still glowing away. Considering the way I looked, I didn't mind the shadows of the Alhambra. I had filled in as hotel detective here twice in the last two years, both times on weekends. There had been no detecting involved, no thefts. The job was to keep the uniformed kids and un-uniformed prostitutes from destroying the place and each other. It had kept me busy. The last time I had held down the duty, I had done almost as much damage to the Allies as the Japanese fleet. Two sailors in diapers had taken umbrage at my telling them to refrain from destroying the lobby. Had they been sober I might have had a problem. They walked away from our discussion with a concussion, broken thumb, badly lacerated thigh, and a black eye. The damage had been divided rather evenly between them.

The guy behind the desk when I walked into the Alhambra lobby on Sunday was named Theodore Longretti, better known on the streets as Teddy Spaghetti. Teddy was about fifty, long, lean, and fairly yellow from whatever it was cheap hotel clerks put into themselves to make the world think they are awake and relatively sane. Teddy's once white hair was even turning yellow again—not the yellow it might have been when and if he had been a kid, but the yellow of white yarn dipped in cheap bourbon.

"Teddy," I said, walking across the empty morning lobby

and listening to my shoes clap the worn linoleum made to look like Spanish tiles.

"Toby?" he said, squinting through the darkness in my direction.

A desk lamp stood on the counter next to Teddy. Light bounced off the counter, making the welcoming clerk look like the skeleton of Woodrow Wilson.

"You've got a Lewis Vance, three-oh-three?" I said, coming near the desk but not too close. A little of Teddy Spaghetti can go a long way. Besides, he thought we were buddies.

"I've got a Lewis Vance," he admitted, looking down at his open book, "and a half-dozen Browns, a sprinkling of Andersons, a Kelly or two, but no Smiths. It's a fallacy that people use the name 'Smith' when they go to a hotel. You know what I mean?"

"I know," I said.

"Even people named Smith avoid saying they're Smith. It looks too suspicious," Teddy said seriously, finally looking up from his book. "So what can I do for you?"

"Vance look kosher?"

Teddy shrugged, his yellow face moving into a thoughtful pout. "Never seen him before. Looks like a straight arrow," he said. "But I ask you, if he's so straight, what's he checking in here for?" Teddy looked around, into the dark corners, past the chipped green former palm holders. I had to admit he had a point.

"Thanks," I said, and headed for the stairway.

"No trouble, Toby," he stage-whispered. "I see you're packing heat. I'm in for two shifts and I don't want to identify the remains of former guests. You know what I mean?"

I patted the holster under my seersucker jacket and winked at Teddy, though I doubted if he could see me.

"I know what you mean," I said, and I jogged up the stairs.

The holster thumped against my chest as I went up and my back told me not to be so athletic. I slowed down and followed the trail of dimly lit landings to the third floor. Room 303 was next to a room where what sounded like a child soprano was singing "Praise the Lord and Pass the Ammunition," with frequent stops for giggling. I knocked on the door of 303, adjusted my jacket, ran a hand through my hair, and tried to look as if I wasn't afraid of anything less than a Panzer attack.

The guy who opened the door looked familiar; at least his outline did against the back light. He was tall, with good shoulders, a full-size nose, and a good head of dark hair.

"Peters?" he said.

"Right," I answered. He opened the door and I walked in.

When I turned to face him, he didn't look quite so much like John Wayne as I had thought, but the resemblance was there.

Vance had a glass of amber liquid in his hand. He was wearing a weary smile and a lightweight brown suit with a white shirt and no tie. It wasn't Beverly Hills but it beat what I was wearing and he was the prospective client.

"How about a drink?" he said, holding up the glass.

"Nothing hard," I said, looking around the small room, seeing nothing but shabby furniture, an open unmade bed, and a dirty window.

"Coke?" he asked.

"Pepsi if you've got it," I answered, sinking into the worn chair next to the splintery yellow coffee table.

"I've got it," he said, moving to the dresser, where a group of bottles huddled together. One, indeed, was a Pepsi. "Even got some ice."

His back was to me as he poured and started to talk. He kept talking as he turned and handed me the glass.

"Job is simple," he said. "I'm John Wayne's stand-in. Maybe you can see the resemblance."

"I can see it," I said.

"I'm doing Duke a little favor here," he went on, swirling his glass and sitting across from me on a wooden chair pulled away from the spindly-legged desk in the corner. "He owes some people and they want to collect. Words out that the Duke was registered at a downtown hotel as Lewis Vance. Meanwhile, the Duke is out calling in some loans to pay these guys off. My job—our job—is to keep them busy and away from Duke till he collects and pays them off. Don't worry about your money. We're talking big bills here. He can pay you with pocket money. No offense."

"None taken," I said, picking up the Pepsi. I wasn't offended by the money insult. It was true. It was the story that offended me. It had more holes than the U.S. Navy ships in Pearl Harbor. There were lots of possibilities here, I thought, as I took a sip of Pepsi. First, the story was true and John Wayne was doing one of the most stupid things imaginable. Second, Lewis Vance, who sat across from me watching for a reaction through dancing brown eyes, was a first-class nut who had thought this up for ends I couldn't imagine. Three, I was being set up for something, though I couldn't begin to figure what that something might be. I took a deep drink of the slightly bitter Pepsi and pretended to weigh the offer. What I really wanted to do was get the hell out of the room before I found out what was going on.

I took another sip of the Pepsi, put the glass down, and stood up. Vance was bigger than me, younger too, but I was used to getting past people or keeping them from getting past me. He didn't look as if he had too much experience with either. I didn't see anything on him that looked like a gun bulge.

"I think I'll pass on this one, Mr. Vance," I said.

He stood up quickly, not losing his grip on his glass.

"Wait," he said with real panic. "I can pay whatever your fee is. Duke authorized me to pay. Cash. Just one day's work. He'll really be grateful."

"Sorry," I said. "Truth is, Mr. Vance, you don't smell right to me."

Something went dull inside my head and should have been a warning, but I've taken so many blows over the years that I tend to regard occasional aches, pains, and ringing bells as natural.

"I'll prove it," Vance said, holding out his free hand to get me to wait. "We'll call Duke. He'll tell you."

Maybe John Wayne had gone mush-headed. My head certainly wasn't feeling too good. Maybe the forty-eight hours straight in Goleta and the drive back were getting to me.

"Make the call," I said. Hell, I needed the money.

"Fine," he said with a smile, his hand still out. "Just sit down again and I'll get him."

I sat down again. Actually, I fell backward.

"Fine," I repeated.

Vance walked slowly to the phone on the desk, his eyes on me all the time, as if to keep me from moving. My upper lip felt numb and my eyes didn't want to stay open, but I forced them to as Vance slowly, very slowly, made his call or pretended to. I was rapidly losing my grip on the room and the situation.

"Right," Vance said. He kept looking at me and nodding his head. "Right. Mr. Peters is right here and he wants to talk to you."

Vance was looking at me now with a triumphant and mean little grin. He held out the phone. "It's the Duke," he said. "He wants to talk to you. All you have to do is walk over here and take the phone."

I tried to get up, but it couldn't be done. It was at that

point, long after a lobotomized chimp would have figured it out, that I knew I had been slipped something in my Pepsi. I could only hope that it wasn't lethal as I gave up, sank back, and closed my eyes.

It rained while I was asleep. I don't know how I knew it while Koko the Clown danced before me, but I knew it and it was confirmed when I woke up with John Wayne, the real John Wayne, holding my gun on me. I looked at the single window and watched the downpour splatter and ask to come in.

"Water," I said.

"That it is, Pilgrim," he agreed, the gun steady and level.

"No, need water," I said, pointing to my tongue.

He nodded, understanding, and pointed to the sink in the corner. I made three tries at getting up and succeeded on the fourth. I staggered to the sink, turned on the tap, and looked down at the brown stain near the drain. The stain looked a little like the state of Nevada. I put my head under the warm water, cupped my hands, and sloshed liquid into my mouth and over my inflated tongue. The tongue deflated slightly, and using the sink for support, I turned around.

Beyond Wayne, who looked at me with his forehead furrowed in curiosity, the Murphy bed stood open and on it lay the former Lewis Vance. He was definitely not asleep, not with that hole through his forehead.

I must have looked sick, surprised, or bewildered.

"You did that?" Wayne said, pointing his gun at the corpse.

"No," I said, as emphatically as I could. I even shook my head, which was one hell of a mistake. The red cotton candy inside my skull turned to liquid and threatened to come out of every available opening.

Slowly, painfully, I told my tale. The call, the offer from Vance, the drugged Pepsi. Wayne listened, nodding once in a while.

"And," I concluded, "I've got a feeling that hole in Vance's face came from a bullet in my gun, the one in your hand, the one with your fingerprints on it."

Wayne looked at the gun nervously and said, "Supposing I believe you. Where do we go now?"

First I asked him why he was in the room, holding my gun.

"Got a call," he said, gun still on me, though he looked over at the corpse from time to time. "Man said I should get over here fast, a friend of mine, Grant Withers, had taken an overdose of something. I came fast and walked in to find you out with the gun in your hand and your friend Vance. He's never been my stand-in. I don't owe anyone any money and no one is looking for me. I was planning on going to a party at C.B. DeMille's to celebrate the release of *Reap the Wild Wind* when the call came. I don't think old C.B. is going to be too happy that I didn't come. Won't surprise me if I've worked for him for the last time."

The rain got louder and the day darker.

"Why should I believe you, Peters?"

"When you were a kid you used to play in the driveway of Pevsner's grocery store in Glendale," I said, making my way back to the chair and dropping into it. "About two blocks from the drugstore where your dad worked. You used to go to that driveway and throw a ball against the wooden wall. You did that for about two weeks till Pevsner's son came out and hit you in the head."

Wayne's mouth opened slightly and his hand went up to his head, a spot right behind the ear.

"That was you?" he said.

"My brother, Phil," I said. "He's a Los Angeles cop now."

I figured Wayne was about thirty-five or thirty-six now, but there was still a little of that kid in him.

"I thought you said your name was Peters, not Pevsner," Wayne said suspiciously.

"Professional change," I said. "I thought your name was Marion Morrison."

"You made your point," he agreed. "But knowing your brother beat me up when I was a kid doesn't exactly prove you didn't shoot that fella over there."

I got out of the chair again and started to stagger around the room in the hope of clearing my head and returning my agonized body to its former, familiar level of constant ache.

"Let's go over it," I said, looking at Vance. "Someone wanted me here. Vance or someone else. Let's figure the idea was to set me up for Vance's murder. Vance thought it was for something else. Who knows what? He put me out with the drink and our killer steps in, takes my gun, and punctuates Vance."

"And then," Wayne interrupted, "the killer calls me and I come over and step into it. Publicity could ruin the DeMille picture and maybe my career. Could be we're dealing with an old enemy of mine."

"Could be we're dealing with an old enemy of both of ours," I said. "The only one I can think of is my brother Phil, and I doubt if he'd go this far to get either one of us. Maybe it's a blackmail deal. The phone will ring and we'll get . . . No. It would have happened by now. It's a frame-up, simple and dirty."

"Let's try it another way," Wayne said, furrowing his brow. "Fella over there puts something in your drink. You feel yourself going out, get out the gun, put some holes in him, and pass out. I come in, find the gun in your hand, and . . ."

"Who called you?" I said. My mind was starting to work again, not as well as I would have liked, but that's the way it usually worked even when I hadn't had a boiled Pepsi.

"Beats me, Pilgrim." Wayne shrugged.

The knock at the door cut off our further exploration of possibilities. We looked at each other, and he delegated me with a wave of the .38 to be the door-opener. I opened the door. The woman standing there was more than thirty and less than fifty but that was about the best I could do with her age. She had a body that could've passed for twenty-five. Her hair was red and frilly. So was her tight dress.

She looked at me, at Wayne, whom she didn't seem to recognize, and over at Vance on the bed, who had his head turned away.

"You didn't say anything about three," she said. "Three is more."

She stepped in, looked at Wayne, and added appreciatively, "Maybe not much more." He had pocketed the gun in his windbreaker and was looking at me for an explanation.

"What did I say?" I said. "On the phone."

She stepped in, put her small red handbag on the yellow table next to my doctored Pepsi, and looked at me as if I had a few beans loose, which I did.

"You said ten tonight," she said, looking now at the body of Vance with the first hint of awareness. "It's ten and here I am." Then she turned to Wayne, looked at him enough to get him to look away, and added, "You really are Randolph Scott."

"John Wayne," I said.

"Right," she said with a snap of the fingers. "That's what you said, John Wayne."

Her eyes stayed on Wayne, who gave me a sigh of exasperation and said, "Thanks for clearing it up for the lady, Peters. I wouldn't want her to forget who she met here."

She took a few steps toward the Murphy bed and Vance out of curiosity, and I eased over as fast as my retread legs would let me to cut her off.

"Are you sure it was me on the phone?" I said, putting my face in front of hers.

"You don't know if you called me?" she said, trying to look

over my shoulder at Vance. "Voice on a phone is all I know. You trying to back out of this? And what's with the guy on the bed?"

Wayne was leaning against the wall now, his arms folded, watching. He wasn't going to give me any help.

"We're not backing out," I said. "You'll get paid, Miss . . ."

"Olivia Fontaine," she said.

"Class," I said.

"Thanks," she answered with a smile that faded fast. "That guy on the bed. Is he hurt or something?"

"Or something," I said.

"He's dead, lady," Wayne said, pushing away from the wall. "And we're going to call the police."

"Dead?" she repeated, and backed away from me. "I don't want no part of 'dead,'" she said, looking for something, finally spotting her red bag and clacking her red high heels toward it.

"You're going to have to stay awhile," Wayne said, stepping in front of the door. "I don't like this much, but you walk out of here and that's one more complication that has to be unwound."

"You didn't talk like that to Claire Trevor in *Stagecoach,*" Olivia Fontaine said with her hands on her hips. "She was a hooker and you was . . . were nice to her for Chrissake."

"That was a movie, lady," Wayne said.

"Me, other girls I know, love that movie," she said, forgetting for a second the corpse on the bed. "I saw it five times. Hooker goes riding off with you at the end to a new life, ranch or something. Only thing is, I thought you were Randolph Scott."

The second knock at the door was louder than Olivia's. It was the one-two knock of someone who was used to knocking at hotel room doors.

Olivia, Wayne, and I looked at each other. Then Wayne nodded at me.

"Who is it?" I asked.

"Hotel detective," came a familiar voice. "Got a call to come up here."

Wayne shrugged. Olivia looked for someplace to hide, found nothing, and sat in the chair I had recently passed out in. I opened the door, and he came in. He was Merit Beason, sixty, a massive white-haired man who had once been shot by a Singapore sailor. The shot had hit him in the neck, and when it had become clear he would survive, it also became clear he would never be able to turn his neck again. Hence Merit Beason became known as Straight-Ahead Beason. The stiff neck cost him his job as a Los Angeles cop but it gave him a strange dignity that got him steady if not high-paying work in hotels. Straight-Ahead looked like a no-nonsense guy, a stand-up, almost British butler in appearance, with strong ham arms and a craggy face. His suit was always pressed and he always wore a tie. Straight-Ahead avoided a lot of trouble just by looking impressive, but he wasn't going to be able to avoid this one.

He took it all in fast, Olivia, me, Wayne, and the body.

"You know the guy on the bed, Merit?" I said.

He stepped into the room, closed the door behind him, and looked at me carefully.

"Before we talk," he said without turning his body to John Wayne, which would have been the only way to acknowledge the actor, "I want the cowboy to ease the radiator out of his pocket and put it nice and gentle on the dresser. You think we can arrange it?"

Wayne took the gun out and did just what Straight-Ahead wanted.

"Good start," Beason said, though he hadn't turned to watch. In the thirty years he had looked straight ahead, he had developed great peripheral vision. "I've seen the gent staining the Murphy around the lobby now and then. Gave him a light rousting. Mean customer. Threatened to cut up Merit Beason. Can you imagine that, Toby?"

"Can't imagine it, Merit," I said, shaking my head for both of us. Something he said hit me gently and whispered back that I should remember it.

"You or the cowboy or the lady shoot him?" Merit asked.

"None of us," I answered.

"Speak for yourself," Olivia said, jumping up. "I didn't shoot him is all I know."

"Sal," Beason said, his body moving toward the corpse, "I thought you agreed to stay out of the Alhambra after the unfortunate incident of the trollop and the ensign. You recall that tale?"

"I recall," she said. "I'm not Sal anymore. I'm Olivia, Olivia Fontaine."

Straight-Ahead was leaning forward over the bed in that awkward stiff-back way he had. When Merit moved, people watched.

"And I am now General Douglas MacArthur." He sighed, touching the body carefully. "The former Mr. Vance has been with his maker for maybe five hours. That how you peg it, Toby?"

"'Bout that, Merit," I agreed.

He stood up, pushing his bulk from the bed with dignity. The springs squealed and the body of Lewis Vance bounced slightly.

"And what do we do now?" he asked.

"We call the police," said Wayne.

"That the way you want it?" Beason said.

"No," Wayne admitted, stepping forward. "It's not the way I want it, but it's the way it has to be, isn't it?" He pointed at the bed and said, "We've got a murdered man here."

"Not the first in the Alhambra," Straight-Ahead said. He now had his hands folded over his belly like a satisfied Sunday School teacher. "You even had one last time you filled in for me, if my memory serves me, right, Toby?"

"You've got it, Merit," I agreed. "Salesman in five-twelve, but it was suicide, not murder."

"Not that time," he agreed. "Not that time." Then to Wayne: "No, you see, Mr. Wayne, hotels usually don't like to promote the number of people who get killed within them. It's not like they keep charts and compete with each other because it will bring in new trade. No, we usually do our best to keep such things from the attention of the populace."

I explained, "It is not unheard of for a corpse to be carted off to some alley by a house dick."

Wayne shook his head and looked at us as if he had been trapped in a room with the incurably insane. "You mean you're suggesting that we just take . . ."

"Vance," I supplied, "Lewis Vance."

"Right, Vance," Wayne said. "That we take Vance and dump him in some alley and walk away?"

"No," I said emphatically.

"Of course not," Straight-Arrow concurred. "Too many people involved now and you're too big a name. Sal—"

"Olivia," she corrected from her chair as she reached for my unfinished Pepsi.

"Olivia," Merit said, "would be happy to walk away and forget it. Toby knows the routine. He'd walk in a twinkling."

I nodded agreement and reached Olivia just as she was bringing the glass to her mouth. I took it from her. She gave me a dirty look, but I weathered it and put the flat, warm drink on the dresser near the gun.

"So," Wayne said. "What now?"

"We get the killer in here and try to work something out," I said.

"That's the way of it," Straight-Ahead agreed.

"But we don't know who killed him," Wayne said, running his hand through his hair.

"Sure we do," said Straight-Ahead, looking straight ahead at Wayne.

"We do now," I agreed. Olivia didn't give a damn.

I moved to the telephone, picked it up, and dialed a number.

"The who of it is easy," said Merit, unfolding his hands and scratching his white mane. It didn't do his image much good but his head clearly itched. "It's the why we have to figure. Then we'll know what to do."

The killer answered the phone on the third ring and I said, "Get up to three-oh-three fast." I hung up.

The rain took this pause in the conversation to get really mad and started rocking the window in its loose fitting. It rocked and rattled and said bad things while we waited.

"Can I go?" Olivia asked Merit.

"Let's all just stay cozy till we wind it up," Merit said. "That's how you put it in the movies, right?"

"Wrap it up," Wayne volunteered with a sigh. "Call it a wrap."

Straight-Ahead nodded and filed that information for future use.

"You think he might skip?" I asked.

"Human nature is a fickle thing. He might skip, it's true, but where's he to go? And going will be a confession. No, he'll bluff it out or try. Besides, he doesn't yet know that we know."

"That's the way I see it," I agreed.

Wayne and Olivia looked at each other for an answer, got none, and joined Straight-Ahead in looking at the door and listening to the rain and the rattling window. I glanced at Lewis Vance's body, trying not to be angry about what he had done to my head and gotten me into. Then the knock came, almost unheard under the noise of the rain.

"Come right in," Merit shouted.

A key turned in the lock and the door opened to reveal Theodore Longretti. He stepped in, eyes darting around, and closed the door behind him.

"What is this all about?" he said, his eyes finding John Wayne and fixing on him.

"Murder," I said. "Over on the bed."

Teddy Spaghetti turned his long, yellow face to the bed and registered fake surprise. "He's dead?" he said.

"You ought to know," I said. "You put the bullets in him with my gun." I nodded toward the dresser and Teddy's eyes followed me.

"Me?" he said, pointing to his thin chest and looking around at each of us for a touch of support, a sign of realization that it was too absurd to consider the possibility of his having killed anyone.

"You," I said.

"I'm calling the police," Teddy said, stepping toward the phone. I stepped in front of him.

"Let's just work it through," Straight-Ahead said, turning slowly to look at us. "Then we'll decide what to do about it. Give it to him, Toby."

I stepped away from Teddy, knowing I had his attention and that of everyone else in the room. I eased back to the metal railing of the Murphy bed.

"Number one, Vance has been seen hanging around the lobby," I began. "Which means you knew him. But you told me you'd never seen him before."

"I knew him, but . . ." Teddy began to say, looking around the group for support. All he got was distant curiosity.

"I get a call on a Sunday to come to a room in this hotel, your hotel, while you're on the desk. You know me. You know Vance. Nothing tight here yet, but it's adding up. You following me?"

"Toby—" Teddy started, but was stopped by Straight-Ahead, who put his finger to his ample lips and said, "Shhhh."

"Then John Wayne gets a call," I said.

Teddy looked at John Wayne, who nodded.

"Then Sal—Pardon me—Olivia shows up. Someone called her. Someone who knows she's for rent. You know Olivia, don't you, Teddy?"

He looked at her and she looked back at him.

"I've seen her," he said. "I've seen lots of whores."

"Seen is right," she said disdainfully. "Just seen."

"I've done plenty," Teddy said, standing straight and thin.

"We're not questioning your manhood," Merit said. "We're trying to clean a dirty room. Hush it now."

"And finally, Merit gets a call to come up here," I went on. "Seems to me whoever did the dealing knew a lot about who was coming and going not just to the Alhambra but to Room three-oh-three. You follow my reasoning?"

"No," Teddy said stubbornly.

"We could be wrong," Straight-Ahead said.

"We could be," I agreed.

"But we're not," Straight-Ahead added.

"We're not," I agreed again.

"Hold it just a minute here," John Wayne said, shaking his head. "You mean this fella here set this all up, killed that fella on the bed, fixed it so it would look like you did it, and fixed it so I'd be found here with the corpse, you and . . . the lady."

"Looks that way to me," I said.

"What in the name of God for?" Wayne asked reasonably.

"You want to answer that one, Teddy?" I asked, as if I knew the answer but was willing to give up the stage to let the supporting cast take over. I had tried to set it up this way with Merit's help and the moment of truth or lies had come. All Teddy had to do was keep his mouth shut and we'd be stuck with having to make a decision. There was about enough evidence to nail him on a murder charge as there was to get Tojo to give up by midnight. A little digging might put him in the bag but a little digging would mean enough time for the newspapers to make John Wayne and the Alhambra big news. That gave me an idea.

"Publicity," I prompted. "You want to talk about publicity, Teddy?"

Teddy didn't want to talk about anything. He looked as if he were in a voodoo trance, his face almost orange as the thunder cracked outside.

"Teddy," Merit prompted. "Merit Beason's got work to do and no one is on the desk downstairs."

Teddy shook himself, or rather a wave or chill went through him.

"It got all crazy," he said. "I'll tell you it got all crazy."

Olivia sighed loudly to let us know she had no interest in hearing Teddy tell it, but she had no choice.

"I didn't plan on my killing him, you see," Teddy said, playing with his shirt front and looking down. "Idea of it was to get you here, Toby, put you out or something, get Wayne in, and then Sal, and have Merit walk in on it. Idea was to give the *Times* a tip about a love nest thing at the Alhambra, have a photographer and reporter maybe right behind. You'd confirm the whole thing and—"

"That was one hell of a stupid idea," Olivia said angrily from the chair. "And my name is Olivia."

Teddy shrugged. It hadn't worked out the way he planned. "Idea was publicity," he whispered to his shirt.

"That John Wayne was making it with a prostitute in your hotel?"

"You think the Alhambra is such a hot-shot address?" Teddy came back defensively, with a little animation thrown in. "Kind of people we got coming here, it could be a real attraction, you know what I mean? Idea was to set something up like this with a whole bunch of movie people, you know, real he-man types, Wild Bill Elliot, Alan Ladd, you know."

"And then the girls would be kicking back a few extra bucks to you just to work the rooms," Straight-Ahead said.

"Never thought of that," said Teddy, who had evidently considered just that. "But it was the publicity. Rooms aren't going as good as they should. Nights are good for soldiers, sailors when the troops are in, and we've got a small health-nut convention Wednesday night, but the Hatchmans, who own the Alhambra, say they need at least seventy-eight percent or they'll sell and I'll lose my job, and where does a Joe like me—"

"Hold it," John Wayne pitched in. He walked over to Teddy, who shrank away from him, almost flopping like a dry noodle over the coffee table. "This is one hell of a harebrained scheme, Pilgrim, and I've got a mind to snap a few pieces off of you, but I want to know why you shot that man."

Teddy was still backing away from Wayne toward the wall. He almost stumbled over Olivia's stretched-out legs, but she pulled them in just in time.

"An accident," Teddy said. "An accident. Vance called me, said Toby had passed out. I had already made the calls to Sal and you, got your phone number from a friend at the Republic. Vance called me up, said he wanted more than the ten bucks I promised him, wanted in on whatever I was doing. I told him I didn't have more than ten bucks to give him, that there might be more money later, but he wouldn't listen. It was not a good situation."

"Not a good situation at all," Straight-Ahead agreed, turning toward him. "So you took Toby's gun and shot Lewis Vance between the eyes."

"He threatened to beat me up, kill me," Teddy whined. "It was self-defense."

"That's the story I'd tell," I agreed.

"It's the truth," Teddy squealed, bumping into the wall as Wayne advanced. I realized what was coming, but I couldn't stop it. It should have been plain to a room in which half the living people were detectives, but it wasn't. Teddy reached over to the dresser at his elbow and came away with my .38 in his right hand. It stuck out from the end of his spindly arm and pointed at the stomach of John Wayne, who stopped abruptly and put up his hands.

"You are making me mad, mister," Wayne said through his teeth, but he took a step backward.

"Teddy, Teddy, Teddy," I said, shaking my head. "You are not going to shoot all four of us. Put the gun down and let's talk."

I could see no good reason why he wouldn't shoot all four of us, but I hoped the prospect of mowing down innocent citizens would not appeal to the shaking desk clerk, whose experience in mayhem, as far as I knew, had been limited to one unfortunate scrape and a lucky shot a few hours earlier with an apparently unpleasant third-rate bully. "Think of the publicity."

Teddy's mouth went dry. He reached over and took a sip of the flat Pepsi to moisten it. I didn't stop him. No one moved. We just watched him and hoped he'd down the whole thing.

"Five bodies in one room, one a famous actor," Straight-Ahead chimed in. "The Alhambra might have a hell of a time surviving that."

"I can shoot you all and get away," Teddy reasoned. He took another sip.

"You'll never get away with it," I said. People always said

that in situations like this. My experience was that they very often did get away with it, but you don't tell things like that to killers holding guns. You just hoped they saw the same movies and listened to the same radio shows you did. The room suddenly went quiet. The rain had stopped.

Teddy blinked his eyes and looked at us. I couldn't tell whether he was considering who to shoot first or was realizing that he couldn't pull the trigger. I never got a chance to ask him.

"I've had just about enough," Wayne said, and took a step, the final step, forward. Teddy, already a little drowsy from the drink, moved his gun-holding hand and fired. It missed Wayne, breezed past me, and shattered the window, letting in a rush of rain-scented air. Wayne's punch slammed Teddy against the wall. The gun fell, hit the floor, bounced a few times, and rested.

Olivia screamed and Straight-Ahead walked slowly straight ahead toward the slumped figure. Wayne, fists still clenched, stepped back to let the house detective take over. It was a show and a half to see Merit get to his knee, lift the now silent desk clerk up, and deposit him on the chair near the desk.

"Let's go," I said, exchanging a look of understanding with Merit when he turned around.

"Go?" asked Wayne, his dark hair over his forehead. "What are you talking about? This man killed that man and we—"

"Can go," I said.

Olivia didn't need persuading. She grabbed her red bag and headed for the door.

"You've never been in this room," Straight-Ahead said to her.

"I've never been in this hotel," she answered. "Nice to meet you, John." And out she went.

"Merit will work a deal with Teddy," I explained to the

bewildered Wayne. "Teddy says he shot Vance in self-defense and no one else was around. Merit backs him up. Story's over. Teddy doesn't want it that way, Merit calls him a liar trying to save his skin, but that won't happen. Teddy will back it up and you're out of it."

"With some embellishments, that's the way it really was," Merit said, looking at Teddy.

"It's—" John Wayne began.

"Not like the movies," I finished. "Not this time anyway. The rain's stopped. You want to stop for a beer?"

"I guess," said Wayne, shaking his head. "It's too late for DeMille's party." He took a last look at the corpse on the bed and the scrawny killer in the chair. The Ringo Kid wouldn't have handled it like this, but what the hell. He looked at Straight-Ahead, who said, "Go on. It's my job."

Wayne nodded and moved into the hall after I said, "I'll be right there."

Teddy was showing no signs of waking up.

"My gun," I said.

"Your gun," Merit repeated, giving up on reviving Teddy Spaghetti in the near future. "We say you left it here for Teddy for a price. Protection. He was threatened by all kinds. That sort of thing. It'll hold up."

"It'll shake a lot," I said, "but it'll probably hold. Take care."

A breeze from the broken window swirled around the room as Straight-Ahead waved his arm at me and sat slowly in the understuffed chair to wait for Teddy to wake up. I closed the door quietly and joined John Wayne in the hall.

"Things like this happen to you a lot?" he said as we got onto the elevator.

"When things are going well," I said. "Only when things are going well."

My head began to ache again and I longed for a plate of tacos from Manny's, a few blocks away. I wondered if I could talk Wayne into a visit.

2

Talking Wayne into a taco at Manny's wasn't too hard. He had already missed his DeMille party and had no place to go. If Manny recognized the Duke when we walked in, he didn't let on, and since there was only one other customer in the place, a fat guy in the corner who needed a shave and demonstrated that he could snore with his mouth open, no one bothered us.

We talked about the bad old days in Glendale. We had both listened to station KIEV on the radio out of the old Glendale Hotel. We had both gone to Glendale High, had both downed beers in Dave Burton's bar, and watched Doug Fairbanks movies at the Alexander Theatre. Wayne didn't seem to be in any big hurry to go home or anywhere else. In an hour he had lined up seven empty bottles of Drerys Beer with the mountie on the label and I had lined up three.

Manny smoothed his bandit mustache and turned on the radio to pick up the news and drown out the snorer in the corner. Two Jap carriers had been sunk at Midway, and the Tokyo Armada was running from Admiral Nimitz. The British were moving in Libya, and Rommel was in Tobruk to rally the Afrika Korps.

"Tried to enlist," the Duke said, scratching at the label of his beer bottle with his thumbnail. "Too old, too many kids, bad shoulder. I'm gonna try again."

I held up my fourth taco to him in a salute to his patriotism.

I knew I was too old to enlist, not that I would have, but who knows. My brother, Phil, had lied about his age and made it into the end of the last war. It had almost got him killed.

"I've got to get going," I said, reaching into my pocket for a couple of bucks. "Tacos and beer are on me. You can leave a tip for Manny."

A guy on the radio was excited and told us that first thing in the morning we should run down to the L.A. Furniture Company on South Broadway to buy a rebuilt Royal Eureka vacuum cleaner. Manny didn't look excited. The idea that a floor might need cleaning was alien to him. He turned off the radio, and the sudden silence almost woke the sleeper, who snorted in fear.

"Colorful place," Wayne said.

"Few people know of it and those of us who do try to keep it to ourselves," I said. "But you're welcome to join the elite."

"*Hasta luego,*" Wayne called to Manny as we left. Manny nodded back without answering as he started to clear away taco plates and empty beer bottles.

"Manny is Greek," I said as Wayne walked to the door.

Wayne looked back at Manny, the sleeper, and the red leather-covered stools.

"He looks Mexican," Wayne said.

"Part of his exotic image. Adds to his mystique for the clientele," I explained.

Outside, the rain had stopped and the night was getting damp and muggy-feeling.

Wayne looked at the sky and zipped up his windbreaker. The seven beers hadn't seem to have affected him. I got the impression that he was used to stronger stuff.

"Helluva thing," he said.

"Helluva thing," I agreed, though I didn't know what we were talking about—the Vance murder, the Battle of Midway, Rommel, or Wayne's inability to get into the war. I was wrong on all four.

"You know where I'd like to go now?" he asked.

"Back into Manny's for another round and a chorus of 'Wang Wang Blues' with the guy sleeping it off in the corner," I tried.

Wayne looked at me, gave me a lopsided grin, and shook his head. "You got one funny sense of humor," he said.

"My brother tells me that sometimes."

"I'd like to go home is where I'd like to go," he explained, putting an arm around me and leaning down to whisper. "But I can't. The wife and I don't see eye-to-eye, so I camp out in hotels."

"I've heard something about it," I said.

"You have?" he asked suspiciously. Maybe now I did catch the first small signs of slurred speech. I knew the three beers I had put away were having a slight effect on my midnight patter. My normal gargle for tacos was a couple of Pepsis.

"I'm a detective," I reminded him. "We keep our ears open and wear flowers in our buttonholes when we can afford them."

There was nothing else to say. The Duke thanked me for getting him out of the Alhambra and popping for the tacos, and we parted, going in opposite directions. I watched him lope down Broadway past a lone couple, who recognized him and turned to watch his familiar walk, then I turned south and went for my own car, which was still where I had left it. I managed to climb in and get it started before the staggering panhandler got to me. He had been advancing slowly, his too warm topcoat flapping in the muggy breeze, his hands already out like Lon Chaney, Jr., as the Mummy.

I made it to Heliotrope in Hollywood and parked in front of home, Mrs. Plaut's boarding house. For the past month or so I had been considering the purchase of a rope ladder, one I could drop from my room window so I could enter and exit without encountering Mrs. Plaut, who, I was now convinced, never slept. But I knew I'd never buy the ladder, would never take time off to buy it and install it and use it. Hell, if I could follow through on an idea like that, I wouldn't be filling in as a night watchman at an old people's home or a substitute house dick in second-rate hotels. There was no moving from Mrs. Plaut's. Rooms were hard to get in the middle of a war. Besides, my best friend lived at the Plaut Palace and I didn't want to insult or hurt Gunther Wherthman's feelings.

I trudged up the walk and the three white wooden steps, not trying to be particularly quiet. Being particularly quiet, even taking off my shoes, had never saved me from Mrs. Plaut. Since she was as close to deaf as one could be without benefit of a precise sign on her chest, I had often wondered by what uncanny sense she detected even the slightest presence in or near her domicile. Gunther was of the opinion that she felt vibrations through the wooden floor. Joe Hill, the postman who lived in the loft, thought she was a witch, but whatever it was, the minute and quite ancient and feisty Mrs. Plaut was better than radar.

I sensed her before I saw her in the shadows on the front porch. She sat on the white wooden porch swing rocking, her feet not quite touching the wooden planks of the porch.

"Photographs, Mr. Peelers," she said.

"It's after midnight, Mrs. Plaut. What are you still doing up?" I knew she wouldn't hear me, but after nearly fifty years of almost normal conversation with people, habits die hard.

"What do you think of photographs?" she went on. The porch swing stopped, ending the rusty creaking. The question, stated in her insistent and too loud voice, penetrated, I was sure, every sleeping house on the block. Now the neighborhood awaited my opinion on the art of photography at midnight.

"I think photographs are great," I said. "I've got one of my old dog, my brother, and my dad on my office wall where I can see them and—"

"Family photographs are the best," she answered relevantly. And then I realized that it was not relevance but coincidence that had created apparent reason. She went on, "I believe we should incorporate photographs in the book."

Now I understood. For more than two years Mrs. Plaut had been submitting to me neatly written pages of her family history. At some juncture and confused moment in our early encounters, Mrs. Plaut had decided that I was both an exterminator and an editor. No amount of explanation had destroyed this illusion, and to preserve what little sanity and the room I possessed, I had found it easier simply to give in and read her manuscript, not knowing that it would continue to grow. It now was more than fifteen hundred pages long. The prospect of including family photographs filled me with delight.

Something, I could see, was in her hands, a rather large wicker sewing box. She held it out to me and I advanced to take it. It was surprisingly heavy.

"Photographs," I said.

"Photographs," she replied. "Going back to 1800."

"That's before photography was invented," I informed her.

She looked at me from the shadows as if my ignorance had no bounds.

"You look through the photographs and counsel me on which would be most illustrative of what you have already edited," she explained. "We can discuss it tomorrow. Each, you will find, is clearly marked on the reverse. Some are copies Harold made from glass plates, tintypes, and the like."

I almost asked who Harold was but even three beers did not drive me to such foolishness. Actually, I considered the price of looking at the photographs a cheap one to pay for escaping from a nocturnal confrontation with Mrs. Plaut.

"I'll do that," I said, turning to enter the house.

"I'm thinking of purchasing a device to aid the hearing," she said behind me, and I was alive with new hope.

"Terrific idea," I said, turning to her and speaking as loudly and distinctly as I could.

"I'd like to be able to hear my canary Sweet Alice," she explained. "And Mr. Peelers, though you may not have noticed it, there has been a slight inclination on my part not to hear everything with perfect clarity. After all, I am—"

And I waited for the disclosure of Mrs. Plaut's age, a fact that had remained secret to all boarders in the Heliotrope house for perhaps a century, according to legend.

"—in my middle years and must recognize that all bodily functions deteriorate, not unlike in a Ford automobile," she concluded.

"I would like the doctor with whom you work to make some recommendation about the proper inconspicuous device to assist my hearing," she went on, "if it should at some point need assistance."

I shifted the wicker basket of photographs in my arms and said loudly, "I share office space with a dentist. Shelly is a dentist, Mrs. Plaut, and I don't think—"

"Doctors get discounts," she explained. "I am interested in an Aurex, which the ads say is like glasses."

I would puzzle out later how a hearing aid was like glasses but now I simply wanted to get my burden to my room and sleep off a long day of work, a murder, and too many beers with the Ringo Kid.

"I'll do it," I agreed, and was relieved to see a smile of satisfaction on her face. I turned and entered the house as the squeak of the porch swing resumed. Somehow I was going to have to go through the box of photographs and come up with a price on the hearing aid for Mrs. Plaut. I climbed the stairs, considered knocking on Gunther Wherthman's door, decided it was too late, and went as quietly into my room as I could.

I took off my rumpled seersucker suit, hung it in the closet, changed my underwear, brushed my teeth in the washroom down the hall, and returned to my room and small table to eat a bowl of Wheaties and milk while I looked at a few treasures from the Plaut photo collection. My room isn't much but I like it that way. Not much to have. Not much to lose. I liked the idea of knowing that if I didn't have to return some night I wouldn't miss anything except Gunther and the Beech-Nut clock on the wall, which told me it was now a little after one in the morning. I had a small refrigerator, a hot plate, a wooden table with two wooden chairs, and a sofa with doilies on the arms that I was forbidden to remove under pain of torture by Mrs. Plaut. I had a bed but I had moved my mattress to the floor because of my bad back. Mrs. Plaut had learned to tolerate this eccentricity, though I'm not sure why. The only other item of interest in the room was a painted portrait, which may have been Abraham Lincoln, a relative of Mrs. Plaut's, or a random leftover from a previous tenant. He was a stern, bearded character in a black jacket and string tie, a no-nonsense dark-haired old guy who needed only a cartoon balloon saying "Shape up or ship out." I had recently taken to calling him Bosco and talking to him, a sure sign of early senility or too close an association with the fringe members of normal society.

The wicker sewing basket contained more than photographs, but I ignored a receipt for fifty-nine cents for a bottle of Pinaud cologne and plowed on through about twenty photographs and had a second bowl of Wheaties before I gave up. Names were scrawled on the back of the photographs with comments—almost legible—in Mrs. Plaut's unmistakable hand. I was sure she had taken penmanship lessons from Cotton Mather and used a goose quill.

I discovered over the next twenty minutes that:

Uncle Dan Seltz was a distinguished traitor, though in what

war and under what circumstances was not clear. It was, however, clear that Uncle Dan Seltz was an expert in disguising himself as a woman. Either that or Mrs. Plaut had been incorrectly labeling the photographs, a prospect that filled me with more dread than the thought of the mummy coming for me.

Cousin Agnes: her house in Buiose (state unspecified) had burned down, making room for the home of Mrs. Amelia Garpol in the photograph. I assumed the woman in front of the house was either Cousin Agnes, Mrs. Garpol, or that master of disguise, Uncle Dan Seltz.

Enough. I left the bowl and the photographs on the table, put the bottle of milk back in the refrigerator, set my watch against the Beech-Nut clock, and turned out the light. My watch would now be correct for a few seconds. It had been the one item of my father's that I had held on to. It didn't work and couldn't be fixed, but I couldn't let it go. It had its own crazy code of time, a code I always thought I might someday break. There was no moonlight from outside, but I knew where the mattress was on the floor and stumbled to it.

I lay back against the pillow I used behind my head and clutched the second pillow I used to keep me from rolling over on my stomach during the night. An accidental night on my stomach would put my back out of commission for at least four days. This had been a simple truth in the glamorous life of the world's foremost detective ever since that day a half-dozen years earlier when I had been unlovingly squeezed by a massive Negro gentleman who wanted to talk to Mickey Rooney at a premiere. Unfortunately, it had been my responsibility to keep anyone but Louis B. Mayer away from the Mick.

Once on my back I knew that the effects of the drugged Pepsi were not completely in my past, nor were the tacos, Wheaties, and beer. Who said a private detective's life isn't full of romance, intrigue, and adventure? It must have taken me all of two or three minutes to fall asleep.

That I would dream was inevitable. That I should remember the dream is unfortunate. I dreamed, at least part of my dream, that I was once again a cop in Glendale. John Wayne and I were on the early night get-your-ass-outta-here run. That was the eight-in-the-evening check to be sure that all Negroes were out of Glendale. They could work there but they had to be on the bus out to Los Angeles or Pasadena before the sun went down. Catholics weren't exactly welcome either, though they weren't as easy to run down. Neither were Jews, of which I happened to be one, a fact the Glendale police chief never discovered.

Well, the Duke, complete with cowboy uniform and horse, and I were routing Negroes when one of them turned and grabbed me in a bear hug. It was the same guy who had gone after Mickey Rooney's autograph. I called for help but John Wayne was riding off into the sunset. Lewis Vance rose out of the ground but shrugged and said he couldn't help because he had a bullet hole in his head and was dead. And then I woke up.

I was on my stomach, with my extra pillow mysteriously on the sofa. I groaned and rolled over to the sound of knocking at my door.

"What, what?" I called.

"May I enter?" came Gunther's precise Swiss-accented voice.

"Enter, enter," I said, trying to sit up with the help of one hand on my back.

Gunther entered, all three-feet-and-a-little-more of him. He wore his usual three-piece suit complete with vest and watch fob. He was clean-shaven, imperially tiny.

"I was concerned," he said. "You called out."

The Beech-Nut clock on the wall told me it was almost

nine. The sun confirmed the hour and Bosco looked down at me critically for sleeping so late and making morning noises.

"I had a nightmare," I explained.

Gunther nodded knowingly and, leaving my door open, disappeared. I tested my back, found that it wasn't so bad, and was starting to get up when Gunther returned with a tray and eased the door shut with his elbow.

"Some coffee," he explained, moving to the table. "And some breakfast biscuits with butter and honey."

"Sounds great," I said.

"May I clean up this disarray?" Gunther asked, putting down the tray and examining the dirty cereal bowl and the basket of photographs, the remnants of my wild night.

"Okay," I said, knowing that Gunther's level of tolerance for mess was very low compared to mine. Actually, I don't have intolerance for messiness. It seems natural to me.

"Nightmares may appear to be, and are, very upsetting," Gunther said as he straightened up and I groped on my trousers. "However, according to Freud, Ernest Jones, Otto Rank, and others, the nightmare can be a therapeutic experience. It is an attempt by the unconscious mind to tell a secret to the conscious mind. But it is in the form of a puzzle, a conundrum."

Normally, I would have had my breakfast without getting dressed, but in deference to Gunther I went to the closet, found my last clean shirt, and put it on. If Gunther hadn't been there I probably would have worn the same shirt I'd had on the day before. It wasn't badly wrinkled and I had no big plans for the day.

"We're feeling very psychotherapeutic this Monday morning," I said, sitting at the table.

"I am in the process of translating an article in German into English for a medical journal," he explained, carefully pouring us each a cup of coffee, in clean cups he had brought in from his own room. Gunther made a comfortable living as a translator. He could handle eight languages, and business had been great since the war, most of it coming from the U.S. government.

"To consummate this translation," he said, after taking a delicate sip of coffee and dabbing his mouth with the napkin that he had also brought from his room, "I have had to do extensive reading in the subject. The human mind is devious, Toby."

"Your mind is trickier than you are, Gunther," I admitted, after finishing the cup of coffee in one gulp and downing a biscuit with a glob of honey.

Gunther smiled and nodded in agreement. "Yes," he said, "the separation of mind and body. A point Jung makes. May I ask? Do you have a hanover?"

"I don't think so," I said, "but you can look around. If I've got one you can have it."

"No," he tried again. "A hanover, the aftermath of too much alcohol in the system."

"A hangover, you mean. Maybe a little," I admitted, "but the coffee and biscuits help." I popped two more into my mouth, finishing off the last of them, and gave Gunther a loopy grin. If my table manners got to him, he never let it show. A little over two years earlier I had gotten Gunther off a murder rap and not only had we become friends, but he had gotten me into Mrs. Plaut's just as I was being thrown out of my old apartment for an excess of broken windows and flying bullets.

I'm not sure where the conversation would have gone next if the phone hadn't rung in the hallway. Neither Gunther nor I was foolish enough to answer it. Mrs. Plaut would beat us to it even if it meant that she had to rush up the stairs or come inside from the garage, where she spent her spare moments keeping her 1924 Ford running. Even if you happened to be lucky enough to get to the phone first, she would arrive from nowhere to take it from you with the aid of a sharp elbow. Her ability to know when the phone was ringing was further evidence of the possible correctness of Gunther's vibration theory.

We sat while the phone rang two more times. I picked at remaining crumbs. Gunther finished his first cup of coffee.

Then the sound of feet clapping up the stairs and the end of the ringing, followed by Mrs. Plaut's voice knifing through the closed door.

"Hello? . . . Yes? . . . All things are possible . . . One thousand or more . . . I'll see if Mr. Peelers is disposed."

Then the footsteps of Mrs. Plaut coming to my door, a sharp knock, and the sudden opening of the door before I could say either enter or stay out.

"The phone is for you," she said, surveying our breakfast dishes. "Did you look at the photographs?"

"Thank you," I answered, getting up. "I looked at some of them, yes."

She considered barring my way as I walked to the door and then, thanks to some intervention of the gods, changed her mind and backed away. I rambled down the hall, with her close behind, and picked up the phone.

"That woman is not reliable," came a familiar voice.

"It depends on what you want from her, Merit," I said, smiling at Mrs. Plaut, who waited for me, hands at her side, wearing a pensive scowl and a purple housedress covered with white flowers.

"Toby, Merit Beason has been shot again," he said.

Straight-Ahead did not make jokes. I took him seriously. "What happened?"

"Teddy," he said. "It didn't go into the book the way we wrote it. The weapon was yours. The circumstances were mine. Can you get down to County Hospital, Room four-oh-three?"

"I'll be right there, Merit," I said, and hung up.

"Exterminating?" asked Mrs. Plaut.

"Maybe," I said, and hurried back to my room to ask Gunther to clean up for me, which he would have done anyway.

The day was sunny. My car started and I had enough gas for the trip.

I turned on the car radio and got a bugle call and a guy telling me to join the civilian army and cut the waste of gasoline. He also told me that "ordinary guys" like me could help save lives by not racing my engine, by turning off the motor when I was waiting for a friend, by shifting gears faster, by reducing speed on the open road, by having my carburetor checked, and by sharing rides with other ordinary guys.

I switched to another station and got Ray Eberle and the Modernaires singing "I Guess I'll Have to Dream the Rest." I tried to sing along, messed up the words, and shut up.

Parking downtown near the hospital was a problem. I didn't want to pay for a parking lot and I didn't want to waste time looking for a space. I didn't know had badly Straight-Ahead had been shot—I might have saved a quarter and lost a business associate.

Luck was with me. I spotted a space being eyed by a well-dressed woman in a black Buick. While she tried to decide if she could fit, I zipped past her and went straight in. It took some maneuvering to straighten my car out, so I was too busy to see if she gave me a dirty look. I wasn't worried about dirty looks. My mission took priority over hers, whatever hers might be. I wasn't quite sure what my mission was, really, but I was curious and worried about my gun, where it might be, and who might be getting shot with it.

3

There were at least six good ways to get into County Hospital without checking in at the main desk and explaining your visit to one of the ex-schoolteachers behind the desk. My favorite, and the one I knew best, was through the Emergency Room, partly because I had had so much business with that part of the establishment. This time, however, I didn't have to sneak in. I had a legitimate reason for being there, so I stopped at the main desk behind a sailor and waited while the woman who looked like Edna May Oliver playing Hidegarde Whithers handed the gob a pass.

When the sailor stepped out of the way, I put on my best Monday morning smile and said, "Merit Beason."

Something about me did not please the woman, who gave me a prunish look and checked through her list of patients.

"Barish, Barbier, Beason, yes," she said.

"Yes," I repeated, reaching for the card.

"No," she said, pulling the card back. "No visitors."

"I'm his brother."

"No visitors," she repeated. "Not today. He was shot."

"I didn't do it," I said, putting my hand to my chest, ready to cross my heart and hope to die.

"No one said you did. No visitors," she repeated, pointing to the card and looking over at the brown-uniformed guard chatting to a nurse about a dozen feet away.

"I'm his son," I tried. "I made a mistake about being his brother. I was nervous."

"No," she said. "Sorry."

"I get the impression here that you don't like me," I said, looking pained.

"That's true," she agreed, looking past me at the young woman holding the hand of a little boy and waiting to cope with the keeper of the gate. "But like you or not, the card says no visitors."

"Why don't you like me?" I said. "I'm nice to my family, pay my taxes, honor my parents memory, want to visit my uncle in the hospital."

"You remind me of my husband," the woman said. "Now, if you please, you'll have to stand out of the way so I can take care of the lady."

"But—" I began, but she put her finger to her lips just the way my third-grade teacher Mrs. Rothcup used to do and I immediately shut up.

"I'm a volunteer here," she whispered. "I do not get paid. I am filling in for the duration of the war to free the regular receptionist, my daughter, to do more essential war-related work. I am, actually, in quite a good mood today, possibly because my husband is in Phoenix on business and partly because I just heard on the radio that the Japanese fleet has been trounced at Midway. I should hate to call that guard and have you escorted out."

"You used to be a teacher, didn't you?" I whispered even lower.

She nodded, pleased that her lifetime of work had so clearly molded her personality. To prove her persona, she pointed an index finger at the door. To prove my conditioning by the California school system, I turned and left the hospital.

Someone must have thought that the Japanese were planning a sneak attack on the hospital, probably intent on eliminating all the dangerous appendectomy patients before they could mobilize. The two side doors were locked. Even the window off the fire escape near the mental wing was locked, though someone had put up a colorful crayon drawing of a smiling round face with three wisps of hair sticking up. The name "Dagwood" was printed in black crayon on the picture. I wondered if it was the comic strip character or the nickname of the mental ward artist.

It was time to try the Emergency Room door. That was always open, and probably only admitting a flow or trickle on this Monday morning. Saturday night and Sunday afternoon were the rush hours for the Emergency Room. On Saturday night they came in drunk and bleeding from fighting over who was winning the war. On Sunday, they came in after accidents and battles. How much of the Sunday funny papers could you read? *Quick as a Flash* and *That Brewster Boy* could only keep you busy for an hour, and another hour in church, in bed, or on a blanket in the front yard listening to the kids only made the natives crankier, reminding them that the next day was work and that the reason they had to work was their wives and families. So they got angry and lashed out or got lashed. At least that was the theory forwarded by my brother, a cop, who did not have my faith in the goodness of your met-on-the-street Los Anglian.

There were six people in the waiting room; one of them looked as if he or she was in immediate danger. Another was a kid who sat with a crude bandage covering one eye as she sat next to her mother, who tried to read a magazine. At the reception desk near the door to the treatment rooms was a dark Latin-looking woman, almost pretty. She was dressed in white and checked something off on a clipboard.

I decided against a smile. It hadn't worked at the front desk. Since I didn't recognize her I walked past her looking a bit disgruntled and grouched, "Dr. Morey in?"

"Dr. Morey?" she said, looking up, puzzled. "I . . ."

"Oh Christ," I sighed, pausing. "I told him . . . listen,

could you call Glendale Hospital, surgery, and ask if Dr. Taylor has left yet. Tell them Dr. Christian is waiting and must leave for Fresno. Also, if a Miss Markhan comes, send her right up to the surgery office. Then page Dr. Cyclops and ask him to report to surgery immediately. You have all that?"

She looked properly confused and repeated, "Dr. Christian at Glendale, find out when he left. Miss—"

"Markhan," I continued, encouraging but looking at my watch to let her know I was a busy man. My watch said it was three, which wasn't bad, no more than six hours off.

"Markham, right," she said with an apologetic smile. "She's to go to surgery and I'm to page Dr. Sy Glopps."

"Right," I said. "Sy's probably in the cafeteria."

I pushed through the hinged double door and strode down the hall past open and closed doors on either side and into the depths of iodine odor without looking back. I went up the stairs instead of taking the elevator. I didn't want to have the elevator operator asking for my visitor's card and I didn't want to play doctor again unless I had to. I had a long day left. Luck was with me on the fourth floor: lots of people were walking around, the nursing station was three-womaned, an eight-year-old doctor was reading a chart, and the hospital paging system called out in vain for my old medical school chum Sy Glopps.

The door to Room 403 was closed. I listened, determined that no one was talking inside, pushed it open and closed the door behind me. The room was small, all white down to the cabinet next to the bed and the patient in the bed. Straight-Ahead's eyes were closed and he was breathing heavily. I walked over to him.

"Merit," I whispered. "Are you—"

"Alive," he finished, his eyes still closed. "Thinking, not sleeping," he explained, opening his eyes and looking over at me without turning his head. His brown eyes strained at their corners, so I moved to hover over him.

"What happened?" I asked. I was still whispering, even though Straight-Ahead had a private room.

"Merit Beason was shot," he said, which he followed with an incredulous can-you-believe-that look.

"Teddy?" I said.

At this point a healthy man, or at least one with flexible neck muscles, would have shaken his head. Beason simply closed his eyes firmly and opened them again before speaking.

"No, an accomplice. It seems our strand of pasta was not in the scheme alone. It seems there was another. It seems someone named Alex put him up to it. According to Teddy . . . how about a sip of water for Merit Beason?" His eyes looked toward the small white table near his bed, though I was sure his eyes couldn't take in the glass.

"Sure," I said, picking up the dusty, not quite clear liquid and wondering how I could get it into his mouth, since he couldn't lift his neck. Maybe there was a funnel in the drawer. I could stick the funnel in his mouth and pour the water in. I'd probably choke him to death. "How do we do this?"

"The bed cranks," he explained.

I went to the foot of the bed and cranked it up. Beason didn't look much better bent at the waist. He took the water, finished it off in a single gulp, and handed the glass back.

"It's not Jim Beam," he said.

"It's not embalming fluid either," I reminded him, and he nodded.

"I didn't see this Alex. Came in behind when I was talking to Teddy. I sensed someone was there, could see it in our Teddy's rusted eyes, but couldn't turn in time. Felt the lead and thought it was over. Then Merit Beason went down and played dead."

"At least they didn't shoot you with my gun," I said. "You want more water?"

"No," he said. "I'm feeling a bit wary, the truth be told."

"My gun," I said after a pause for Merit to catch his breath.

"Gone," he said.

"The body of Lewis Vance?" I tried.

"Gone. They took the body, planted it somewhere, maybe in the Alhambra, maybe in the lobby of the Brown Derby, maybe in the desert."

"So," I said with a sigh.

"Yes," Merit agreed, closing his eyes. "Someone who killed a gent in the Alhambra and who bears an ill will toward John Wayne is out on the streets of this city with your thirty-eight. It gives us pause."

"It gives us pause," I agreed.

"Merit Beason thinks that Alex should be located, disarmed, and manacled before he makes headlines."

"How are you doing? I said, getting ready to hit the streets.

"Bullet went in, went out," he said. "Not the first time and, possibly, not the last." His hand went up unconsciously to his stiff neck, his body remembering the last bullet he had taken, the one that had given him his dignity and his nickname.

"The doctors say Merit Beason will be out in a week, working in two. Nurses say it will be a day or two. Let's go with the nurses."

"I do when the opportunity arises," I joked.

Straight-Ahead did not smile and neither did the white-uniformed doctor who stepped into the room. "Can't you read the sign on the door?" he said angrily.

I recognized him before he realized who I was, though I was sure Dr. Marcus Parry had changed a hell of a lot more than I had in the past year or two since I had last seen him. He looked shorter, thinner, paler. His blond hair was darker and his forehead higher. He was somewhere in his late twenties but he looked my age.

"Peters," he said.

"Guilty," I agreed.

"Get out," he said.

"Good to see you again, too," I answered with a grin.

Parry was not charmed.

"My fault, Doc," whispered Straight-Ahead. "I called him, told him to come."

"This is your closest relative?" Parry asked, shaking his head incredulously and plunging both hands in the pockets of his white hospital jacket.

"Got no relatives in California," Merit said with what looked like a smile. "Beason clan remained in Nevada. Friends are few. We come into the world alone, leave it alone."

"Those are his cheery words for the day," I said.

Parry was still not amused.

"Last request from the recovering patient," Straight-Ahead said as I walked to the door. "Call Jack Ellis. He's between jobs. See if he can take over at the Alhambra for a night or two. Merit Beason would ask you but you have to hit the streets in search of our Alex and Teddy. The call would be made from here but the Axis seems to have snuck in this morning and removed the phone."

"I'll take care of it," I said, and eased past Doc Parry and into the hall. Parry followed me, closing the door behind us. Before he had been drafted, Parry had done his residency in the Emergency Room of County Hospital, and I'd used him as my personal physician, a job he had taken reluctantly and out of curiosity, wondering how long my skull could survive the forces of evil using it for a Chinese gong.

"Glad you're back," I said, putting out my hand. Parry didn't take it.

"That man is sixty years old," he said, nodding at Straight-Ahead's door.

"He's as strong as a bull."

"Bulls get slaughtered by the thousands every day," he said. "He's alive because he's strong, but things go wrong.

One minute a patient is recovering nicely, the next we're fighting to save his life."

"I'll stay away," I said. "How are you?"

He took one hand out of his pocket to push his few strands of mousy hair back.

"Shorter," he said with a bitter smile.

"Shorter?"

He reached down awkwardly to pull up his right pant leg. His wooden leg was as black as Henry Armstrong's. I couldn't tell if it was ebony or mahogany or something else, and I didn't feel like asking.

"I'm sorry," I said.

"And I'm now an internist," he said.

"I thought you were a surgeon."

"Surgeon's have to stand up and do surgery, sometimes for hours," he explained. "I can't stand up for more than twenty minutes without pain. Ever hear of a surgeon who operated sitting down?"

"Why not," I tried.

"Go to medical school for four years, then do an internship and a couple of years of residency and we'll talk about it," he answered.

"I got in a couple of years of college," I said, "and lots of years in the field."

"Different fields," Parry said, nodding at the burly nurse who passed us. "You want me to hire you to go back to that island and find my leg? I don't think it can be put back on but this war is a devil's send for surgeons. We get to do so many things, try new ideas. The human guinea pigs are carted in by the dozens. I got to be one of them."

"Well, I'd love to stay around here and have you cheer me up, but I've got work to do," I said. "Did you know Herbert Marshall has a wooden leg? Sarah Bernhardt had one. That pitcher for the White Sox, Monty Stratton, had one."

"Surgeons all," he said.

"Hell, maybe you can pitch or act," I said.

The smile was there. Not much of a smile, but a smile. I considered it a small triumph.

"Get out, Peters," he said.

I saluted him with two fingers to my forehead, like Jimmy Cagney in *The Public Enemy,* and hurried down the hall in search of a telephone.

I didn't find one till I had made my way back to the lobby. The Edna May Oliver receptionist spotted me coming from the bowels of the hospital and rose from her chair in indignation, ignoring the old man who was leaning forward to take the visitor's card from her hand.

"It's a boy," I called, heading for the phones in the corner. The uniformed guard smiled and a young couple waiting on a bench near a window looked up beaming, the woman's large stomach extending empathy.

I made three calls with my three nickels. One was to Shelly Minck, the dentist with whom I share space in the Farraday Building. Shelly had things to tell me. I didn't have time to listen. I told him I'd be coming to the office later.

"Toby," he insisted. "I've got a new idea for drumming up business."

"And I've got a life to save, a gun to get back, and a body to find," I said.

"Well, what the hell is more important?" Shelly asked.

"Business first," I agreed. "The oral hygiene of an ignorant public that yearns for the talents of Dr. Sheldon Minck."

"A half-page ad in the telephone directory and the *Times,*" he said. "Plates."

"You're going to sell plates, Shel?"

"Not plates you eat off of," he said with exasperation. "Plates you eat with, in your mouth."

"Right, Shelly. I've—"

"See yourself as others see you," he said, probably reading a copy he had written on the wall. "Take the mirror test. Plates can look natural. Happy days are here again. Pay later. Don't worry about money. Plates repaired while you wait. What do you think?"

"Sounds terrific, Shelly. Now I'm hanging up."

"And my picture pointing at a mirror. I mean a picture of a mirror," he said dreamily. "If I can only get Mildred to invest a little of her money in the ads, I'm sure it will pay back in a matter of weeks."

The chances of Mildred Minck dipping into the money she had inherited from her Uncle Abel were about equal to those of MacArthur calling it a day and giving up on the Pacific.

"I'm hanging up, Shelly," and I did.

A chunky balding man in a suit and carrying a briefcase bounced impatiently on his heels waiting for the phone.

"It's a boy," I said, dropping my second nickel into the phone. The businessman was not touched.

Information didn't have a phone number for John Wayne. That didn't surprise me but it had been worth a try. There were other ways of reaching him, but they would take a little time. I dropped my last nickel into the phone and didn't turn to explain to the bouncing businessman behind me. I let my voice rise when I said, "Wilshire Station? I'd like to speak to Captain Pevsner."

"Wait," came the raspy man's voice on the other end. I waited, imagining my gun being used in a series of murders, robberies, and assorted displays of public mayhem.

"Busy," came the male voice in a few seconds.

"How about Lieutenant Seidman?" I asked.

"Vacation."

"I'm coming in to see Captain Pevsner. Tell him his brother's on the way."

"Brother," said the voice on the other end.

"Get it?" I tried.

"Got it," he answered.

"Good," I said, happy to have gotten more than a one-word answer. I hung up and made way for the businessman.

I turned on the car radio and found that Jinx Falkenburg wanted me to try Royal Crown Cola. I decided to try it once for Jinx, though I didn't think I could be disloyal to Pepsi. I daydreamed my way onto Pico and took in the fact that the Pico Theater was showing Hitchcock's *Suspicion*. If I could wrap this up quickly I would try to persuade Carmen, the cashier at Levy's on Spring, to join me for a taco or two and a movie. I would have liked to call my ex-wife, Anne, recently widowed from husband two, and push her for a cup of coffee, some conversation, and a further crack in our thawing relationship, but she was not back from her trip East to visit her parents and get away from the messy demise of Ralph.

For some reason I started to sing "Mississippi Mud" like Bing Crosby and the Rhythm Boys, while tapping time on the steering wheel, and just managed to avoid a collision with a beer truck. At ten-fifteen "Vic and Sade" came on and I shut up while Sade recounted the tale of the mailman with different color eyes who was drawing the attention of the neighborhood spinsters.

It took the sight of the Wilshire Station to erase the sweet smile from my face, but though clientless, I felt that things were going my way in spite of the missing gun, missing body, and missing killer. Almost anything was better than wearing a uniform and guarding the Goleta gate house.

I parked a block away. There were spaces right in front of the station but I didn't know how this session was going to go and I didn't want people who were less than pals, including my brother the cop, taking things out on my helpless vehicle. A good portion of my meager income over the past decade had gone to replacing cars and paying for parking tickets that were all too often gifts of police wanting to teach me a much-needed lesson in civic responsibility.

The sky was clear and the wind gentle as I climbed the stone steps and entered the grayness of the reception area. The area was empty except for the overage police sergeant who sat at a desk behind the low railing.

"Veldu," I said.

"Peters," he responded. "Hell of a world."

"Hell of a world," I agreed, walking past him to the dark wooden stairway.

"He's not in a good mood," Veldu called after me.

"I wouldn't have it any other way," I said. His laugh echoed up the stairs and mixed with the stale smells coming down from above.

In an effort to conserve energy, the janitors in all the Los Angeles police stations had been told to replace bulbs as they died with ones with lower wattage. The result was an estimated saving of $18,000 a year in electric bills and the medical loss of about $24,000 from overage and overweight cops and robbers falling down unlighted stairs or plowing into the walls of darkened toilets.

My brother's office was upstairs and down the hall to the right. He had graduated from the cubbyhole inside the squad-room he had had as a lieutenant to this private space across the hall.

I knocked. He didn't answer. I knocked again.

"Who the hell is it?" he shouted.

"Toby," I said.

"Shit," he shouted.

I opened the door and stepped in. Phil gave me a gray look and swiveled in his chair, the phone in his hand pressed against his ear. I sat down in one of the two wooden chairs in front of his desk. The room looked like a monk's cell. At least it looked like the monks' cells I'd seen in a few movies. It was big and empty, with the exception of Phil's desk, the chairs, and a cabinet in the corner. The windows had incongruous curtains made by Phil's wife, Ruth. Instead of brightening the place, they reminded the visitor of how much in need of work the rest of the room was. The wooden floor was uncovered and worn from the weight of cops and robbers crossing it since the turn of the century. Phil fit the room perfectly. He was pushing 240 pounds, fifty-two years, and a bad temper he had trouble keeping in check. His steel gray hair was cut short and bristly. Phil ran his hand over it absently, when he wasn't adjusting his tie or rearranging his desk, while he talked or worked. His hands longed for the old days on the street when he had been able to reach out and put his pulpy fingers around the neck of some grafter, grifter, or grabber and teach him the error of his ways. Promotion and respectability were ruining Phil, and the increase in salary wasn't compensating. The conversation he was having on the phone seemed a case in point.

"That's the shore patrol's job," he said, pulling at his collar. "I didn't tell them to put those thirty-two taverns and bars off limits . . . I know. I know, but before, it took us five officers to patrol Fifth and Main Street. If we enforce this, it will take fifteen officers. I don't have fifteen officers to change diapers for swabs and GIs."

Whoever was on the other end of the call took over, and Phil had to sit and listen, nodding his head and looking at me with distaste. I shrugged and examined the decor, the dirty walls, the backs of the photographs of Ruth and his three kids on his desk.

"I know there's a war on," Phil got in. But whoever the other person was, he took over again and I could see that Phil was losing. Phil hid his impending defeat well, but, as his brother, I could tell the truth from subtle hints like the gritting of his teeth and the hurling of a pencil across the room. I watched the pencil fly like an anemic miniature javelin, mark the wall with a small graphite check, and clatter to the floor.

I got up, retrieved the pencil, and returned it to the desk. Phil took it and aimed his next throw at the wall behind me. I let the pencil lie there this time and sat quietly, my hands folded in my lap till the conversation ended and Phil hung up.

"They're fine," he said before I could ask about his family. "What do you want?"

"Well—" I began, but he stared at the phone and interrupted me.

"Where am I going to get six policeman a night?"

I shrugged.

"I've got a multiple murder in the valley," Phil said, turning his back to me and talking to the curtains. "I've got kids, little kids, seven-, eight-year-olds down at the farmers' market, dozens of them stealing anything that isn't nailed down. You know how many policeman are needed to patrol that?"

"Seven," I guessed.

Phil swiveled around and plumped both hands on the desk.

"Who asked you?"

"You did," I reminded him.

"What do you want?"

"Hotel dick at the Alhambra, Straight-Ahead Beason," I said.

"Used to be a cop," Phil said, touching his forehead to see if he had a fever.

"Used to be a cop," I agreed. "Got himself shot yesterday. I just saw him at the hospital. He thinks the guy who did it is out there and looking for John Wayne."

"Looking for John Wayne," said Phil, looking up from his troubles for the first time and actually listening to me. "Why the hell would someone who shot a hotel dick be looking for John Wayne?"

"Straight-Ahead heard something when he got shot," I explained.

"And what part aren't you telling me?" Phil said, his knuckles turning white on the desk.

"Nothing," I said, which was the truth—with the exception of the fact that my gun was gone, Vance was dead and missing, and Teddy Longretti was involved.

"Bullshit," he said. "What do you want?"

"Someone to keep an eye on Wayne till we find the guy with the gun," I answered.

"Didn't you hear what I said when you came in? Everyone wants a cop. I don't have a cop for you. The young cops are in the Army. I've got officers who are too few and too old. If it weren't for the damn war I'd be one of them. I never would have been promoted."

"Well—" I tried, but, once again, was interrupted.

"No protection," he said. "Wayne will have to get his own protection unless you come up with something stronger than the maybe of a stiff-necked house detective who was passing out with a bullet wound in his pride. Cawelti took the Alhambra call. Go see him."

Sergeant John Cawelti and I were not friends. We had not been friends since our first meeting. I had that effect on people, from hospital desk clerks to cops. Cawelti had the same effect on people. We were not a good pair to co-star in *The New Moon.*

"Phil," I said, playing with the idea of telling him about the gun and body.

"Out," he said.

I knew better than to argue with Phil, especially when his eyes were turned down and his outstretched hand was pointing at the door. I knew better but I never acted on that knowledge. Bile ran too deep between us. I couldn't slink out that door, even though I knew that the next step might be a violent chapter in the tale of two brothers.

"Would it make a difference if I said please?" I asked.

"O-U-T. Even Lucy knows what that spells," he said between clenched teeth.

Lucy was his year-old daughter and my niece. Phil tended to equate our emotional development.

"Okay," I said, getting up. "Okay. But this attitude of yours seriously jeopardizes the possibility of my getting you a birthday present next month. I was seriously considering a Fred Waring album."

Phil's head was down. This was the moment of truth. I could get to the door before him. I was sure of that. He had too much weight on him and had picked up more since his promotion. I wasn't sure I could make it down the stairs in the dim light before he caught me, however.

I saw the smile. He kept his head down and hid it, but I saw it. Instead of speaking, he simply waved his hand and shook his head as the phone rang. I left as he said on the phone, "Of course, Mrs. Borrows, I haven't forgotten the neighborhood bond drive."

I closed the door and walked the long mile to the door of the squadroom. Like Wyatt Earp in *Frontier Marshall,* I took a deep breath and stepped in to meet the equivalent of Ike Clanton.

4

The smell of food hit me when I pushed the doors open and entered the squad room. It was the familiar smell of a room where men work around the clock and sometimes the people and food they bring in are a bit ripe. The room, cluttered with desks and files, was cleaner than usual. It wasn't clean, but on Sunday an old colored guy named Nero Suggs had peeled away the top layer of filth and found someplace to dump the waste baskets.

There were four or five cops around beside Cawelti and a couple of citizens and citizens who prey on citizens. Cawelti was sitting at his desk off to the right, just a little removed from his fellow officers. He was one-finger typing a report, and his red face and poor complexion and his reddish straight hair parted down the middle like a comic bartender's stood out across the room. A thin guy of about sixty in a suit was sitting on the chair within easy reach of Cawelti. I couldn't tell if the graying wisp was a good citizen or a bad guy. I could see he was scared, as if someone were about to hit him. I took two steps toward Cawelti's desk and Cawelti reached over and slapped the man in the head.

"Don't hit me in the head like that," the man said, recoiling and holding his slapped head with an open palm.

Cawelti didn't apologize or promise better things for the future. He went back to his report. When I was a foot or two from the desk, the wispy man looked up at me ready to protect himself from an attack on a new front.

"Cawelti," I said, but he didn't grunt, just pondered over the spelling of some troublesome word. He made a decision and went on. In the corner a couple of fat cops thought of something funny. One of them thought it was so funny he spilled half his coffee on an unoccupied desk. He didn't bother to clean it up.

"Sergeant," I tried. The wispy man in the chair shivered.

"Peters," he said without looking back at me, "go away."

"I'm here about the Beason case," I said.

"There is no Beason case," Cawelti said, getting in two more letters on his typewriter. "Hotel dick gets shot by hash-headed hotel clerk. Clerk grabs ten grand from the safe and runs. What do you think we're going to do, send out an all-states on Teddy Spaghetti? Maybe we should call back the troops from Europe, go house to house. I've got to work here."

"A man's been shot," I said. "I've always been able to rely on your compassion."

"Go tell your jokes to your brother," he said. "I've got a murder case I'm wrapping up. Beason will get better. Longretti will turn up on a garbage heap some morning. Case closed."

"But—" I began, and he turned to face me. As he turned, his eyes met those of the thin man with the white hair and the neat suit. Before the man knew what was coming, Cawelti reached out and hit him again with an open palm, this time on the other side of the man's head.

"I told you, don't hit me," the man said. Then he looked at me for help. "You heard me tell him. It hurts to be hit like that."

Cawelti shrugged and gave me his attention. "I've got paperwork on this weed," he said, nodding at the slapped man. "Mr. Patterson of the firm of Patterson and Walker owns the New Hollywood apartment building on La Cienega. You know it?"

"New building, about fourteen stories, went up just before the war started," I said.

Cawelti nodded yes and went on.

"Mr. Patterson here made a mistake. He gave the tenants long leases and reasonable rents. Times were still a little hard. Then the war comes and rents fly and everyone's moving to Los Angeles to make war money building boats and airplanes and Mr. Patterson starts feeling sorry for himself for all the money he could be making so he tries to get his tenants to move. Mr. Patterson here is ingenious at making his tenants move and breaking their leases, aren't you, Mr. Patterson."

Patterson cringed, expecting another blow, but didn't answer.

"Threats from hired hands, mysterious break-ins, plumbing problems," Cawelti went on. "Then Mr. Patterson makes a mistake. Up on the tenth floor lives an old guy with a heart problem."

"Ninth floor," Patterson corrected.

"Mr. Patterson fixed the light on the elevator so that when the old guy gets on, the lights go bam-bam-bam. The old guy looks up and thinks maybe the elevator is falling and he's only going to be fit for burial in a Mason jar when it hits bottom. Old guy gets a heart attack. Vacant apartment. Only trouble is, Mr. Patterson didn't have time to fix the elevator lights again before we found the naughty little trick."

"I didn't do this thing," Patterson protested to me, turning in his chair, palms up, pleading. I was unconvinced.

"Proving it is proving hard but not impossible," Cawelti went on, giving Patterson a look that promised pain. "And Mr. Patterson is not cooperating. He is not confessing like a good citizen."

"So you haven't got time for Beason," I concluded.

"You got it," he said, returning to his report.

"Beason tells me that Teddy and some guy he's working

with named Alex are out to get a movie star," I said. "Two hash heads loose with a gun shooting at a movie star could embarrass you, John."

"Don't call me John," he said without turning. "You want to walk out of here instead of crawl, don't call me John. In fact, don't call me at all, just get out now."

"Right," I said. "If John Wayne catches a bullet in his teeth, I'll tell the *Times* how interested the police were in keeping him alive."

Cawelti spun around, suddenly very angry or very interested. The move was so quick that Patterson leaped from his chair with a howl.

"Sit down," Cawelti yelled. Across the room the cops stopped joking for a minute in the hope of seeing some real mayhem, but Patterson sat down and Cawelti just stared red-faced at me. The cops went back to their coffee and ringing phones.

"John Wayne, someone might be trying to kill John Wayne?" he asked.

"Could be," I said.

"Shit. They can't do that." His right hand went out and grabbed the nearest piece of paper, crunching it into an ugly Christmas ball. He stood up leaning toward me. He had me by about three inches.

"I'll find that little son of a bitch," he hissed. "Kill John Wayne. What the hell is this world coming to?"

Patterson shrugged, but Cawelti didn't see him.

"Wayne's the only damn movie star who means anything except for Spencer Tracy," Cawelti explained. "I'll get on it but you better be giving me this straight. And what's it all got to do with you?"

"It's my gun Teddy has," I explained.

Cawelti's red face looked like a traffic light.

"Beason borrowed it," I improvised. "He had trouble with

his own. Both of us have permits. When this Alex shot Beason, he took my thirty-eight from him."

Cawelti looked down at his desk, his hands supporting him amid the pile of papers. He turned to Patterson and said, "Do you believe this guy?"

Patterson knew a cue when he heard one. He shook his head no.

"I know I'm going to get shit for an answer, but I'll ask anyway. It's my job. Why John Wayne? Why the Duke?"

"Wayne's a client." I plunged in even deeper. "Maybe Teddy's gone off the top. He knew me, doesn't like me. Maybe he saw me with Wayne. In fact, I had a late dinner with Wayne last night at Manny's on Broadway."

Cawelti cocked his head like a bird.

"Check with Manny if you don't believe me. Check with Wayne."

"I could meet John Wayne," Cawelti said.

"Sure, I th—"

"I'll look for Teddy and the gun. You stay with Wayne," Cawelti said. "And I want to talk to Wayne. That's part of the deal."

I could have pointed out that citizens shouldn't have to make deals to get the police to protect them, but I had some part of my brain still functioning. I nodded in agreement.

"Now get out. I think there's a lot of shit about this thing you're not dumping on my desk," Cawelti said, and he was damn right. "I'll find out what it is and we'll have that little talk I've been promising you. I can be a persuasive talker, can't I, Mr. Patterson?"

"Very persuasive," Patterson agreed.

"I'll be in touch," I said, turning to leave and almost bumping into a cop dragging a man in a trench coat behind him. The cop, named Bresnahan, was handcuffed to the trench-coated guy, who wore a little white cap. The trench coat flopped open for a second as the man teetered, revealing nothing but his scrawny body.

"Toby, how's it going?" Bresnahan said, yanking the flasher up to his feet.

"Fair enough," I said. "There's an Army Boxing Show at the Hollywood Legion Wednesday."

"Naw," said Bresnahan, who had done some amateur fighting. "Their hearts aren't in it unless rankings are on the line. I'll wait till the war's over and the guys with heart come back."

Behind me I could hear Cawelti explaining to Patterson how John Wayne got his nickname "Duke."

"It was his dog," Cawelti said seriously, as if explaining history to a dense student. "He had a dog named Duke when he was a kid. Glendale firemen started calling the kid *and* the dog Duke and it stuck."

Someone moaned behind me as I went out the squad room door. I would have put my money on Bresnahan's flasher, but Cawelti's good moods didn't last very long and Patterson might be on the floor with remnants of some cop's Italian beef dinner and the blood of the guilty and innocent alike.

Cawelti had given me two things I hadn't had when I came in, a headache and the information that Teddy not only had my gun and Vance's corpse but $10,000. Ten grand was a lot for a dump like the Alhambra to have in the safe. I'd have to ask Straight-Ahead about it when he was up and marching.

I got my first death threat of the day when I got back to my office in the Farraday. I had parked in No-Neck Arnie's garage, answered politely when he asked me how the car he had sold me was doing, told him I wasn't ready to fix the door that wouldn't open, and hiked the two blocks to the Farraday. My back jingled nervously and I told myself to call Doc

Hodgdon, the old orthopedic specialist who I played handball with at the Y on Hope and who, occasionally, got me back on my feet when my limbs creaked or cracked.

The office I shared with Dr. Minck was on the top floor of the four-story Farraday Building on Hoover near Ninth. The Farraday was owned by Jeremy Butler, a mountain of a bald man who had made a reasonably good living and a good name for himself as a professional wrestler before retiring to write poetry and manage property he had bought with his sweat. He lived at the Farraday and dedicated himself to keeping the building clean of dust, decay, and neighborhood bums who found their way into the cool recesses of the building.

The steel elevator sat on the main floor, waiting for the unsuspecting to climb in and be trapped into the longest ride this side of the Orient Express. I started slowly up the fake marble stairs, listening to the early afternoon sounds of tenants, the distant whirl of a printing press, the sound of arguing voices, and someone who might have been singing or might have been calling out for help.

On the fourth floor I wandered through the not unpleasant smell of generously sprinkled Lysol and opened our outer office door. The pebbled, opaque glass window had a neatly printed notice in black letters:

DR. SHELDON MINCK, DENTIST, D.D.S., S.D.
PAINLESS DENTISTRY AND PERFECT
PLATES SINCE 1916

TOBY PETERS, INVESTIGATOR

Shelly had agreed to this compromise after pleas, promises, and threats from me. His idea of door lettering was much more fanciful and less given to truth.

The small anteroom held two chairs, a small table, overfull ashtrays, and a pile of magazines in disarray and with covers missing. Jinx Falkenburg looked up at me from one of the magazines. She was everywhere. I wondered if it was time for me to write her a fan letter, maybe try to talk her into trying Pepsi. I pushed through the anteroom door expecting to see Shelly torturing a patient or sitting in his dental chair reading, but the room was empty and silent except for the dripping of water into a cup in the sink near my office. The sink was, once again, piled with dishes and coffee cups. For almost a month after a dental association inspection, Shelly had kept the place reasonably clean, but old habits, like old house detectives, die hard. I turned the handle to slow down the dripping water and noticed that the door to my office was open slightly.

My office off Shelly's was slightly larger than a toilet stall at Union Station. There was a very small desk with a chair and one window behind it. There were also two chairs across the desk, which could be squeezed into comfortably by normal-size people. The chairs needed replacing, as did the plaster on the ceiling. The walls were dirty white and undecorated except for my dusty framed private investigator's license and a photograph from when I was a kid. The photo showed me, my dad, and my brother, Phil, plus our dog Kaiser Wilhelm. It wasn't much, but it was home, except when I had a client. I did my best to keep clients away from Shelly and my office.

Shelly, who was seated behind my desk, didn't seem surprised or embarrassed by my entrance. He was writing something with one of my pencils, leaning close to the paper, peering with myopic eyes through his thick glasses. His ever-present cigar was shifting from side to side in his mouth, and tiny beads of sweat were dancing on his brow.

"Toby, advertising is the key to the future. I'm convinced of it," he said, removing his cigar to point its wet end at me.

"What are you doing in my office, Sheldon?" I said, leaving the door open behind me.

"I'm writing," he said, pointing at the paper. "I'm working on our futures, both of our futures. Translucent teeth." Then he read: "'A size for every face. A size for every case. A shade for every complexion.' How do you like that?"

"I've heard it somewhere," I said. "I've got work to do, Shel."

He waved my work away with a free left hand and then wiped the hand on his unclean white smock.

"Listen." He read again: "'Toby Peters, Investigations. You may know but can you prove it? True facts secured and submitted in confidential reports. Local and national investigations. Missing persons our specialty.'"

"Our specialty?" I asked, still standing. "There's only me. And I haven't got money for ads. I can't pay for my gas as it is and if you don't get out from behind there and let me work I may have trouble coming up with my rent for this place."

Shelly got up with a sigh and looked at me as if I were a pathetic child.

"You don't understand," he said. "You've got to invest to earn."

I came around the desk, looked out the window, vowed to clean it, and sat down, easing Shelly out of the way. "Did Mildred give you the money for your ad campaign?"

"Not yet," he admitted, "but I'm working on her, got tickets for *Life with Father* at the Music Box. Dorothy Gish and Louis Calhern. Might try to talk to Gish. Her teeth—"

"Any messages for me, Shel," I asked, handing him the sheet of scrawling he had left on my desk.

"I'm talking about your future here, Toby," he said. "You're not getting any younger."

"Thank God one of us isn't," I said, shuffling through the junk mail. "Messages?"

Shelly put the cigar back in his mouth, adjusted his slipping glasses, and slapped his sides.

"Yeah, you got messages. Let's see. I wrote them down somewhere. Your landlady called. Something about a photograph she found. Hy called—"

"Which. . . ?"

"The one from Hy of Hy's Clothes for Him on Hollywood," said Shelly. "He says you owe him eight dollars and something."

"That it?" I asked, hearing the door to the outer office open.

"No, some guy called. Said his name was Alex. Said something nuts like stay out of it or away from it if you don't want what Lance got."

"Lance? You mean Vance?"

"Vance, Lance." Shelly shrugged.

"You think you might have passed on this death threat a little earlier," I asked amiably.

"I had a patient," Shelly said. "You get nut calls all the time. How am I supposed to know what's a threat and who's a nut? I got to go." Someone entered the outer office and Shelly left, closing the door behind him. I searched the top of my desk for the message from Alex. I found it sticking to a letter from Hollywood Tennis and Golf Shop promising me a great discount on restringing my racket.

The note from Shelly didn't help much. I could make out the name "Alex" and the words "Stay up" or "Stay out."

I spent the next twenty minutes trying to find John Wayne and listening to the groans from one of Shelly's patients over Shelly's off-key singing of "I've Got a Gal in Kalamazoo." I finally got through to Wayne at the Allegheny Hotel through a tip from a guy in the security office at Republic Pictures.

"Hello," came Wayne's voice, a little boozy or sleepy.

"It's me, Toby Peters," I said. "We've got to talk about cleaning up after the party last night."

"I thought the party was all cleaned up."

"Not quite. Can you talk?"

"I can talk." He sighed. "I've got a friend here but he's all right."

"Vance's body is missing. Teddy the clerk shot Straight-Ahead with my gun and got away with ten thousand dollars. There's also reason to believe that Teddy is working with some guy named Alex, who may have a grudge against you."

"You and your friend really cleaned things up," he said with reasonable exasperation.

"It happens like that sometimes. I've talked to the police, and a cop named Cawelti who's a fan of yours is working with me to find Teddy and Alex. I just want to be sure nothing happens to you. If I tracked you down, Alex might be able to, too."

"I'm going on a fishing trip with a couple of friends this afternoon," Wayne said. "We won't tell anyone but my manager where we are and I'll tell him not to tell anyone. I'll be gone about a week."

"Your friends are . . ." I started.

"Their names are Wardell Bond and Grant Whithers. They drink too much, can't shoot straight, and are damned ugly, but they are friends. And before you ask it, I don't remember anyone named Alex who might not like my face. In my business you make friends and enemies without knowing it. Any more questions?"

"None I can think of," I said.

"Good, I'll send you a check for fifty dollars this week and another fifty next week for finding this guy. Will that cover things?"

"It's a little less than I usually get," I said.

"Amigo," Wayne said with a sigh. "I'm generous to a fault but my business manager has me on a hundred-dollar-a-week budget. He hopes to make me a millionaire. I just signed a hundred-thousand-dollar-a-picture deal with Republic, so maybe I can get Bo to cough up something more reasonable. Hell, if your friend Alex gets me, there won't be any money for anyone, me, my soon-to-be-ex wife, and all four of my kids."

I wished him good fishing, told him my address, and said I'd get messages to him, if there were any, through his agent, whose name and phone number he gave me.

With Wayne officially my client, I felt a lot better. I also felt hungry. The next step was something to eat and a trip to wherever Teddy Spaghetti dwelled, but first I had to get past the horror chamber of Dr. Faustus.

"I'm going, Shel," I said, glancing over the hunched shoulders of Dr. Minck and the twitching legs of a woman.

"The ads," Shelly grunted in farewell.

On the stairway going down I encountered Jeremy Butler. Jeremy was mopping his way downward step by step. He wore double-extra-large shirts but they didn't completely cover his almost three hundred pounds of flesh. At first glance Jeremy looked a bit fat, but after an encounter, the unwary realized that he was a sensitive pile of muscle.

"Toby, I was hoping to meet you today."

"How are things, Jeremy?" I asked.

"The battle with decay and ignorance never really ends," he said, looking around and listening to the echo of his voice through the Farraday. "But there are bright corners. Alice and I are planning to be married on Friday, a simple ceremony in my office. We'd like you to attend. Four o'clock."

"Congratulations, Jeremy," I said, reaching out a hand, which was engulfed and almost devoured. I wondered how many people besides Jeremy and Alice Pallice could fit in Jeremy's third-floor office and apartment. Alice almost matched Jeremy in bulk. She had been and still was a Farraday tenant. Her profession had involved the publication of pornographic books. Her talent had been the fact that she could tuck the printing press under her arm and escape from oncoming police in seconds. Jeremy had converted her to poetry and children's books. It did not do to dwell too long on the image of the two of them locked in love, though I assumed Jeremy would be a most gentle suitor.

"I'll be there," I said. "Wouldn't miss it."

"A simple ceremony," he said. "A service and perhaps one of my poems. I'd also like to extend an invitation to Gunther. I'll invite Dr. Minck also."

"Great," I said, "I'll be there."

An hour later, with a couple of bowls of chili and a Royal Crown Cola in me, I felt better. I also felt worse, but there was more better than worse.

The lobby of the Alhambra seemed to have lost no further illumination since the night before, but it hadn't picked up any either. I didn't know the woman behind the desk and there was no one in the lobby to witness our momentous introduction. She was a corrugated box of a woman, neatly suited, brown hair pulled back tight and tied with a rubber band. She looked more like the turnkey in a woman's prison picture than the desk clerk at a seedy hotel.

"You want a room?" she asked as I approached. There was none of the warm greeting of the innkeeper for the weary traveler in her tone.

"My name is Peters," I said, holding my wallet open to reveal my investigator's badge. Actually, I had a certification card from the state but I usually flashed the badge my nephew Dave gave me. It had been issued by the Dick Tracy Club and at six feet looked better than my brother's real badge. The gray-suited woman took in the badge without comment. "What do you know about last night?"

"Last night?" she asked, playing games.

"Merit Beason getting shot, Teddy Longretti running away with the cash in the safe, little things like that that might have slipped your mind."

"I am very concerned about this theft. My husband and I own this hotel and several others," she explained. "I told the other police all about that this morning."

Her hands had been folded in front of her on the desk but they must have been getting a bit wet. She reached under the desk and came up with a handkerchief to wipe her palms.

"And what about the money, Mrs. . . ."

"Larchmont, Adrienne Larchmont. The money is missing."

I moved closer, now that my badge was safely tucked away, and leaned over the counter, intruding on her space. She backed up.

"That was a lot of money," I said. "A lot to be in a hotel like this on a Sunday night. Didn't the policeman, Sergeant Cawelti, ask you that?"

Mrs. Larchmont definitely looked nervous now. Her mouth quivered a bit.

"He did not think that entirely relevant, but I explained that my husband and I sometimes kept cash from our various properties in the safe over the weekend pending the opening of the bank on Monday morning and the opportunity to deposit."

"Which in this case never came," I said.

"I am less concerned with the recovery of the money than in the apprehension of Mr. Longretti," she said, looking around for something to do with her hands. Someone blundered into the lobby behind me. I didn't turn around. "Why don't you get this from the other policeman? I really have nothing more to add."

I could hear two pairs of feet moving toward the desk and the whispering voices of a man and woman, but I kept my eyes on Mrs. Larchmont, who was squirming more than she should have been.

"I read minds," I whispered, leaning in closer. "There was more than ten thousand dollars in that safe Mrs. L., maybe more money, maybe something else that's missing, something you didn't mention to Sergeant Cawelti. Maybe you and the mister are not too anxious for Teddy to be caught."

Her mouth dropped open, but I didn't expect her to call out bingo. I had hit something but it would take more to get it out of her.

"We'd like a room," a voice from behind me said. Mrs. Larchmont couldn't take her eyes from mine. Sweat had formed on her upper lip.

"A room," Mrs. Larchmont repeated.

"Right, this is a hotel ain't it? You have rooms," the voice repeated.

"Give us a minute," I said, keeping my eyes on Mrs. Larchmont. I didn't want the spell I had cast broken, but it wasn't to be. The voice repeated, "A room. We haven't got forever."

I turned, ready to do some insisting, but my eyes were level with a thick neck. The owner was about six-four, wearing an army uniform and carrying a lot of weight, and he was no kid. The woman at his side matched him year for year and looked just as tough. They had no luggage and I wanted to stay alive.

"Sorry," I said with a grin, and stepped back to give them room. By the time Mrs. Larchmont had checked the two war lovers into their room, I knew I had lost her.

"I'm afraid you will have to leave," she said. "I can help

you no further. My attorney will have to be contacted before my husband or I will deal with the police further." Her handkerchief was a mess.

"I want Teddy's address," I said. "Where does he live?"

"I don't—"

"He worked for you. The law says you have to keep tax records, personnel records. You want to obstruct justice, I can call in building inspectors. If we have a violation here, I—"

She reached under the counter and came out with a little box filled with index cards. Her lips were drawn thin and her hands trembling. "I don't like working here, not even for a few hours," she said. Then her fingers touched a card and paused. "He lives at—"

I reached over and took the card from her hand. Teddy's address was on Witmer.

"Did you give this address to Sergeant Cawelti?"

"He didn't ask for it," she said primly.

"Ten thousand dollars," I said with an evil grin. She didn't comment but her eyes danced. Something was going on and Teddy's apartment might tell me what it was.

Witmer wasn't far. I listened to a few minutes of "Young Widder Brown" and caught a few seconds of Hollywood news, enough to learn that Myrna Loy had gotten married and Alice Faye and Phil Harris's two-week-old baby, Alice Junior, was doing just fine.

Teddy "Spaghetti" Longretti's room was not doing nearly as well as Myrna Loy's love life and Alice's baby. Teddy's room was in a six-flat building. The downstairs door was probably supposed to be locked but the lock had long since given up trying to keep anyone out. The halls were colorfully decorated with obscenities and incoherent war slogans. Teddy's name had been scrawled on the downstairs mailbox with the number of his apartment. I had no trouble finding it on the second floor. I knocked but didn't expect an answer.

The door wasn't open but it wasn't ready to protect the domicile either. I hit it with my shoulder and popped in, accompanied by splinters of wood. No one stirred in the apartment across the way as I stood and listened. So I closed the door and turned to look around.

In the next half hour I discovered where the publicity officers for the major and minor movie studios in Los Angeles dumped their garbage. There were one-sheets from Monogram Westerns, photographs of actors and actresses whose names were lost in the antiquity of Hollywood's rapid history. Press books, lead pencils with Richard Arlen's name on them, and even a napkin autographed by both Douglas Fairbanks and Don Ameche.

My trip down memory lane revealed no money and a lot of memories. I was considering giving up when I came on what seemed to be more memorabilia in a desk drawer. This stuff was different. It was in a nice clean envelope and the papers were letters, signed letters, one by Charlie Chaplin. Then a second by Chaplin and a third.

Most of the letters in the file were from Chaplin to Sydney Larchmont. They moved chronologically from September 1941 to March 1942. The letters started cordially, inquiries about "the donation." By the end of 1941, the letters were no longer so cordial, and by March, Charles Spencer Chaplin was definitely not enamored of Sydney Larchmont. In fact, the Little Fellow was threatening legal action if there was no answer to his inquiries.

I took the file and letters and continued my search for ten more minutes, finding nothing of interest besides a closet with some clothes, $28 in a sock, and the sorriest-looking collection of food in the refrigerator and small cupboard in the corner.

It didn't look as if Teddy had come back home after his scrape with Straight-Ahead at the Alhambra. It also didn't look as if either Vance's body or my .38 were on the premises.

Instead of answers, I had more questions. What were the Larchmonts up to? Where was Vance's body? What did Charlie Chaplin have to do with all this, if anything? How much money would John Wayne send me in the mail? Did I have time to stop for a hot dog at Maury's on Sepulveda?

I thought of these questions as I drove through a sudden drizzle back downtown. I would have thought of more questions and maybe even a few answers if I hadn't found Lewis Vance's body when I got back to the Farraday. He was sitting in the waiting room outside Shelly's office.

5

I left Vance sitting there wondering where he might wander to next and opened the door to Shelly's office. Something smelled all wrong and it wasn't just Vance's two-day-old body.

"Shel," I said, watching him hunched over a victim in the chair.

"Busy," he said. "Busy now."

The patient in the chair was wearing cowboy boots, but I couldn't tell if it was a man or a woman. Shelly's body obliterated gender and sensibility.

"You've got a patient out there waiting and he's getting a bit fragrant," I said.

"Almost, almost," Shelly answered, his right arm moving back and forth, a metal tool plunged into his patient's mouth. The patient gave off a constant, gurgling, sexless *urghhh.*

"Shel," I repeated.

"Now," he groaned, and his arm pulled back holding a plierlike tool, which in turn held a tooth. "Damn," Shelly said, beaming as he turned to show me the tooth. Sweat beads vibrated on his red face. He turned to show his catch to the creature in the chair but the creature, a man whom I didn't know but could now see clearly, didn't seem to care. His mouth remained open, his eyes blank.

Shelly moved over to me and whispered, still clutching the tool and tooth.

"Damn thing wouldn't come out but it didn't have a chance against me."

"You and the tooth were enemies," I said, hoping to get him over this professional outburst so I could deal with our dead visitor.

"Enemies, yes," he said, adjusting his slipping glasses and relighting his cigar after plunging the tooth in the dirty pocket of his once-white smock. "Oral hygiene takes a backseat to no rotted tooth."

"Get rid of him, Shel," I whispered. "We have another patient to take care of in the waiting room."

"The three guys?" he said, blowing a puff of smoke into the stale air of his office and glancing at the still unmoving man in the chair.

"Three?"

"The two guys with the yellow shirts and the sick one," he said. "I told them I'd be with them in a few minutes."

"There's only one guy out there now, Shel," I whispered. "And he's dead."

Shelly looked at me over his glasses. It gave him an air of intensity, but I knew it eliminated his minimal sight. "I haven't worked on him," he said, his hand moving to his heart.

"No one's accusing you of killing him," I said. "Just get rid of Buffalo Bill quick."

I gave Shelly a little push to urge him on, but he almost slipped as he approached his patient.

"Mr. Guerero," he said. "Mr. Guerero?"

"Urghhh," said Mr. Guerero, a common response from a patient on a first visit to Dr. Sheldon Minck.

"Mr. Guerero, the tooth is out." Shelly patted his pocket. A spot of blood from the extracted souvenir had seaped through.

"I don't give a shit," moaned Mr. Guerero, trying to sit up. "That hurt, you know. That hurt like—"

"A little pain—" Shelly began.

"I'm not talking 'a little pain' here," Guerero said, standing on uncertain legs. "You said 'painless.' That means 'no pain.'"

Shelly nodded his head sagely and looked at me knowingly, as if to say the poor man simply did not understand the subtle lies of the dental profession. I pointed to the waiting room.

"Pain tolerance varies," Shelly said. "That will be five dollars."

"I paid when I came in," Guerero said. He was no longer leaden-legged behind Shelly. He was lanky, solid, somewhere in his thirties, with straight black hair and a nose like the American eagle. He wore chinos and a denim vest.

"You paid for routine work," Shelly said slowly and distinctly, as if to a child. "There were complications."

I leaned against the wall and checked my watch. It told me nothing of value.

"I'm not paying you another cent," Guerero said, leaning toward Shelly.

Shelly removed his cigar from his face and pulled out his pliers for self-defense. "My associate will have something to say about that," Shelly warned. "Won't you, Mr. Peters."

Guerero paused and looked in my direction. Pain ticked in his jaw, anger in his black eyes.

"Yeah," I said, pushing away from the wall. "I wouldn't pay another cent either. I'd get the hell out and go to another dentist, one with respect for human suffering."

Guerero shook his head, thinking it was a good idea, and Shelly looked in my general direction with sincere disappointment in his chubby face.

Guerero walked past me to the door and Shelly said, "Tell the next patient to come in as you—"

Guerero slammed the door of the alcove and less than a beat later slammed the outer door.

"Betrayal, Toby," Shelly said.

"You shouldn't have called me in on it, Shel. I've warned you. We'll talk about it later. We've got to get that body . . ."

Shelly took out the recently extracted tooth, sighed, and put it on the cluttered table near the chair. Then he walked past me to the door to the alcove, opened it, and stepped out. About five seconds later he stepped back in, his face white and dry, his cigar out.

"There's a dead man out there," he said.

"I already told you that," I said. "He was shot with my gun. My gun is missing. I think someone planted him out there. They probably called the police, who will probably be here any second."

"Get him out. Get him out," Shelly screamed. "For God's sake, get him out."

"Calm down, Shel," I said calmly. "My guess is the police have my gun or it's somewhere around here."

"Shit and hell," Shelly said. "Damn and crap. Why did you have to kill him in the waiting room? Why did you have to kill one of my patients?"

"He wasn't one of your patients and I didn't kill him in the waiting room," I explained. "I didn't kill him at all."

Shelly pointed at the door.

"He should have been one of my patients. He has a pair of cavities in the lower bicuspid that are as bad as any I've seen in months. Well, Mr. Stange has a comparable—"

I put a hand on Shelly's shoulder to shut him up, but that was no easy task.

"Shel," I said calmly. "If they find him here it won't do your business a hell of a lot of good. They might even think you were part of it, an accessory, an accomplice, a—"

Far off, the Farraday elevator ground into action, a sure sign that the rider was unfamiliar with the ins and outs of the Farraday. No regular would ride the cage, not if they wanted to be anywhere within the decade. I went out the door, noticed that Vance had slumped over, and hurried into the hall to look over the railing at the elevator. From this angle I could see the distinct center part in the hair of Sergeant John Cawelti of the Los Angeles Police Department.

I got back into the waiting room, surveyed Vance, and called for Shelly. About a minute later John Cawelti, who had gotten off at the second floor and walked up, stepped into the room.

He saw me drinking a cup of solid Shelly coffee and saying, "So I bought the coat . . . Sergeant Cawelti, I didn't know you were one of Shelly's patients. You couldn't have come to a better dentist."

"Just have a seat in the waiting room," Shelly called over his shoulder. "I'll be finished with Mr. Kerensky in about twenty minutes."

"I didn't come here to see the fat dentist," Cawelti said, adjusting his tie. "A gun, your gun, was dropped off at the station about an hour ago, with a note saying you had shot someone and the body was here now."

I pretended to savor the coffee and shrugged. "No body here, at least not till Shelly gets finished with Mr. Kerensky. You see a body here, Shel?"

"No," Shelly said.

"Mr. Kerensky?" he asked.

Shelly hovered over the corpse of Vance, who was covered in a white cloth, and answered, "He can't talk. He's got cotton in his mouth."

Shelly reached over for his drill, flipped the switch, and started enough noise to give me an excuse to lead Cawelti into my office. The drill was buzzing away when we closed the door and sat down, me behind the desk, Cawelti in front of it. He was smiling as if he had a great secret he didn't plan to let me in on. He made a house of his fingers and bounced them together.

"Now," I said, casually opening a letter from a detective school in Van Nuys, "what's this about my gun? Remember, I reported it missing. When can I get it back?"

"When we find the body and match the hole in it with your thirty-eight is when," Cawelti said, bouncing his fingers.

"I'm still on the John Wayne case," I said, glancing down at the letter promising to turn me into a sleuth in three weeks for $40.

"And I'm still on your case," Cawelti said. "I think your John Wayne story was turkey fart."

I decided not to go to detective school as we sat looking at each other for a few seconds and listening to Shelly drill away at Vance's corpse.

"I can't help you, Big John," I said with a heavy sigh. "I've got no body for you and not much time either. If I shoot anyone, I'll let you know, but at the moment I don't have a gun. Someone gave you a story, John, and you came running here hoping I had a—"

He stood up and pointed his chimney finger at me. "I'm going to check every office on this floor and I'm going to check your car."

"Car's at No-Neck Arnie's on—"

"I know where it is," he said, still pointing.

"Who is this guy I'm supposed to have dusted?"

"Shit. Lewis Vance. Lewis Guy Vance. Small-time grifter," Cawelti said. "Three minor convictions and one major-league job for assault. Played in a few double cheap movies over at RKO, even had a walk-through in Chaplin's *The Great Dictator*. You never heard of him, right?"

"Never heard of him," I said with a smile, picking up my coffee cup. "Why am I supposed to have shot him?"

"Fight, extortion, something like that," Cawelti said, moving to the door. "I don't know. Don't care much. I find the body with your bullet and I'll think of a motive."

And out went Sergeant John Cawelti. He left the door open and I heard him go out and slam the doors over Shelly's drill. I gave it a count of twenty and then went into Shelly's office.

"Okay, Shel," I said. "He's gone." Shelly went right on working. I walked over to him and tapped his shoulder. "Shel, he's gone."

Shelly shrugged me off. "I've almost got this cavity cleared," he grunted.

I looked at Vance, who was definitely pale and dead, the dot in his forehead caked with blood.

"Sheldon, the man is dead. He doesn't need his teeth fixed. He needs to be buried."

"A second, give me a second, can't you," he bleated.

Cawelti could have come back. We might even have run into him in the hall, but I'd learned to give Shelly Minck his ground when dental surgery was involved, as long as I wasn't the one in the chair. He had managed to get me in that chair only once.

Shelly finished, inserted a silver filling, patted it down, and said, "Finished," as he proudly turned to face me.

Shelly's suggestions for getting Vance's corpse out of the office with Cawelti around were not helpful. He thought we might simply throw the body out the window into the alley, hoping it didn't land on some dozing derelict. I vetoed this idea, and we compromised by lowering Vance out the window with forty feet of rope purloined from Jeremy's janitor's closet. The body might have surprised a few people on the way down but no one opened a window. The dubious tenants of the Farraday had their own problems and a healthy lack of curiosity. The body and the rope ended up in the alley behind a worn-out sofa.

I left Shelly panting from the exertion and headed down the stairs. No Cawelti. Nobody. When I picked up my Ford, Arnie said that a cop who looked like a bartender had made him open the doors and the trunk and then left after sprinkling a few threats here and there.

Five minutes later I had Vance's dentally correct body in the trunk of my Ford. I had some vague ideas of what to do with him, but they had to wait while the two guys who had brought the body to the Farraday tried to kill me.

6

My '38 Ford coupe had its problems, most of them a result of frequent encounters with overly large people with bad tempers and a willful disregard for other people's property. That "willful disregard" expression came from my lawyer, slick Marty Leib, who tried to get a lunatic political party to repair my right front door after one of their members kicked it in. They didn't pay and I wound up fifty bucks in the hole for Marty's fees. The least he owed me was a good legal phrase I could toss around to impress clients. Another problem: the gas gauge didn't work, never had worked since I bought the car from No-Neck Arnie the mechanic. I could live with that, and the hot sauce stains on the upholstery, and the radio that wouldn't get one of my favorite stations, KHJ.

I didn't think about all this as I turned up a side street off Alvardo past St. Vincent's Hospital. What I thought about was the uncertain lock on my trunk and the body of Lewis Vance bouncing at each stop. Traffic was light on the street of small factories and I was vaguely aware that I had turned on the radio and that Belle was warning Lorenzo Jones to keep out of the whole situation till Mary had time to talk to Biff and his brother. It sounded like good advice to me.

The car that hit me was a '42 Chrysler New Yorker, a four-door sedan, a solid car, maybe the last of its ilk till the war ended. With new cars off limits to the public for the duration of the war, the guys who hit me had to be rich, determined, or drunk. The first whack sent my Ford's rear end shimmying to the side. I tried to keep the front of the car steady as an announcer on my now sputtering radio suggested that I pick up a can of Swift's Prem for only thirty-one cents. My right rear skipped over the sidewalk, bounced off a brick wall, and made an old guy wearing a beret do a hell of a ballet leap to keep from getting killed. I heard a hubcap clatter down the street and felt my stomach being kissed and mugged by the steering wheel. The Chrysler was in front of me now. There were two figures, big ones, in the front seat. One, the passenger, looked back at me to see if I was hurt. I wasn't, at least not enough to suit him.

As I bounced forward trying to control my Ford, the Chrysler stopped and began to back up toward me, the passenger guiding the driver.

The Basque ballet dancer I had almost hit was charging at me. I could see him in my now cracked rearview mirror. He was shouting and twirling a bony fist. I hit the gas, hoping my hopping tires would grasp the street and send me out of the path of the oncoming Chrysler, but the Ford had had enough. The radio went on about Prem. The Basque cursed and hit what was left of my right fender and the Chrysler plowed into me, crushing the passenger side of the car.

My left shoulder and head hit the door, which popped open. The Ford spat me out into the street like a bitter peach pit. I rolled over two or three times and lay on my back, looking up at the sun. It was too bright. I closed my eyes and heard what must have been the dancing Basque shout, "Craziness. Craziness. Crazies all over the streets."

Something was grinding inside my head or near it. I opened my eyes and saw what was left of my car moving sideways toward me, the door open like a mouth ready to scoop me up and digest me. The damned radio was still playing and Lorenzo was sighing as he and my Ford, urged on by the Chrysler beyond, skidded toward me.

I rolled, tried to get up, crawled a few feet, wondering where the hell the people of Los Angeles were when I needed them, and fell on my face. I kissed the curb and prayed to Pearl Buck, sure I had ingested my last taco. Then the grinding stopped.

A car door opened and I turned my head to see a square head looking over the top of my wreck. It was the Chrysler passenger. He came around one side of my former Ford while his partner came around the other.

They were slightly-off bookends, barrel-chested, wearing identical yellow Hawaiian shirts with pineapples on them. The driver was humming something. I couldn't tell what it was till he came around the car. It was a passable version of "Love in Bloom." The passenger, slightly bigger, wasn't humming at all. He did grunt a little when he pushed aside the Basque, who tried to stop him.

"There's an injustice here," the old man shouted. "What, do you think you own the streets, you cossacks?"

I managed to make it to a sitting position on the curb, though I knew my stomach would have preferred I stay in the gutter. I didn't know what the two fugitives from a demolition derby had in mind.

My .38 was normally in the glove compartment of the piece of modern sculpture that had recently been my car. I didn't know where the .38 was now. I've never had particularly good luck with the gun. Sunday's soiree had been one in a long series of firearms fiascos over the past few years. Just the same, I would have felt better having it to wave at the oncoming pineapples.

A car came down the street, saw the mess, swerved just in time to miss the party, and sent the Basque leaping again. This time the old guy finally got the point, decided to leave the battle zone, and hurried down the street shouting about the madness of civilization.

"Peters?" the bigger pineapple said.

"No," I said. "You've got the wrong guy. My name is Ross, Barney Ross."

"Barney Ross is a fighter," said the second pineapple.

"It's Peters," the big pineapple confirmed. He reached into his pocket and I tried to get to my feet for a gallant lunge before he could shoot me. My legs had been through this kind of thing too many times. They just wouldn't cooperate. I sank back and thought, "The hell with it."

Banana fingers came out of the big one's pocket and the walking fruit salad threw something in my lap. "This is a warning," he said. "Consider it a warning."

"A warning," the driver repeated, in case I had periodic sieges of deafness.

"Stay away from the Alhambra," the top banana said. "Forget about Longretti."

"Larchmont," I said. "Two and two makes Larchmont. The Larchmonts sent you. Correct me if I'm wrong."

Another car came around the corner and paused while the big pineapple corrected me with an open-palmed slap to my forehead. I rolled back. The car took over, made it around the mess by going up on the sidewalk, and rolled away. The two pineapples were in no hurry.

"See a doctor," the bigger one said. "You hit your head when you fell out of the car."

"I didn't fall," I reminded him. "You shot me out the door. You have a goddamn short memory. Think back. There I was, driving peacefully down the street, when you two decided to turn me into scrap metal."

They looked at each other again. Rapid thought was not their greatest strength.

"You are trying to be funny?" the smaller one asked.

I looked around for a more appreciative audience, maybe a cop, but none was around. Irony is useless when you have no audience.

"This is very serious business here, Peters," the big one said, leaning down to talk to me.

"Very serious," agreed the other one.

Theirs was not a class act.

"Don't I look serious enough for you?" I tried.

"You should be frightened."

"I'm frightened," I conceded, though I wasn't, at least not anymore. They probably weren't going to kill me, though they might kick me once or twice for good luck. Kick a private eye and make a wish.

They had exhausted their repertoire, at least the verbal one, and were deciding what to do next when a police siren called from not too far away.

After exchanging looks the big one said, "No Alhambra."

They walked slowly around my car to the tune of the siren, got in their slightly battered Chrysler, and drove away. My right hand touched the wad the big guy had thrown in my lap. It felt like money. My eyes tried to focus on the paper. It looked like money. I had just finished counting the $400 in $50 bills when the siren, attached to a black-and-white police car, screamed into my ear. I looked over at my former Ford. The trunk had held and Vance was safely tucked inside. Two uniformed cops I didn't recognize came out and walked over to me even more slowly than the pineapples. Both cops were in their middle forties and in need of a rigid diet. I didn't think now was the time to advise them on the diet.

I pocketed the money and tried to grin.

"What the hell is going on here?" cop one said.

These two didn't promise to be any more alert than the pair who had just left. I had the dim hope, however, that the ones in the blue uniforms might be on my side, or at least not against me. I was proved wrong.

"Hit-and-run," I explained. "Two guys dressed in pineapple shirts driving a Chrysler plowed into me and then came back and did it again. I'm lucky to be alive."

"We're all lucky to be alive," said the second cop, who wore glasses. I looked up, shading my eyes from the sun with my hand. This one had the makings of a street-corner philosopher.

"I don't buy it," the other one said, looking down at me with suspicion. "Why would two guys plow into you? What's the motive?"

"Lust," I tried. "Or greed. How the hell do I know? Maybe they're German spies disrupting normal life by random acts of terror against innocent citizens."

"Citizen," the first cop said. "I think you've been doing some afternoon drinking and plowed your vehicle into the wall is what I think you did."

I gave him a long withering look and then tried to stand up. The cop with the glasses pushed me back down.

"Stay there till the ambulance comes," he said.

"You called an ambulance?" the first cop asked.

"No."

They stood for a few beats listening to the distant sound of music, waiting to see who would go back to the car and call for an ambulance.

"I don't need an ambulance," I said finally, getting up. "Ambulances take you to hospitals and send you bills. Nothing's broken." I felt my body. Nothing seemed to be broken.

"Suit yourself," the first cop said with a shrug. "You're going to have to get your car off the street and I'm going to have to give you a ticket."

"A ticket?"

"Reckless driving, suspicion of driving under the influence of alcohol, disruption of a public thoroughfare," he ticked off, as I staggered to my lump of a car. The radio was playing and Dinah Shore was singing and the sun was shining.

"Thanks," I said as I lurched forward.

"We won't arrest you this time," cop one said.

"I appreciate that," I said appreciatively.

The cop with glasses caught up with me and handed me the ticket, saying, "You better get this wreck off the street in half an hour. We'll be back to check."

"God bless you, Officer," I said.

I didn't watch them get in the car and drive off. I tucked the ticket into the same pocket as the $50 bills, shook my head, which failed to make things any clearer, and looked around for a telephone. There was none. I had to walk four blocks to something approaching civilization and found a phone in a Thrifty drugstore and called No-Neck Arnie, who grunted in response to my sad tale and said he'd be right there.

Twenty minutes later he drove up in his truck and found me sitting listening to the music slowly fade out as my car battery died. No-Neck climbed out of the truck, spat in the street, wiped his hammy hands on his greasy overalls and walked over to where I leaned against what had once been my hood.

"It's a total wreck," he said, hands on hips.

"You're kidding," I said.

"Just look at it," he said, pointing to the wreck to prove his point. "I ask you."

"A total wreck," I agreed.

A car or two negotiated past us as we negotiated, but I was feeling hot and still a little dizzy. My seersucker suit was dirty, which was no great problem. It had been dirty before the encounter with the Chrysler.

"I'll tell you what I'll do, Peters," No-Neck said, looking for a cigar stub in his pocket and finding none. "I'll take this in trade, give you thirty bucks for it, and charge you only fifteen to tow it away."

"You'll give me fifteen dollars," I said, employing my lightning-fast mathematical brain.

"And," he said, still circling the car, "I'll let you apply the insurance to a payment on one of the cars I've got back at the garage."

"I'm not insured," I said.

"Tough."

"I've got four hundred dollars," I added, showing him the wad of fifties and the ticket.

Arnie's eyes went from sandpaper brown to shiny amber.

"I've got a yellow '41 Crosley," he said, wiping his hands again on his overalls in anticipation of touching the cash.

"I don't think a normal-size human can fit into a Crosley," I said.

"Are you kidding? There's plenty of room. What do you want for four hundred dollars? A new car. You can't get new cars unless you're a doctor or a nurse."

That wasn't quite true. I knew it and Arnie knew it. Ministers and people in certain civil services could buy new cars, in addition to all persons directly or indirectly employed in the prosecution of the war, including factory workers, miners, farmers, and lumberjacks. What Arnie meant was that I was one of the few people in Los Angeles who couldn't buy a new car even if I could afford one.

"Crosley's a good car," he whispered confidentially, though there was no one within five blocks. "Four-cylinder cobra engine made out of brazed copper and sheet steel, weighs about sixty pounds and gives twenty-six point five horsepower at fifty-four hundred rpms."

"Arnie . . ."

"Only eight thousand miles on the little beauty," he said, patting my Ford wreck. It wasn't much of a pat but it knocked out the radio. In the silence, I made the deal and handed the money over to Arnie, who wrote out a receipt on the back of the ticket the cop had given me.

"One more thing, Arnie," I added, and then I told him about Vance's body in the trunk. For another fifty bucks Arnie promised to put Vance on ice.

Less than an hour later my wreck was off the street and I was driving down Wilshire heading for home in my two-seater Crosley. Crosley's weren't bought new from dealers. You got them from your local hardware and appliance shop. They were made by the Crosley Radio and Refrigerator Company and were about the size of a refrigerator. At least this yellow beauty had a radio and a working gas gauge.

7

To secure California for Spain before the French, English, or even the Russians could grab it, in 1781 a series of small towns, called pueblos, were established. The second pueblo was Los Angeles. The first settlers didn't come seeking a land of sunshine and promise. They were recruited in Northern Mexico and forced to march four hundred miles or more to build shelters and plant crops.

By 1840, Los Angeles had enough bodies, willing and unwilling, to qualify as a city or *ciudad*. It had earned a reputation for the beauty of its location and for the largest congregation of gamblers, thieves, drifters, and cutthroats in the New World. When the United States annexed California after the war with Mexico in 1848, hordes of Yankees streamed into the city led by Marine Lieutenant Archibald Gillespie, who made it clear that he held no love for the Mexican residents. A few months later, Gillespie and his garrison were surrounded on Fort Moore hill by the L.A. residents he and his boys had been stepping on. The Marines were kicked out and promised never to return. They were back in a few weeks with reinforcements and had a hell of a time retaking the city. Los Angeles became an occupied territory chest-deep in soldiers at odds with the sullen cutthroats they had defeated. The peaceful citizens were caught in the middle.

Almost a hundred years later things were pretty much the same. The Yankees were still coming by land, sea, and air to the last stop on the trail of Manifest Destiny. If they came running too fast, they found themselves in the Pacific Ocean before they could stop or catch their breaths. If they did stop, they discovered that serpents slithered in the New Eden and the Angels in the City of Angels were mostly fallen ones.

I had plenty to do in my little Crosley. I could go back to the Alhambra and have another chat with the Larchmonts. I could look for the Dole pineapple twins. I could pick up the trail of Teddy Spaghetti and his partner, Alex. I could also find Charlie Chaplin and see how he fit into all this. I decided to go for Chaplin, not because it was the best lead, but because it might be the most interesting.

Besides knowing Chaplin was funny, I knew where he lived. Anyone who had ever taken a guided tour in Hollywood knew where Charlie Chaplin lived. I also knew from reading the papers that he and Paulette Goddard were "estranged," and that Charlie had stuck his oversize shoe in his mouth by speaking at a San Francisco rally a few days ago held by the American Committee for Russian War Relief. America's love affair with Charlie was a little strained. A couple of columnists had started wondering why Charlie had never become a U.S. citizen. Others thought he was too chummy with our friends the Russians. There was even a rumor that the income-tax people were having long, serious talks with him.

It was a pleasant afternoon. Vance's body was on ice and I had a new car. I headed for Beverly Hills on the chance that I'd get past the gates and that Chaplin would be home. I got there in about fifteen minutes and turned down Summit Drive. I parked in front of the gate and looked at the house, a combination of Basque and modern Spanish architecture I'd glanced at a few dozen times before. The house was yellow like my car, a big stucco box, probably forty rooms or more, with a tile roof. There was a circular drive, from which I was barred by an iron gate. Fortunately, there was a black button in the brick post on one side of the entrance to the driveway. I pushed the bell, adjusted my gray jacket, straightened my tie, tried to wipe off a few of the more obvious dirt spots, and succeeded in grinding them in deeper. I was certain to make a great impression. I clutched the folder from Teddy's apartment under my left arm and waited.

I rang again and looked in at the house. The door opened and a head peeked out, followed by a body and a thin, bald man in his forties wearing a dark suit with shiny lapels. It took him a few months to walk down to the gate. When he got there, he did a great job of resisting the urge to raise his eyebrows. His accent was British and his manner superior.

"Yes?" he said.

"You should install a speaker," I suggested. "How many times a day do you have to make this trip?"

No expression.

"Your business?" he asked.

"I want to talk to Charlie Chaplin," I said with a pleasant smile.

Madmen in shabby suits probably kept him busy for most of his workday and he knew how to deal with my ilk.

"If you'll leave your name and address," he said, the gate still separating us, "I'll inform Mr. Chaplin that you were here. He'll answer your inquiry by mail and send you an autographed photo."

"I'm not a fan," I said. "I'm not selling scripts. I'm not with the income tax service. I'm not an actor. I'm not an anti-communist. And I'm not selling anything."

A tour bus drove by, its windows open. I could hear the driver identify me as John Garfield, "a frequent visitor to Charlie Chaplin's." I waved my purloined folder at the bus while the servant stood erect and waited through this indignity. When the bus rolled down the street, I said, "They thought I was John Garfield."

He was unimpressed. "I am frequently identified as Arthur Treacher," he said. "I'm afraid I must get back to the house. If—"

"Tell Charlie I have information on the Larchmonts and the donation," I said, holding up the file.

"The Larchmonts," the servant said dryly.

"And the donation," I reminded him.

"If you'll give me—"

"I'll wait," I cut in.

He was a pro. No sigh, no shrug, no sarcasm. He turned and walked at the same pace back up the drive, crunching gravel beneath the soles of his finely polished shoes. I resisted the urge to look down at my shoes and maybe shine them up a bit on my pant leg. Should a man who has been mistaken for John Garfield do something that crude? I examined the black metal gate, counted the drifting clouds in the sky, glanced at the house to see if curtains were moving, and hummed a medley of tunes. I was well into "Sleepy Lagoon" when the front door opened and the world's slowest servant made his way back to me and opened the gate.

He didn't even say "Follow me" or "Walk this way." He let me in, closed the door, and started up the driveway with me a pace behind. The house was surrounded by tall trees and woods. As we got to the rise at the top of the drive, I could see down a slope to a swimming pool and nearby tennis court. Someone was playing, a small man in a white polo shirt and white pants. His curly white and black hair bobbed as he rushed to hit the ball. His opponent was lanky and young and wore shorts and a matching polo shirt.

The servant opened the front door and held it while I entered, and then he closed it behind me. The wooden floor creaked under our feet as we stepped in. I found myself in a massive hall two stories high and extending deep into the house. On one side was a winding stairway leading up to a balcony. About halfway up the stairway was a suit of armor and a big brass gong with a black-handled knocker on a peg above it. Dangling from the ceiling was a massive chandelier. I was impressed.

"You will wait here," the servant said, and then he took off toward the rear of the house, taking small creaking steps.

While I waited I looked at a black cabinet with little drawers, dozens of little drawers. The cabinet was against one wall. It was covered with colorful pictures of dragons. I squinted at one fire-breather that snaked around to the rear of the cabinet.

"It's more than five hundred years old," came a voice behind me, a high male voice with a touch of British in it. I turned and found myself about ten yards from Charlie Chaplin, who was looking at me and my folder with open curiosity. Chaplin was a little older than I was, somewhere in his early fifties. His hair was mostly white but there were still dark strands in it. His face looked unlined. I had known he was small but I hadn't known how small till this moment. I was five-nine and had at least three or four inches on him, maybe five. He was dressed in white, had a tennis racket in one hand, and a pink towel draped over his neck.

"It's nice," I said.

"Yes, it is," he agreed. "I don't wish to be rude Mr. . . ."

"Peters, Toby Peters," I said, still a first down away from him. Our voices echoed in the hall. I felt as if I were being interviewed by the Duke of Westphalia and my answers had better be good or I might find myself separated from my head. "I'm not a blackmailer. I don't work for the Larchmonts. Here."

I stepped forward and handed him the file. His hand was small, long-fingered. He took the file, pursed his lips, and glanced at it.

"I found this in the apartment of a hotel clerk name Teddy Longretti, also known as Teddy Spaghetti."

"Colorful," said Chaplin.

"The name, yes. The man, no," I said. "Teddy shot a grunt named Vance on Sunday. Killed him. Then he shot a house detective named Beason. He did it with my gun."

"Your gun," said Chaplin with a smile designed to humor the madman who had tricked his way into the castle.

"I'm a private investigator," I said, pulling out my wallet and flashing my Dick Tracy badge. "I'm working for John Wayne."

"John Wayne," he said with a smile, as he shifted his racket to his right hand in case he had to hit me with it.

"Right," I went on. "Look, I thought you'd like to have these. It might be embarrassing if they were found in Teddy's place."

"Ah, yes," said Chaplin. "And you'd like a reward for keeping them from public scrutiny."

"Right," I said, watching Chaplin begin to circle nonchalantly toward a telephone on a small table near the stairs. "But I don't want money. I want information on the Larchmonts and what they're up to."

Chaplin stopped his circling maneuver, put his racket and the folder on the table near the phone, and turned to me, his head tilted to one side, his hands on his hips.

"You really are a private detective," he said.

"I am."

"I suppose I could check this with the police," he went on, surveying my less than shabby ungentility.

"My brother is Captain Phil Pevsner, Los Angeles Police Department, Wilshire District. The desk sergeant on duty about now is Veldu. The number—"

His right hand came up like a traffic cop's to stop me. "That won't be necessary," he said. "I've never met a real private detective before. I am intrigued."

I turned around in a circle so he could get a good look, and he laughed, a sudden short laugh.

"Come," he said, and bounded up the stairway. I came. As we passed the gong, Chaplin reached out to ping it with his fingertips. "Listen to the muted answer," he said as he went on. The gong murmured.

"My sons are not home today," he said, leading the way when we got to the top of the stairs. "They're visiting their grandparents in the valley." There were three doors. Chaplin plunged through one with me behind. The room was a big bedroom; a musky odor of men's cologne filled the air. The room was bright with big windows. In one wall was a fireplace. A writing table and chair stood under the window. There were neat stacks of paper and a one-ton Webster's dictionary on the desk. Against one wall were twin beds and a nightstand between them. A pile of pulp magazines were piled on the stand. Near another window was a telescope. The rug on the floor was Persian and strangely shabby.

"We'll not be disturbed here," he said. "This is my sanctum. My refuge."

"Nice," I said. I wandered over to the dark oak writing table and glanced down at the manuscript on it.

"*Shadow and Substance,*" he said, moving over to look through the telescope. "The play you are looking at. It will be my next film. The story of a young Irish girl of simple faith and a most cynical canon. I'll be the canon and—"

Something caught his eye in the telescope and he stopped speaking to adjust the lens.

"Ah," he said. "Harold Lloyd is at his croquet on that ostentatious meadow of his. His smile is most genuine when he makes a decent point. None of the affectation . . . out of sight." Chaplin turned to face me. "Your question?"

"What kind of donation did you make with the Larchmonts?"

Chaplin rubbed his palms together, removed the towel from his neck, and dabbed his forehead.

"A sizeable check for the establishment of a center for the improvement of Soviet-American cultural relations," he said. "The world will not always be at war. The hope for prolonged peace rests on the United States and the Soviet Union living in respect and harmony."

I leaned against the writing table, careful not to sit on *Shadow and Substance.*

"The Larchmonts share this desire," I said.

"The Larchmonts share in the more than ten thousand dollars I foolishly placed in their care to use as seed money to establish this project. They have had the cash for more than a year and my efforts to discover what has been done with it have been met with silence or lies."

"Did the Larchmonts ever mention John Wayne?"

Chaplin laughed again. "I doubt if they would have approached John Wayne in the expectation of getting his support for this enterprise. Mr. Wayne is known for his lack of sympathy for the Soviet endeavor and sacrifice. Mr. Larchmont, in the two meetings I had with that infamous individual, may have mentioned Mr. Wayne in a less than complimentary context, but I don't recall."

"Two men, look-alikes, one a little smaller than the other, probably wearing loud Hawaiian shirts. That ring a gong?"

Chaplin smiled and tapped his cheek. "I believe a pair answering to that description did accompany Larchmont to a meeting here. They drove Larchmont to the gate and then departed. I got a very good look at them through the telescope. As I recall, the one I could see most clearly was wearing a gauche red shirt with hula girls imprinted on it. Would you like something to drink?"

"Pepsi if you've got it."

Chaplin picked up the phone near the pile of pulps on the

nightstand and ordered a Pepsi and an Alka-Seltzer. Then he sat on the edge of his bed.

"It will take a few minutes," he said. "My regular servants are gone. They were Japanese. All of them are in the camp at Manzanar. You're familiar with it?"

I nodded.

"Do you know why they are in that camp?" he asked. And then he answered. "Because the United States government recognizes the intellectual superiority and determination of the Japanese. Couple that with gross prejudice and unreasoning fear and we have the insanity of Manzanar."

We went on for a while talking about my job, the detective pulps he read every night to get to sleep, his nervous stomach aided somewhat by the Alka-Seltzer, and the Larchmonts.

"I suspect," he said, "that others were and are equally displeased with the Larchmonts, but I shall now count myself lucky to be rid of them. I plan to burn this file when you depart. It has been a most illuminating discussion, most illuminating. Tell me, Mr. Peters, would you consider taking on a job for me? I'd be willing to invest a few hundred dollars more to recover my investment with the Larchmonts. You could serve as a collection agent. Do you do such work?"

Chaplin had downed his second Alka-Seltzer and it was getting late in the afternoon.

"Five percent of anything I recover," I said, rattling the melting ice cube in my glass. "That's a maximum of five hundred dollars."

"More than fair, more than fair," said Chaplin, bouncing forward to shake my hand on it. His hand was firm and strong.

Since I wasn't going to take any cash upfront from Chaplin, I wouldn't feel guilty about not pursuing his investment with too much zeal. I'd bear it in mind as I went after my gun, Teddy, and Alex. With Chaplin as a client, I also had some cover for harassing the Larchmonts. It was a good deal all around.

"I'm having a few people over on Sunday for tennis and swimming should you like to return with a report," Chaplin said at the front door. "I'm sure you could tell us some interesting tales of mayhem."

"Mostly lost grandmas, stolen cars, and people who need a few hours of protection," I said.

"Nonetheless," Chaplin added, "you are welcome to join us."

"Thanks for the Pepsi," I said.

"My pleasure," Chaplin countered, and I bounded down the gravel driveway with another client and a little more information.

The radio in the Crosley was pretty good. I listened to the news and found out that coffee and tea would probably be rationed soon, which meant that millions of people who didn't even like tea would soon be running out to stock up on it. Basements would fill with boxes of tea, more tea than a hoarder could drink in a lifetime, even if he or she loved tea.

Traffic was heavy heading back to the Farraday, so I stopped for a hot dog, some fries, and a chocolate shake at a stand on Gower.

Inside, the guy next to me asked for the mustard. I told him I had just had a couple of Pepsis with Charlie Chaplin. The guy with the mustard looked like a leather bulldog.

"What'd Chaplin drink?" he said humoring me.

"Alka-Seltzer," I said. "Nervous stomach."

"Too bad," the bulldog man said, and walked off dripping mustard.

8

It was after five when I got back to the Farraday. At that hour I found a space on the street half a block down. The workers, shoppers, and sightseers of the daylight hours were on their way out of town and the shadowy night crowds hadn't yet made their way in.

The people on the streets now were mostly young men in soldier and sailor uniforms. They had nowhere to go but shared hotel rooms and afternoon bars till the prostitutes, feeling the shade of night, knew it was time to get up and go to work.

Madame Carpentier was coming out of the Farraday as I walked up. I would have avoided her if I could, but it was too late. Her "study" was in the office on the second floor. Her specialty was the past and the future. Mine was the present. You'd have thought we had nothing in common, but she kept seeing me in tea leaves and Tarot cards. I didn't want to be seen in tea leaves or Tarot cards or even in my mirror.

Madame Carpentier, also known as Vera Krachnovitz, was about fifty or eighty, carried a knitting bag that weighed her down, and wore loose-fitting black dresses with colorful beads. Her too-black hair was always tied in a tight bun.

"Tobias Leo," she said when I tried to ease past her. "You've been trying to avoid me."

"I've been busy," I said.

"Too busy to learn the future?"

"Takes the fun out of now," I said. "I'd rather not know."

She shifted the knitting bag into her left hand and stared at me.

"How's business?" I asked politely.

"Murder," she whispered. A pair of kid sailors heard the word as they passed by and grinned at us.

"That's too bad," I said.

"No," she corrected, holding up her free hand. "I'm not talking about my business. Business is good. These children stream in with their dollars to discover if they will live and prosper," she said. "I put on a show. I give them their money's worth. Incense, sometimes even raising the table. They eat it up. No, I mean you and murder." She shifted the knitting bag back to her right hand again. "Damn thing weighs a ton, but I can't leave my stuff in the office. Thieves."

"Murder," I said.

"Tobias Leo," she said, remembering the subject. "There will be two murders."

"Just one," I corrected her, feeling like a kid who needed a toilet but couldn't get away from the teacher in the hall.

"Listen to me," she said. "Pay attention, don't fidget. Three will die, two of them murdered. This is free information. You could pay some attention here. I've had a long hard day. You want me to buy you a drink?"

The first sign of night appeared on the street like a robin in spring. A prostitute named Boom-Boom stepped out of the Anchor Bar across the street, blinked at the setting sun, saw her shadow, and went back inside.

"No thanks, Madame C.," I said. "I've got to work . . ."

"Suit yourself," she said with a shrug, finally putting down her load to exercise her fingers. "I wasn't going to make a sexual attack on your scarred body. Watch yourself."

"Thanks," I said, taking a step toward the Farraday before she could say more, but I wasn't fast enough.

"Damn, I almost forgot," she said, lifting her burden again. "Two men in yellow are looking for you."

"Madame C., you are one amazing woman," I sighed.

"They were here about ten minutes ago. I heard them asking Jeremy about you," she said. "Stay away from them."

"Is that from the cards?"

"Hell no," she said, looking down the street and gauging the journey. "It's from someone who's seen too many things on these streets."

The outer lobby of the Farraday was tiled, clean, and dark. Jeremy had been at his task of scrubbing. The inner lobby echoed my footsteps as I headed for the fake marble staircase. Then a voice came out of the shadows.

"Toby."

I stopped and Jeremy Butler came out, a pail in one hand, a wet rag in the other. He was wearing dark slacks and a gray T-shirt. His shaved head caught a small glint of dusty light from a small, high lobby window.

"Some men were looking for you," he said with concern.

"I know. I ran into Madame Carpentier in the street. How are the wedding plans?"

Jeremy looked up into the heights of the Farraday in the general direction of Alice Pallice's office.

"Perfect," he said. "Remember. You are coming."

"I wouldn't miss it," I said.

"What else is new?" I asked politely.

"The war," he said. "The echoes of war on life and art are difficult for people to grasp. The War Production Board plans to order the halting of manufacture of almost all musical instruments except violins, cellos, and some guitars. This, they say, will result in striking savings of strategic material."

"A tough war," I agreed.

"It's the metal," Jeremy explained. "The musical industry used about fifteen thousand tons of war related metals last year including ten thousand tons of iron, three thousand tons of steel, fifteen hundred tons of brass, three hundred and seventy-five tons of copper, and twenty-five tons of aluminum."

"That's a lot of music," I said.

"According to the War Production Board, that iron could have been used to make the casings for eleven thousand five hundred six-ton army tanks; the steel, eighty-three medium tanks; the brass, fifty million rounds of thirty-caliber cartridges; the copper, five hundred hundred-and-fifty-five-millimeter field pieces; and the aluminum, forty thousand aircraft flares."

"Jeremy, how do you remember all this?"

"It's a curse," he said. "The bathos of human existence brands itself on my soul. I'm working on an ironic poem on the curse, which I will read at the wedding ceremony. Alice thinks it appropriate in this day and age."

"Sounds fine to me."

Somewhere above us a door closed, a man coughed.

"The instruments of the orchestra are the first cousins to the weapons of destruction," he said. "An ordinary piano contains enough steel, copper wire and brass to make a dozen bayonets, a corps radio, and sixty-six thirty-caliber cartridges. A bass drum contains the steel for two bayonets and a trumpet enough brass for about sixty thirty-caliber cartridge cases. If this war continues for three or four years, the orchestra will die, chamber music will be the norm. The irony Toby, the irony. As the war continues, music will be more gentle, thoughtful. I haven't worked it all out . . ."

"It's a job for a poet," I said.

"Till they take away our pens and scrolls," he said sadly, looking into his bucket of soapy water for the muse.

"Jeremy, cheer up. You're getting married," I said, starting up the stairs.

The thought of the gargantuan Alice brought a small smile

to the massive, scarred face of the former wrestler, the onetime Terror of Tarzana.

"I've got to get back to work." Jeremy sighed. "It never stops. As Sisyphus discovered, if you don't keep pushing the rock upward, it will roll back and crush you. Civilization is the realization that the rock will never be pushed to the top. Our meaning lies in the style in which we push and our attitude toward the other pushers."

"Check," I said, as Jeremy strode back into the darkened depths of the Farraday Building to push against endless dirt.

Having encountered a mystic and poet within five minutes, Shelly would have been an interesting contrast, but Shelly was already gone, the outer door locked. I had to use my key and was pleased to find that no more of the bodies Madame Carpentier had promised were waiting in the waiting room.

Shelly's office was dark, but since the sun wasn't quite down, there was enough light coming through his window for me to walk toward my office without fumbling for the light switch. I touched the coffee pot. It was warm. I knew there'd be some coffee at the bottom. Shelly never cleaned the pot. I rinsed a mug that had *Venga a Tijuana* enameled on it in red. The coffee was awful but it was coffee.

I stepped inside my office and almost tripped over one of the Hawaiian pineapples. The coffee spilled, some of it, on the floor, but I straightened up and reached over and put the cup on my desk before all of it was lost.

The bigger pineapple on one side of the door closed it behind me. The smaller pineapple moved to block my possible exit. I knew the office better than they did. There was only one way out now, the window through which Shelly and I had lowered Vance a few hours earlier.

I inched past the lesser of the two evils and got behind my desk to face them. My desk was tiny, the room small, my options limited, and my senses alert, partly from the awful coffee.

"We gave you four hundred dollars," said the big one, sitting in the chair opposite me. The smaller one stood, his back to the door.

"You destroyed my car," I said, sipping slowly and considering my options. "That was a family heirloom. The four hundred dollars bought me new transportation, not my loyalty. You almost killed me."

The setting sun over my shoulder was hitting him in the face. His face, less than comely in the best of light, was beet red. Even Josef von Sternberg couldn't have given the gentleman a look of normalcy.

"If we wanted to kill you, you'd be dead," he said. "Am I right, Sutker?"

"You are right, Lyle," the smaller pineapple said.

"We told you to stay out of this," Lyle said. He seemed to have memorized his lines. I wondered who was writing his material.

"I'm working for Charlie Chaplin," I said, trying to remember if there was anything in my desk I could use to claw my way out of here. "The Larchmonts owe him ten grand."

"They don't owe Chaplin anything," the big pineapple said. "What did you do with the body?"

"Vance's body was in the trunk of the Ford when you hit me," I said. "Now I've got him on ice."

"We never killed anyone, did we, Sutker?" Lyle said.

"We never," Sutker agreed.

"See?" said Lyle to me, having offered the evidence of Sutker's unshakable testimony.

"I didn't think you killed Vance," I said, wondering if I could fool them with the broken stapler in the bottom drawer. The light was behind me and it might look like a gun in the shadow. "But you did plant his body here. You or the Larchmonts did find the gun in the Alhambra and gave it to the police. The Larchmonts want me out of this, fine. I'll get out when I find Teddy and Alex. I've got a client to protect. Now get out."

I reached down for the drawer, opened it, fumbled for the stapler, and aimed it at the big yellow lump. He looked surprised.

"That's a stapler," he said. I put the stapler down. "We'll get Teddy. We'll get the money back. You stay out. You know what we do now, Sutker?"

"We demobilize Sam Spade," said Sutker.

Lyle looked pleased with his protégé's answer. The phone rang and I grabbed it before they could stop me.

"Hello," I said.

Lyle stood up and gave me a red-faced warning. The pineapples and bananas were wrinkled.

"Hello, Mr. Peelers?" came Mrs. Plaut's high voice.

"It's me, Captain," I said. "Come right up. I've got visitors."

Lyle looked at me warily and then at Sutker for help. Sutker had no help to give. Lyle was the what little brains the outfit had.

"Mr. Peelers," Mrs. Plaut went on, "I've been trying to reach hold of you for many hours with rationing and all."

"I understand," I said, looking smugly at Lyle.

"Good," she went on. "We must discuss the photographs. Aunt Donna's glass plate photographs seem to have gotten mixed with the Easton side of the family and it is difficult to tell whether the woman with the long hair and feather is Cousin Eunice Marie Ann or a Sioux who worked in my Great-Uncle Caution's General Merchandise Store in Hanley, Missouri."

"We'll straighten that out as soon as you get up here," I said seriously.

"I cannot come up there, Mr. Peelers," Mrs Plaut said with a wary sigh. "I do not know where 'there' might be and since the photographs are here and heavy and you reside here, my 'here' is here."

"Makes sense to me," I said.

"There are details of identity to be worked out—" she said.

"Captain," I cut in. "We can save that for later. I've got a life-and-death situation up here. If you don't hurry, there could be bullets, falling bodies, and death."

Mrs. Plaut did not answer for a few seconds and then she said, "Mr. Peelers, do you have a radio on there?"

"No, that was me. I said—"

But before I could repeat it, Lyle pulled the phone from my hand and held it to his ear. I could see from his face that Mrs. Plaut was speaking. Puzzlement bespangled his brow. He reached over and slammed down the phone.

"Captain Irene Plaut," I said. "She's downstairs with two men from homicide and —"

Lyle was shaking his bulky head no. "Sutker, we must alter Mr. Peters and rearrange his office and face," said Lyle, moving around the right side of my desk. Sutker began to move slowly to my left. And then the door opened and the last of the sunlight struck Jeremy Butler, who held an envelope in his hand.

"Toby, this letter just arrived by special—" he began and then stopped as his eyes took in my two visitors.

"Go out and close the door behind you," Lyle said.

"Go out and play D and D, Deaf and Dumb," agreed Sutker.

"What is this, Toby?" Jeremy asked, ignoring Lyle and Sutker, who had paused to menace him.

"I think they plan to rearrange me, Jeremy," I said.

"Back out and close the door, blimp, before we—" Lyle began, but we failed to discover the extent of his violent inventiveness. Jeremy stepped forward and threw both of his arms out. He hit both Lyle and Sutker solidly, Lyle in the throat, Sutker in the face. The fight was over.

Lyle sagged against the wall, clutching his throat with both hands, his face strawberry red, his tongue out, mouth open. Sutker's hands covered his broken nose and his moaning mouth. See no evil and speak no evil were in pain.

"What shall we do with them?" Jeremy asked. "The police?"

"No," I said. "I think they're getting the Farraday dirty and should probably be escorted out with a warning."

"As you think best," Jeremy said, reaching over to grab Lyle by the neck. Lyle slouched back as Jeremy's massive hand approached, but he was caught. He was breathing a bit now but no intelligible sounds were coming through the damaged throat. Sutker saw Jeremy's hand coming through his bloody fingers but had nowhere to hide in my closet-sized office. Jeremy picked them up by the neck and went out the door calling, "I'll be back when I've deposited them in the alley."

"Thanks, Jeremy," I called as he dragged his burden into the twilight of Shelly's office.

I finished my coffee and reached for the envelope that Jeremy had brought and dropped on my desk. I had to lean back to catch the departing light to read the note that went with the two hundred dollars in cash. It read:

> *Peters. This should cover expenses for a while. If you need more, get back to me. My business manager says this is more than generous. One more problem. My secretary says someone named Alex, didn't give his last name, called, mentioned you, and said he'd be seeing me. Might be your Alex. Keep in touch and take care of yourself.*

It was signed John Wayne. I pocketed the cash and called County Hospital. Straight-Ahead had been released, according to the ward nurse. She tracked down Dr. Parry for me and he got on the phone.

"What do you want, Peters?" he said.

"Beason. I thought he was—"

"This isn't a prison," Parry said. "He signed himself out. He said he was fine and had to get back to work."

"And you didn't try to stop him?"

"Peters," he said slowly, carefully, "I've seen men who I knew were dying get off of operating tables and insist on going back to combat. I've seen men with scratches whimper to be sent home, pretend they were blind, deaf, insane. I didn't stop any of them, I'm not God."

He was shouting now. I wondered how many nurses and patients were listening.

"Doc . . ."

"I'm just a one-legged doctor," he went on. "People are responsible for their own lives. I do . . . forget it. I'm sorry."

"Listen, Doc, I just came into some money. How about dinner, on me?"

His voice went from shouting rage to a low whisper I could hardly hear.

"Not tonight," he said. "Not tonight."

"Saturday," I said. "I'll pick you up at the hospital at seven."

"Saturday," he said, and hung up.

During Parry's absence, I had taken my pains and breaks to Doc Hodgdon. Doc Hodgdon was a wiry man, about seventy, whom I played handball with down at the Y on Hope Street. I had never beaten Doc Hodgdon, who played the angles of the court like a three-rail billiard pro. Doc Hodgdon had made me a few meals and shared a few Pabst Blue Ribbons in his kitchen behind his office. Doc's wife was long dead and his two kids lived back East. My plan was to get Hodgdon and Parry and me together over one of Hodgdon's lamb roasts. I might sucker them into a poker game and get them to swapping army stories of the two big wars they had met the world in.

I called Hodgdon, who was finishing with his last patient of the day, and he agreed to provide the lamb if I brought the beer.

Jeremy came back in after I had hung up. He flipped on the light and I blinked up at him.

"The war has done this," Jeremy said, shaking his head.

"Done this?" I asked.

He looked back over his shoulder. "Them," he said. "The formidable ones are in the services. Those two are retreads, cheap extras, second-rate actors playing at evil. Remember that one last year? That was monumental."

I remembered Jeremy's encounter with an ex-wrestler who had tried to kill us both. For me it had been a nightmare. For Jeremy it had been a pleasant reminder of the good old days.

"We need poetry now more than ever, Toby. The world is permeated with malice. Malice breeds malice. I have a book for you to read, a new book by Steinbeck, *The Moon Is Down.* I'll leave it for you tomorrow."

"Thanks again, Jeremy," I said. He nodded and departed to further consider the fate of the world.

I sat there for another twenty minutes deciding on my next step. Then the next step was decided for me by the ringing phone.

"Mrs. Plaut," I said patiently when I picked it up, "I'll be home in a few hours and we'll—"

"Toby," came the quivering voice of Teddy Spaghetti.

"Teddy," I said. "People are looking for you."

Someone said something behind Teddy. I couldn't tell what or who. Teddy put his hand over the mouthpiece and said, "Yeah, yeah" to whoever was behind him.

"Toby, I got to talk to you. Can you get here, the Alhambra? I'm holed up in a janitor's room in the second basement. Back behind the furnace. Can you get here fast? I mean like fast?"

"I can get there fast, Teddy. Tell Alex to stay there. I want to talk to him."

"Alex—" Teddy began, and then the phone went dead.

I got up, turned off the light, and hurried out doing a reasonably good, I thought, job of imitating Ray Eberle singing "I Guess I'll Have to Dream the Rest." All I needed was the Modernaires. I patted my wallet with the two hundred dollars, wondering if I was being set up by Alex and Teddy or the Larchmonts and the pineapple goons. I considered asking Jeremy to come with me. I knew he would, but I also knew there was no way Jeremy Butler would ever fit into my new Crosley. No, I was on my own again.

Night had fallen on Hoover when I stepped out of the front door of the Farraday, night and the night people. And I was one of them.

9

I picked up "Counterspy" on my Crosley radio as I headed for the Alhambra. It wasn't far. I could have walked but I didn't want Teddy to change his mind. I only caught the last few minutes of the show but I head David Harding consoling some rich guy who had fallen for a Nazi spy. Harding told the rich guy and me that we had to be careful, that Nazi spies were clever and ruthless and seductive. I believed him.

Night traffic had taken over. Nobody was car-pooling on Broadway or Main. All the soldiers and sailors who were now barred from the thirty-two downtown taverns were looking for new bars and hotel lounges. I had to park in a lot and pay a quarter of John Wayne's advance to a skinny woman with stringy pigtails wearing a gray uniform.

"Busy night," I said amiably.

"Park your own," she said, pointing to an empty space near the far wire fence. I parked my own, wished her "Top of the Mornin'," and left her shrugging her shoulders. I could but imagine the madness that paraded through her parking lot each night of the full moon.

The Alhambra lobby was jammed with uniforms and ladies of almost every imaginable ilk and persuasion. The air was thick with smoke, and the last few bulbs looked down with yellow, bleary light.

Larchmont of neither gender was on the desk. It was a near Teddy clone who tried to take care of the line of waiting registrants, almost none of whom had luggage.

"Going to be one devil of a night for Merit Beason," Straight-Ahead's voice came from behind me.

I turned to him. He looked a bit pale but steady enough.

"Doc Parry says you should be in bed," I said.

"Not the first time I've been shot," he said, surveying the crowd and speaking just loud enough to be heard over the frantic rapid talk of the desperate seekers of a few minutes of forgetting. A heavily made up woman with yellow hair piled high on her head eased between me and Straight-Ahead. Her cigarette came within a lash of my nose.

"Merit Beason can take care of these kids with one hand and a cold stare," Straight-Ahead said. To prove it, he fixed a cold stare on a nearby sailor, who responded by taking off his hat.

"I see, Merit. How do I get to the basement?"

"I know, I know," screeched a woman from across the room. She wasn't answering my question.

"Why?" asked Straight-Ahead reasonably.

"Teddy called my office. Said he was hiding right downstairs in a janitor's room behind the furnace. You know where it is?"

"Second basement," said Beason. He reached over to touch his still tender and bandaged wound. "Teddy has things to explain."

Straight-Ahead led the way, wending slowly through the crowd, his eyes forward. I followed in his wake and we took the stairway next to the elevator. Voices echoed from somewhere below. A blond Marine had a murmuring dark woman plastered against the wall near the basement door. The Marine couldn't see us, but the woman did. Her dark eyes made it clear that she recognized Straight-Ahead. She pushed the Marine away. Her blouse was open.

"That's enough," said Straight-Ahead. "The two of you up and out."

The girl buttoned up and hurried past. The Marine put his head down and brushed past us, embarrassed.

"Can't blame them," said Straight-Ahead. "But can't let them either. You can't let social order break down or what are we fighting for?"

Straight-Ahead proceeded through the door and into the damp darkness of the basement. A generator pounded away like an earache, and a single bulb on a chain gave us a beacon but not enough light to see by. Straight-Ahead turned on the row of bulbs from a switch near the door and headed to the right. I followed him to the beat of the metal heart of the Alhambra.

"Back this way," Straight-Ahead said. "Mind the walls."

I minded the dirty walls and followed him down a narrow walkway. My hand touched the cool furnace and my eyes watched Beason, whose shadow danced black against gray.

"Here we are," he said, stopping before a closed door. A thin bank of light crept under the door. I turned the handle and pushed the door open, stepping to the side in case Teddy had a gun and an itching finger or his pal Alex had set me up.

There was nothing to fear in the small room unless the sight of a corpse provokes frightening thoughts of mortality. The room was small: a single cot, a little lamp, a metal bar sticking out of the wall with empty hangers. Teddy Spaghetti was lying on the cot, his eyes open, his mouth open, his hands open. He looked as if he were about to sing an Al Jolson song to the waiting ceiling.

"Dead," said Straight-Ahead, crouching near the cot and touching Teddy's chest. "Two through the chest."

He stood up, straight-backed and dignified. "Don't suppose we'll find the missing money here," he said.

"No," I agreed, but we knew we'd look. You had to look. We found the gun on the floor under the cot. Actually, I found it. There was no way Straight-Ahead could retain his dignity and balance when he looked under a bed. I left it there.

"At least it's not mine," I said.

"That's something," he said. "No cash here. No papers. No Alex."

"I have a feeling the men in uniform will be coming down here any second," I said.

"You've been set up. No doubt," Merit agreed.

"And I know the folks who did it," I said.

"Let's just get you out of here," came Merit's answer.

I was almost at the door when Merit said, "Wait."

Pinned to the back of the door where we wouldn't have seen it without closing it behind us was a note. The note was typed and brief:

The Duke is next.

Straight-Ahead handed me the note and I folded it once and put it in my pocket.

We hurried down the walkway. I tried to think fast but the pounding noise of the generator cut through any ideas I might have had. We went through the door to the lobby and I spotted Cawelti and the two uniformed cops at the desk. If it weren't for the crowd, I would have been spotted when the clerk pointed to the door to the basement and Cawelti looked over. I crouched behind Straight-Ahead.

"Back through the door, up the stairway," Straight-Ahead whispered. I took my first good look at Straight-Ahead in the light. His face was white, his legs unsteady. He was sixty and should have been in a hospital bed instead of running around a cheap hotel finding bodies. I wanted to tell him, but I didn't have time. Cawelti was moving toward us. I went back through the door and took the stairs two or three steps at a time. I was on the second floor when I heard the sound of a voice below me and Cawelti's tenor cut through the general din with, "Downstairs, you moron. Basements are down."

I pushed through the door and found myself in a hallway. The stairway was out. There might be a cop in the lobby, so the elevator was out. The fire escape was a possibility. I ran down the hall, had some trouble getting the window open, and carefully looked down into the alley. A black-and-white police car was down there, its lights on and fixed on the fire escape.

I closed the window and turned. A door opened and Olivia Fontaine stepped out. "What the hell are you doing?" she said.

"Looking for a friend," I said.

She was wearing a tight red dress, not the one she had worn on Sunday. She looked pretty good to a trapped man.

"You're the guy with Randolph Scott," she said, remembering.

"John Wayne," I corrected.

"Right," she agreed. "Did Teddy shoot somebody else?"

"*No,*" I said, looking at the hall door. "Teddy's dead. Somebody named Alex killed him. I've got a feeling the police think I did it."

"You didn't?"

"Do I look—" I stopped. Sure I looked like a murderer. "They'll be up here looking for me in a few minutes."

Something, a memory, crossed her face, softened it.

"What the hell," she said with a big sigh that did nice things for her chest. "Come in."

I moved past her into the room and she closed the door. She smelled sweet. I knew what I must have smelled like.

The room was a small one—a bed, two chairs, lamp, small dresser, and a view of Broadway through the window.

"I should be working," she said.

"I'll pay for your time," I countered, reaching into my wallet and pulling out a John Wayne $10 bill.

"Well," she began, "it'll buy you time but nothing else."

"That's all I'm after," I said.

We stood awkwardly for a few minutes and then she said, "I'll go see what's going on." She picked up the ten, put it into her purse, and went out the door. There was no place for me to go so I opened the door to the bathroom. It was small, with one permanently closed window over the tub.

What the hell. I ran a tub full of hot water and took off my clothes. A hot bath would feel good, cleanse my troubled mind and dirty body. I hung my fragrant suit on the hook near the door, scratched myself where I itched, and climbed into the tub.

The worst that could happen would be for Cawelti and his troops to come back in with Olivia, who, I realized, might well be turning me in. I still didn't have a decent lead on Alex. I didn't know if he knew how to get to John Wayne.

I turned off the water and heard the outer door open. No voices, only one set of footsteps. Olivia crossed the room and turned on the radio and then she came over to the bathroom and opened the door.

"The place is full of cops," she said, looking down at me. "You're right. They're looking for you. You sure you didn't shoot Teddy?"

"I'm sure," I said.

She didn't leave. She stood with her hands on her hips and said, "That's one hell of a body."

"It's been through a lot," I admitted.

She stood thinking for a while.

"I've seen worse," she said finally. "Scars aren't bad. You want company?"

I looked up at her.

"I didn't give you the ten to—"

"Hey," she said angrily, "I'm talking about my own time. I'm a sucker for losers who don't give up. You want company? You don't want company?"

In the other room Fibber McGee said, "I thought it was provocative of mirth."

"I would be honored to have your company," I said, putting the soap aside.

A few seconds later she was out of her dress and in the bath with me. It didn't do my back much good but it did a hell of a lot for my self-image. Olivia was good. No, Olivia was great. We moved from the bathroom to the bedroom and I turned McGee and Molly off.

Olivia didn't lie. She didn't push. She didn't demand. She did talk a hell of a lot about movies, a future she probably didn't have, and her mother back in Cleveland. No cops came into the room.

Just before ten, Olivia called a thousand-year-old bellhop named Stanley, who picked up my suit, which Olivia gave him while I hid in the bathroom.For ten bucks he found a way to get it cleaned and pressed by midnight.

"You want to sleep?" she said when the suit came back. "Or you want to go? Lobby's probably clear now. I can check."

"I'd like to stay," I said.

She smiled. "I'd like you to stay."

And I did. In the morning I tried to give her another ten. She wouldn't take it.

"That was on my own, I told you."

"Thanks," I said. Strangely, without makeup she looked younger, not pretty but younger, softer. I kissed her. She kissed back and touched my cheek.

"Take care of yourself," I said.

"You know it," she said. "Stay in touch."

Five minutes later I stepped into the parking lot, paid an extra $2 for parking overnight, and drove out down Broadway toward the rising sun.

10

Mrs. Plaut was out or finally sleeping when I got back to the boarding house on Heliotrope. I made it to my room, took off my neatly pressed jacket, counted my money, found I still had $168.43, and poured myself a bowl of Kix with milk and too much sugar. I was on my second bowl when Gunther knocked and I told him to come in. It was seven in the morning, according to my Beech-Nut clock, and Gunther was dressed in a gray three-piece suit complete with tie.

"I was concerned that you did not return during the night," he said, coming across the room and hopping up to sit in the chair across from me.

"How about a bowl of Kix, Gunther?" I offered.

The look of distaste didn't quite make it to the little man's face, but I saw it approach and knew that it wasn't far off.

"There really is no nutritional value in these cereals you consume," Gunther explained. "If you did not add sugar and milk, they might even be of a negative value, though some of them are fibrous. I made some yogurt, which I would be happy to share."

I shook my head. Gunther had introduced me to yogurt, an old family recipe he had brought from Switzerland. There was no future for the stuff in America but I didn't want to hurt his feelings any more than he wanted to hurt mine.

"Are you an insomniac, Gunther? I mean, no matter what time I get up, you're already awake and fully dressed and I get the feeling you've been working for hours." I finished my second bowl of Kix and thought about a third while I poured Gunther a cup of coffee. He examined the cup carefully, trying not to let me see. Apparently it was just clean enough for him to take a sip.

"I need little sleep," he said. "I sleep with depth, deeply. I accept my dreams."

"To your health, Gunther," I said, raising my coffee cup to him and holding back a belch.

I told Gunther about Jeremy and Alice's wedding. He was happy to be invited and suggested that he buy a gift we could give together. I hadn't thought about a gift. I fished out five bucks and gave it to him. He said he would think about it and make a suitable purchase. I suggested one. He told me about a government job he had, translating a nineteenth-century military strategy book from French to English. He could think of no reason why the American government would want such a book and I couldn't help him.

"The idiomatic nature of the terminology makes it somewhat of interest," he said, "but the content will not challenge the imagination. Military writers, I have discovered, often have an unfortunate inclination to attempt a poetic style."

I sympathized with him and then brought him up to date on what had happened. I didn't give it to him in order and probably left out something besides my night with Olivia Fontaine. Gunther took a little notebook from his inside jacket pocket and began writing. He asked me to repeat some details, fill in some blanks. Then he gently pushed away the coffee cup in front of him and placed the notebook down where he could examine it. I noticed that he had drunk no more than that first polite sip of coffee. I cleared the cup away and stacked it with the other dirty dishes in the sink.

"Two men are dead," Gunther said. "Both shot. Both in the Alhambra Hotel. One with your gun. One with a gun of unknown source. In both cases, an attempt is made to suggest that you should be suspected of the murder."

"Right," I agreed, finishing my own coffee and pouring another, which went well with the Salerno butter cookies I had put out. I refrained from dipping them in the coffee because of Gunther.

"In both cases, and that of Mr. Beason, an Alex who apparently harbors a dislike for the actor John Wayne is involved."

"Right," I agreed, crunching on a cookie and watching Gunther's intense little face.

"Apparently too, this Alex and his second victim . . ."

"Teddy Spaghetti," I supplied.

"Colorful name," Gunther said. "A *nom de plume.*"

"A moniker," I agreed, "but not one of his own choice."

"To resume," said Gunther. "Alex and Noodles—"

"Spaghetti."

"Yes, they removed cash and possibly some papers from the safe of the Alhambra, perhaps more than ten thousand dollars. And you have concluded that the cash and papers are related to certain illegal activities of a dubious couple named Larchmont who own the Alhambra Hotel."

"So far, so good, Gunther," I agreed.

"The Larchmonts, you believe, have sent two thugs—"

"Goons," I corrected.

"Goons?" Gunther said, writing the word in his book. In a few days he would be back to tell me the origin of the word "goon." "The goons wish to recover the stolen papers and money for the Larchmonts, to keep them from falling into the hands of the police," added Gunther. "To this end they fear your interference. Hence, though they probably know full well that you have not killed Mr. Vance or the man with the name of an Italian pasta—"

"Let's just call him Teddy," I suggested.

"Yes, they know you have not killed them, but they wish you to cease the pursuit of the money and papers, so they are doing their best to make the police believe that you are indeed the murderer. Is this not the situation?"

"That's the situation," I agreed. "And I have to protect John Wayne from Alex, find Alex and pin the rap on him, keep clear of the goons and the Larchmonts, and, if I'm lucky, get Charlie Chaplin's money back."

Gunther hopped down from the chair and removed his jacket. He rolled up his sleeves and went to the sink to do the dishes.

"There are some enigmas present," said Gunther, turning on the hot water and carefully rinsing my cereal bowl. "Why," Gunther began, "did Mr. Teddy remain in the Alhambra Hotel instead of fleeing after he and Alex removed the contents of the safe? Surely, remaining in the hotel would be most dangerous?"

I had no answer and none for the rest of his questions either, not yet.

"Why did this Teddy call you? Why is this Alex informing you of his hostility toward John Wayne? What function does it serve?"

"He's nuts," I suggested.

"Even the mad have motive," Gunther responded. "I have translated the works of Adler, Jung, and Freud himself. What does this Alex gain from informing you? Perhaps it is the hope that you will tell John Wayne and John Wayne will be apprehensive, but it would be better to threaten Wayne directly. And why is it that this Alex who knows Teddy, the Alhambra, and, apparently, the value of the contents of the safe, why is it that no one seems to know who he might be?"

I shrugged. Gunther finished the last few dishes. They filled the drainer near the sink. I found a relatively clean towel in a drawer and dried the dishes while he rolled down his sleeves and put his jacket back on.

"We must look at the facts," he said, returning to his notebook.

"Why?" I asked reasonably.

"Because the facts when arranged properly will present a pattern which reveals the truth."

"That's not the way it usually works for me," I said, moving over to sit on the one worn stuffed chair in the room, careful not to upset the basket of photographs from Mrs. Plaut. Gunther stood at the table.

"The way it works for me," I continued, "is I put all the facts I've got on the table and look at them till I get a pain in the head. They never tell me anything. I always mean to do what you just did, lay it out, keep it neat. But the wires on my notebook always come loose and I can't find a pencil with a decent point."

"So, what is it you do, Toby?"

My back twinged. The chair was too comfortable. I got up.

"I just keep gathering facts and hope a voice inside will click in and give me an idea of what to do with them. Then I know what facts to use and which ones I don't need anymore. There are always too damn many facts. Problem is, the voice never kicks in when I hope for it or wait for it. It only comes when I forget about it. I send up balloons and wait for someone to try to shoot them down."

"I see," said Gunther. "And on occasion, you get shot down with the balloons."

"It's the only way that works for me," I said with a shrug, as I wound my watch and reset it to coincide with the big Beech-Nut on the wall. That way it would be almost correct for about three minutes.

"So," Gunther said. "What is your next step?"

A knock on the door followed by Mrs. Plaut answered the question. She stood, a blue dress up to her neck, her hands on her hips, surveying me with tired patience. Her appearance made Gunther even more erect. Still, he was a good five inches smaller than the landlady.

"Mr. Peelers," she said. "You spoke nonsense to me on the telephone yesterday night."

"Two men were about to beat me senseless, break my arms, face, and spirit," I explained.

"And that is an excuse for rudeness? Mr. Wortman is always polite," she said with a pleased smile to Gunther, who returned the smile and didn't bother to tell her that his name was Wherthman, not Wortman.

"I'm sorry, Mrs. Plaut," I said. "It's been—"

"The photographs," she cut in. "Ordered, arranged, captioned, integrated with the words. This is a monumental task. And I am not getting any younger."

"None of us is getting any younger, Mrs. Plaut," I agreed, "but some things can age us much faster than others."

"That is sarcasm and irony," she said, pointing a finger at me. "You'd best knuckle down if you wish to make something of yourself."

"It's too late for that, Mrs. Plaut. I am what I'll always be."

"The photographs," she said, pointing at the box near my feet.

"I have a killer to catch, a life to save, money to return to its rightful owners," I explained.

"Those will pass," she said, "but history will always be upon us. I hear there will soon be a scrap rubber drive."

Gunther winced at the transition.

"So I understand," I said.

"There are messages for you from yesterday," she suddenly remembered, and reached into the pocket of her dress to withdraw several scraps of paper. "Two men were here looking for you, said they would return. They were gaudily attired and rather large and quite indifferent to history. I attempted to engage them in conversation. They would not be engaged."

I got up, determined to escape as she went on.

"A police officer named Caldi called."

"Cawelti," I corrected.

"Does it really make a difference?" she said impatiently. "I have a busy day ahead. Finally, a man called and said to inform you that he would dispose of the Duke very shortly. His name was—"

"Alex," Gunther finished.

"Alice is correct," said Mrs. Plaut. "Am I to assume that Duke is a family pet that you are having disposed of or are you planning more dead bodies? I will tolerate no more dead bodies, Mr. Peelers. We have an agreement on that."

"We do, Mrs. Plaut," I said, moving toward the door, but she cut me off with a step.

"Saturday we do the photographs," she said.

"Saturday," I agreed.

Satisfied at last, she left.

I fumbled in my pocket for some change and the phone number in my notebook. Gunther handed me four nickels and I hurried into the hall and to the pay phone near the head of the stairs. I plunked in a nickel and dialed while Gunther stood six feet off. After five rings someone answered.

"My name is Peters," I said. "I'm doing some confidential work for Mr. Wayne. He said I could get in touch with him through you. Tell me where the boat is supposed to dock and—"

"Duke told me who you are, Peters," came the voice. "He's not on the boat. He's back in town. You can reach him at the Roosevelt Hotel, where he's having a business conference with Republic. But if it's not an emergency—"

"It is. What room is he in?"

I got the number, thanked the man, hit the phone cradle, and called the Roosevelt, asking for the right room number. A woman answered and I told her I wanted to speak to John Wayne. She said he was busy. I told her to give him my name. About ten seconds later, Wayne was on the phone.

"Peters," he said, "how's it going?"

"I thought you were safe on some boat in the ocean catching barracudas and drinking beer."

"Coast Guard turned us back," he said. "Jap subs were spotted off San Diego yesterday, or they thought they saw Jap subs. Then I got this Republic call and—"

"Teddy's dead, the one in the room at the Alhambra. The one you hit, and this Alex guy claims he's going to get you. You've got to go someplace safe for a few days while I—"

"Nothin' doing," said Wayne. "Listen, mister. Our boys are dying, people are dying all over the damn world. Do you read newspapers?"

"I read—"

"That goddamn Hitler killed twelve hundred Czechs today in some place I never heard of called Lidice. He killed them because someone assassinated Reinhardt or Reingold or something Heydrich, the monster he set up to step on the Czechs. I'm sitting here safely making movies and going on boat trips and people are getting killed every day. I'm not hiding. I'm goddamn mad. I don't know who the hell this Alex is but I'd be happy if he takes a look-see for me. I'd be obliged to meet him. I've got a big family to feed and I am not hiding. You find this Alex before he finds me, if you can. If you can't, then I'll just have to take my chances the way thousands of our boys are doing it every day."

"It's your life," I said.

"That it is," he agreed. "When we finish up here in about an hour, some friends and I are going over to a friend's boat moored at Harris's Marina in Santa Monica. We're going to stay just off shore doing some fishing and drinking. Boat's called *Mad Anthony.* You're welcome to come."

I declined the invitation, told him I had the money he had sent, and said I'd stay in touch. Then I hung up and turned to Gunther.

"Can I be of service?" Gunther offered. "I am well ahead on my current assignments and would welcome the opportunity to assist."

I couldn't turn him down. I put in a call to Straight-Ahead at the Alhambra. The clerk on duty told me that Straight-Ahead wasn't due in till evening. I had no trouble getting Straight-Ahead's phone number from the phone company.

Another nickel from Gunther got me through to the house detective.

"Merit Beason," he answered.

"Merit, Toby. How are you feeling?"

"The police are searching for you, Toby. We were right. The bad guys have somehow suggested that you did Teddy in last night."

"I'll live with it, Merit," I said. "Our Alex has made another threat on John Wayne. I know you didn't get a decent look at him, but is there a chance you'd recognize Alex if he walked past you?"

"There's a chance that Merit Beason would recognize the man who shot him," Beason said. I imagined him sitting straight up in bed, eyes fixed on the future.

"Are you up to a few hours of parking and watching?"

"The bullet missed the ticker," he said. "It's beating like a new Elgin watch. Where'll it be?"

I said I'd pick him up, and a few minutes later Gunther and I were heading for Santa Monica in the Crosley. The car was about right for Gunther. Instead of being cramped in the backseat, he had plenty of leg room.

I made a stop before we went to Straight-Ahead's. First, I

went to a pawn shop on Sepulveda where I had done some business before. I also made a deal on something I wanted to give Mrs. Plaut. That set me back another ten.

"I would especially like to be of service to Mr. Chaplin," Gunther said as I searched for Beason's address on 14th Street. I couldn't see Gunther. His head was below the sight line of my seat. "When I worked in the circus during that difficult period of my early days in this country, I retained my sense of dignity only by bearing in mind the image of Mr. Charlie Chaplin's tramp. Dignity, tradition, skill. I modeled myself after the character of Chaplin, as did so many others. I should like to think that I could repay him in some way for his inspiration."

"We can repay him ten grand worth if things work out," I said, finding Beason's place. He was standing in front of the place as ramrod-still as a cigar store Indian, a little out of place in the shabby neighborhood. His apartment building had never seen better days. It looked as if it had been built knowing it was a loser.

I was a little worried about Merit making the fit since he couldn't duck his head, but he knew how to maneuver his way into tight spots.

I introduced Gunther and brought Merit up to date as we headed for Harris's in Santa Monica. We got there ahead of Wayne and his pals and found the *Mad Anthony* docked along with four other boats.

"We'll spread out here and keep out of sight," I suggested. Straight-Ahead was looking out the front window and not at me. Since he couldn't nod, he gave a simple "Yes."

"And afterward," I went on, "we follow Wayne in shifts. I'll stay with him through the day, but I'll need relief at night."

"I shall relieve at night," Gunther volunteered. "I am conversant with firearms. You can allow me the use of your weapon."

"Check," I said. "If you're up to a few hours in the morning, Merit . . ."

"Merit Beason will be on the job," he said. "There they come."

We all looked out the window as a car pulled up near the dock and four men piled out. One of them had apparently told a joke. They were all laughing as they walked down five stone steps and onto the wooden dock. I was parked about three car lengths behind them in a small lot for the marina. Through the window we could look down at the bubbling ocean and anyone who approached.

I recognized the three men with Wayne, though I didn't know their names. They were all movie actors, gangster types, and they already had had enough to drink to keep them happy and their minds off the war for the rest of the day.

When they were on the boat, Merit and I got out of the car. Gunther agreed to stay and keep his eyes open from the slope. I went up the coast along the shore about twenty yards and Straight-Ahead, looking like a lead soldier, paced down the coast and out of sight around a bend. For the next hour, we sat watching as the fishing boat pulled out and anchored about a hundred yards from shore. The sound of voices carried on the wind over the water. The Duke and his buddies laughed, fished, told jokes. We waited.

After another hour, a man in a yachting cap spotted me and walked over. He had a pipe in one hand and wore white pants and a white shirt.

"Can I help you?" the commodore said. He had gray-tinged sideburns. He should have been battling Chinese pirates.

"No," I said from the wooden barrel I was sitting on. "I like to just sit here and meditate."

I guess I didn't look like the meditating type.

"Meditate?"

"Rest my mind and soul," I said. "This is a troubled world and these are troubled times."

"I see," said the commodore, examining his pipe to see why it wasn't working. "That's my ship there, *The Sahara.* I thought you were looking at it."

"I was looking through it to the sea, to infinity," I said with a grin. "I'm a poet."

"A poet?"

"Yeah," I said. "I'm trying to get in touch with the muse, so if you'd just get your ass out of here and let me get to it, I'd be very grateful."

He looked like a commodore but he wasn't built like one. He turned and walked away with his dead pipe, heading for his ship. During the third hour of our wait, he popped his head up five times to see if I was still there. I was. He never took *The Sahara* away from the dock.

Somewhere in the fourth hour, the *Mad Anthony* headed back for shore. The boys aboard were whooping it up and a few of them had some trouble negotiating the short leap from the deck to the dock. None of them carried any fish.

I stood up, stretched my legs, and was taking a step toward the parking lot when the shot came. I didn't see what, if anything, it hit, but I looked at Wayne and his four cronies, who were standing straight up, their eyes toward the shore.

"Get down," I shouted. "Get down."

Wayne was the first to wake from his daze. He grabbed the man nearest him and went face down on the dock. The third man followed. The last, whom I recognized as Ward Bond, just stood there like a lineman, hands on hips, looking angrily in the direction of the shot.

"What in the Sam Hill is —" Bond shouted.

The second shot tore a piece of the dock at his feet and Bond dove back on the boat and hit the deck. I ran down the shoreline past the dock and jumped down to the rocky beach, my gun in hand.

"Merit?" I shouted. "You see him?"

"On the ridge, parking lot," came Beason's voice. Then he stepped out and pointed with his pistol. I thought I saw something behind a Chevy coupe. Merit saw it too and fired. His bullet took a line of paint off the Chevy.

"Cover," I called.

"Covered," returned Straight-Ahead, standing straight up, a perfect target, but what choice did he have. His body wouldn't let him stand any other way. I crouched and went up the slope. I ducked behind the Chrysler Wayne's crew had come in, took a breath, and stepped out at the sound of footsteps near the wounded Chevy.

I came within a rat's breath of killing Gunther, who had ducked behind the Chevy.

"He was over there," Gunther said, unaware of his brush with death. His small finger was pointing down the shoreline to a stack of metal drums.

I leaned over so Straight-Ahead could see me and motioned to the barrels. He waved a hand to show that he understood, and we moved in on the place where I assumed Alex had fired from. I was moving on the high ground, Beason on the low. I kept my back away from the ridge line so I wouldn't be a target, but Beason, gun at his side, strode right for the drums. It was showdown time and he was doing for real what John Wayne did in the movies. I wondered if Wayne and his boys were watching the show.

I went about fifteen yards past the drums, dropped to the shore behind some rocks, and came from behind as Straight-Ahead advanced from in front. If Alex had been there, we would have had him, but he wasn't.

"Got away," I said.

"Like the wind," agreed Straight-Ahead, holstering his gun. I did the same. There wasn't much likelihood that Alex had stuck around after Beason had taken a shot at him. He was in no hurry.

"Gunther," I shouted. "Anybody drive away up there?"

"I don't know. I don't think so, but there are cars farther down on the street," Gunther's small voice came back.

Straight-Ahead and I moved side by side back to the dock, where John Wayne was now standing.

"The son of a bitch tried to kill me," Wayne said. He had sobered quickly. He was wearing blue slacks and a light blue shirt. The wind was blowing his dark hair and he looked like something out of one of his movies.

"You?" bellowed Bond. "That bullet almost took my right foot. I'd like to get these paws on that bastard."

The other two passengers looked scared, which is damned reasonable when someone has just shot at you.

Wayne did the introductions and I found out that the other two passengers were Paul Fix and Grant Withers. None of them had seen who had shot at them.

Beason found the hole from the first bullet in the dock bulletin board. The bullet had smashed through the glass and hit a poster of a cruiser over which was written "Build the Cruiser Los Angeles. Buy an Extra War Bond This Month." The bullet hadn't sunk the cruiser. It had also come nowhere near Wayne or the small boat.

"Lucky the fella can't shoot straight," Fix said.

"That we are," agreed Bond. "Now who the hell is he and what's going on?"

I let Wayne do the explaining while Beason, Gunther, and I looked for any sign of the elusive Alex. There wasn't one. Back with Wayne, we had a quick meeting, with the Wayne entourage contributing the identities of various Alexes they knew. Gunther dutifully recorded each name and whatever they remembered. None of the Alexes sounded very promising, though a few of them were interesting, especially Alex Schwoch, a stunt man who had doubled for John Wayne on a Republic Western in 1935. Schwoch had insisted on doing a belly first slide down a lumber sluice. He had hit bottom, landed on his head, stood up in a daze, and shouted that he was tired of waiting for his drink and would henceforth bring his business to Mooney's Tavern.

The fellows thought this was a great tale establishing Alex Schwoch's image and possible motive. The only problem was that Grant Withers was sure the man's name had been Arthur, not Alex.

Sobered by Alex's bullets, the Duke agreed to take things easy for a few days and make it a little less trouble to keep an eye on him. He was going to do some tests at a set in the hills just off Coldwater Canyon sometime the next morning, a new Western, part of the agreement with Republic. Wayne was going to produce and he had a location he liked picked out for a gunfight. Other than that he could stay holed up playing cards at Bond's house.

On the way back to town in the Crosley, Gunther, Straight-Ahead, and I said very little. We had failed to catch Alex, who was obviously damned resourceful or lucky. He had managed to find Wayne at the Roosevelt, follow him to Santa Monica, and get a couple of shots off at him.

We trailed Wayne's car to be sure Alex wasn't following him. Merit adjusted the mirror, Gunther looked out the rear window, and I checked anything that passed us. We were sure no one was on the trail.

I dropped Straight-Ahead off at his apartment building on 14th after he declined an offer to lunch with me and Gunther.

"Few hours rest and Merit Beason has to be back on the job," he said, awkwardly getting out of the Crosley. "Let me know where to pick up Wayne tomorrow and I'll stay with him through the morning."

"I can get—" I started, but Straight-Ahead lifted a hand as he moved away.

"Wound's healing fine," he said. "This is time number two

for Alex getting the best of Merit Beason. There won't be a third time."

Two dark men got out of the way as the house detective walked straight to the door and into the unnamed building. Then I headed for Spring Street, found a space, and treated Gunther to a late lunch at Levy's. Gunther had the chicken noodle soup and chopped liver plate. I had the corned beef with a sour pickle on rye, with lots of ketchup.

The voluptuous Carmen was on duty at the cash register as I knew she would be, the silent, elusive, and ample Carmen.

"Carmen," I said as I paid the bill. "How about Monday? Boxing, a movie; *The Gold Rush* is at the Hawaii on Hollywood."

"I've seen it," she said without looking at me as she plunked down my change.

"Everyone's seen it," I said. "It's worth seeing again. I'm working for Charlie Chaplin. I can tell you things about him that will make it a new experience."

Her massive bosom heaved in disbelief under her yellow blouse.

"He is, indeed, in the employ of Charlie Chaplin," Gunther said.

Carmen leaned forward to see where the voice was coming from and I saw as much of Carmen as I had ever witnessed.

"Carmen," I gulped when she sat back. "I know I've been less than responsible in the past, but believe me—"

"No fights, wrestling," she said.

"Wrestling's a fake," I said. "Jeremy will tell you. It's a show, a sham."

Carmen was unmoved. A couple behind us reached over Gunther to pay their bill.

"Wrestling and a real dinner," Carmen insisted. "No tacos. No hot dogs. Chinese."

"Chinese food and wrestling," I agreed. "It's a date. I'll pick you up at seven at your place."

"Three dollars even," Carmen told the couple behind us, and Gunther and I left Levy's.

My social calendar was filling rapidly. Alice and Jeremy's wedding on Friday. Dinner with Doc Parry and Doc Hodgdon on Saturday. Chinese and wrestling with Carmen on Monday. If I could stay alive and out of jail, it looked like a promising weekend.

Since Gunther wasn't in a hurry, we stopped at the May Company and picked up a pair of brown-and-white shoes for $6.95 before I returned Gunther to Heliotrope. I didn't park in front of the house because John Cawelti's car was across the street and John was in it. I dropped Gunther at the corner with the box I had purchased for Mrs. Plaut. He reminded me that he was ready for future service. I thanked him and watched him walk down the street, package under his small arm, suit still neatly buttoned.

The two little girls who had a persistent lemonade stand a few doors from Mrs. Plaut's tried to strong-arm Gunther into a purchase. They were both bigger than he was but they didn't know Gunther's commitment to cleanliness. He bought no lemonade.

I pulled into a driveway, turned around, and headed back downtown, beginning to worry about what the Crosley was doing to my back.

Lyle and Sutker played it smart this time. Someone had probably laid it out for them. They got me when I stepped out of No-Neck Arnie's garage. Arnie had assured me that Vance was still safely on ice and I had decided to make my way back to the Alhambra in search of the Larchmonts. I was crossing Olympic when they came up on each side of me. Fortunately, they had changed shirts. The new ones were light blue with pictures of seals on them. Each seal was balancing a yellow ball.

"Someone wants to see you," Lyle said.

I had a pretty good idea of who that might be.

11

I sat in the backseat of the Chrysler with Lyle, the gun in his hand bouncing with every pit in the road. Sutker, whose nose was covered with bandage and tape, drove silently. We went south on Avelon, made a turn on Rosecrans, and wheeled into a small, apparently nameless dead-end street in Compton. There were some reasonably nice looking two-story houses on the street, including one at the end facing a small open airstrip. We parked and got out.

Having nothing to say to Lyle and Sutker, I followed them into a two-story brick house. There should have been a mom, a dad, and two kids inside. Instead there was Adrienne Larchmont in a dining room seated at one end of a big table, her hair tight, dress black, her look determined. Seated behind the table and facing me was a man in his fifties, tall, a bit thin, gray hair combed neatly back, a small nose, and smaller eyes. He lacked only a monocle for his Conrad Veidt imitation.

Lyle stepped to one side to block the door, and Sutker took up residence on the other side. All we needed were some candles for the man behind the table to induct me into his fraternity.

"Here he is," said Lyle.

"We can see him," said Adrienne Larchmont.

"I know," said Lyle, explaining. "I was just being . . . polite."

"Larchmont?" I guessed, taking a step forward toward the man. The room still smelled of something from lunch, probably pork. I had the feeling this had all been set up for me, Monogram serial stuff or a Columbia B picture.

"I am Sydney Larchmont," the man agreed, folding his hands on the table.

"Ask him about Chaplin," Mrs. Larchmont said.

"I'll ask him, Adrienne, as soon as I establish a relationship here," he said. "Kindly give me some credit for knowing how to conduct myself in situations such as this. Mr. Peters, we are in a somewhat awkward situation."

"All right if I sit?" I asked.

I had broken Larchmont's train of thought. He looked at Lyle and Sutker.

"He asked if he could sit," said Mrs. Larchmont.

"I'm well aware that he asked if he could sit," Larchmont said. "I am not deaf. He may not sit."

"Oh God," groaned Mrs. Larchmont.

"Adrienne," Larchmont said, looking at her. "You are only undermining my authority in this situation. I want to impress Mr. Peters with the seriousness of his position. That is difficult to do if you undermine . . ."

Adrienne Larchmont looked around the room for someone with a backbone and intelligence to sympathize with the burden of stupidity she had to bear. She looked at me and I shrugged a what-are-you-going-to-do shrug.

Larchmont tried to take control again but he didn't know where he was going.

"Would you like a glass of wine, Mr. Peters?" he asked.

"Make up your mind Sid-Ney," Mrs. Larchmont said. "First you're going to treat him like a Turkish prisoner and now you're offering him wine."

I checked Lyle and Sutker. They seemed to have heard the

Larchmonts at it before. They stood with folded arms and vacant stares.

"Adrienne," Sydney whispered, though we could hear him clearly. "You said that I shouldn't—"

"Get on with it," she whispered back.

It was like being interviewed by the dark side of Fibber McGee and Molly. I knew how Mayor LaTrivia must have felt.

"Let me help," I said. "You want to know if I know where your money and papers are. I don't know, and the way I figure it, the money isn't yours. It belongs to Charlie Chaplin, at least he has a claim on it. My guess is that a lot of people have a better claim on it than you two."

"Now just a—" Larchmont began.

"Why did you kill Teddy?" I demanded, placing my hand on the table and leaning forward like a trial lawyer.

"I—we didn't kill—" Larchmont stammered.

"Sydney," Mrs. Larchmont said slowly, "he is in our house, our guest. Lyle and Sutker are right there. He should answer our questions."

"I know that, Adrienne," Larchmont said. "Let me use my own methods. Peters, you will answer the questions, not ask them. We didn't kill Teddy. We want only to recover that which has been stolen from us and we want no further trouble from Mr. Chaplin. It is you who killed that Vance man at our hotel. It is you the police are seeking for the murder of Longretti. Mr. Peters, you are jeopardizing our business."

"Sydney," Mrs. Larchmont said, this time with the patience of a teacher talking to a child she has had to discipline so many times that tranquility carries its own sarcasm. "You didn't ask him anything. You made a speech."

"Are you married, Mr. Peters?" Larchmont said, wiping his brow with an unlined white handkerchief and looking at me.

"I was. Not anymore. Didn't get along with my wife," I said. "My fault. She thought I would never grow up. She was right."

Larchmont smiled. I guessed he was envying my unwed state.

Sutker or Lyle shuffled behind me.

"What we want," Sydney Larchmont picked up, "is for you to cease whatever investigation you are conducting on Charlie Chaplin's behalf, to cease looking for our stolen money and documents unless you agree to turn them over to us for a reasonable fee if and when they are found. They could be damaging to us and embarrassing to others if made public. We are engaged in many causes, Serbo-Croatian Relief, the Irish Front, Orient for the Allies, Friends of the Occupied Nations, The Fifth—"

"Why don't you give him a typed list of all our enterprises?" Mrs. Larchmont said, throwing up her hands in exasperation.

"Well, in any case, Peters, you must stay out of this," Larchmont tried again. "In exchange we will stop suggesting to the police that you are responsible for murder."

So far my trip to Compton had been very informative. I looked around the room, giving the impression, I hoped, that I was weighing the offer. I imagined the Larchmonts at breakfast across the table from each other like Citizen Kane and his wife, the years passing. They hadn't killed Teddy. They didn't have the papers or the money.

"Alex," I said. "What does Alex have to do with this?"

"Alex?" asked Larchmont puzzled, then, turning to his wife, repeated, "Alex?"

She shrugged. Larchmont tried Lyle and Sutker. They looked blank.

"Did this Alex take the files and the money?" Larchmont asked.

"John Wayne," I tried.

"John Wayne took the files and money?" Larchmont said, looking at me as if I were insane.

"No," I said. "What has John Wayne got to do with this?"

"I don't know," said Larchmont, gripping the sides of his chair. "What does John Wayne have to do with this? We've never gotten a nickel from him, never tried really except for a letter, general mailer, but—"

"Sydney," Mrs. Larchmont said, standing and shaking her head. "Why don't you just give him a taped confession while you're at it."

"Adrienne," Larchmont said, standing, his voice coming through clenched teeth. "If you would kindly stop interfering, I might get someplace with this, but all I get is your criticism, which, I feel, Adrienne, is completely unmerited."

"All right with you two if I leave," I said.

"I don't—" Sydney began.

"No," said Adrienne. "You are not to be trusted, Mr. Peters. We are not killers but we are not going to be . . ."

"Thwarted?" I suggested.

"Deterred?" tried Sydney.

"Pissed on," said Lyle behind me.

"We sent you to Mr. Peters earlier," Adrienne said, looking past me at Lyle and Sutker. "We wanted him immobilized. It is my opinion that we return to that plan."

"Adrienne," Larchmont nearly shouted, "I'll handle this. You two," he said pointing at Lyle and Sutker. "Do something to Mr. Peters, a limb or something."

Lyle grabbed one arm, Sutker the other. They wheeled me around.

"I'll see you two again," I promised over my shoulder. I could have told them I'd be back to give them a taste of hell, but they had created their own hell together and there wasn't much I could do to match it.

"They always like that?" I asked Lyle.

"Pretty much," he agreed, giving my arm an unneeded pull.

"You embarrassed us," Lyle said, opening the Chrysler door and urging me in while Sutker moved around to the front to drive. "Back in your office when your blimp friend threw us out. No blimp is going to embarrass us."

Sutker started the car and I eyed the pistol in Lyle's hand.

"We have our pride," Sutker said, gently touching the bandage on his broken nose.

"If Jeremy hadn't thrown you out, you would have stomped on me," I said.

"So we're gonna stomp on you now," said Lyle. "What'd it gain you, I ask you."

We drove down Alameda. It was dark and I had no plan.

"The hills," Lyle said. In the front seat Sutker nodded. There were lots of dark rocks in the Dominguez Hills where a battered private detective could be left to reacquaint himself with nature.

I was thinking about how much longer it took for broken limbs to mend when you got to be as old as I was when the flash appeared in front of us on the street. It scared the hell out of Sutker and it didn't do me any good either. Lyle was looking at me and didn't see it.

"What was that?" Sutker said.

"What?" asked Lyle.

"Something on the street, up ahead," I explained. "A flash."

"Bullshit," said Lyle, glancing out the front window to the second giant spark now about forty yards in front of us.

"What was that?" Lyle said, making it clear he had no answer to Sutker's question.

In five more yards we could see what it was, but it didn't

make any more sense: a giant metal chain dipping out of the sky to scrape the street and send up a flare of sparks. Sutker pulled off to the side, almost hitting on oncoming Buick, which kept right on going. If we had stayed on the street, the chain would have missed us. As it was, it turned, snapping like a clanging snake, and lashed across the front of the Chrysler.

"Holy shit," screamed Lyle, bolting out of the door. Sutker followed him. I went to the floor listening to the chain play a Gene Krupa riff on the roof. It stopped and I looked out the rear window. In the dark sky I could make out the shape of a barrage balloon, the kind that was usually moored on the coast to keep away the feared Jap airplanes, but this one had, as two or three others I had heard of, torn loose. It was losing air and dragging its chain, causing more damage and fear than a Zero on a rampage.

Lyle had left his door open. I could see him in the trees at the side of the road. I couldn't see Sutker. I got up, dove into the front seat, and shifted the idling Chrysler into gear. I hadn't bothered to close the driver's door that Sutker had left open when he jumped. I should have. Sutker grabbed my arm as I hit the gas. The jerk forward slammed him against the side of the car. He held on to my arm until I jerked forward again and he had to let go to keep from hitting the asphalt of Alameda with his already broken nose. I didn't turn around to look for Lyle. I drove. About two hundred yards down the street I stopped to close my door and reach back to close the rear door. Running down the road toward me in the distance were Lyle and Sutker, their red shirts catching the light of oncoming cars not curious enough to slow down to see what they were up to.

On the way back to Los Angeles I listened to Fred Waring and the Pennsylvanians singing "Ain't We Got Fun." I hummed along for a few bars. When the song was over, I stopped for a hot dog and Pepsi at a roadside stand. The car hop said her name was Melinda and that she had been entered in the Car Hop of the Year contest. She also told me she was seventeen and had a brother and father in the Army. I wished them all luck and finished a second hot dog as I drove. I spilled ketchup and Pepsi on the front seat.

Back in town I parked the Chrysler on Main and hoofed it to No-Neck Arnie's to retrieve my Crosley. Arnie wasn't there. He had left a few hours earlier. His night man, Otto, a wiry grunter, grunted hello to me. I asked if I could use the phone. He grunted. I didn't have the Larchmonts' phone number but I looked up the Alhambra and called. Straight-Ahead came on about three minutes after I asked for him.

"Leave a note for the Larchmonts," I said. "Their car is on Main near Twelfth."

"Will do," said Straight-Ahead. "Officers of the law are looking for you, Toby. You might check in with them."

"No time," I said. "I've got to figure out a way to find Alex."

"No problem," he said. "Merit Beason thinks he's up in Room one-twelve right now. Checked in last Saturday. I did a double check on the registration book. Alex Tuster from Meridian, Mississippi. I checked Tuster's room when he was out just on the name, nothing to lose, you know?"

"I know," I said.

"Merit Beason found what may be one of the missing files from the safe in the desk. You want to come on over?"

"Toby Peters is on the way," I said, and hung up.

When I reached the Alhambra, I knew something was different from the night before. Gone were the sailors and Olivia's sisters in the profession. The place had been taken over by men and women in white pullover shirts, white shoes, and white pants. Straight-Ahead was at the entrance. A few new light bulbs had been put in the ceiling, probably to be removed when this group of starched characters departed.

"Health fiends," Straight-Ahead explained as he motioned for me to follow him. "Three floors booked. Miracle Mineral Water all over the place. Guy over there has a booth in the ballroom. You buy ten gallons, you get one free."

I caught snatches of conversation as I followed Straight-Ahead, who moved as always straight ahead to the elevator.

"Alkaline . . ." said a woman.

"Saline . . ." countered a man.

"Tried a glass," said Straight-Ahead as I pushed past a pair of white even teeth surrounded by a woman who looked like a compact refrigerator. "Maybe it was imagination, but it made the bullet hole ache. Thought the stuff would come pouring out. Don't recommend it."

"I won't," I promised.

"Arthritis, acidosis, neuritis," said a man on one side.

"No, high blood pressure, autointoxication, rheumatism," echoed a woman on the other side.

"Magnesiac, antacid, diuretic," came a third voice as we stepped into the elevator.

"Up?" asked a woman with teeth almost as white as the little refrigerator woman.

"Up," I agreed. "Two."

"These are self-service elevators," Straight-Ahead said, turning his large body toward the woman, a rather small, straight-backed creature of no certain age, with short black hair and in uniform white.

"Dr. Miracle asked me to run the elevator as a service to the members," she explained. "To keep track of where they are going and remind them that the convention is primarily in the first-floor boardroom. You two are not with us?"

"We're not against you either," I said.

"Merit Beason thinks you'd better not run the elevator," Merit Beason said.

"Who?" she asked.

"Him," I said, nodding at Straight-Ahead.

"Dr. Miracle—" she began.

"He can see Merit Beason," Merit said. "The house security officer."

We were at two and stepped off.

"Larchmonts might not like your disciplining the nonviolent paying guests," I said.

"Tojo's ass," he said. "I'm getting too old for fools and fads. I have a feeling Merit Beason's not long for the Alhambra."

He found the right door, inserted his pass key, and stepped in.

"Your employers and I just had a short talk," I said. "They're worried about the files that Teddy and Alex took out of the safe Sunday. They are so worried that they want me to stay out of the whole thing, or two of their other employees named Lyle and Sutker will be sure that I stay out."

"A pair of melons," sighed Straight-Ahead, turning on the light. "No art to either one of them. They don't seem—"

"A runaway barrage balloon was sent by God to rescue me from them tonight," I said, looking around the small, obviously unoccupied room.

"Right," said Straight-Ahead. "Heard it on the radio. Broke loose on the coast. Came to rest in Lynwood. Lots of danger. What a world."

"What a world," I agreed, as Straight-Ahead opened the drawer to the desk and pointed to an envelope. I picked it up, opened it, and read part of the contents.

"Son of—" I started.

"James Farley, John Nance Garner, Willie Randolph Hearst," said Straight-Ahead. "You name 'em, the Larchmonts had 'em hooked. You'd think people like that would see through the phony fronts. They got less for their money than Dr. Miracle's Mineral Water."

"For a lot more per gallon," I said. "Where are Alex's things?"

"Gone," said Straight-Ahead. "Nothing here but that envelope. Don't ask why he left it. Oversight. Maybe a little teaser for us. Got a feeling that this is only the topsoil of what was in that safe."

"Well, we'll keep these and contribute some erosion," I said. "No point in going over the place?"

"Merit Beason already did so," he said. "From rolled up window shades to plumbing. Nothing else here. Did you get to the last page?"

I hadn't. I flipped through the dozen or so stapled pages and found a handwritten note with John Wayne's name repeated about thirty times. A third-rate cartoon of a gun in the left-hand margin was shooting a bullet at Wayne's name. The bullet was moving. You could tell from the straight lines behind it indicating the retreating air.

"Merit Beason's off at four in the morning and," Straight-Ahead said, "will get himself down to Ward Bond's house and keep an eye on Wayne and out for Alex. No real description on our Alex. Teddy checked him in. Clerk downstairs doesn't remember him checking out. Ledger showed he paid cash. Guy who might have been him was seen checking out this morning. But it might not have been him."

"I'll take these," I said, tucking the envelope under my arm.

"Okay with Merit Beason," he said.

"Merit, I can keep an eye on Wayne in the morning. How about you getting some rest. You got shot three days ago, almost . . ."

"Time to rest when we're under the ground," he said. "People say Bat Masterson used to say that back in Kansas. Always thought he had a truth there. A job gets started, a job gets seen through to the end. You keep bulldogging Alex. Merit'll watch your client's back."

I pulled out my wallet and counted off two twenties and handed them to Merit, who took them.

"Client money?" he said.

"The Duke's," I answered.

"Fair is fair," he said, putting the two twenties in a wallet that looked as if it had been sewed by the Indians who greeted the first Pilgrims.

Someone screamed in the hall.

"Back to the front," Straight-Ahead said, walking slowly to the door.

"Thanks, Merit," I added.

His back was to me as he answered, "My business, too. Two murders in my domain and me an almost third. Finding our Alex is a mission."

With that he went out, leaving me alone. I went over the contents of the envelope again, essentially a listing of people who had given the Larchmonts money for a variety of organizations, each one of which was listed after the investor or donor's name, along with the amount donated or invested. Someone, probably Sydney Larchmont, had totaled the whole thing up on page three, exactly $214,327.68. Charlie Chaplin wasn't even on the list of top contributors.

Straight-Ahead was a pro. There was no point in going over the room again to see if I could turn up something on Alex that he had missed. As I stepped to the door, it began to open. I expected Straight-Ahead. I got John Cawelti.

"Surprise," he said.

I was surprised.

"Hey," he said, grinning. "You want me to just turn around and leave? We can forget the whole thing."

"We've played this scene before John," I said, trying to think of a way to swallow the envelope in one quick gulp without water.

He touched his hair to be sure it was still parted in the

middle, adjusted his jacket and tie, and smiled an unfriendly smile.

"That was a tank full of crap about John Wayne the other day," he said.

"No," I said. "It was true. Someone tried to shoot him this afternoon. I was there. Fellow named Alex. Alex shot Teddy last night, the clerk and . . ."

"And . . ." Cawelti prompted with the evil smile of a leprechaun.

"A guy named Lewis Vance on Sunday," I said.

"We found Vance this morning in a freezer at the San Luis Ice House. They're slicing him now. Frozen solid. Doc says it gives him an idea about taking tissue samples. Thought you might like to know you contributed in a small way to forensic science."

"I'm pleased," I said, watching him bounce on his heels.

"Waiting for a ballistics report," he went on. "I think the bullet in Vance is going to match your thirty-eight, the one turned in by your two friends. And I think we're gonna get you on the Longretti killing last night. You got troubles, Peters, and I don't think your big brother will even want to get you out of them."

Cawelti took a step toward me, teeth set, face a little redder than usual. "Why don't you try to get by me," he suggested. "Maybe I couldn't stop you."

"You couldn't," I said, putting the envelope down on the desk, "but that bulge under your jacket could. Let's go see Phil."

He stepped back, giving me a few yards to pass, reached over, and picked up the envelope, which was a mistake. I didn't have much choice now. That list and the note on Wayne would have me tied up for a week. I didn't see how they could get me for anything long-term on the two stiffs, but Cawelti could lock me in the can for a night. I threw an elbow as he turned for the package and caught him in the chest. He reached for his gun. I grabbed the envelope with one hand and with the other pulled at his jacket to make it a little hard for him to kill me. It was a great plan, well thought out, well executed. The problem was that it didn't work. Cawelti had one free hand, which he used to hit me flat on my already flat nose. There was nothing left to break in my nose but that didn't stop it from bleeding, and it didn't stop me from staggering back, still clutching the envelope. I went over the bed and neatly rolled to a position on my knees, facing him. An unprejudiced audience would have appreciated the acrobatics, but Sergeant John Cawelti was not one of my fans.

His gun was out and pointed at a spot around the center of my chest. At seven feet, even I would have hit a kneeling man.

He looked happy.

"Resisting arrest," he said, pulling back the hammer of the revolver to extend his pleasure.

"Murder suspect," he went on.

"I'm a Rosicrucian," I said. "I'm also unarmed."

"I'm not going to kill you," he said, his hair dangling in front of his eyes. "I'm just going to shoot a kneecap or two. Hurts like sin. I know. I've done it three times. Twice to the same guy."

I was on my feet now and the spirit of fear and feeling of I've-had-enough were on me. My legs were almost fifty years old. My back was a dry rubber band and I had a mouth full of blood. I knew I was going to make a leap for the good sergeant. Somewhere not too deep down I also knew I probably wouldn't make it, but John Wayne had tried something crazier in *Randy Rides the Range.*

The door moved behind Cawelti and bounced as it flew open.

"What's the discrepancy here?" Straight-Ahead said.

Cawelti didn't turn. His eyes and gun were leveled at me. "Murder suspect here is resisting arrest," he said. "I'm going to subdue him with minimal force."

"Streets are yours," Beason said. "Alhambra belongs to Merit Beason. It's not much of a territory, but what there is in these ten floors is mine. Now put the weapon up."

Cawelti shook his head, holstered his revolver after releasing the hammer, and brushed back his hair. Then he turned to Straight-Ahead.

"You're on my list, Beason," he hissed. "My Christmas list, right under Peters."

"I'll take a tie," I said.

"You'll take a ride to the Wilshire Station with me," Cawelti said, rubbing his chest where I had thrown the elbow. Straight-Ahead removed a white handkerchief from his pocket and handed it to me as he walked around the bed. It was ironed and clean. I pressed it to my nose and it wasn't clean anymore, probably never would be. I had a sudden image of Straight-Ahead in a one-room apartment in the run-down building he lived in, standing straight up in a pair of shorts and a white undershirt, ironing handkerchiefs by the bushel. I laughed.

"Crazy bastard," muttered Cawelti.

"Merit will take care of our friend in the morning," Straight-Ahead assured me.

Cawelti stayed behind me on the elevator and through the lobby, where he zigzagged through glittering people drinking glasses of mineral water. I figured out now what was wrong with this gathering. This convention of health fadists included old men and women, people of odd shapes and sizes, and even some kids, but no young men. This was an army of those unsuited for combat, uniformed in white and obsessed with staying healthy. I shivered and heard the blast of disease and remedy words and decided that the crowd from last night, the drunken kids and the tarts in uniform, were probably healthier than this bunch.

I tried not to bleed on them and they tried not to notice me. It was what we both wanted.

Cawelti cuffed me and guided me into the backseat of his Pontiac. We didn't talk much on the way to the Wilshire Station. I asked him how he knew I was in that room in the Alhambra. He said, "A tip." It was the most cordial conversation I had ever had with John. Maybe we were on the way to a friendship. Maybe not.

12

By the time we got to the Wilshire Station I had succeeded in bleeding over most of the backseat of John Cawelti's vehicle. The bleeding had stopped, but he didn't appreciate my redecoration.

"Christ," he shouted, pounding the upholstery when he opened the door. "Look at that."

I looked at the blood. If my hands weren't handcuffed I might have pointed out to him that his punch was at least partly responsible.

"Get out," he said, and helped me through the door. With my hands cuffed behind me, I did a rather neat dance to keep from falling on my face. He had parked in a space right in front of the station. He prodded me up the stairs and through the door. The sergeant on duty at the desk—McConnell—was a little knot with glasses.

"One of these days, Peters?" he said, turning from the two women who were chattering away at him in Martian.

"One of these days, Frank," I agreed.

Cawelti took the cuffs off and prodded me to the washroom near the stairway leading up to the squad room and my brother's office. It was a washroom that would have made a slum gas station's look like home. Even the soap was too dirty for a civilized human being to touch and the towels were stiff and almost black.

"Hurry up," Cawelti grunted. "Wash."

Cawelti didn't want Phil to see me bloody. We both knew it. Phil had no objection to my being bloody. He just wanted to be sure he was the one who did it. It was a commission he had taken on when we were kids and he objected to others cutting into the shelf life of his merchandise. Our old man was a grocer. Sometimes I can't help thinking in grocery images.

There was an ancient bum in the grime-speckled mirror. I looked at him with sympathy, washed his face with the crusty soap, dried it with my jacket lining, and smiled at him. He looked like shit.

"Let's go," said Cawelti, and we went.

We had to wait for about ten minutes outside Phil's office. I was getting hungry again. The night was dark and I was tired. Cawelti checked his jacket pocket to be sure the envelope with the names and numbers was safely there. It was. He grinned, and for the first time I thought I had found a person who really deserved the care and attention of Dr. Sheldon Minck.

Phil stuck his head out the door, looked at us, and grunted. We got up and went into the office. He sat behind the desk and looked at me. I couldn't read the look. He looked terrible. Not as bad as the bum in the mirror, but bad enough. His tie was open and dangling from the wilted collar of a white shirt. His short white hair was sweat-dampened and flat and he needed a shave. If he had let his beard grow, Phil would have made a hell of a Santa Claus. On the desk in front of him was half a sandwich and a cardboard cup filled with what was probably coffee. I couldn't tell what was in the sandwich besides wilted lettuce. The only light in the room came from the desk lamp, which bounced a deadly white on his face.

"Give," he croaked, reaching out his ham hand.

Cawelti stepped forward and handed him the envelope. "If you—" he started.

"Shut up," Phil said, reaching into his pocket for his glasses.

Cawelti shut up and looked at me. I shrugged in mock sympathy. Phil read. He took a bite of his sandwich and some tepid coffee and read some more. Then he put the papers down, open to the sheet with John Wayne's name. He took off his glasses, pocketed them, and pointed to the drawing of the pistol and the bullet.

"What is this?" he asked, rubbing the bridge of his nose.

"Evidence," said Cawelti.

"Of what?" Phil said, running his right hand over his bristly hair.

"Some kind of scheme," Cawelti said, looking at me for help.

"You know what time it is?" Phil said. He looked first at Cawelti and then at me. I shrugged and pointed to my watch. Phil recognized our father's watch and shook his head. "It's almost two in the morning," he answered himself. "I haven't seen my wife and kids in three days. We've got a killer out there in Watts with a machete, a gang of fifty, sixty kids stealing cars in Culver, an impotent rapist in Echo Park, assorted goddamn lunatics, half-assed gangsters, and a whole set of new war crimes, counterfeit sugar and gas stamps, stealing armed services uniforms, and pretty soon we're going to have rubber thieves, paper thieves—"

"Musical instrument thieves," I added.

Phil's fist came down on the desk, sending stale toast, wilted lettuce, and something that looked like cheese dancing into the air.

"Cawelti, out," he said.

"Hey," Cawelti said, stepping forward.

Phil looked up calmly, the worst of all possible Phil Pevsner looks. "You want to argue with me, Sergeant?" he asked, folding his hands.

Cawelti straightened his tie and shook his head no. Phil said nothing and I looked at a blank spot on the wall as innocently as I could. Cawelti went to the door.

"Slam it and I lose my temper," Phil said.

Cawelti left without slamming the door. It was my turn.

"Where's Steve Seidman?" I asked socially.

"Vacation," Phil said. "Where's your goddamn brain? Is that on vacation too? Sit down."

I sat in the chair opposite him. If my office was too small for business, his was too large. His desk and single lamp were an island in a dark room the size of Shelly's entire office. Maybe Phil didn't plan on staying a captain long. Maybe he didn't think he could survive as a schedule maker and problem solver. His hairy hands longed for the throat of a back-talking holdup man. He looked at me for a few seconds and then reassembled his sandwich as best he could.

"You hungry?" he asked.

"I'm hungry," I admitted. He fished in one of his desk draws and threw me a box of Wilbur Buds. He watched me eat them, finished his coffee, and threw the empty cup at the battered brown metal waste basket at the side of the desk. He missed.

"Talk," he said. "Whole thing, start to finish. No jokes. Include Vance, Longretti, John Wayne, and this who's who list.

I talked. I could have used a drink of something to get the chocolate out of my teeth but I knew I was going to get nothing until I finished.

I finished and Phil looked through the list again.

"This is no evidence of anything," he said. "It's a damned list. Anyone can write lists. Any of these people willing to make a complaint against the Larchmonts?"

"I don't—"

"Hell no," he said. "The hills around here are filled with

con men and grifters. Biggest damn industry since the gold rush. They came out here to mine the rich."

"Phil, I didn't shoot anybody," I said.

"Who gives a shit, Toby," he said. "I mean who really cares. Vance had a record with more sales than Bing Crosby. Longretti was vermin. Arrests for junk like picking his nose in public. I don't care who swept them away. It's the goddamn book work that keeps me here. Reports, reports. You think Wayne is in real trouble?"

"Someone shot at him," I reminded Phil.

He picked up his phone, dialed, and screamed at someone, giving them Alex Tuster's name. "And fast," he added before hanging up. Then back to me, "I'm thinking of quitting when the war ends. I've got my twenty in. Short pension. I can get a job doing security in San Diego or back East."

"Sounds like a good idea," I said.

"I won't do it," he said, picking up his reconstructed sandwich.

"I know," I said.

"I'll pick up the Larchmonts," he said, looking at the sandwich with distaste but continuing to eat it. "I'll pick up those two goons who work for them, too. I'll have a nice talk with them, very friendly, maybe persuade them to share a confidence or two with me."

The prospect of getting Lyle and Sutker alone in a room did a great deal to brighten Phil's night. He looked dreamily at the last bite of his sandwich and then downed it.

"Can I leave, Phil?" I asked.

He returned from his reverie and remembered I was there.

"No," he said. "You can spend the damned night in the lockup. You can stay off the streets so if another body turns up no one can drop it in your lap."

"What's the charge?"

Phil burped and let his belt out another notch.

"Suspicion of murder, obstructing justice, fleeing the scene of a crime, resisting arrest . . ."

"I didn't resist arrest," I said.

"If you don't shut up, you will be," Phil explained.

Then the phone rang. Phil picked it up and kept his eyes on me as he talked and listened.

"Okay . . . Spell it . . . Take the rubber ball out of your mouth and speak clearly . . . Then what . . . You sure? No. I said no."

He hung up and looked at me.

"Your killer Alex Tuster is on his way home to Meridian, Mississippi. He is a salesman. He has no record. He is thirty-seven, has flat feet and a punctured eardrum. Four-F."

"You got the right guy," I said.

"He was at the Alhambra," Phil said. "Business trip. Sales. The right guy."

"He did it," I insisted.

"Little salesman down in Mississippi suddenly goes nuts, gets a bug up his ass about John Wayne, teams up with Teddy, shoots Straight-Ahead Beason, cleans out the Alhambra safe, blasts Teddy, and—"

"Revenge," I said. "We're missing a link."

"You're missing a link, Toby." He picked up the phone and called for someone to come for me.

About five seconds later, a uniformed guy about a thousand years old came in. The retread said, "Yes, sir," to Phil, and Phil told him to take me to lockup for the night.

"You got it, Captain," the old guy said, motioning for me to rise.

"Phil," I tried.

"Out," said Phil, returning to the list of names from the Alhambra safe.

We got out.

"You're lucky," the retread cop said, keeping a few feet behind me. "He was in a good mood."

"I know," I agreed, leading the way down the corridor, looking forward to a few hours of sleep.

"Don't think of trying anything," he said behind me. "I'll blow your head off."

"I'm in on a drunk driving," I said.

"Makes no never mind to me," he said. "You try something and I turn you into shashlik. I got nothing to lose. My pension's safe and I'm collecting. I didn't ask to come back. It's the damn war. We all have to do our part."

I was hoping to be alone in the lockup but I was hoping in vain. There were two bunks in the cell. The old cop let me in, locked the door, and shuffled off. I went to the empty bunk and sat on it. The guy on the other bunk was overweight and maybe thirty. It was dark in the cell but I could see his wide eyes. He was sitting and holding on to the blanket with tightly clenched hands.

"I didn't do it," he said.

"I did," I said. "And I need some sleep."

"Listen to me," the fat guy cried. "They won't listen."

"I need some sleep," I said with a yawn, and lay back on the bunk.

"They say I smashed my father's face while he was sleeping," the fat guy said. "Said I hit him with a wrench. Said I did it to my brother Byron, too."

"While he was sleeping?" I asked.

"Yes," he said, his wild eyes opening even wider.

"I think I'd like to hear your side of it," I said, sitting up to face him.

"God, thanks," the fat guy said, wiping away a line of grit from his neck. "It all started when I was about seven. No, I better go back to when I was four. Yes, four is the place to start . . ."

When the first light of dawn came through the window, my roomie was up to his fourteenth birthday. In the process of getting up to the point where he didn't use his father and brother for batting practice, he had thrown in offhand confessions to a few dozen atrocities on which the statute of limitations had probably run out, but he was just warming to his subject. I stayed awake by encouraging him, trying to listen and imagining myself looking like a lump of ground beef.

My nose was mildly sore. I needed a shave and I had to make a decision about whether or not to go to Meridian, Mississippi. I decided that Alex had not taken off for the South. Somewhere in his past he had met John Wayne, and he was prepared to do him ill before he took off with the money from the Larchmonts' safe and the files that were probably worth their weight in real rubber.

A tired-looking guy in uniform whom I knew by name—Warnek—brought us coffee and a jelly roll for breakfast.

"Long night," I said.

"I just came on duty," said Warnek.

The fat guy finished his doughnut in one gulp and eyed mine with murderous longing. Sugar sprinkled his face and I didn't feel like finishing. I handed him what was left of my doughnut and watched him gulp it.

He started talking the second it was gone, but I was rescued by Warnek, who let me out.

"You'll help me?" the fat guy said, still sitting on the bunk.

"As much as I can," I said with an encouraging yawn.

I left without ever knowing his name or wanting to. I could only handle one case at a time.

Warnek gave me the things—wallet, keys, belt—that had been taken from me the night before by the old guy. I thanked him and made my way through the stale morning darkness of the station. Somebody hacked the cough of the tubercular or the working cop. I didn't look around. Outside I found a restaurant, a small place where cops went. I'd been there before. I finished off a few bowls of Wheaties with cream and the one spoon of sugar I was allotted by the waitress, put down two cups of coffee to wake me up, and was hit by an idea. I didn't like the idea, but it wouldn't go away. Everything didn't fit but it told me where the killer was and why a gun was being aimed at John Wayne. It made some sense. I didn't like it, but it made sense.

I paid my bill, caught a cab to Arnie's, retrieved my Crosley, and listened to Arnie apologize for letting Vance's frigid body fall into the hands of the cops.

I didn't care. I had things to do, a head to clear, a life to save.

It took me ten minutes to get back to Heliotrope. Five more minutes to get past Mrs. Plaut after again promising her all of my Saturday morning. Gunther was in and agreed to talk to me while I ran a hot bath and shaved. I went over things with him again and told him my theory as I sat waiting for the trickling water to get up to a respectable level. I lay back with a towel over my sore nose.

"It responds to many problems and answers many questions," he said. "But, if it is indeed true, why are we sitting here? Why are we not in motion?"

"You've got a point, Gunther," I said wearily. "But I've been punched and chased and forced to sit up all night listening to true horror confessions from Fatty Arbuckle's ghost. My body is bruised and the hair on my chest is, as you may have noticed, mostly gray. But what the hell."

I forced myself up, touched my clean-shaven face, got out of the tub, pulled the plug, dried myself, and put on my underwear. With Gunther right behind I went to my room, leapt over a basket of photographs, and got dressed. It was time to catch a killer.

13

The Crosley had one good point: it didn't eat much gas. With gas rationed, that made a difference. The major bad point was that the Crosley wasn't built for the hills of Hollywood. It panted, grunted, strained, and pleaded as I forced it up and around the streets of Coldwater Canyon looking for the place where John Wayne was setting up locations for his new movie. I knew one possible place, near the old reservoir, but no one was there except two teenage kids doing some illegal hunting.

Gunther sat quietly, hands folded in his lap, neck straining to see out the window.

"It is almost ten," he said finally, looking at his well-polished pocket watch. I didn't bother to look at my watch.

For the first forty minutes I had been going on energy fueled by insight, but now the lack of sleep was getting to me. I could have used one of the unnamed pills Shelly kept in his bottle-ladened desk drawer. He had pills for sleeping, staying awake, causing insanity, clearing up an itchy scalp. The problem was that he threw all the pharmaceutical company samples into the same drawer and usually lost the information on each one. It wasn't unusual for Shelly to give a little orange pill to a suffering patient resulting not in the loss of pain but in distraction from pain by the temporary onslaught of double vision. Still, I would have tried for a pill if one were available.

"Shall I drive a while?" Gunther asked, looking at my drooping eyes.

Even with the cut-down size of the Crosley, there was no way short of a big pillow and blocks on the pedals that Gunther could have safely driven the car. I could imagine some guy watering his lawn and looking up to see this little yellow driverless car coming down the street.

"No thanks, Gunther," I said, yawning. "It keeps me awake. If I stop driving I'll fall asleep and we've got a life to save."

"As you think best," Gunther said with dignity, adjusting his little vest. "It is possible, of course, that your killer will not actually attempt to shoot Mr. Wayne. It may be sufficient to simply make another attempt which—"

I had turned a corner down a dirt road that seemed familiar to me from some past life or dream. My reflexes were dead. I took the corner on two wheels and Gunther was thrown against the door.

Pretending that things were in control, I said, as I straightened the swerving car and managed to avoid a lone telephone pole, "We can't take a chance on that, Gunther."

"I would truly enjoy to drive," Gunther repeated once again, putting himself in order.

What the hell? I pulled over, got out, and let Gunther slide behind the wheel. I got in the other side and closed the door.

"Just keep looking," I said, seeing that Gunther's eye level wasn't too bad. He might be able to make something out through the steering wheel and maybe he could see over the dashboard. I opened the window to let the breeze hit my face, unzipped my windbreaker, and started to look for some telltale sign of a movie company as Gunther pulled into the road. Within two minutes I was asleep.

Koko the Clown jumped out of the inkwell, winked at me, touched my sore nose, and danced through the corridors of the Alhambra. I went after him, but someone had tied Charlie Chaplin's telescope to my leg. I dragged after Koko, who seemed to have something important he wanted me to see. I lost him down a long corridor and then he popped his head out of a door. I took a step toward the door and Koko popped out of another door. I took another step and Charlie Chaplin in his tramp suit kicked me in the can. I turned around just in time to see him leap up, click his heels, twirl his cane, return to the ground, and disappear around a corner. Koko whistled at me and I turned to follow him again. Mack Swain and Ward Bond both stepped into the hall and blocked my way. By now I was desperate to find Koko. He had something important to tell me. Bond and Swain picked me up by the shoulders; the telescope tied to my leg clanked and clanged as they pulled me into a room where the bodies of Lewis Vance and Teddy Spaghetti were seated watching the Larchmonts and Straight-Ahead planting a Victory Garden.

"Have to use every inch possible," Straight-Ahead said. He was holding an extra-long-handled rake because he couldn't bend. The Larchmonts were on their hands and knees plunking seeds into little holes in the dirt they were making with their fingers.

"Seeds of doubt," said Sydney Larchmont, who wore farmer overalls and a straw hat.

Adrienne Larchmont, similarly clad, said, "Tell me about Alex."

"I was about to," replied Sydney. "Give me some credit, Adrienne."

"Let's plant these two," said Straight-Ahead, pointing at Vance and Teddy, who were playing gin rummy on the bed. I turned to Bond and Mack Swain but they were now Lyle and Sutker dressed as pineapples.

"We're gonna plant you too," said Adrienne, pointing a soiled finger at me. "Call Alex."

"Alex," called Sydney. "I was about to do that without prompting, Adrienne. Alex."

A door behind the garden started to open and everyone looked toward it: the two corpses, the two Larchmonts, the two pineapples, Straight-Ahead, and me, but before the door opened all the way, something scuttled behind us and Koko and Charlie Chaplin grabbed me and pulled me into the corridor, where John Wayne was standing. He was wearing a Marine sergeant's uniform with a cowboy hat.

"I'll just take a look-see in there and hold them off while you get away," he said.

"But Alex," I said. "I have to see Alex."

"Never you mind," said the Duke evenly, pulling out a .45 automatic and a Smith and Wesson revolver. "This is just a dream."

"There they are," came a voice at my side. I tried to pull loose from Koko and Chaplin, who were grinning at me.

"Toby, there they are," came the voice again.

Koko let go and dived into a keyhole. Chaplin let go, doffed his little hat, and waddled down the hall as John Wayne hitched up his gun belt and walked into the room to face the Larchmonts, corpses, and assorted fruit.

I opened my eyes and tried to say something.

"Down there," said Gunther.

He was standing and pointing. I followed his finger and found myself looking down a hill at a group of men and a woman.

"Time," I grunted, dry-mouthed.

"Almost eleven," Gunther said. "You have been sleeping an hour. I did not wish to wake you until and unless we achieved some success."

"Straight-Ahead," I said, sitting up and blowing out some air. "He should be around someplace. He's supposed to be keeping an eye on—"

A shot echoed through the small valley. It could have been a hunter. The group of people in the little valley looked up.

Then another shot. A puff of dirt exploded about ten feet from the little group and they ran for cover.

"Uncanny timing," Gunther said.

"No," I groaned as I opened the door. "Our friend Alex was waiting for us to arrive before he played out the scene. Where the hell is Straight-Ahead?"

I had groaned because my back was sore. I took my newly purchased pawn shop beauty and scanned the ridge. Something glinted. Straight-Ahead appeared through the brush and pointed with his pistol at a spot about thirty yards to his left. Something glinted there, too. I nodded. Straight-Ahead motioned that he was going to circle behind the spot and I nodded in agreement.

Straight-Ahead looked good standing there, like a monument, but I didn't think he could get to that spot in less than three or four minutes. He strode into the trees. The next shot came toward me and pinged the right headlight out of my Crosley. It exploded.

"Gunther," I yelled.

"I am safely ensconced behind the automobile," he shouted.

I aimed my pistol at the spot on the hillside where Straight-Ahead was making his way. I held the pistol in two hands and balanced it in the crook of a small tree. I hit a tree about ten yards from where I was aiming, which was one of my better shots at that distance. I considered another shot but realized I might accidentally have killed Straight-Ahead.

"Stay here, Gunther," I said. "I'm going down."

And down I went, through bushes and brushes, dirt and small scurrying animals, probably scattering a rattler or two.

I took the last ten yards at a roll and landed covered with dirt and dust at the foot of John Wayne.

"Peters," he said, hands on hips. "What the hell is going on?"

My breath wouldn't come. Still seated and looking up at the frightened and puzzled faces, I pointed with my gun at the spot where Straight-Ahead was headed. Then a few words came.

"Up there . . . Trying to . . . Same guy."

Wayne looked up at the hill just as a shot came down. It fell short. The woman, dark-haired and overly made up, screamed and said something in Spanish.

"This is some stupid joke by one of your drinking friends," said a bald guy about sixty.

"Rein it in, Herb," the Duke said. "This is no joke."

I sat up, took careful aim, and shot at the spot from which the shot had come. I was about five yards off this time, even though I was much closer than I had been when I'd fired from the ridge. I consoled myself with the fact that I was aiming low to keep from accidentally hitting Straight-Ahead, but I was hoping for five feet, not five yards.

"Give me that thing," said the Duke with exasperation. Still trying for a good breath and unable to make sense, I let him take the pistol and watched him hold it up with one hand and aim for the hill.

"Straight-Ahead," I gasped.

"That's the way I always shoot," he said, and fired.

The shot tore leaves right at the spot where the glint had been. Wayne fired again and tore more leaves only a foot away from where his first shot had entered. He tried for a third shot but the pistol jammed.

"Peters," he said in further exasperation, "where the hell did you get this thing, in a dime store?"

"Pawn shop," I said, getting up.

"Why don't you—" he began, but shots rang out on the ridge. Everyone ducked for cover but no bullets hit nearby. The shots were coming from the ridge and into the ridge. There were four shots and Straight-Ahead popped up through the brush shouting.

"Up the hill," he said. "Merit Beason's going after him."

I waved and Straight-Ahead disappeared.

"Who the hell is shooting at me, mister?" Wayne said. He was wearing a dark windbreaker like mine, except that his was clean. "I'm getting a little tired of this."

I stood and tried to dust myself off. I also took the pistol back from Wayne and plunked it in my shoulder holster.

"I'll get back to you later," I said, gulping for air.

"Toby," came a small voice from above.

I looked up and waved at Gunther.

"He's getting away," Gunther called.

"No," I tried to shout. "I know where to find him."

I got some quick introductions as I caught my breath. The dark woman was a friend of Wayne's, Chata Bauer. One of the men was Herbert Yates from Republic Pictures. I don't remember the others and they didn't look as if they were interested in polite conversation. They all looked scared.

One of the people in the group, a vaguely Indian looking guy Wayne called Yak, led the way to a path up the hill. I had trouble navigating but I didn't want to show it. I was dirty, tired, and thirsty. My back ached and I had some bruises and a mouthful of dirt. All I needed was someone to feel sorry for me and help me up a hill.

I made it and Gunther greeted me.

"Toby," he said, taking my arm. "Are you intact?"

"I'm intact," I said. "This is my friend Gunther Wherthman," I told the assemblage.

They stepped forward and leaned down to shake his hand.

"Mr. Wayne," he said. "We met yesterday during the unfortunate and somewhat similar incident at Santa Monica."

"Couldn't forget you, Mr. Wherthman," John Wayne said with a smile.

Wayne had more questions, but I had no answers, none I was ready to give. I wanted a drink, some cleaning up, and a meeting with a killer. I made excuses and got in the Crosley

with as much dignity as I could, which wasn't much. A burr had latched onto my pants. I sat on it. Charlie Chaplin should have been around taking notes. I didn't yell but I did pop up and put a hand under me to find the offender and rip it out while Wayne and his crew watched my performance.

"Just got an idea," I said lamely.

As I pulled away, I heard a male voice say, "And you trust him?"

"Old boyhood friend," came John Wayne's voice. "He'll do the job."

"Well?" asked Gunther, looking at me with concern.

"Not very," I answered.

Half an hour later I pulled up in front of the Farraday and parked in a loading zone, leaving Gunther in the car to wait. He'd drive around the block and probably survive if a cop tried to ticket. I limped into the building and into the lobby. Now I was faced with saving time or pain. I opted to save the pain. I got in the elevator, pressed the button for the fourth floor, and leaned back as it lurched into action.

"Toby?" came Jeremy's voice, echoing through the dark corners.

"Jeremy," I answered.

He appeared on the stairway next to the elevator and began to walk up, easily keeping pace with me. In fact he had to slow down.

"More pain?" he asked sympathetically.

"More pain," I admitted. "But I'm almost through this one. Don't worry. I'll make the wedding tomorrow. Wouldn't miss it. Just have to pick up a killer and tie a few strings. Won't take long."

"Alice is doing the cooking and baking," he said. "We have two small cakes, one in the shape of a book and another in the shape of a printing press."

"Cute," I said, as he inched past the second floor.

"Maybe a bit too—" he began.

"Not a bit," I said, as he trudged along with me up past three. "Love."

"Yes," he sighed, probably imagining Alice, all two hundred plus pounds of her, a gentle coming together of titans.

When we hit the fourth floor, Jeremy was standing there waiting and helped me pull open the steel-grate doors.

He wanted to help me to the office, but having been through hundreds of public battles in wrestling rings he valued the need for dignity.

"I've got to go make further preparations," he said. "If you need me I'll be in my place."

"Thanks, Jeremy," I said, and waved as he went down the stairs, his footsteps echoing. I stood for a few seconds holding the rail, took a deep breath of Lysol air, felt better, and went down the corridor into the offices of Minck and Peters, dentist and detective, an enemy of decay and an enemy of disorder. Shelly was sitting in his chair, cigar in mouth, looking at the newspaper. He wiped his hands on his white smock and looked at me through his thick lenses.

"Toby, you look terrible," he said, and returned to his paper.

"Thanks, Shel," I said.

"Paul Whiteman's coming to the Shrine Auditorium next week," he said. "Bing Crosby, Harry James, The Kings Men, and Dinah Shore are going to be with him."

"Sounds terrific," I said, shuffling over to turn on the water tap and push some dirty dishes out of the way so I could put my mouth under the trickle.

"That all you can say?" he said. "I'm taking Mildred. You curious about why?"

I washed my face and hands and looked at myself in the mirror above the sink. Then I washed my face again, which helped a little.

"Why?" I finally said, seeing Shelly waiting in the mirror.

He beamed. "Take a look. A celebration." He jumped from the chair and held out the newspaper. I dried my hands on his jacket, which he didn't seem to mind, and took the paper. It was page thirty-four of the *Times*.

"Admiral Nimitz," I said. "He looks great."

"Not Nimitz," Shelly groaned, adjusting his slipping glasses. He needed a bath or fumigation. I stepped back, paper in hand.

"The ad," he prompted.

My bleary eyes found the ad. There was someone vaguely resembling Shelly in it. No glasses, no cigar, a shirt and bow tie. He was earnestly looking up at me and below him were the words: "Translucent teeth—A form for every face, a size for every case, a shade for every complexion." It went on the same way with one-line quotes from satisfied customers. The third quote down was from me. "Dr. Minck's translucent teeth have changed my life," the quote ran. "I've learned to smile again without embarrassment." I was identified as Tobias Leo Pevsner, Criminal Investigator.

"I don't have false teeth, Shel," I said. "I don't have a dental plate."

He shook his head and took the newspaper back.

"Quibble. O. J. Quibble. Are we friends or are we friends?" he asked.

"I don't know what we are, Shel, but what few acquaintances I have who read the newspaper now think I have a mouthful of fake teeth. What's worse, they'll think I was stupid enough to let you put them there."

Shelly sulked back to his dental chair. "Vanity," he sighed. "It's a vain world we live in, Toby. That's why this is going to work. That's why Mildred and I are celebrating. She agreed to invest in the ad."

"In exchange for. . . ?" I asked, feeling a little better with a few more feet between me and the dental destroyer.

"The show, a few promises, things," he said vaguely.

"Like what things?" I asked.

"Things," he said, retreating behind his newspaper. "Keeping the place clean, sterilizing the equipment, taking Mildred on vacation, getting you to move out or pay more rent."

"Little things," I said. "There's an open office on two. Jeremy said I could have it for the same thing I'm paying you for the closet."

Shelly lowered the newspaper and glared at me with an open mouth. "That's what we get for loyalty," he said. "Betrayal. Now I know how Chamberlain felt at Munich."

"This isn't global, Shel, and I didn't threaten to raise your rent or kick you out," I said. "Look, we can talk this around later. I've got a killer waiting for me. Did I get any messages?"

"On your desk," he said, pouting. "Who's going to take messages for you in the other office? That's a service I don't charge for."

"I take messages for you, too. It works both ways, Shel."

"I'll work things out with Mildred," he said.

"Fine." I thought of asking for one of the wake-up pills in the drawer but I was feeling better and a forkful of Shelly's coffee would probably be enough. I poured a cup and went into my office.

Before I could close the door, Shelly called, "Just you wait. In a few hours they'll be waiting in the hall for my translucent teeth."

I closed the door and went behind my desk and looked at my messages. One was from Alex, reminding me that he was going to get John Wayne today. It had apparently failed to penetrate Shelly's consciousness as a potentially important piece of information. A second message marked IMPORTANT was from Mrs. Plaut. *About the photographs,* Shelly had scrawled. A third message was from Sydney Larchmont. There was a number and a message: *Let's work this out.*

Shelly was still sulking in the chair when I left a minute or two later. Toothless millions had not lined the halls. Someone coughed from the bowels of the Farraday and an echo answered, "Fraud."

I made it down the stairs without falling and tiptoed past the first floor, where Madame Carpentier had her sanctum. I didn't want her to come out, point a finger at me, complain about her lumbago, and tell me that lightning was about to hit me. She took the fun out of life and scared me. I had enough to scare me without the Farraday seer. I also remembered that she had prophesied three bodies, one more than already existed in the case.

"A policeman did inquire," said Gunther as I got in the car. "He wanted to know why you had only one headlamp and how long I would remain in the zone."

"And you told him?" I asked, pulling onto Hoover.

"I told him that you had been the victim of a child throwing a rock and that we would be leaving as soon as you came down with a shipment of batteries."

"Simple," I said.

"Simple is usually more effective than imaginative," he replied. "That is a concept articulated frequently in the works of Stendahl."

"And Henry Armstrong," I added.

We listened to the radio and discovered that San Gabriel wine was now seventy-three cents a quart, Hinds Honey and Almond Cream was forty-nine cents, and Rip Sewell of the Pittsburgh Pirates had shut out the Boston Braves 3–0.

"Want to stop for lunch?" I asked Gunther.

He looked at me and then checked his watch. It wasn't much past noon.

"You are procrastinating, Toby. The solemn task can be postponed, delayed, but it must be faced," he said like a little father.

Finally, he agreed that lunch couldn't hurt, so we stopped at Simon's Drive-In at Wilshire and Fairfax. It was lunch-time crowded but we found two bar stools at the counter. I had a barbecue sandwich and a pair of Pepsis. Gunther had a tuna club sandwich and iced tea. We both ate slowly and had little to say.

People around us talked about the war, the food, and bus-load of guys dressed as Indians who had taken up most of the seats in Simon's. The Indians were complete with feathered bonnets and war paint.

"You guys in a movie or what?" a pug with a flannel shirt asked between bites of a hot dog.

"Yeah," answered one of the Indians, capturing a ketchup and attacking his burger. "We're the first wave of an invading army of Comanches. We're in cahoots with the Japs."

The other painted Indians laughed. The pug turned to me and Gunther for support, saying, "There's a war on and we get smart-asses. My brother and oldest son are somewhere in the Pacific or France and who the hell knows where or if they're alive and I got to listen to jokes. I think we should teach these cigar store Indians a lesson."

"They're not real Indians," I said, washing down some bar-becue. "Besides, we're outnumbered. Like the Little Big Horn. Ambushed at Simon's."

"I don't care how many of them there are," said the pug, inches from my face. "I say we teach them a lesson."

"That's what George Armstrong Custer said," I told him, picking up Gunther's and my check.

The pug looked at Gunther.

"What's he?" he asked.

"Short," I said so Gunther couldn't hear.

I had a whole series of suggestions and things Gunther and I could do instead of our duty. We could go watch a ship launching at San Pedro or take a ricksha ride around China City for a quarter.

"Toby," Gunther said, without looking at me.

"Okay." I gave in. I made a phone call. Then we got in the car and drove where we had to go.

There was a parking space on the street. There were plenty of parking spaces.

"How do I look?" I asked, getting out of the car.

"How do you feel?" he countered.

"Tired, bruised," I said, zipping up my jacket. "But the teeth are still mine. Stay here and watch the car."

Gunther looked properly puzzled as he sat there ready to protect my Crosley, and I crossed the sidewalk and entered the small dark hall. I found the right name. There was no bell. I tried the inner door. It was open. The stairway was dark and somewhere a baby screamed and a woman answered the cry in hysterical Spanish.

I found the right room and stood waiting with the smell of cooking tortillas around me. I wasn't hungry. I knocked again and a voice called, "Who is it?"

"Toby," I answered.

"Be right there."

It took another five or six seconds for the door to open.

"Alex," I said.

"Yes," he admitted, and stepped back to let me in.

14

The room was small, neat. In one corner was a bookcase. A bed with an old-fashioned quilt covering it stood in the other corner near the window. There was a table with a white salt and black pepper shaker, an ancient sofa, and a matching chair. Another small table held a hot plate. Near the bed was a dresser. It reminded me of my own room at Mrs. Plaut's on Heliotrope.

When he turned to face me, Straight-Ahead Beason held a pistol in his hand. The pistol was aimed at my stomach. I walked carefully past him and looked out the open window. It looked down on 14th Street. I couldn't see my car.

"Merit Beason figured you'd work it out," he said, "but it was worth a try. You want a seat, Toby? A cup of coffee?"

"Coffee would be fine, Merit," I said. He was fully suited. I imagined him spending long nights in the chair, listening to the radio, reading, hearing the night sounds of the street, ironing handkerchiefs, getting older alone.

The coffee was on the hot plate. He poured me a cup. I drank with Straight-Ahead seated across from me at the wooden table, pistol aimed at my chest.

"Good," I said.

"Chase and Sanborn," he said.

"Want to tell me the tale?" I asked. "You got a little sugar?"

"Sure," he said. "Sorry."

He got up, moved to a small cupboard covered by a piece of flowered cloth, and came out with a sugar bowl. He handed me a spoon and I shoveled in two spoonfuls.

"I could give it a shot," I said, "but I've got holes to fill."

Straight-Ahead sat again.

"Merit Beason will have to shoot you, Toby," he said.

"We'll talk that through later," I said. "Tell me a story."

"Look around you," he said. I took a sip and looked around.

"Merit Beason is not in the chips," he said.

"Neither is Toby Peters," I said.

"Merit Beason is getting old," he went on.

"So is Toby Peters," I said.

"You're kibitzing," said Straight-Ahead.

"Sorry."

"It went down on Sunday the way it looked," he said. "Teddy had put away Vance with your gun. Then you and Wayne took off and Teddy tried to talk his way out, talked about big dollars in the safe. Papers that were worth even bigger dollars to the Larchmonts. It's difficult to be loyal to the Larchmonts."

"I've met them," I said by way of agreement.

"I've saved nothing. Lost my police pension by early retirement for injury. Didn't lose all of it but wasn't left with enough to live on. The Alhambra doesn't pay the big dollar either. So, Merit Beason was tempted. Teddy led the way to the safe, opened it, and proved he was right. Ten thousand, the papers. We were looking it over when Merit Beason made a mistake. Teddy grabbed your gun from my pocket and took a shot at the house dick. Old Merit got it back, held on to the papers and money and busted him, told him to hide out in the basement room with the papers, that we'd get him off the murder charge and share the wealth."

"Merit—" I began.

"A moment of madness," he interrupted. "Might even happen to you some day. Cash and hope in your hand. Dry years ahead and fading memories behind. More coffee?"

"No thanks," I said.

"Cookies? Mexican bakery down at the corner is good, clean."

We went through the ritual of his bringing out the Mexican pastry. They were large cylinders covered in powdered sugar and filled with fruit, damn good.

"Told you they were good," he said, pointing at the last one with his gun. "Have another."

I did and he went on.

"Next thing, Merit Beason was in the hospital. Larchmonts' boys must have found Vance's body in the hotel. Found the papers and money gone. They got a tip to be on the lookout for you."

"A tip?"

"From Alex," he said. "Merit Beason respects you, Toby. Merit Beason invented Alex when you came to the hospital. Alex began to take on a life of his own."

"Frankenstein monster," I suggested.

"Whatever," he agreed. "Idea was to keep you busy looking for Alex, who had a grudge against John Wayne. Then Teddy began to get a little feisty, a little frightened. Not a man to be trusted."

"No," I agreed, finishing off the last pastry and wiping the powdered sugar from my mouth.

"Had to shoot him," Straight-Ahead said. "Tit for tat. He had shot Merit Beason."

"But Merit Beason shot straighter."

"No argument," he said. "Down at the dock, Alex took those shots at Wayne. Not trying to kill. You figured that."

"I began to get the idea, but nothing for sure," I said.

A traffic jam on 14th set horns blaring. Straight-Ahead got

up, closed the window to cut down on the interference, and returned to the table.

"Then this morning Alex took the shots at Wayne when you drove up. All show."

"Creating Alex," I helped.

"Creating Alex," he agreed. "Fortunately, Teddy had checked someone named Alex into the Alhambra the day before Vance checked out.

"Merit Beason was playing for time. Couldn't just run. Merit Beason is too much a figure to hide, too easy to spot. Had to hope Alex could make it through a few days, then Merit could quit the Alhambra in anger over the way the Larchmonts were playing."

"Not bad for ad-libbing," I said.

"Not good enough," he said.

"Where are the papers and the cash?"

"Box under the bed," he said. "No need to be too fancy. Not too many places to hide things here anyway. Any other questions?"

"Give me some time and I'll think of one or two," I tried. "You fire that gun and —"

"No," he said. "In this neighborhood, shots are as regular as flushing the toilet."

"How about another cup to wash down the cookies?"

"Last one," Straight-Ahead said. He got up and had to turn to reach the pot. I pulled out my jammed pistol. Straight-Ahead had class. He turned, coffee pot in one hand, pistol in the other, saw my gun, and reached over to pour.

"More sugar?"

"I'll take it black," I said. "What now?"

Straight-Ahead didn't sit.

"You didn't shoot. You let Merit Beason turn with a gun in his hand, maybe shoot you. Makes a gumshoe wonder why he isn't lying dead."

"I'd rather take you in," I said.

"No. You're not a fool. No bullets? Gun jammed? Doesn't matter. Even if you've got a working piece there, Merit Beason hasn't much choice. Been shot once already this week. Might survive another. Cole Younger took more than twenty and died an old man. Can you see this ancient cop doing time? How about the chair?"

"You'd go with dignity, Merit," I said. "Better than a bullet."

"Don't see how it would be better," he said. "Let's play it out, Toby."

He lifted the gun at my chest and I considered throwing my pistol at him. But I knew it was useless. He was an old police horse. I might hurt him but I wouldn't stop him from shooting.

"Someone's outside," I said. "Waiting for me."

"Chance Merit Beason will have to take."

"Right outside the door," I went on, starting to get up. If he didn't hit me in a crucial place, I might have a chance going for him.

"Call them in, Toby," he said. "You're playing your final chip."

"Come in," I shouted. "He confessed."

The idea was to distract him for a second, half a second, and go to his left over the table. He couldn't turn his head. I might survive.

Instead, the door opened with a kick and Merit in surprise fired a shot toward the sound. Phil fired three quick ones. They all hit Straight-Ahead Beason in the chest. He staggered back, crashed into the closed window, and fell through it, creating an even bigger traffic jam on 14th Street.

Phil, tie undone, jacket unbuttoned, belly out, walked to the window and looked down to be sure Beason was dead before he put his gun away.

"That was Straight-Ahead Beason, wasn't it," he said. "Used to work Culver City?"

"That was him. How much did you hear?"

"Enough," he said, looking around. "Looks like your place."

"Yeah," I admitted. "Gunther called you?"

"Yeah," Phil said, checking the coffee pot to be sure it was hot. People were shouting on the street. Straight-Ahead Beason's body was drawing more attention in the neighborhood than he ever had alive.

"There's a squad car down there. They'll take care of the remains."

"Thanks, Phil," I said, stepping toward him.

He grabbed me by the collar and threw me back against the table. "Thanks? What kind of shit are you shoveling? You call me, get me running here, and push me to kill someone who didn't have to be killed," he said. "I'll sleep all right but I don't like your playing Jesus H. Now we've got a cleanup and paperwork, and Tobias, you are too damn old to be playing cops and robbers."

I got up from the table and shrugged. "We're both playing cops and robbers."

"I'm not playing," he said, stepping toward me again. I backed away. "I'm for real. I'm the man with the badge."

"I concede," I said, and Phil stopped.

"I'm going downstairs. You sit down and stay seated till I get back and don't touch anything or I'll break every damn finger on both your hands. That's a promise."

He stepped out the open door. No one had gathered in the hall. The baby was crying louder than before.

Phil may have heard enough to clear me of a pair of murders but he hadn't heard about the box under the bed. If he had, he wouldn't have left without it. I went for the box, found it, a worn rough wooden gift fruit box, and took it into the hall. I went up the stairs to the top floor, found a ladder to the roof, and went up with the box under my arm. The overhead door opened easily. Kids must have used it a lot. I climbed through and looked around the pebble-covered roof. There was a pigeon coop in one corner. I scurried over and shoved the box under it. There was just enough room. Then I hurried back down the ladder. Someone was coming up from below. I ran down the stairs and got back to Straight-Ahead's a dozen steps before Phil.

"Come on," he said.

I came on. Gunther drove the Crosley to the Wilshire Station and I went back with Phil.

There was nothing to say on the ride. I didn't want to think about Merit Beason. I had liked him. I had a feeling I'd be seeing him in mirrors in a few years. There was a lot to say when we got to the station. Gunther talked. I talked.

"So where's the file from the Alhambra safe? Where's the money?" Phil said. The stenographer, a broom of a woman, paused and waited for an answer.

"Probably hid it somewhere," I said. "Some locker. Someplace in the Alhambra. Who knows? You may never find it."

The stenographer took it all down dutifully. Phil looked at me suspiciously.

"That's it," he said when I was done. "That closes it. I've got slicers, rapists, lunatics out there. This one is closed tight. Get out, Toby, and take the midget with you."

Gunther got off the chair with dignity. He had run into Phil before. Something about Gunther got to Phil. Gunther had learned to take it. You learn to take a lot when you're three feet tall.

I asked for my .38. Phil told me it was evidence in a murder. I'd probably never get it back. We drove to Heliotrope in silence and I parked.

"I'll change for the wedding," Gunther said, stepping out of the car.

"Wedding?"

"Miss Palice and Mr. Butler. This afternoon," he reminded me.

Gunther needed no changing, but I did. I was prepared to strangle Mrs. Plaut if she tried to stop me. She stood on the porch waiting as we walked up. She wore a clean white dress, with lace around the collar and pearls around her neck.

"Mr. Peelers, I left messages for you all about," she said.

"I've been busy catching a killer," I explained. Gunther eased past her and into the house, but she stepped in front of me.

"You are always catching a killer or being caught by one. That is no excuse. We have work to do."

"Tomorrow," I reminded her. "All morning tomorrow."

Gunther came back out, a package in his hand. He handed it to me. I handed it to Mrs. Plaut.

"The wedding is not mine," she said. "I was married to the mister in eighteen and ninety-one."

"Open it, please," I said.

She opened it. "What is this?" she said.

Gunther cleared his throat. She didn't hear. I pointed down at him and she turned. He handed her the written material that went with the hearing aid.

"Amazing new Aurex," she read. "Brings hearing to ninety-five percent of even the most difficult cases. Mr. Peelers and Mr. Wortman, are you suggesting that I am unable to hear?"

"Maybe a little," I said. "You, yourself said—"

"I'm not lying," she said indignantly. "The Plauts, the Wainwrights, every branch of the family has had the hearing of a hawk."

"Sorry," I said, reaching out to take the Aurex back. She

didn't give it to me. "I'll consider this," she said instead. Then she turned and went back into the house.

"Worth a try," I said to Gunther.

"We have done what can be done, as Goethe said," Gunther added. We went inside. Gunther hurried up ahead of me to get ready for the wedding. I went up more slowly, nursing an aching body and a tender nose. When I got to the top of the stairs and took a step toward my room, Mrs. Plaut called up, "Oh, Mr. Peelers. You have some visitors in your room. Your sister and brothers have come for the wedding."

It was too late to run. Besides I wouldn't have made it. Lyle opened the door and aimed a pistol at me. I moved forward and went into my room to find Sydney at my table with Adrienne standing behind him. Sutker, a fresh dressing on his broken nose, was ripping up furniture. My clothes were on the floor, my refrigerator open.

"Papers?" said Sydney, as Lyle closed the door behind us. Lyle and Sutker were wearing bright purple. They looked at me with less than brotherly love.

"Papers?" repeated the greatly irritated Adrienne. "You expect a reasonable response from that? Threaten him, Sydney."

"Adrienne," he said, smoothing his hair. "Of course I was going to threaten him. If you deprive me of style, how am I to earn respect?"

"I've got the files," I said.

They all stopped and looked at me.

"They're not here," Sutker said.

"They're not here," I agreed. "And you're not getting them. I've got a deal for you. You're out of the extortion business and I don't turn those files over to the police."

Lyle prodded me urgently in the right kidney.

"Don't irk me, people," I said. "I have a friend who has

orders to send the file to the police if I get seriously hurt. And I don't respond well to torture. It makes me very angry."

Lyle stepped in front of me and said, "I'd like to make you angry."

"No," Adrienne Larchmont said behind him.

"No," agreed Sydney belatedly.

"Do I keep looking or what?" asked Sutker.

"You can stop looking," said Adrienne Larchmont.

Lyle stepped out of the way and she approached me.

"The money?" she said.

"Goes back to a victim," I said.

"Can we trust this man?" asked Sydney, who got up and joined her. They were looking into my eyes for answers. My eyes didn't have any answers.

"If he betrays us, we simply return and deal with him," she said, her dark eyes fixed on mine. "It was time for us to move on anyway. We've exhausted our welcome in California. It's time for us to move south."

"But Adrienne," Sydney pleaded.

She walked past me and out the door. Sydney followed without looking at me. Lyle and Sutker went next, and then I was standing alone looking at my mess. They had even rearranged Mrs. Plaut's packet of family photographs.

The hell with it. I left things the way they were, closed the refrigerator, and got ready for the wedding.

15

I still had $147 of John Wayne's fee for services but I didn't have time to buy a new suit. The old gray seersucker, a little the worse for wear and the only one I had left, would have to do, along with the brown-and-white shoes from Macy's, which polished up reasonably well in spite of the beating they had taken in Coldwater Canyon.

"We are ready, Mr. Peelers," Mrs. Plaut shouted from below while I was trying to tie my blue-striped tie to hide the spot left by my bloody nose. It worked reasonably well if you didn't notice that the tie was a little short in front and long on the downside.

"Coming right up," I shouted as I came through the door. "Got a phone call to make first."

I looked over the railing at Mrs. Plaut, with her neatly wrapped wedding present, and Gunther, who stood patiently at her side carrying a large gift box, and then I called John Wayne. It took three calls to find him at Republic.

"It's over," I said when he came on. "You were a decoy. There was no Alex. Remember Merit Beason?"

"Fella with you at the hotel and the dock and Coldwater with his neck all messed up?"

"He did it. It's a long story with a couple of bodies," I said. "Beason's dead. Case is closed and you're safe. I'll send you a full report in writing and a refund."

"Keep the difference," Wayne said. "You did a good job."

"I was hoping you'd say that."

"Mr. Peelers," Mrs. Plaut shouted. "I do not wish to miss the canapes."

"Listen," the Duke said languidly. "We're having a preview showing of my new picture, *Shepherd of the Hills,* at the Los Feliz Monday night at nine. If you can make it, I think you might get a kick out of it. Remember my dad?"

"Doc Morrison?"

"The druggist, right. Back in Glendale. I play a frontier druggist named Doc Morrison in the picture. Means something a little special to me. I'd like you to be there."

"Can I bring—"

"Anyone you like," he pitched in with a laugh. "See you."

"Time is money," Mrs. Plaut shouted as I hung up the phone. I didn't see how the homily applied in this case. I dropped another nickel and called Chaplin's house. The slow butler answered and I told him I'd like to come over later to give Mr. Chaplin something. The phone went silent and I waited, listening to Mrs. Plaut begin a story to Gunther about one of her relatives named Trumpeter who dug up Indians.

"Mr. Chaplin says you are welcome to drop by anytime after four and before seven."

"Suits me," I said, and hung up.

We took the Crosley instead of Gunther's Oldsmobile with the built-up gas pedals because the Crosley used less gas. Mrs. Plaut was not wearing the Aurex, but I could see as she sat next to me, clutching the box in her lap, chattering about tardiness, photographs, and the rationing of tea, that she was playing with it in her open purse. Gunther fit neatly into the small rear seat below eye level. Since he said not a word all the way to the Farraday, I had to fight the urge to lean back and be sure he was still there. The wedding gift sat in the front seat by my side.

It was an odd time for a wedding, a Friday afternoon, but

Jeremy and Alice wanted a weekend honeymoon. It made parking a little tough. I couldn't park at Arnie's and make Mrs. Plaut walk. She had never demonstrated the slightest inclination toward frailty, but the afternoon was hot and she was wearing her best dress and I knew that Gunther didn't enjoy two-block hikes with people staring at him.

I think I made it into a legal space on Ninth. It was close. A heartless cop could have given the city the benefit of the doubt. I took the chance. I had the money for the ticket and the prospect of getting more.

Nothing was different in the Farraday lobby. Our footsteps echoed and distant sounds of voices and doors echoed in the darkness. We took the elevator, and Mrs. Plaut, when we hit the second floor, asked me if I knew how the hearing aid worked. I told her I thought so, but Gunther indicated that he had done the translation for the directions to a hearing aid and was sure he could explain. He explained quickly and Mrs. Plaut listened intently with a squint as the elevator came to a stop on three.

I opened the door and let Mrs. Plaut out. Gunther, carrying the gift, paused and motioned for me to bend down to catch a secret.

"Did you see the vehicle following us?" he said.

"I saw it Gunther, Pontiac. One man. Car needed some body work. He was looking for a parking space behind us."

"Why?" Gunther asked.

"Who?" I asked. Since we had no answers for each other we followed Mrs. Plaut down the hall, got ahead of her, and led her to Jeremy Butler's office-apartment. We were late. Not very late, but late. Music was playing when we opened the door. The music was provided by a man with a thatch of white hair wearing a frayed shirt and dark tie. He was playing the flute.

"The second movement of Bach's Brandenburg Concerto No. 2," Gunther informed me as we eased into the room.

The ceremony was about to start and the room wasn't all that crowded. Jeremy, suited and tied, nodded at me and I nodded back across the room. Alice the broad-beamed beamed in a new pink blouse and blue skirt that covered her muscles. It would be nice to say she looked beautiful. She didn't but she did look a little softer. Her brown hair was loose in the back and turned out to be almost down to her waist. The minister was a guy named Jacomo Huston from the Church of Shiva on 16th. Jeremy and Jacomo carried on long arguments on philosophy and religion in Pershing Park. They drew great crowds. I'd heard their act a couple of times and thought someone should grab them for an educational radio show.

I avoided the eyes of Madame Carpentier and those of Mildred Minck, who tried to make contact, maybe to hypnotize me into paying Shelly more rent. I wondered if Shelly had told her I wouldn't pay. From her look I guessed he hadn't. From Shelly's pale smile I could tell he hadn't. The two cakes were laid neatly out along with bottles of Roma white wine and Pepsi plus a big pot of coffee. Gunther placed our gift on the table in the corner with the other gifts.

"If we are—" the Reverend Jacomo Huston began, but the door burst open and Phil entered. I thought at first he was looking for me, the $10,000, and the papers from the Alhambra safe. I had visions of the two of us punching it out and rolling over cake and guests. But right behind Phil came his pale, thin wife, Ruth, carrying year-old Lucy and behind them my nephews, Nate and Dave. Dave spotted me downing a Pepsi and shouted over flute and reverend, "Uncle Toby, Uncle Toby, did you shoot anybody yet today?"

Nate put his hand over his brother's mouth but Dave struggled free and made his way over to me.

"I don't see any new cuts or holes," Dave said, looking up.

"I'm a mess under the suit," I confided.

Dave smiled. "Great," he said.

"If we can now begin," the reverend tried again, and he began.

The ceremony was brief and didn't make a hell of a lot of sense to me, stuff about merging with the all, being tranquil, being what one is meant to be. The kids fidgeted, Lucy made demands, and the guy with the flute used his instrument to scratch his head. Madame Carpentier kept glancing at me and I did a good job of pretending to concentrate on the ceremony. I couldn't see Gunther. He was below and behind someone or something.

"Bombs and bodies fall,
Spirits in turmoil call
and claim our vision,
our hearing or senses
demanding that we place
one foot in the past and
one in the future straddling
the present; But we are in the hall
of now and the shadows standing tall
should not move us from the one
at our side; The present is our obligation.
Forsake not history or tomorrow's dreams
but honor the now and abandon schemes
that promise whispers instead of sweat
and love."

"Amen," said Mrs. Plaut and everyone added their "amens," though I wasn't sure we had heard a prayer.

"Is it over?" Nate whispered hoarsely to me so everyone could hear.

"I now pronounce you man and wife," answered Jacomo Huston. Jeremy and Alice embraced and exchanged a small kiss before turning to the small gathering with gentle smiles. The flutist started something else and Gunther appeared at my side, slightly smaller than ten-year-old Nate, to tell me that the piece was Vivaldi's Recorder Concerto in D.

A good time was had by all, at least by most. I kept Nate and Dave nearby for protection, but it didn't stop Phil from coming over to me after he had picked up a piece of chocolate cake.

"Nice," he said. He was sweating with about twenty extra pounds.

"Nice," I agreed, looking over the group.

I glanced at Phil, who appeared ready to say something more, changed his mind, and moved away. I waved at Ruth and Lucy across the room. Lucy had spilled Pepsi over herself and her mother.

The presents were opened. Shelly and Mildred gave a card promising six months of free dental care to the newlyweds. Madame Carpentier's gift was a pair of matching Egyptian health necklaces. Mrs. Plaut's gift was a pair of hand-knit sweaters, both of which looked too small for the happy couple. Phil and Ruth gave an orange juice squeezer, and Gunther and I gave a vacuum cleaner, a rebuilt Royal Eureka, bought for $12.95 from the L.A. Furniture Company on South Broadway.

When I finally made my way to Jeremy to wish him and Alice good luck, he asked me, "Is everything settled, with those two in your office?"

"The pineapples? All settled. My life's in order, Jeremy. Enjoy your honeymoon."

"Darkness and light, Toby," he said, clutching my hand. "Remember there can be no light without darkness. No joy without sorrow. Life is not life without contrast."

"I'll remember that, Jeremy," I said, which proved to be the right answer. He released my hand, and I turned around to find myself facing Madame Carpentier.

"Nice dress," I said.

She finished off the glass of white wine and shook her head at me. "You can call me Charmaine," she said.

"Nice dress, Charmaine," I said, trying to ease past her to the strains of Vivaldi and conversation. I pretended to wave to someone I desperately had to get to in the corner. There wasn't room to get by unless Madame Carpentier backed off.

"The three are dead," she said.

"Yes, but—" I started.

"And now someone follows you," she added, licking cake frosting from her fingers.

"I'd rather not—"

"You have no choice. He will find you. This cake is too dry. Not enough butter."

"Butter is hard to come by," I said. "There's a war on."

Half an hour later, after telling Dave and Nate how their father had saved my life by putting a pair of bullets in Straight-Ahead and avoiding Shelly and Mildred downing two more Pepsis and a piece of cake shaped like a book, I scooped up Mrs. Plaut and Gunther and departed.

"Weddings make the Plaut women weep," said Mrs. Plaut, clutching her purse. She wasn't weeping. Gunther looked unusually sober and said nothing.

I drove them back to Heliotrope, noting the Pontiac on my tail.

"Toby," Gunther said from the backseat.

"I see," I answered.

When I dropped them at the door, Mrs. Plaut said, "Photographs tomorrow morning."

"I tremble with anticipation," I said, grinning.

"I've told you about sarcasm," she said, her face at my open car window. "Cousin Gaylord never recovered from it."

"Try the Aurex," I said. "It'd be a shame to have it go to waste."

"Be careful, Toby," Gunther called, looking back down the street to where the Pontiac had pulled in.

I pulled away and spent the next twenty minutes losing the guy in the Pontiac. He wasn't a pro but he was determined. He ran a couple of lights on 8th Street, cut off a flower truck on Alameda, and almost kissed my bumper on Banning. Luckily for him he was trailing a yellow Crosley that was easy to spot and had the pickup of a kiddie car. I pulled into a driveway on Inez right near Hollenbeck Park when I lost eye contact with him after a left turn. I drove right into some guy's open garage and cut the engine. In my rearview from the shadows of the garage I saw the Pontiac speed down the street.

"What are you doing?" came a voice and then a face through my passenger window. The face belonged to a man who looked like Lionel Barrymore.

"Good afternoon," I said. "Mr. Barrymore?"

"No," he responded. My name is Harris, Anton Harris."

"You're not an actor?"

"I'm a tree surgeon," he said. "And you're in my garage. You really think I look like Lionel Barrymore?"

"Yes," I said, checking for the Pontiac in the mirror.

Anton Harris smiled. "I always thought so," he said. "But Betty and the kids don't think I look like anybody."

I left Anton Harris, sure he would make for the nearest mirror, and backed into Inez. No Pontiac. I took a right, watching my mirror, and slowly made my way back to 14th Street. I parked a block away from Straight-Ahead's apartment and locked the car. I also paid two Mexican kids who should have been in school fifty cents to watch my car, with the promise of another fifty cents when I came back.

No one stopped me from entering the apartment building. No baby cried this time as I went up the stairs. I looked at Straight-Ahead's door. There was a padlock on it and a sign indicating that no one was to enter without police permission. Someone had already written an obscenity on the sign. I went up to the roof. No one was there. No one had found the box with the files and cash.

I made my way back to the street and to my car. The two kids were there and my hubcaps were still in place. I gave them each another quarter as I had promised and drove away.

I hit Chaplin's place at five and went through the same procedure to get in. The butler walked even slower this time but he didn't lead me into the house. We walked around it and he pointed down the hill and beyond the tennis court. That was as far as my guide was going to go. The rest of the safari was up to me.

Chaplin was sitting in a clearing beyond the tennis courts. The clearing was covered in concrete and in the center was a sewer with a manhole cover. Chaplin was sitting on a rock with his legs folded and his chin on his fist. He wore a loose-fitting white shirt with the sleeves rolled up to the elbow and a pair of dark trousers, creaseless and trim.

"Mr. Chaplin," I said softly.

He seemed to be hypnotized by the manhole cover. Finally, he sighed and spoke without looking up at me.

"There are comic possibilities to a manhole cover that have never been explored," he said. "I mean the cover itself, not the hole. The trick is to take a natural object and turn it into a symbolic prop."

"Like the globe balloon in *The Great Dictator* or the buns in *The Gold Rush,*" I said.

Chaplin looked up at me and cocked his head to one side like a small bird. "Precisely," he said. "The manhole cover can be made of wood, a light wood but not too light. It must look heavy and have a sense of solidity, but not the weight. It is the door to our foul refuse. I'll open that Pandora's box and engage in a display with the cover, balancing, dancing, perhaps using it to ward off villainous pursuers. No, it lacks meaning. A plate to eat from? No . . ."

"A wheel you can put on a car that just lost one," I suggested, getting into the spirit. "The manhole cover replaces the missing wheel so you can escape. Then the guy following you falls into the open hole."

Chaplin eyed me for as long as a minute.

"Possibilities," he said. "I doubt I'll use it at all but it has possibilities. You've come to report on your investigation of the Larchmonts. Bascomb said you have something for me."

Chaplin's eyes fell on the box under my arm. I sat on the rock next to him and made a show of opening the box. The money was in an envelope. I opened the envelope, showed him the contents, and handed it to him. His eyes opened wide.

"It's all here?"

"Count it," I said. "The Larchmonts are out of business, at least in California. You want the details?"

"That won't be necessary," he said. "Neither will I need to count this other than the five hundred dollars we agreed upon."

He counted off the five hundred in fifty-dollar bills and handed them to me. I stuffed the wad into my front pocket.

"You'll stay for dinner, I trust," he said, rising. "My sons are home and we are having squab. After which I plan to tell some particularly blood-curdling ghost stories."

"Not tonight," I said, standing.

Chaplin walked me up the hill. He looked even smaller outdoors than he had inside a few days earlier, but he also looked healthier.

"You'll come Sunday to the little party I have planned?" he said. "I would like to propose a small but not insignificant role for you in the film on which I am now working."

"If nothing else comes up, but I think I'll pass on the acting."

"As you wish," he said at the gate, holding his hand out. I shook it and he said, "And the papers. What do you plan for them?"

"I'll build a little raft and burn them at sea, like *Beau Geste.*"

Chaplin shook his head. "A romantic, but, ah, so too am I."

He let me out and I turned to watch him hurry back up the path. He didn't waddle like the tramp and he wasn't wearing the costume. The hair was almost white instead of black but it was the same curly hair. All the scene needed was "The End" to come up out of the lawn.

I got in the Crosley and drove back downtown. It was too late to get to the bank. I had six hundred bucks. The world was mine. I could move into a new office. I knew I wouldn't but it was good to know I could.

Instead of heading for the office, I drove over to Spring and went into Levy's for the Friday special. I asked Carmen if she wanted to go to a John Wayne premiere on Monday. Maybe even meet the Duke. It was fine with Carmen, who managed a dark smile. Before the waiter served me the soup at the corner table I had picked out so I could watch Carmen breathe, I went into the kitchen. The chef was a Negro named Walter. We had talked a couple of times. He was the best Jewish cook in Los Angeles.

"Got a fire going?" I asked.

Walter, sweating from the heat of the kitchen, pointed to the stove.

"You mind?" I asked.

Walter was too busy with the dinner trade to answer with more than a nod. I burned the letters and papers two or three at a time and swept the ashes into the garbage can in the corner. It took about five minutes.

"Thanks, Walter," I said.

"I gave you the stuffed peppers 'stead of the fish," he said. "Trust me."

"I do," I said. "Thanks."

When I got back to my table the cabbage soup and the stuffed peppers were waiting. So was a well-dressed blond young man.

"You're Toby Peters," he said in a foreign accent.

"And you've been following me around in a Pontiac," I said, crumbling some crackers into my soup and smiling over his shoulder at Carmen.

"A friend of mine needs your help," he said.

"I'm going on vacation," I said, taking a mouthful of cabbage soup. When I was a kid I had hated cabbage soup, but at some point I couldn't remember, I had decided I loved the stuff. It didn't beat a good bowl of Wheaties, but it was close.

"My friend can pay," he said.

"I just came into a pile of money," I said. "You want to eat the stuffed peppers? I'll get another order."

He didn't want them, so I finished my soup and moved on to the peppers while he considered his next move. Walter was, as always, right. The peppers were terrific.

"What's your friend's problem and who is he?" I asked, feeling in a good mood.

"Someone is trying to convince the United States government that he is a spy," the young man said, looking around the restaurant to see if anyone was listening or watching.

"Who is he?" I asked, finishing off the second and last stuffed pepper.

"Albert Einstein," the man whispered.

"I think I'll have dessert," I said. "They make a great rice pudding."

your FOUR-YEAR-OLD
Wild and Wonderful

by Louise Bates Ames
and Frances L. Ilg

Gesell Institute of Child Development

Illustrated with photographs

DELACORTE PRESS/NEW YORK

RODMAN PUBLIC LIBRARY

649.123
A513

B-2

To our daughters,
Joan and Tordis,
and our grandchildren,
Carol, Clifford, Karl, and Whittier

Copyright © 1976 by The Gesell Institute of Child Development,
Frances L. Ilg and Louise Bates Ames.

All rights reserved.
No part of this book may be reproduced
in any form or by any means without
the prior written permission of the Publisher,
excepting brief quotes used in connection with
reviews written specifically for inclusion
in a magazine or newspaper.
Manufactured in the United States of America

First printing

Designed by Giorgetta Bell McRee

LIBRARY OF CONGRESS CATALOGING IN PUBLICATION DATA

Ames, Louise Bates.
Your four-year-old.

Bibliography: p.
Includes index.
1. Child development. 2. Children—Management.
3. Child psychology.
I. Ilg, Frances Lillian, 1902– joint author.
II. Gesell Institute of Child Development, New Haven.
III. Title.
HQ772.5.A398 649'.123 76-8471

ISBN 0-440-09884-X

Photo credits appear on page 152

RODMAN PUBLIC LIBRARY

CONTENTS

chapter one

CHARACTERISTICS OF THE AGE

The Four-year-old is a funny little fellow, and if you can accept him as such, you will appreciate and enjoy him for what he is. If, on the other hand, you take a sterner stance and feel that his boasting, his swearing, his general expansiveness, and his often out-of-bounds behavior is *wrong*, both you and he may have an unnecessarily hard time of it.

For the most part, we have found the boy or girl of this age to be joyous, exuberant, energetic, ridiculous, untrammeled—ready for anything. What a change he offers as compared to his more difficult, demanding, Three-and-a-half-year-old, just-earlier self! If at times he seems somewhat voluble, boastful, and bossy, it is because it is so exciting for him to enter the fresh fields of self-expression that open up at this wonderful age.

The child at Three-and-a-half characteristically expressed a strong resistance to many things the adult required, possibly because in his own mind the adult was still all-powerful. Four has taken a giant step forward. All of a sudden he discovers that the adult, though still quite powerful, is not *all*-powerful. He now finds much power in himself. He finds that he can do bad things, from his point of view, and the roof does not fall in.

More than this, following its seemingly built-in plan

of interweaving, nature sees to it that whereas the Three-and-a-half-year-old was rather withdrawn and insecure much of the time, Four operates on the expansive and highly sure-of-himself side of life. Four, as Figure 1 shows, is an age when the child is characteristically in a nice state of equilibrium.

Emotional exuberance has its positive as well as its negative side. The typical Four-year-old *loves* adventure, loves excursions, loves excitement, loves *anything* new.

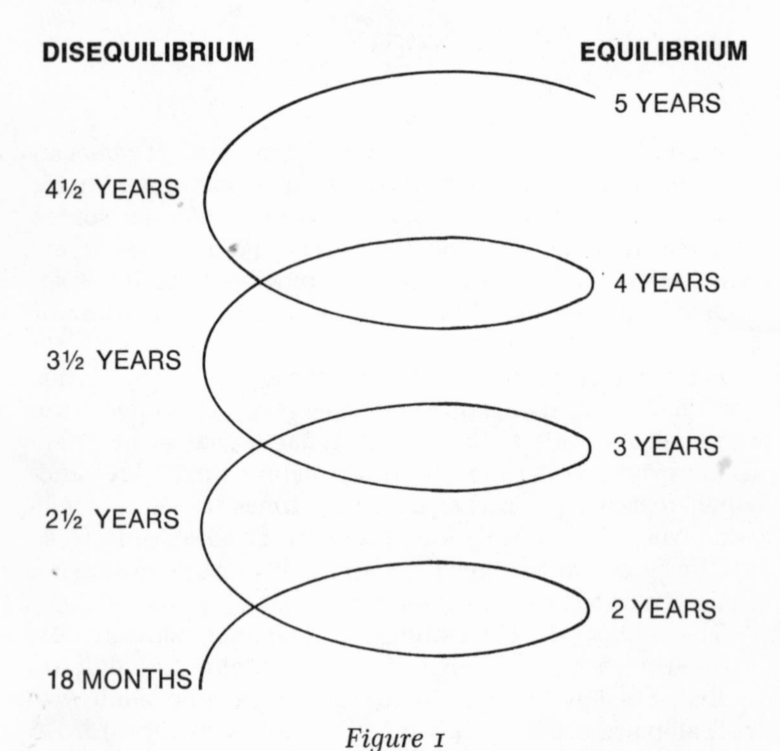

Figure 1

Alternation of Ages of Equilibrium and Disequilibrium

He adores new people, new places, new games, new play-things, new books, new activities. No one is more responsive to the adult effort to entertain. He will accept what you have to offer with delightfully uncritical enthusiasm. So, it is a pleasure to provide the child of this age with new toys, books, clothes, experiences, information—because any of these things make his eyes sparkle so, because he is so wholeheartedly appreciative.

In fact, Four *loves* many things, but his emotions tend to be definitely extreme. He loves a lot and he hates a lot. In fact, his hates may be equally as strong as his loves. One can never be quite certain what it will be that will stimulate his hate, but whatever it is, his feeling should be fully respected, at least within reason.

With those children who have a tremendously strong attachment for their mothers (and that is most) there may be especially strong hatred expressed for anything that changes her in the child's eyes. He may hate certain jewelry she wears; he may hate it if she changes her way of wearing her hair. Or, he may especially hate a special look on her face that tells him that she is displeased with him.

He may hate squash, or any other food to which he takes a dislike. Or, he may (alas) hate certain people. He especially hates things that he considers *ugly*, and may at times express a quite remarkable aesthetic sensitivity.

Four loves things that are *new*. The Three-year-old has a conforming mind. Four has a lively mind, and new thoughts and ideas or bits of information may please him as much as do new toys. That is why it is so much fun to talk with him. His incessant "whys" may sometimes pall, but often they lead the way to enthusiastic information-giving on the part of the adult. It is fun to inform somebody who so enthusiastically wishes to be informed.

The key to the Four-year-old's psychology is his high drive combined with his fluid imagination. Four is, indeed, highly versatile. What can he not do? He can be quiet or noisy, calm or assertive, cozy or imperious, suggestible or independent, social, athletic, artistic, literal, fanciful, cooperative, indifferent, inquisitive, forthright, humorous, dogmatic. He is many people in one.

The typical Four-year-old is also speedy. Each thing he does, he does quickly, and he is also speedy as he moves from one interest to the next. For the most part, he does a thing once, and *that's enough*. He isn't interested in perfection; he is interested in getting on to the next activity. Behavior is fluid, and if he does stay with a single activity, that single activity may change so rapidly as to make your head spin.

A good example of the often quite remarkable fluidity of Four's imagination can be seen in his drawing. A Four-year-old in spontaneous drawing may quite typically start with a tree, which turns into a house, which turns into a battleship. Or, even more fluidly, his "person's foot" can grow so large that it develops large toes that turn out to be the back of a bird. And that turns out to be a roller coaster. And that turns out to be the *back* of the roller coaster. (At that point, your Four-year-old may very likely run out of paper.)

Fluidity can be expressed in media other than pencil and paper. For instance, two boys, playing in a sand-pile, decide that they are making volcanoes. However, when it is suggested to them that the volcano's *erupting*, as they had planned, might be too messy, they themselves spout a little and then give up the volcano plan and decide they are digging for dinosaur bones. No bones being forthcoming, they talk awhile about how old dinosaurs get to be (nine thousand years, they think) and then turn their sand into imaginary snow and make snowballs (which do not stick together very well even with the addition of water). So, they turn their snowballs into rotten eggs and say that the last one to talk is a rotten egg. (All this within five minutes of play.)

It is no wonder that adults have to keep on their toes to keep up with speedy, fluid, fanciful Fours. But, fluid as they are, there still remains some of Three's "me-too" quality. If you ask one child in a group what street he lives on, each child in the group then wants to tell where he or she lives, and all may be surprisingly patient and

polite until everyone has had a turn at giving this interesting information.

It may be that Four's expansiveness is sometimes a little too much even for him. At any rate, he likes and respects boundaries and limits, which he does not always

have within himself, and which, therefore, often have to be supplied. In fact, we find that many Fours like very much the verbal restraint of "as far as the tree," "as far as the gate." Others can be reasonably well contained if told, "It's the rule that you do (or do not do) so-and-so."

In fact, many seem to seek for regularity and rules in the happenings around them. Thus, a Four-year-old may come up with the spontaneous conclusion, "It's always so-and-so." This "always" seems to give him security. He may sometimes break the rules, but he likes at least to know what they are.

Also, he sometimes spontaneously restabilizes himself, even in his wilder play. Thus, two boys may pretend they are in a cave (a large pasteboard box) with monsters, but then they protect themselves by pretending that the monsters have disappeared and that they (the boys) are "all safe and sound."

And, for all his expansive and often out-of-bounds tendencies, Four can, when he puts his mind to it, sometimes be very reliable. Many can go on small errands outside the home if these do not involve crossing the street. And many, by Four-and-a-half, have reached the point where they can be trusted to play outdoors without much supervision or checking.

However, when his customary expansiveness combines with his exciting need to see just how far he can go before the grown-ups call a halt, the Four-year-old generously and characteristically very often expresses what we consider the outstanding trait of his age—his love for going out-of-bounds.

A normally vigorous and well-endowed child of this age may seem out-of-bounds in almost every area of living. Motorwise he not only hits and kicks and spits (if aroused) but may even go so far as to run away from home if things don't please him. Whether he is happy or not, his motor drive is very high. He races up and down stairs, dashes here and there on his trusty tricycle.

Emotionally, too, he tends to be extremely out-of-bounds. He laughs almost too hilariously when things please him; howls and cries more than too loudly when things go wrong. (But he laughs more than he cries, and he loves laughter in others. In fact, he may tell you of his parents, or of other adults, "When they're happy they always laugh." He can, on frequent occasion, be extremely silly.)

But it is his verbally out-of-bounds expressions that are most conspicuous. He exaggerates: "as high as the sky," "ten million bugs," "as big as a house." He boasts: "I have bigger ones at home," "I can do better than that," "My father is stronger than your father." Along with his boasting, he swaggers. Boys like to emphasize their own masculinity by calling each other what they consider to be very masculine names, not their own: "Bill," "Mike," "Joe."

There is much interest in both the products and the process of elimination. Children are especially fascinated by bowel movements. Out for a walk, they may spot every deposit of a dog's bowel movements. Their own buttocks are especially important to them, and when asked what they think with, they may even point to their behinds.

Elimination swearing has its beginning at Four. When angry with a friend, the child may call him an "old poo-poo." In fact, in general, nouns and adjectives tend to be on the unacceptable side, and there is considerable talk about "wee-wee" and "doo-doo." (Even though right in the midst of such a conversation by one child, another may criticize and say, "That's not nice.") There is also much reference to garbage.

This concern about elimination is also seen in the child's great interest in bathrooms, especially in other people's houses. The minute he enters a house, Four may want to see the bathroom. But, though he is much interested in bathrooms and other people's toilet functioning, he tends to be extremely private about his own. He may even go so far as to lock the bathroom door, and many a Four-year-old has locked himself into the bathroom.

And (alas), all too often Four lapses into outright profanity. "Jesus Christ!" is a not-uncommon expletive, even though Four may not fully appreciate what he is saying. When one Four-year-old was heard to repeat the phrase "Goddamn it to Hell!" for each step as he climbed the stairs, his father got the message and became more careful about his own language.

And we have the (supposedly true) story of a little Boston girl whose mother, discouraged by her profanity, told her that if she swore once more, she (the mother) would pack the girl's suitcase and ask her to leave home. The little girl did swear once more. The mother did pack the suitcase and put her and it outside the door. After a few minutes, feeling guilty, the mother went to look for her daughter. The child was still sitting on the steps.

"I thought I told you to leave home," said the mother.

"I would have if I could have thought where the Hell to go," was her daughter's reply.

True or not, this story is all too typical. Or, if not with actual profanity, the child may criticize the adult with epithets and threats: "You're a rat," "I'll sock you." And, not content with unacceptable language, all too often a Four-year-old departs from truth to an extent that any literal-minded adult can label only as outright prevarication. If you meet this, as any other exuberance, with a calm "Is that so?" or with a knowing wink rather than with anger and admonition, he tends to come rather quickly back to reality.

FOUR INTO FIVE

And just in case you are curious about what happens next, here's a word about that interesting transition time —Four into Five.

We know that the typical Four-year-old girl or boy tends to be, as we have told you, extremely exuberant, enthusiastic, outgoing, out-of-bounds. We also know that at Five the same child will in all likelihood be, much of the time, calm, collected, quiet and self-contained, adaptable, conforming, well-adjusted, easy to get on with, happiest and most comfortable while engaged in conservative, close-to-home activities.

How does he get from Four to Five? What is the transition like? Does he all of a sudden one day simply forget his earlier exuberant ways and settle down? Or, is the change more gradual?

It tends to be rather gradual, and sometimes the child

himself seems a bit confused, as if he really does not know whether he is a wild Four-year-old or a calm and quiet Five. At any rate, adults often find his behavior highly unpredictable.

A clue to his own uncertainty is the strong interest of the Four-and-a-half-year-old in whether or not things are "real." Making a drawing of an airplane, he may include a *real* electric cord so that people can plug it in. "Is it real?" is a customary question.

At Four-and-a-half, the child does tend to be a bit more self-motivated than he was just earlier, and he tends to stay on the job better than he did before. Children of this age are much interested in gathering new information, in perfecting old skills. Play is less wild than at Four, and most are better able to stand frustration. But emotions may be quite uncertain, with laughter and tears following each other in quick succession.

And, the child may be less easily shifted than he was just earlier. Some Four-and-a-half-year-olds can be persistently demanding, especially to secure certain objects such as sparklers for the Fourth of July. This kind of demand may be so persistent that it becomes obnoxious. In fact, when crossed, the child of this age may become obnoxious, sticking out his tongue and making dreadful faces. It may now be less easy to distract him with humor than it was when he was just Four.

At Four-and-a-half, the child is becoming aware of authority, and a new kind of confused but listening expression, mixed with a bit of fear, crosses his face when a parent reprimands him. Parents may like to temper their demands when they see this expression. This may be a time for bargaining.

Now the awareness of "good" and "bad" things begins to dawn. Nothing delights a Four-and-a-half-year-old more than to hear real true stories at bedtime, either about himself or about his parents. He loves stories about how bad his parents were when they were little, and also stories about how good they were.

Prayers, especially spontaneous ones, are welcome at this age and often allay children's bedtime fears. The thought of God the Father, and the thought that He is everywhere, can be comforting to some. Children of this age may like to tell God about their troubles and why they happened. They like to bless all who are near and dear to them or tell God about the people they love.

All in all, the Four-and-a-half-year-old is unpredictable. But if you will keep in mind where the child has been and where he is going, it can help you to define and to understand where he is now.

WARNING!

Here, as at any age, we give you an important warning: *Do not take too seriously what anybody (we included) tells you about how your child will or may behave.*

Child behavior, for all reasonably normal children, does develop in a highly patterned way. Stages of more mature behavior follow those of less mature behavior in a remarkably predictable manner. To a large extent, when we see a child expressing some one certain kind of behavior, we can tell you what will very likely happen next.

We can also, on the basis of having studied thousands of children at every age, give you an estimate of when, *on the average*, your child may be expected to reach each stage.

Almost every child does go through almost all of the stages, and in a rather standard order. What we cannot tell you for sure is *exactly* when your own child will reach each and every stage.

Age norms (our story of what behavior is like at the different ages) are only *averages*. Your child may quite normally be ahead of or behind these averages. So, if we say that a certain behavior is characteristic of Four years of age, and your Four-year-old has not reached this stage yet, you should not feel that you have cause to worry. Your child may be, and quite normally so, a little slower than the average in his development (though the quality of his behavior might be quite superior, indicating that a fine potential will express itself in time.) *Every child has his own timetable. Do not expect that your own child will always perform right on our schedule.*

And then, of course, there are individual differences. Not all Three-year-olds are gentle; not all Four-year-olds are wild.

We tell you about behaviors that are characteristic of the different ages not so that you will check and worry. We tell you what behavior is usually like so that you can, within reason, know what to expect and then *not* worry when your own child's behavior sometimes departs from your ideal.

It is comforting to many parents to know that children do not always behave in a desirable, conforming way; that many perfectly "good" children are often, at some stages, quite normally less than good.

"Now I know he's normal" is what many parents say when they read our often seemingly somewhat lurid descriptions of what behavior can be like at different ages. This is why we write for you—hopefully to prepare you for, and to make you feel comfortable with, the many sometimes rather remarkable ways in which even completely normal children behave as they grow older.

Then you can protect yourself from feelings of guilt, or simple embarrassment, at your child's sometimes unorthodox behavior. Or, you can protect yourself from striking out at your child in an unknowing way or in aroused anger. With knowledge, you can appreciate what the laws of growth are expressing through your child, can smile within yourself at his forms of expression, and can act with confident and loving authority, knowing that this, too, will pass.

chapter two
THE CHILD WITH OTHER CHILDREN

The typical Four-year-old loves adventure, and other children, for him, can be a big adventure. Especially if they are of his own age they will be, as he is, exciting, active, enthusiastic, out-of-bounds, always ready for something new. And, like him, they will be somewhat unpredictable. This adds spice to playtime.

Children at this age enjoy each other so very much that often playtime goes smoothly without too much interference, though it may go much better if a mother or teacher is in the offing to settle disputes, patch up quarrels, provide something new when play bogs down.

Any two Four-year-olds still express the tendency to exclude some unwanted third, but somewhat less than just earlier. Now friendships may be quite positive and based on shared activities and not merely on the exclusion of some unwanted other.

Cooperation, sharing, taking turns now tend to come quite easily to most. Interest may be directed more to the excitement of shared, cooperative activity than to attempts to control the actions of other children. In fact, the Four-year-old's love of big projects often makes the help of several other children necessary.

There is much less difficulty than earlier about owner-

ship of possessions as several can now play cooperatively with the same material.

Children of this age enjoy the notion of "friend," and a nursery school teacher can often stimulate a friendship simply by announcing to a child, "Here is your friend who wants to play with you."

Fours are not as rigid about interpersonal relations as

they were just earlier, so a mother or teacher can often solve any momentary tangle by humorous verbalization, by shifting the scene of play, or merely by suggesting some interesting elaboration of any current activity.

Or, the child himself may solve his own social problems: "First let me have a turn," or, "It's my turn now. OK?" Or, "Pretty soon will you let me use that red?" or, "Please, may I have my iron now?"

Four-year-olds, obviously, have all the words they need for any and all social relations: "Let's play with this. OK?," "I'm the dairy-farm man. Want some dairy cream? Who goin' help me get milk? Who goin' help me unload the barn?," "Put it on top. Yes, that's pretty good," "Feel my forehead. It's so hot," "My belly button's sticking out." Or, cuttingly, "Richard, you have big ears."

If, in a play group, several should sit at a table, crayoning or playing with clay, there is much interchild interchange. They may quarrel mildly over materials, show the teacher what they have made or what others have made. Or, while they work with their hands, they may discuss topics quite unrelated to what they are doing.

Four's typical violence and exaggeration express themselves in play with friends as in other activities. "I just set your coat on fire," a quite usual Four-year-old may say to his friend. When his friend ignores this bit of (untrue) information, he may repeat, "Can't you see? I set your coat on fire!"

(As a matter of fact, Fours tend to be obsessed by fire. A fire engine may be a favorite Four-year-old present. Or, the child wants a fireman's hat. And above all he may want to be a fireman when he grows up. But at the same time he might be deathly afraid of the fire alarm and need to be protected from his fear.)

Violent and excitable as he may often seem, the child of this age mostly wants his friends to like and approve of him. "OK?" is a frequently used expression: "I'll just take this one now. OK?," "Let's build a garage now. OK?"

In a group situation at this age there is very little isolated play. Children are now tremendously interested in each other as people, and they are also tremendously interested in, and ready for, group activity. Most children in any play group will spend most of their time in rather elaborate constructive or imaginative cooperative play. Frequently, now, children can organize a cooperative activity by themselves, without adult help or suggestion.

They may, as earlier, emphasize imagination. Or, they may emphasize actual construction and activity. One group may, spontaneously and without help, build a large block church and then conduct a service. They may build a store and then sell groceries. They may build a boat and then go for a sail. But their talk about any of these activities may be more important to them than the activity itself.

Friendships are strong at Four. Children not only like to play with their special friends but like to sit with arms around each other and whisper. Even boys can be seen hugging and kissing each other. If one of a pair of friends initiates an activity, such as painting, his friend will probably want to paint, too.

This warm interest in others can, and often does, lead to sex play if children are left unsupervised. Such play is probably not particularly harmful to children, but most parents don't like it. And obviously it can be overindulged in if not put in its right perspective. When it does occur, no one special child should be *blamed*, since any child, no matter how nice his mother may consider him, could be the one who starts it. Careful supervision can usually prevent such play.

But parents need to remember that tensional overflow often does have its outlet through the genital region at this time, especially in boys. Grabbing the penis in a socially tense situation is quite usual. This is no time to tell the child to "stop that." Better to direct the child's mind toward something of interest, such as going on an excursion through the house or yard.

In older Fours, especially in boys, certain children tend

to stand out as leaders. Others in a group quite willingly carry out their orders and do what they say. Girls tend to lead in a more romantic way. In a nursery school group, one or more of the boys may consider that they have fallen madly in love with some special girl, and these friendships may last for several weeks.

In a nursery group there tends to be strong identification with the group. Children will bring in food to share with everybody. They like to invite other children, as

well as teachers, to their homes to visit them. They love parties, and like to celebrate their birthdays, either at school or at home.

SIBLINGS

The Four-year-old can be an aggressive little fellow, with brothers and sisters as well as with those outside the family. Actually he may get on less well with siblings than with others. In a play group he tends to gravitate to those other children who appeal to him and whom he likes —his friends. At home he may be involved with children he has not selected and may not always like—his siblings.

A Four-year-old is usually old enough that unless he is having real emotional problems in growing up and in being superseded by somebody younger, he will much of the time be reasonably good to a baby sibling. But even now he should not be trusted alone with a baby, at least not for any long periods of time, as he is still not entirely predictable. (And if he is one who actively dislikes his baby sibling, they should not be left alone together for even a short time.)

With other siblings, Four is unpredictable. He may play nicely, but he may be extremely quarrelsome and rambunctious, even with those somewhat older than he. It is often surprising to parents that a Four-year-old can, on occasion, get into real trouble with a brother or sister considerably older. In fact, Fours can, for their own reasons, sometimes unfathomed, become extremely aggressive and directive toward much older siblings. Perhaps their own sense of superiority is threatened by greater competence. At any rate, a quite typical command, by a Four-year-old to an older sibling, may be: "Don't do it like that. That's wrong. If you do it again, I'll cut you in pieces and throw you in the garbage."

And though often good to those much younger, a Four-year-old may be surprisingly mean even to a baby, like the boy who, quite unprovoked, said to his little sister, all dressed up in a new pink dress, "Pink, pink, you stink." (Perhaps here he is exercising his sense of superiority.)

Households vary, and children differ. Some, especially quiet little girls, may get along with their brothers and sisters a good part of the time. Others are extremely quarrelsome and "always fighting." When such fighting occurs, parents should: 1) appreciate that fighting among siblings is not only normal but tends to be much enjoyed by them, no matter how much they scream; 2) separate them when possible; 3) figure out what times of day or what situations bring the most difficulty, and then, so far as possible, avoid or minimize those situations.

NURSERY SCHOOL

Though nursery school attendance is not essential for a happy childhood, one of the most satisfactory and exciting opportunities you can offer a Four-year-old is the opportunity of attending a lively, lovely, nonacademic nursery school.

Your normally endowed, characteristically exuberant, bursting-with-energy-and-with-a-desire-for-new-experiences Four-year-old may all too quickly exhaust your own most enthusiastic and generous efforts to keep him entertained. A good nursery school teacher has that second wind so necessary to keep up with the vigorous and demanding child of this age.

Equipment in a good nursery school can, quite naturally, be both more abundant and more varied than even a well-equipped household can be expected to provide.

Teachers, unlike mothers, are not looking after the child in the midst of other duties. Setting up a situation in which the child can fully express his own creative and dramatic interests is her job, her full-time job. And she is less likely to be called on to take part in his play than is his mother at home.

Not only is equipment more plentiful, adult help and guid-

ance more available in a good nursery school than in the ordinary home, but there are all the other children.

Other children at times excite but also at times calm down the sometimes too exuberant Four-year-old. There is perhaps no better learning situation for any child of this age than one in which he finds himself at the tender mercy of his contemporaries. Here, rather than from books or in forced learning situations, is where the child of this age *really* learns.

However, there are some children who either resist going to nursery school or who tend to develop one cold after another to such an extent that the disadvantages of the school experience may seem to outweigh its advantages. Three is the ideal nursery school age. Four demands more of school, and if it is not up to his liking he may prefer to stay at home.

There is much at home to please the child of Four. He loves all the things that happen there—the arrival of the deliveryman, the milkman, the garbageman, the mailman. He re-enacts all these activities in his own yard with such simple props as big cartons or boxes and odds and ends of toy equipment.

And, above all, whether nursery school is part of his life or not, he likes to go neighborhood visiting, just to talk. How he loves to talk to an older person who has the time and interest! But limits must be set even to this, and a parent must see to it that such visits do not last too long.

chapter three

TECHNIQUES

The techniques with which one can best handle the bouncy Four-year-old stem directly from a knowledge of his basic personality. Obviously, the better you understand him, the better job you will do in helping him behave in ways that will please you rather than grieve you.

To begin with, Four is one who loves adventures. Share them with him. Create them for him. A simple trip around your own neighborhood, with its inevitable points of interest, takes on new luster when seen through the enthusiastic eyes of a Four-year-old. And when you plan an excursion, plan it with him in mind. A short walk, perhaps past a spot where a new building is going up (or, better still, being torn down), and an ice-cream cone on the way back will be a lot more satisfactory to a Four-year-old than a cultural expedition to a nearby town.

The best way to calm Four down when some of his wilder ways (his profanity, his boasting, his supersilly way of talking) bother you is to ignore him. "He only does it to annoy," as the old rhyme tells us. So, if you show that you not only are not annoyed but do not even notice, the thrill of profanity or exaggeration dies down, in most, rather quickly.

An opposite technique, and one that is more fun and perhaps equally effective, is to join in and enjoy. You will

not enjoy his profanity, but you can often enjoy his exaggerated stories by countering with your own—obvious—exaggeration. That is, rein in when you feel that you absolutely need to, but do not always rein in.

Certainly you can join in with and truly enjoy some of the wonderfully silly poems and stories now available for the Four-year-old. You haven't lived if you have never shared with a Four-year-old the delightful nonsense of a book such as Ruth Kraus's *I Want to Paint My Bathroom Blue*, which tells you of

A doorknob a doorknob, a deer little doorkn
A deerknob a deerknob, a door little deerkno

Or, try some of the gorgeous rhymes in *Somebody Nut Tree*, also by Ruth Kraus:

There was a girl
and she had a cat
and a dog
and a chicken
and she wanted a horse.
On her birthday
she got a horse
and that day the horse had horses.

Four loves his own familiar stories and songs, but, unlike the just-earlier child who must have everything just *so*, he may enjoy having a familiar story or song read or sung in a silly way. Thus, "Twinkle twinkle little star" might become "A bat and a rat sat on a hat." With each repetition, the song may be sillier and sillier. Many parents find that they are better at these games and exaggerations than they thought they were.

A very important thing for any parent of a Four-year-old is to try not to be aroused in a negative way by his often unacceptable behavior. If you appreciate that this kind of behavior is potentially there, you are less likely to be thrown by it.

If your child attacks you, as he sometimes will, with rude remarks, play a game of "insulting" to release his (or your own) pent-up feelings as though your name calling were real. Try such foolish epithets as, for instance, "You're a toasted marshmallow," "You're a squashed worm," until laughter takes over.

To be certain that you take the time for the excursions and adventures that the Four-year-old so loves, especially if you are very busy with his younger brother or sister, you may like to set aside one afternoon a week, or part of

an afternoon, that will be *his*. He may choose (from a list prepared by you to be sure that things don't get *too* wild) the destination or activity that will please him for that particular week. He (or she) may even like to keep a little notebook, with considerable help from you, of course, that tells about these weekly excursions.

Since the child of this age does tend to go out-of-bounds, you will need, for safety, to find the most effective way of containing him within what you consider to be acceptable physical limits. Environmental restrictions such as gates or closed doors are not as effective as earlier, but most at this age do respond pretty well to verbal restrictions, such as "as far as the corner." In fact, the Four-year-old seems to like and respect boundaries and limits, which he doesn't have within himself. He seems to appreciate it when you supply them.

Most respond rather well to the statement, "It's the rule that . . . ," even when they do not understand why it is the rule. The statement "It's the rule" can, of course, apply to almost any situation throughout the day. It is wise, however, to use it only in fairly big and general situations, such as, "It's the rule that we don't hit other children," or, "It's the rule that we don't grab other people's toys." Don't waste this good technique or fritter it away on single situations, such as by saying, "It's the rule that you mustn't hit Johnny."

"It isn't fair" is another similar stricture that many will respond to even when they don't fully understand it.

Boundaries, or at least *shape*, can be provided if you give your Four-year-old a structure within which he can function. If, for example, he is visiting his grandmother, and his behavior becomes a little too wild, she can help him by telling him, "You are the *guest*." She can then outline a few restrictions that pertain to *guest*'s behavior, and it may be interesting enough to him to be a guest that he may to a large extent conform to reasonable restrictions.

With some boys and girls, a very good technique at this

age is bargaining. If it bothers you to do this, or if it seems too much like bribing, don't do it. But with Fours many parents find that a little bargaining goes a long way. That is, you give a little, and your child may be willing and able to give a little in return.

Since this is an age when children love "tricks" and new ways of doing things, sometimes, if a child balks or stalls, you can motivate him by suggesting that he hop or skip toward some desired destination.

Transitions do not present the difficulty they did some six months earlier, but if there is trouble with transitions this can often be countered by enthusiastic talk about the next proposed activity.

One general rule that may save you and your child much anguish is to try to avoid known trouble areas. There may be some things you do together, or some situations, that almost inevitably spell trouble. When you have identified such an area, do what you can to change the whole situation, instead of allowing it to arise and then disciplining on the spot.

One thing that from now on can make a great deal of difficulty is that most children *hate* it when their mother is on the telephone, especially when her conversations run on and on. They hate it; they behave badly and get into trouble and then make a fuss; and then their mother scolds and yells and punishes.

It is probably hard for a mother who may feel that she has little enough fun or time to herself during the day to appreciate how shut out a child feels when his mother is gossiping on the phone. It would be an act of great kindness, and would prevent much bad behavior and the accompanying need for punishment, if long, chatty phone calls could be restricted to some time when your child is having his nap or is otherwise out of the room.

A child of this age, since he so loves silliness, may respond better to some silly noun, adjective, or verb than to a more conventional instruction. If you tell him not to push a friend, he may go right on pushing. If you tell him, "Don't be a goober [pusher]," he may respond more positively.

Although positive instructions tend to work better than negative—that is, tell him what you want him to do, not what you do *not* want him to do—the negative can at times be used effectively. An exaggeration of the negative, such as "Never, never, never!," if expressed forcefully, may engage his attention and his compliance.

It's best, in general, though, to keep things positive if you can. If you tell a child how nicely he is going to behave, he sometimes does so.

As just earlier, the child tends to respond very well to the notion of newness. Such words as "different," "surprise," "guess what" are still highly effective as motivators.

Or, some made-up word that has specific meaning only to the child and his mother, such as "cushalamacree," may at times be extremely useful. Such a word can roll off Four's tongue with ease and enjoyment. And when its meaning is secret, it can produce magic results, to the astonishment of those not in the know.

Thus one girl of Four always ran and hid when her mother came to fetch her from a friend's house. But just the saying of that special word, by her mother, helped her to organize at once, helped her gather up her things and walk out the door holding her mother's hand, feeling safe in the knowledge of this word that nobody else understood.

Whispering may, as just earlier, be more effective than shouting. At least it calms the child and catches his attention.

Distraction, at any preschool age, can be, as some have put it, a truly "magic wand." This technique will be less necessary with a fluid, fast, ever-changing Four-year-old than with the child just younger. But even at Four your boy or girl may sometimes get stuck on a point, and the two of you may find yourselves at loggerheads. If this occurs, rather than fight things through, you may be best advised to change the subject or the scene very quickly by any distracting device that may occur to you.

Since Fours love exaggeration, in your efforts to motivate or restrain, as well as in your efforts to entertain, you will find exaggeration to be very effective. "As big as the world," "in ten million years," or just plain silly language, such as "mitsy, bitsy, witsy," "goofy, woofy, spoofy," can often interest or distract when distraction is needed.

At Four, perhaps even more than at other ages, praise and compliments work wonders. Later on, children may be aware of exaggeration; but no compliment and no amount of compliments seem too much for Four's insatiable appetite. You can comment on a handsome shirt, a pretty dress, nice new shoes. Or, you can praise the way the child accomplishes any given task or any creative activity. Or, if he is playing with others, you can praise his relations with others: "I bet he appreciated the way you helped him with that."

In fact, if you don't praise enough, he will praise himself. You can often hear your Four-year-old expostulate, "I'm smart." You can smile and agree with him.

You can always win by telling the child how much you love him. It is easy and natural to criticize and to try to improve your child. If words of praise come less naturally, then they need to be cultivated.

Along this same line, remember that at this or any other age the simple act of conversing with your child can work wonders. Almost any child loves to feel that he has his parent's full attention, and he loves to talk. If you want to know what is on your child's mind, you don't necessarily need to ask directly. Just talk with him. Good communication is vital in those difficult teen years soon to come, but it is important even here. So, listen to your child and talk to him. Conversation provides one of the best routes to a good relationship, and in the final analysis *it is your relationship with your child even more than the use of good techniques that gets you smoothly through the day.*

There is one special aspect of the world today, often criticized and seldom praised, that can nevertheless help you out beautifully, especially on a rainy day. Do take advantage, freely though carefully, of one of the great new things society has to offer for the preschooler—television. All of a group of Four-year-olds recently studied by us did watch television.

All parents of boys and nearly all parents of girls felt strongly that TV did add to their children's lives—if only to their enjoyment. So, don't be afraid, within reason, to take advantage of what your television screen has to offer. It can be one of your best techniques for filling some of the day and for meeting Four's high demand for excitement, activity, and drama.

The choice of suitable programs may be difficult, especially if there are older siblings. So, try to select some one program that you consider good for your child that will become *his* program. Then he can be more easily controlled in not being exposed to other programs that may be both frightening and beyond his comprehension.

And if some program he watches attempts to teach letters and numbers or sizes and shapes, and he responds to this teaching, let his interest be your guide. It won't make him smarter, and it probably won't make him read any earlier than he otherwise would have. And it is just as well not to encourage him to show off any such skill to friends and neighbors. But if you and he enjoy this exercise, fine!

Last of all, remember that once you appreciate what a child of this age (or any age) *is* like, it helps you to appreciate what he *will* like. You can tailor your techniques accordingly.

DISCIPLINE

This discussion of techniques attempts to convey, at least implicitly, our attitude about discipline. Discipline, as most of you appreciate, is not the same thing as punishment. Discipline, rather, is a way of setting up the child's life situation so that good, effective, desirable behavior becomes possible. Techniques themselves are a form of discipline.

As to your own *philosophy* of discipline, you may be an old-fashioned, authoritarian parent who expects your child to do what you tell him to, regardless, even when the demand may be unreasonable or beyond his ability. You may be a *permissive* parent who permits anything and allows the child to follow his own whim.

Or you may, as we recommend, follow a policy of what we call *informed permissiveness* (or controlled flexibility). That is, you try to fit your demands and expectations to things that it is possible for a child with the maturity level and personality of your own to perform. Knowing that your demands are reasonable, you make them, firmly and consistently.

The more effectively you manage this, the better your discipline, the fewer will be the incidents of rebellion, disobedience, or "bad" behavior, and the less need for punishment. (Though no parent succeeds entirely. There will, in any family, be some unhappy incidents.)

As to what kind of punishment you should use, if and when punishment becomes necessary, this depends partly on your own temperament and partly on what works with your child. Temporary isolation works with some. Deprivation of privileges works with others. Some respond to scolding, some to more physical measures. An occasional spanking, if it works, is not immoral; but spanking should never be relied on as a chief form of punishment.

The so-called behavior-modification people hold that you can get any child to do anything you want him to by praising the good and ignoring the bad. This kind of handling seems complicated or unnatural to some, but for those of you who would like to try it, we suggest that you read *For Love of Children* by Roger W. McIntire.

Other disciplinarians have used (for some sixty years now), with reasonable success, a common sense kind of discipline called "logical consequences." That is, if the child does something he shouldn't do, or fails to do something he should, he must take the consequences. For example, he leaves his tricycle outside, and it gets stolen.

Each of you will, of course, work out your own philosophy of discipline and methods of discipline, keeping in mind both your own temperament and that of your child. Most important of all, perhaps, is that, if possible, Mother and Father agree, if not about every detail, at least about the basic approach. Two parents working together, especially if they have a reasonably good understanding of what it is reasonable to expect of their particular child, have a very good chance of helping him to behave in a comfortable and effective manner, at least much of the time.

THINGS TO AVOID

1. Don't worry excessively if your Four-year-old, as he very likely will, goes out-of-bounds. A certain extra exuberance is natural, usual, and quite probably necessary at this age to give balance between uncertain Three-and-a-half and quiet, adaptable Five.

2. Don't fuss too much and certainly don't worry if your boy or girl lies, swears, and/or exaggerates. Such behaviors are almost the essence of Four-year-oldness. You can, and undoubtedly will, discourage and disapprove of such behaviors, but try not to worry about them.

3. In fact, try to avoid excessive "moral" judgments about your child's often somewhat antisocial behavior. In another year he or she may be as conventional, as docile, as conforming as you please.

4. Avoid that wild search for things that will motivate an uninterested or underactive child. *Success* is the best motivator at any age. The likelihood is that any child will be motivated to activity if you provide for him materials and opportunities that by his temperament and matu-

rity level he will be able to cope with and to deal with effectively.

5. Don't worry that you should be doing something to increase your child's IQ. Basic intelligence level is, so far as we know, largely determined by genetic factors. You can and should give all children reasonable stimulation, but don't be self-conscious about level or quality of intelligence.

6. Don't feel that you should be teaching your Four-year-old to read. Read to him. Make books available. And when the time comes that he starts picking out initial letters in books or asking, "What does S T O P spell?," by all means respond. But don't push. Be sure that any interest in reading (or in numbers) that may be shown is his and not merely your own.

7. If your child is still sucking his thumb, fondling his blanket, or indulging in any other earlier tensional outlets, try not to feel that it is now "time" that he give these up. Another few months may see the behavior ended.

8. Don't feel that you have a "bed-wetting problem" if your child still wets the bed at night—some nights or even every night. Many quite normal children do not develop the ability to stay dry until they are Five or even Six, or even later. (Pad them up good and tight to save on laundry, and don't fuss or worry.)

9. Don't blame your child's playmates for behaviors in him or her that you don't like—exhibitionism, bad language, sex play, and the like. Today it may be a neighboring child who initiates the activity. Tomorrow it may be your own!

10. Don't fail to enjoy this extremely amusing, lively, enthusiastic age while it lasts, even though some aspects of your child's behavior may not be entirely charming.

chapter four
ACCOMPLISHMENTS AND ABILITIES

As long as your boy or girl is developing in what seems to you a reasonably normal way, if he behaves about as other children in your family have at his same age, or about the way other children in the neighborhood seem to do at his age, you should not be too self-conscious about specific abilities and inabilities.

It is important to remember that intelligence and maturity are two separate things. A child may obviously be very bright, but young for his age. Or, he may be not so bright, but mature for his age. And whether he is bright or not so bright, mature or immature, keep in mind two important things.

First of all, remember that intelligence is to a large extent an inherited capacity. You will, of course, want to give your child all the reasonable stimulation possible, make his life full and interesting. But even your best efforts will not, in all likelihood, make him more intelligent than nature intended. Even if he is not one of the more superior, intellectually, there can be a very good life ahead for him if you do not make his lack of A-quality intelligence a matter for major concern.

The same with maturity. Our expectations of what a Four-year-old should be able to accomplish are only averages, and a child might be quite a bit ahead of, or quite a bit behind, any time schedule that we or others set up, and still be perfectly normal. If your Four-year-old by chance does not seem quite up to usual Four-year-old maturity standards, this may mean that, when the time comes, you will want to have him go a bit more slowly in school than the law permits, but it still is not necessarily a cause for anxiety.

Any listing of the activities and accomplishments of the supposedly typical child of any age should be preceded with the clear warning that perhaps there actually *is* no truly "typical" child. When we describe Four-year-old behavior (or, for that matter, behavior typical of any age), we mean that most or many children of that age do behave that way.

But there will be many children who, because they follow the usual path of behavior change at a faster or slower rate than the average, will reach the behavior in question sooner or later than the average time. There will be many others who, because of their own individual personality, may actually never behave in quite that special way.

Consider an age characteristic such as the expansiveness and out-of-bounds behavior that we think of as so highly typical of the Four-year-old. If you have a gentle, quiet, moderate, restrained little boy or girl, he or she will in all likelihood be more expansive at this age than at Three or Five, but may not even at this lively age go to any great extremes. Or, if his or her whole rate of development may be a little on the slow side, even though intellectual endowment may be fully adequate, it could be on toward Five before the customary Four-year-old expansiveness appears. That is, the behavior in question may come in early or late.

As to specific abilities described in this chapter, here, too, you must allow your boy or girl considerable leeway. A child could be as much as a year ahead of, or behind, any supposed "average" and still be quite within normal limits.

For instance, interest in books and in formal learning varies tremendously. Or, a child may be ahead of age in some one behavior (language behavior, for instance) and not up to age in motor behavior. Each child has his own individual rate and pattern of growth.

MOTOR BEHAVIOR

Your typical Four-year-old, with his high drive, enthusiasm, expansiveness, is a motor person *par excellence*. He loves to run. He loves to climb. He loves to gallop. He loves sheer movement for its own sake. And, he loves to talk, to shout, to carry on. He loves exaggeration, of sound and movement as well as of actual words. He loves to talk about big (or enormous) things, and he loves to make big things. His drawing strokes are dashing, and he needs lots of room for his productions.

His drive seems boundless. There is strength and push behind everything he does, and he gives the impression of being ready for anything. A difficult motor situation, which may have brought out all his sensitivity and insecurity six months earlier, is now a welcome challenge. He loves the difficult and the daring. He loves the different. He loves to show that he is master of space and incline.

As we've said before Four is speedy. There is a quickness of decision and of action apparent in almost everything he does. He moves quickly and with very little wasted motion.

Four coordinates the movements of the parts of his body much better than formerly. In fact, he often shows a remarkably good ability to move his body effectively and to move it in relation to other things in the world. His increasingly good sense of balance allows him to play games requiring complex motor skills and to enjoy body-building skills and stunts. This may be a good time to introduce a few body exercises such as toe or knee touching, or making angels in the snow. The child appears

especially to take pleasure in stunts that stimulate the semicircular canals: whirling, swinging, somersaulting.

In fact, there seems to be an inner awareness of what he or she can do. More feelings seem to be unfolding now, combining the control of physical ability to move with the awareness of self and feelings inside one's body. This is why a child of this age enjoys creative movement, with perhaps the addition of drumbeat or song. (An inner awareness is also evident in his interest in stomach, heart, and bones. His frequent reporting of stomachaches makes one aware of this concern.)

At times, his motor drive is so extreme that if he is *not*

given opportunities for motor activity, for blowing off steam, he may become a difficult young person for those in charge to manage. If any Four-year-old is giving you trouble with his exuberant demand for action and variety, see to it that he spends as much time as possible out-of-doors, and hopefully that he is provided with plenty of physical equipment that will give him the opportunity to use and display his muscular effectiveness. He feels his muscles in activity, and he also wants *you* to feel his muscles and to tell him how strong he is. He may like to tell you, "I'm tough!"

Specific motor abilities of both balance and action have improved impressively in the past few months. The child not only walks upstairs a foot to a step but also walks down a foot to a step, at least on the last few steps. He can stand on one foot from four to eight seconds, can skip on one foot. He can accomplish either a running or a standing broad jump. He can jump down from a two-foot height with feet together. He can hop on his toes with both feet off the ground at the same time, seven or eight times in five seconds.

Many can learn to use roller skates. And some of the better coordinated can even ride a small bicycle if it is equipped with training wheels.

By Four, most children have acquired strength, ease, and facility in the use of their legs, which lend considerable grace to their movements. Most walk with long, swinging steps, in the adult style.

Boys, especially, and some girls, are rapidly becoming athletic, and take real pride in attempting motor stunts that require delicate balance. In ball play, most now use their hands more than their arms in catching a small ball. They can judge their direction of throwing better now than they did just earlier. Boys throw a ball overhand with a horizontal motion from above or to the right of their shoulder; girls from above the shoulder with a downward sweep.

Fingers are now much more skilled than earlier and

under better control. Children can handle small objects, button or unbutton buttons, lace shoes, string even rather small beads. Most can cut on a line with scissors and can carry a cup of water without spilling. They enjoy games that involve many little pieces that need to be manipulated.

Though the Four-year-old is by nature active and athletic and loves to cover considerable space both on the level and in climbing, his increased attention span means that he can stay longer than he could before in a single area of activity. In fact, though he so greatly loves physical activity, he is able to sit for relatively long periods of time at an especially interesting manual task.

Hyperactivity. We hear a good deal nowadays about a way of behaving that has probably always been with us but that currently has a new name. When a child is overactive and seems never to stay still, can't quiet down, can't stick with one thing, can't turn his motor off even if he wants to, we label his behavior *hyperactivity.*

The truly hyperactive child finds it almost impossible to slow down and concentrate. As a preschooler he wears everybody out, and as he grows older he frequently finds it difficult or impossible to behave "properly" or to succeed in school because of his overactivity.

It is often difficult for parents of the active preschooler who is quite normally "always on the go," always "into everything," to distinguish between normal preschool activity and real hyperactivity. Your best bet is to check with your own doctor or child specialist.

If no such help is available, you may like to use a checklist offered by Dr. William Crook. In *Can Your Child Read? Is He Hyperactive?* he lists thirty-five behaviors characteristic of hyperactivity (or hyperkinesis) and suggests that you rate your own child as to how often he displays each of them.

Give a score of 0 if your rating is "rarely or never"; a score of 1 if it is "occasionally"; a score of 2 if it is "often"; a score of 3 if it is "usually or constantly." The highest

score possible would be 105. Any score over 60 suggests the probability that your child is hyperkinetic. (But remember, any child at times may be expected to show almost any of the behaviors characteristic of hyperkinesis. It is the extent and frequency of his behavior that determines the diagnosis.)

The kinds of questions asked include the following: Is he overactive? Does he not finish projects? Does he have trouble sitting still at mealtime? Does he wear out his toys? Is he generally destructive? Is he impatient, accident-prone, clumsy? Does he get into things? Is he always on the go?

VISUAL BEHAVIOR[1]

There is a fluidity, flexibility, and looseness in the visual patterns of the typical Four-year-old. He is definitely more stable visually than he was at Three, and definitely more outgoing in his visual response. His attention is to the horizon, and he often goes far afield in his pursuit of that horizon.

As his space world enlarges, he enjoys outdoor play, while indoors he prefers not to be confined to a single room or play area. In nursery school, his activities spill over from one room to the next, and even into hallways. Outgoing he is. Boundaries need to be carefully established lest he go too far and endanger himself, such as following a dog across the thin ice of a pond.

Four's high energy drive results in a new burst of physical activity. He is a charmer who has trouble telling the difference between fact and fable. He exaggerates as he practices using new and big words. He may roll his eyes in a delightful manner as he talks.

There is greater interest and participation, now, in both gross and fine visual-motor activities. Outside, he likes climbing equipment, ball play, a tricycle, and sometimes even a two-wheeler. The availability of plastic bats and balls makes a simple game of baseball even more fun. The newer, small-size two-wheel bikes make learning to ride without training wheels easier. If the youngster can touch the ground while the bike is upright, he will have less trouble learning.

The secret to balancing on a bike is through the hands, which tend to be in better control if the trunk is bent forward. Once a child can trust his hands, he'll be able to ride. Newer versions of the old-fashioned tricycle, with the sitting area closer to the ground, reduce the danger of

tipping. The heightened motor activity is not limited to boys alone. Girls enjoy it, too.

Drawing, coloring, and painting are becoming more successful for the Four-year-old than they were earlier. A good pair of blunt scissors is appreciated by the young craftsman or craftswoman. Puzzles, blocks, and other building materials are enjoyed. Four may try his hand at hammering nails—best into a log that does not demand precision.

Seeing is now action oriented. For this reason, the child may like to sit close to the television as if participating in the action on the screen. Parents should remember that television viewing is a poor substitute for activity at this action-oriented age.

Spatial language is well developed. The child can now react correctly to such prepositions as "on," "under," "in back of," "beside" or "in front of," when asked to place a ball in relation to a chair. And the child is now better than he was at following directions at home. He can find his own clothes. He understands about picking up toys and putting them away.

If there has not yet been a visual or eye examination, now is a good time to have it. Four can attend to directions, answer questions, and he is capable of concentrating for a period of fifteen to twenty minutes while such an examination is being made. When he has had enough, he may get down from the examining chair and leave the room. He escapes!

Good cooperation is possible if the examiner works quickly. The Four-year-old responds well to the simple E letter test, or he may know some of his letters, especially those in his name. Both of his eyes participate in the total act of seeing. There is better eye teaming and less need than earlier to support vision by bringing hands into the seeing act. There should be a normal amount of farsightedness measurable. His visual acuity may be close to 20/20 if not already there.

ADAPTIVE BEHAVIOR AND PLAY

Wild as your Four-year-old may be in motor ways, and even emotionally, when it comes to working with his hands you may be surprised to find a beautiful fining down. Eyes and hands coordinate with increasing skill, and fingers increase in their ability to make even rather fine and intricate adjustments.

Four can do many things that his Three-year-old self could not accomplish. Building with cubes becomes so increasingly skillful that he can now imitate a four-cube gate with delicately tipped center cube. By Four-and-a-half, he can make such a gate from a model, without watching it being built.

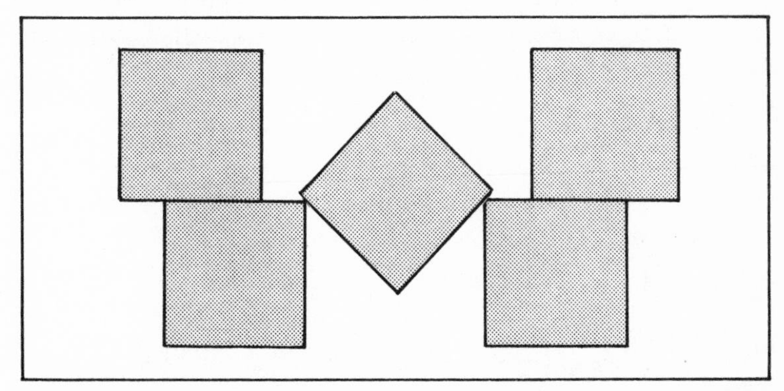

Figure 2

With pencil or crayon, too, he is becoming increasingly skillful. Whereas at Three he could imitate a cross, he can now *copy* a cross if you show him a drawing of one. And, at Four-and-a-half he can copy a square, a rather mature skill.

Or, he can copy the order of a group of things, such as stringing differently colored or differently shaped beads in the order provided in a model. Many can match all shapes, such as square, circle, star, etc., in a ten-hole formboard.

If asked to draw a person, the child can make a recognizable person, though it may still have a potato-shaped body and facial features may be included inside this body. Or, he may be able to draw a man with head and eyes, body, arms, and legs.

If asked to complete an Incomplete Man, most can now add five parts, including, usually, leg and foot, arm and hand, eyes or hair or ear. At Four-and-a-half, most add seven parts to the Incomplete Man—those seen at Four, plus, in many, a body line in the neck area—and their man often appears rather wild, with longish hair, longer arm and leg than six months earlier. Many now, with their characteristic special interest in bathrooms and belly buttons, add a belly button to their man. (*See* Figure 3.)

Four years *Four-and-a-half years*

Figure 3
Typical Response to the Gesell Incomplete Man Test

Most children now really enjoy drawing things, and many enjoy coloring books, filling in the outlines reasonably well. Many adults feel that coloring books deaden the child's presumably innate artistic ability. We feel that they are not harmful if you are careful also to permit the child free artistic expression. Actually, many Fours especially enjoy tracing over the lines of the figure in a coloring book. They also enjoy drawings that provide dotted lines that when linked up make a picture.

The use of scissors is becoming rather effective. Many can cut on a line well enough to cut out pictures and then paste them onto paper or into a notebook in consecutive order. Or, they can cut a picture into parts and then put it back together again, puzzle-fashion. They also enjoy large and not too complicated picture puzzles, response to such puzzles becoming increasingly adept as they move on toward Five.

Adaptive behavior that also includes language expression may now have developed to the point that the child can give likenesses and differences between familiar objects. Or, he can tell the biggest and the longest of three things, and can order five blocks from the heaviest to the lightest, with few mistakes. He masters form both in matching and in placing.

Some Fours, especially older Fours, are becoming much interested in trying to print their letters and numbers. Some may even be able to print their whole first name, though usually in large, two-inch-high, capital letters. Though children should never be pushed into this kind of activity, when it occurs *spontaneously* it should be supported and encouraged, as should early efforts to read.

Play. Four's playtime is seldom a problem. He is ready for anything. Almost any kind of toy or material appeals, and whatever is lacking can often be made up for by his vivid, fertile imagination.

But he moves so rapidly, running through materials and situations and even space, that he may need a rather large quantity of whatever it is that he (or she) is using. Parents need to budget larger supplies of material, such as paper, at this age, but at the same time they need to determine limits of use. They will also find that it is better to set these limits prior to an activity than to clamp down when it is in full swing.

Fours may be happiest with rather active gross motor play, preferably out-of-doors. Most enjoy fully any opportunity for outdoor play. This does not have to be constructive or planned for. Almost any Four-year-old, with his exuberant energy, his vivid imagination, and his ability to turn almost anything into a good play opportunity, loves to be outside where space permits him the kind of activity he so much enjoys.

By Four, or certainly by Four-and-a-half, most can play outside in their own yard unsupervised, with only occasional checking by a parent.

One can readily see why the freer, more outdoor-oriented activities of the usual nursery school are better for the Four-and-a-half-year-old than the more structured and confined, indoor, kindergarten types of activities offered by some schools.

A Jungle Gym provides ideal equipment for the Four-year-old to climb on or on which to perform interesting tricks, such as hanging upside down or holding on with one hand. A slide for sliding, a good place to dig, a flat surface on which to ride his trusty tricycle will obviously add to his enjoyment, but even a relatively unequipped yard can be turned, by him, into a joyous place to play.

Hopefully, in summer there may be a short visit at the beach or in the country. Four is not too young to begin to appreciate the birds and trees and flowers—even though, unfortunately, many children in our cities are, and remain, far away from all the wonders of nature. Watch a Four-year-old hold a flower in his hand. Or a bug. He is full of awe and wonder.

In fact, for many, religious stirrings are there, and God may become a part of the child's vocabulary, his being, and his thinking. One Four-and-a-half-year-old boy, when asked what he liked best, summed up his feelings with "I love the sky and the mountains and the flowers and the whole world." The concept of wholeness now includes the

Greens
electrosol
CREST
2 for 24¢
Crest
JOY
BAND-
AID
IVROY

world, and Four may even think that the Fourth of July is the whole world's birthday, not just that of the United States.

Both boys and girls, but especially boys, relish almost any vigorous physical activity, such as riding their tricycle fast, sliding, digging. Building with big blocks is also a favorite physical, as well as constructive, activity. Big blocks are often combined into impressive structures—houses, stories, forts. The child's big muscles seem to want to lift heavy objects. Once such structures are built, children often play imaginative games inside. (Or, they love any corner of a room, any secret place where they can have privacy to giggle and whisper.)

Or, big blocks may be combined with trucks and wagons, or cars and trains. Boys, especially, may construct elaborate roads and tunnels or tracks, one or two leaders often bossing a "gang" of workers. Whether they combine them with block structures or not, boys love cars and trucks and trains and airplanes—anything with wheels.

Fours, also, in their search for adventure and for anything new, very much appreciate excursions, exploring trips, visits to museums, or even simple walks in their own neighborhoods.

Four's vivid imagination often leads to dramatic play of the most creative sort. No kind of "pretend" is beyond him. Within half an hour, children in a group may be monsters, astronauts, robbers, storekeepers. Or, the child may pretend he is a photographer taking somebody's picture with a Polaroid camera, waiting a minute, and then showing the imaginary result.

Of course, inevitably, they play house, little girls usually taking the part of mothers, grandmothers, and babies; boys of fathers, grandfathers, or people coming to sell something. (Or, if no better role is available, that of the family dog.) Playing store is almost as popular as playing house, with everyone wanting to be the salesperson behind the counter.

Or, less imaginatively, children love to "help" wash cars, wash floors, wash windows. In fact, almost any sort of water play is extremely popular. Parents tend not to be too friendly toward this. They are afraid that their children will spill the water or get themselves wet. With a little effort and ingenuity, most could make more readily available this interesting, satisfying, and soothing kind of play. Blowing bubbles is especially delightful to Four and can as a rule be quite easily controlled.

Doll play, the most conventional form of imaginary play, is becoming increasingly elaborate. Dolls go to a picnic, go to nursery school, or even move to another city.

Dressing up is very big at Four. Boys as well as girls love to dress up, preferably in adult clothes. Boys, as a rule, prefer cowboy hats and holsters; girls love long gowns, veils, hats, handbags. Boys are less likely than earlier to dress up in high-heeled shoes or women's hats. Make-believe weddings, with the bride, especially, dressed elaborately from the old-clothes box, are popular.

All the usual creative activities are still great favorites: crayoning, painting, fingerpainting, cutting, pasting. Some are starting to make letters and numbers spontaneously. Play-Doh and clay are still much used by younger Fours, but as children move on toward Five this kind of play may seem too tame for them.

Many other forms of earlier play are still enjoyed. Children like to build with plastic blocks or tiles or Lego or Tinkertoys or small wooden blocks. Most Fours like dominos or puzzles or simple card games. As they move on toward Five, they may begin to like games where points are scored, though it will require a mother or teacher to tell them how many points they have earned. Also, winning and being first are very important.

Books are still great favorites with most and make up a big part of the lives of many Four-year-olds. Whether being read to or "reading" for oneself, many now have special favorites and can stay a long time with a single book. This is the age when humor in stories is especially appreciated. Nearly all love such silly books as *I Want to Paint My Bathroom Blue*, *Somebody Else's Nut Tree*, or Stoo Hemple's *Silly Book*.

By Four, tastes in reading, aside from the general love of the ridiculous, are often rather individual and well defined. Some like whimsical or imaginative stories like *Curious George*, *Mulberry Street*, or *McGillicut's Pool.* Others prefer books about "real" things.

Since Four is an "out-of-bounds" age, it is not too surprising to find that the Four-year-old has a voracious appetite for the dramatic, and that no storied situation seems fantastic enough to overtax his constantly inventive imagination. Thus, complexity of event and even horror of situation seem to add value to many of the Four-year-old's favorite stories. Executioners and miraculous rescues from destruction have much the same appeal that the

Grimms' fairy tales afford. However, caution must be exercised to protect the vulnerable child who cannot tolerate a fear- or tension-provoking story.

Children of this age like complexity in illustrations. They enjoy an abundance and diversity of tiny details. Whereas the Two-year-old preferred a single large picture to a page, the Four-year-old delights in searching out minutiae in illustrations to stimulate and satisfy his constantly expanding interest and imagination.

Music is now a source of great enjoyment for many—not only the somewhat passive pleasure of listening to

favorite records but, especially in groups, more active participation. Older Fours can beat out a rhythm rather well and may like to "conduct" group singing with a conductor's stick. They also like circle games that combine singing and skipping around.

Television, as mentioned earlier, is becoming of increasing interest. Nearly all Four-year-olds do watch television except in those rare instances where there is no set in the household. Girls, usually more amenable, as a rule accept their parents' ideas of what and when to watch. Boys, too, usually accept parents' decisions as how long they should watch, though they may on occasion object to their parents' choice of programs for them.

Most parents do admit that, though it may create some problems, television viewing does add to the young child's life since it keeps him quiet and entertained. Many do feel that it must be limited or it becomes too engrossing. Some object because they feel that it is a passive activity. Others complain that it gives a distorted view of life. Most adults, however, do appreciate the relief it gives them, even while they may complain.

Programs watched most at this age include (1975) in order of popularity: cartoons, "Lassie," "The Brady Bunch," "Captain Kangaroo," "The Lucy Show," "The Flintstones," and "Sesame Street."

Pets provide a good deal of pleasure and experience about life for Fours as for children of other ages. There is much to be learned from pets, and if not too much is expected from him the young child can learn a great deal not only about living and growing but also about responsibility from the care of simple and relatively undemanding pets. But if the parent will not take the major responsibility, it may be best not to have a pet.

Short-time pets—snakes, frogs, caterpillars that can be contained in a terrarium—can offer much interest and excitement and may need not too much care. And turtles are all-time favorites. They may even develop a personality for the child and are often much loved.

Even less demanding is the care of sturdy plants, which still require a certain amount of responsibility. Even a Four-year-old can identify strongly and can enjoy the fact that his plant is surviving and growing partly because of the care he may be giving it.

LANGUAGE AND OTHERS

The Four-year-old tends to be an egocentric little person, but his egocentricity, perhaps happily, includes his contemporaries. Any Four-year-old who may be playing in a group that includes other children and one or two adults directs nearly all his conversation to the other children and is also reasonably responsive to conversation directed to him by the other children. Though he may from time to time speak to an adult, or acknowledge something the adult may say, his chief and outstanding interest tends to be in other boys and girls.

At this outgoing age, there is relatively little solitary play, and even when there is, it is accompanied by very little verbalization. Even when a child is not talking to others, what he says tends to have a social implication, as when a boy comes into a playroom and remarks, "Oh boy! What a noise!" Or, mimicking an adult's admonition, he may remark, "If I don't stop that noise!" Four is a noisy age—the Four-year-old is loud and active in most things he does.

Children by no means ignore an adult who is present or playing with them. It is merely that they are much more interested in other children than in adults. Thus, a child may give what he considers interesting information to the adult: "I don't mind anything. Anything 'cept when Mommy washes my hair," "I live next door to a haunted house."

He may tell or boast of his own abilities: "I can write," "I can count," "I can swing by my knees," "I'm awful strong," "Watch me jump. Awful high." And he boasts about possessions, comparing them favorably to any that others may have: "I have bigger blocks at home," "I got more blocks than the other children have."

He still is not above asking the adult for help: "How do you do this, anyway?," "Will you put this somewhere it won't get lost?" He may still, for all his improved social skills, sometimes ask for help *against* other children: "They won't let me have my car," "They won't let me come in."

If no other children are present or available, he may carry on elaborate imaginative play with an adult. Thus, a boy may initiate an elaborate game of telephone repairman, telling the adult what he is going to do and then carrying it out elaborately, with appropriate verbalization.

But his chief conversation now is definitely with other children. As at Three, he is most interested in conversation he initiates himself, though he is now highly responsive to things that other children say to him. And, conversation now reflects a much more secure sense of self. The child no longer seems to need to protect his every product or possession.

So, there is less talk about ownership, more asking permission to use things that others are playing with, more use of the word "let's," more friendly suggestions in cooperative play: "Could I have those tickets?," "First let me have a turn?," "Let's play with this," "Shut dat door. You see, we don't want any germs to come in," "May I please have the iron?" ("Please" is a favorite word for many at this age.)

Imaginative play tends to involve delightful verbal fantasy: "I'm the farmer. Who's going to help me unload this hay?," "I'm off to work. You put the baby to bed."

Or, cooperative play may involve the use of real objects, especially constructive materials, and practical conversation: "Put a roof on that house, why don't you?," "Ready?," "That's pretty good, but we need another one," "I'm holding it so you can get down." In cooperative play, Fours are quick to accept suggestions from each other. Any one incident of cooperative and/or imaginative play may continue for as much as twenty minutes, with good, sustained reciprocal conversation throughout.

As six months earlier, some children still seem to define those they like by emphasizing those they do *not* like, so excluding and rebuffing remarks are still very strong: "You can't come in," "Get outta here." Or, when one child, in imaginative play, remarks, "I need some more milk," another may retort, "That's not milk. That's only blocks."

They exclude children they don't like but often verbalize strong expressions of friendship for those they *do* like (of either sex): "You're my playmate," "I'm sitting with you," "I like you." They may show jealousy of a friend: "Barbara, don't you talk to him."

Fours love whispering and secrets. They now seem to have fun with language. They enjoy rhymes, and most adore silly language: "My mother's gone goo-goo," "Ready weady, steady weady."

The Four-year-old is, above all, a boaster: "I'm bigger than you are," "I can jump higher than you can." He boasts about his parents, or quotes them as ultimate authorities: "My mother says you can't have that truck." (Sometimes this boasting gets him into trouble with Five- and Six-year-olds. A fight may be the only way out, and the poor Four-year-old usually ends up in tears.)

Silly language is so loved by many that it provides an excellent technique for getting cooperation. Four seems captivated by any silly approach. And, language of any kind is extremely important now. In fact, in some episodes of imaginative or cooperative play, there may be more talking than action.

VARIANT BEHAVIOR

Inevitably at stormy Four, some violent physical resistance and even an occasional tantrum may be expected when things go wrong. For the most part, though, when he does not wish to comply or conform, the child's objections can be expressed quite effectively in his colorful language. He tells you in words, rather than in actions, why he doesn't want to do as you wish.

The child of Four, in a standard behavior examination situation,[2] which permits a fair comparison from child to child and from age to age, as just earlier, refuses with words and not with deeds. As Figure 4 shows clearly, at Four the child refuses things that do not interest him or look too difficult, in very close to what will also be his Five-year-old manner. Quite maturely, he neither fights nor cries. He just talks.

LANGUAGE AND THOUGHT

The child of Four loves language. He loves to talk, to rhyme, to whisper, to sing. Or even to shout. He is his

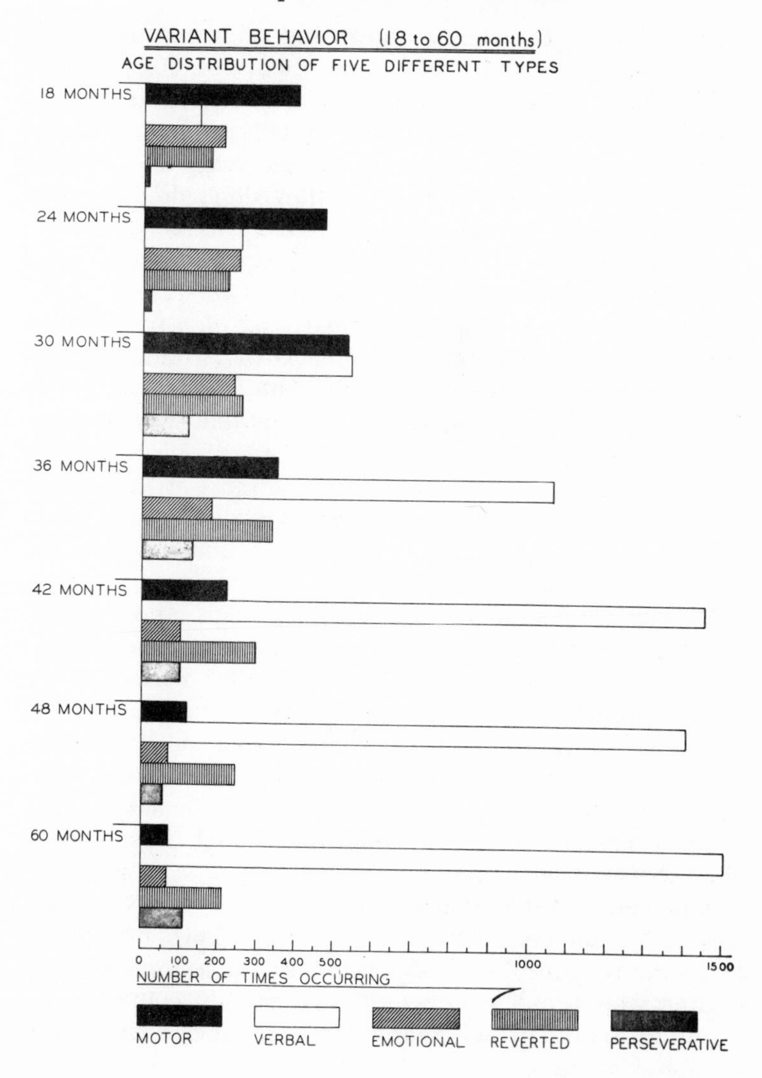

Figure 4

Age Distribution of Different Kinds of Variant Behavior, from Eighteen months to Five years

own self-appointed commentator and often his own audience. He loves words, likes to try them out, likes to play with them. He likes new and different words. He likes to do silly things with words, such as to say "smarty-warty" or "batty-watty" or "ooshy-wooshy." He even likes to talk to his play objects, especially if they don't do just what he wants them to: "You silly red ball," "You foolish block."

He especially loves the word "big," a word that is soon superseded by "enormous" or "gigantic." Four just naturally exaggerates, as we have mentioned: "as high as a mountain," "five million years," "as long as the world." In fact, much of his prevarication, which his parents probably call lying, may at times result from his tendency to exaggerate.

By Four, most children begin to use most of the sounds in their language fairly well. Some estimate that most English-speaking American children use about 90 percent of the American English vowels at this time.

Vocabulary has now increased by leaps and bounds. Some estimate that an average Four-year-old vocabulary may contain as many as 1,550 words. Most Fours can express themselves freely and well. They are now even more interested in stories than earlier, will look on when read to, may even ask what certain letters spell. If the child has been a television watcher, he may even be surprisingly good at saying letters and numbers, though it should be of no concern if he cannot.

The Four-year-old doesn't really *need* to know his letters and numbers, though as children move on toward Five, many quite naturally become much interested in written words and in knowing what certain combinations of letters spell. In fact, many can print their own names in capital letters.

Sentence structure, grammatical usage, and correctness of tenses is improving. As Laurie and Joseph Braga[3] point out, "Children do not learn to speak by copying adults. They listen to adults, learn the rules, and then make up their own sentences based on the rules they have at the time. Children seem to have a built-in language-learning device that lets them learn to use certain rules about their language from what they hear. They even make mistakes in a systematic way."

For example, when they begin learning the rules for making plurals, children who previously had used the correct plural forms for "mouse" and "foot," now, at Four, say "mouses" and "foots." This is called overgeneralization, and is a sign of growth, a sign that they are learning the rules. Later they will learn the exceptions to the rules—again through listening, not through lessons, and will again say "mice" and "feet."

Somewhere around Four, most begin to learn the following word-changing rules: 1) When using "she" or "he," there is an *s* added to verbs in the present tense. Thus, "She walks," "He runs." 2) An *-ed* added to the verb means the past tense. Thus, "Today I walk to school; yesterday I walked to school." 3) An *s* added to a noun indicates more than one: "one dog; two dogs." 4) When something belongs to somebody, you use words like "my/mine," "your/yours," "his/hers," "their/theirs."

Irregular verbs come in due time. But Four goes by his own simpler rules; thus, he "builded a house" and "knowded" he was right, before he takes on the irregular verb forms of "built" or "knew." He also adds extra *s*'s for possession, as "This is hers house."

All these things come in in their own good time, and some children, especially boys, are slower than others. Enjoy these transition forms as a part of growth, and be concerned only if the child doesn't move on to the usual forms by Five or Six. *It is important not to correct your child's language.* Fear of failing can make a child anxious and might even lead to stuttering or not saying anything. If they make a mistake, you can answer them, or repeat what they have said, correctly, but don't emphasize their own mistakes.

Between Four and Five, most learn to say some of the more difficult speech sounds such as *l, r, s, t, sh, ch,* and *j.*

And what they say is now largely intelligible even to those outside the family. Children who have trouble with these sounds can be helped to hear and say them through special books such as those by Jan Slepian and Ann Seidler (*see* page 143).

This is a top age for questions. Endless "whys" and "hows" are uttered, partly in pursuit of knowledge, partly just for the fun of keeping a conversation going, and partly in resistance, such as "Why?" meaning "Why do I have to?" However, the word is used most as a request for information: "Why does the wind blow?," "Why does the sun shine?," "Why does it rain?"

Since children of this age tend to be insatiably curious and avidly seeking for information, try to answer these "whys" as long as you feel that real curiosity and interest motivate them. Don't hesitate to cut short their conversation when they use their "whys" for stalling or resisting.

Not only does the child ask the adult for information, but he, too, likes to *give* information. He has a great deal to say, to adults as well as to other children. He likes to tell outsiders about things at home, and he especially likes to talk about his mother: "My mommy has a brand-new washing machine." He likes to provide facts: "Dogs can run very fast," "A pencil is a simple thing."

Or, he makes extremely touching personal remarks, like the little boy who said to his teacher, "You know, I often think of you. You could come to my house some time, and we could play ball."

Words aplenty he now has under his command. Conversation now truly enriches his life and his relationship with others.

By Four, most children can even define a few words by telling how they are used. Thus, they can tell you that an apple is to eat, a coat is to wear. Most also know four prepositions, such as "off," "in," "next to" or "beside," and "on." They can also repeat after you a short sentence, say their numbers from one to ten, count three pennies with correct pointing. They can also carry out somewhat complex commands. A "test" that most Four-year-olds can pass is the instruction to "Close the door, put the book on the chair, bring me the key," or some variation of this kind of command.

Also, the child of Four usually has enough understanding of the relationship of parts to wholes to be able to tell you when something is missing from an ordinary object, such as an arm from a coat, or a leg from a table or chair. Or, he can tell you what everyday objects are made of, such as a chair is made of wood or a window of glass. Somewhere between Four and Five, on the average, comes the ability to name correctly the four basic colors, though actually some children are able to do this much earlier. Color naming seems to be a highly individual matter.

Most Fours can also respond correctly to such questions as "What cries?," "What swims?," "What sleeps?," "What bites?" And they can also answer correctly one of two such questions as "What must you do when you have lost something?" or "What must you do before you cross the street?" Language has come a long way for most.

chapter five

THE FOUR-YEAR-OLD BIRTHDAY PARTY

Four is perhaps the first age when the very characteristics of the age lend themselves ideally to party giving and party going.

The average Two-year-old is not really certain what a party is. Is it the cake? The ice cream? The guests?

Three enjoys a party more or less as he would a morning at nursery school or an afternoon of play with a friend. He is on the verge of awareness that a party is something special and exciting, but often only on the verge.

Four, however, can be an ideal party age. The Four-year-old tends to be a creature of boundless energy, enthusiasm, and appetite for the new and different and exciting. He *loves* an occasion!

Though Four's enthusiasm can sometimes go out-of-bounds, he can be truly cooperative if things are exciting enough and are going his way. He tends to be extremely appreciative of adult attention. He throws himself fully and positively into plans for his own entertainment.

It is easy to entertain a party-giving or a party-going Four-year-old if you yourself have time, energy, goodwill, and imagination. He tends to accept quite uncritically the games you suggest, the food you serve, the favors and surprises you provide. (Five may say, "Oh, I have one of those." Thirteen may mutter, "Oh! One of those!" Not so with the Four-year-old.) Four's demand for something special or something new and different is easily satisfied by simple favors or attractive decoration.

Discipline should not yet be a major problem, at least for the mother who understands children of this age. She knows that a party is not the place for lessons in sharing, behaving, minding. Quarrels should be settled as quickly and inconspicuously as possible by removing one of the quarrelers or by providing some different but acceptable toy for one of two grabbers.

KEYS TO SUCCESS

The keys to a successful party at this age are speed, simplicity, and novelty. Speed is necessary because Fours react quickly and they tire rapidly if the party drags or if it lasts too long. Simplicity is important because children of this age are not mature enough to understand or to participate in complex games. Some novel element is important because Fours, unlike Threes, have a general notion of what a "party" is and expect something to go on other than just to go and play. This surprise should be something quite simple, such as a distribution of favors.

Number of Guests. Six guests is a good number and definitely not more than eight (both boys and girls). It may be safe to invite one or two extras, or at least to have some in mind who can be invited at the last minute. There are apt to be casualties among invited guests, so that they do not get to the party. They may be ill from overexcitement, their mother may not be able to get a baby-sitter and so cannot bring them, or other difficulties may get in the way.

Number of Adults. The host or hostess's mother and one adult helper need to be available. One or two of the mothers may need to stay as at Three—that is, mothers of children who are extremely shy or extremely aggressive, or who for other reasons may need to be there.

SCHEDULE

One and a half hours is plenty, ideally from 3:30 to 5:00. This timing allows for a nap beforehand for those who still need one, yet doesn't bring the refreshments too near dinnertime.

3:30–4:10 Guests arrive and play with toys. Parents bring, or earlier may have brought over, something for each child to play with (in addition to what the home may provide) for this initial period. So, the living room somewhat resembles a nursery school playroom, with a good assortment of toys, including big cars and trains, a rocking horse, dolls and carriages, stuffed animals, Blockcraft, Tinkertoys, big musical tops. Children play, usually quite individually, with these toys. The host or hostess opens presents as they come.

4:10–4:15 As children go into the room where refreshments are waiting, each one is given a favor. Fireman's hats and badges make good favors. These may be available on a table, and are given to each child as he or she goes into the dining room.

4:15–4:40 Refreshments have all been set up in advance on card tables or on low children's tables. (Tables may have to be borrowed.) Use a paper tablecloth, napkins, plates, and bright cups. And provide some kind of favors—for instance, little toy frying pans filled with candy. Balloons—all blown up—hang in a cluster on the wall. These are given to the children toward the end of the party.

The refreshments can consist of simple small sandwiches, the smaller the better, but in interesting shapes. Better for children to eat several small sandwiches apiece than to half-eat one big one. Or, sandwiches can be omitted and you can have just ice cream, cake, and milk. Individual frosted cupcakes may be better for eating, but there should be a central cake with four candles on it, which can be blown out.

4:40–5:00 Informal play period. Children play with the toys in the living room and with balloons, which have been distributed. (If balloon play becomes vigorous, it may be necessary to push toys to the edge of the room to allow space.)

If the children are on the other side of Four, some slightly organized play, such as singing games, play with instruments, marching, or dressing up in costumes, could be introduced at this time. Also, this is a good time for giving out special surprise favors. These are wrapped separately and may be presented in a big cloth bag that the children reach into, taking turns. They unwrap and play with these. Good favors include small figures of animals or humans, small balls with elastic, toy wristwatches, toy rings, fire trucks.

5:00 Departure. Mothers who are already there leave with their children. Other mothers call for their children. However, by the end of the party most Fours are tired and excitable and may cry or go to pieces if they have to wait to be called for. Thus, it may have been arranged for the mothers already there to take all the children home.

EXPENSES

This can be an inexpensive party. Favors might cost around $4, refreshments $7, balloons $2, extras $2. Total around $15.

HINTS AND WARNINGS

Remember that you can count on only minimal group activity. Individual informal play is better than organized games for most. In fact, it is not only unnecessary but may

be dangerous to introduce even simple games. Ring-Around-the-Rosy or Farmer-in-the-Dell would be better than something complex, such as Pin-the-Tail-on-the-Donkey, if games must be played.

Every child is likely to think that it is *his* birthday, wish it were his birthday, or pretend that it is his. So, all may want to blow out the candles. If someone other than the host or hostess gets there first, you will simply have to relight the candles.

There are almost bound to be some tears, some spilling, some disagreements or quarreling. Be especially careful that the party does not last too long. Fours tire easily and become overexcited.

As to favors and gifts: If you have hats, sturdy homemade ones are better than purchased ones, which are apt to rip and tear. Blowers may become a menace as children blow them into each others' faces. Don't have favors, surprises, hats, etc., all at the refreshment table. It makes for too much confusion. Have the surprises spread out a bit through the party instead of giving them all at once.

chapter six
HELP WITH ROUTINES

EATING

By Four, most children can feed themselves completely except for cutting. They are competent enough now at feeding themselves that they don't have to think so much about it or try so hard. Most can talk and eat at the same time now, though, in some, talking may definitely interfere with eating.

If the child's incessant talking interferes with adult enjoyment of the meal, some families still find it works best for the child to eat apart from the family. If he does eat with others, he tends to become restless long before the meal is over, and may need to interrupt his meal to go to the bathroom.

If parents are relatively relaxed about what the child eats, and unless a feeding problem has been built up in the past by poor management, there should not be much fuss about *what* is eaten. But many parents still worry about *how much* is eaten and may insist too much on quantity.

It is important to remember that the Four-year-old appetite may still be only fair, even though as the child moves on toward Five appetite may increase. Refusals and preferences are not quite as definite as earlier, but the child may still go on either food jags (insisting on the same thing over and over) or on food strikes (certain foods or types of food being definitely refused).

By Four-and-a-half, most can pour milk from a pitcher without spilling, and most drink their milk rapidly and well.

Those who eat alone are apt to dawdle, but they do not need to be fed, merely encouraged to speed up a little. Sometimes such incentives as eating to get big, racing with the baby, finishing within a certain time, or working toward a dessert goal may help. However, in general, the less gimmicky things become, and the less emphasis is put on the whole thing, the better. If children think that their eating matters a good deal to their mother, they are likely to use the power this seems to give them. A very casual attitude on the part of the adult usually works best.

By Four-and-a-half, children not only feed themselves nicely, but may even help to set the table. Both speed and appetite pick up. The child can usually manage more meals with the family, and is beginning to find a reasonable balance between talking and eating.

Though it is not within the scope of this book to discuss in any detail matters of either diet or health, and we do not wish to make any parent overly anxious about the kind of food eaten, we would like to give one warning. This is that some of the foods your child may like best may conceivably be harmful to him.

Obviously, if they make him sick to his stomach, or make him break out in a rash, you will know it and will avoid such foods. But as physicians concerned about child behavior[4] are now pointing out, many foods harmful to the individual child may do no observable physical harm but may have a disastrous effect on his *behavior*.

Food or drink, or even things that are inhaled, may produce hidden allergies, which, in turn, can cause extremely deviant behavior. In some children, dizziness, listlessness, fatigue, irritability, violence, and hyperactivity all can be induced by foods liked best.

Doctors report many striking examples of this, like that

of the boy who at Five had for two years been wetting his pants several times a day as well as having to get up several times during the night. This urinary difficulty, as well as other symptoms of overactivity, cleared up when he stopped eating tomatoes. Unfortunately, in this case, as so often, the boy craved the very food that was harmful to him. For two years he had had tomato soup for lunch every day, and would eat five or six ripe tomatoes at a sitting. His symptoms returned when (as an experiment) he was given tomatoes again, and cleared up when they were once again removed from his diet.

Or, even without there being an actual allergic reaction, harmful food products, especially artificial colorings and flavorings, have been shown to produce dizziness, listlessness, fatigue, irritability, violence, and hyperactivity, and, in school-age children, problems usually described as learning disabilities.

If your child seems healthy and happy, and if his behavior is reasonably satisfactory to you and to him, that is, if he or she is getting along all right in major ways, chances are you don't need to worry about all this. But if behavior is disappointing or unsatisfactory in major ways, and you can't find the reason, at least consider the possibility that something in your child's diet may be at the root of his difficulties.

SLEEPING

Bedtime is now relatively uncomplicated in most. In fact, some seem to know when they are tired and may even ask to go to bed. As at earlier ages, the child will enjoy some special attention, as a story read by his mother or bedtime singing. He may also enjoy half an hour alone in bed with books or crayoning, and often takes dolls or toy animals to bed with him.

The highlight for many a Four is that he is old enough to have earned the right to sleep in a big bed. Parents often produce their own bedtime problems by moving the child from crib to big bed too soon, as early as Two-and-a-half, especially if a new baby has come along. It would have been better to have two cribs, one for each.

Parents can often utilize this momentous experience of having a big bed at Four for potential transitions into release of younger behaviors. The crib shaker and head banger may even be cured overnight. The bed wetter may suddenly become dry. And the lovely, cozy expanse of a big bed may encourage a happy going-to-bed time, with room for a parent to lie down, too, as bedtime stories are read or prayers are said.

Bedtime is usually around 7:00 or 7:30 though with daylight saving time it may be later. If the child can read the time on the clock, and some can, he may respond better to the fact that the clock says it's time to go to bed than if Mother tells him.

A few children need to have not only a going-to-bed time but also a putting-out-the-light time. Without this extra few minutes to settle down in their beds with the light on, they may be very demanding.

Most sleep well, waking only, if need be, to go to the toilet. Some can manage this by themselves; others need substantial help from a parent. And still others resist being wakened and therefore should not be disturbed. This is not a big age for nightmares, though especially around Four-and-a-half some do have troubling dreams.

Many sleep eleven hours or even longer, waking around 7:00 A.M. The child is now able to put on his bathrobe and slippers if they have been laid out for him, can close the window, go to the bathroom, and then will usually play in his room until it is time to go into his parents' room. (Very young children may stay in bed not at all after they wake up. By Three, they *may* stay in bed until you tell them they may get up. By Four, many will wait until a certain hour [the clock says such-and-such] before getting out of bed.)

Though a few still really nap at this age, most have only play naps or no nap at all. Boys are more likely to go to sleep at naptime than are girls. Even if they do not sleep, here as just earlier even a play nap gives both parent and child a welcome change of pace, and a rest from each other.

The day's schedule, at Four, is often helped by the fact that many Four-year-olds enjoy the idea of a routine or schedule. They seem to like to know what comes next and to be able to count on it.

ELIMINATION

By Four years of age, things go pretty well with most. Most children are dry during the day and can manage this entire routine themselves, "Accidents," if any, tend to occur simply because the child does not want to interrupt his play and puts off going to the toilet until too late. If this happens repeatedly, a mother had best take some responsibility here. She can either see that the child comes in to go to the toilet at fairly regular intervals, or, if he resists this idea, she can tell him that she is going to blow a whistle when she thinks it is time for him to come in.

Many demand extreme privacy for their own bathroom functions now but show much curiosity about the activities of others. They are also very curious about strange bathrooms and may insist on seeing the bathroom, if visiting.

Out at play, especially if play is unsupervised, boys may like to urinate in front of other children, and there may be much silly talk about this function.

Perhaps the majority by now can stay dry all night if picked up around midnight. But it is not unusual for a child still to be wet at night. This, as a rule, should cause no concern. And if the midnight pickup does not ensure a dry night, it may be best to skip it altogether. Just pad the child up good and tight to save on laundry, and make very little comment about this immaturity.

(In fact, many quite normally developing boys and girls are Six years old or even older before it is easy for them to stay dry at night. So, it may be helpful for you to know that there are now available effective and reasonably inexpensive conditioning devices that in many instances can serve to dry up a child in a matter of weeks. Some that we have found most satisfactory are listed on page 122.)

Bowel movements in most are also usually rather well routinized, and this function, too, causes no problem in most. One movement a day, after either breakfast or lunch, is a common Four-year-old pattern, though some have more or fewer than one a day, or their functioning may occur irregularly.

As with urinating, most consider this an extremely private functioning and usually want the bathroom door to be closed or even locked.

Unfortunately, there are a few boys who are not up to standard in this department. There are some troublesome children, usually boys, who though they may be trained for dryness, seem to be making no progress whatever with regard to bowel functioning even as late as Four. They refuse to use the potty chair or toilet, and continue to defecate in their pants.

This refusal and continued immaturity of behavior tends to be related to severe mother-child battles. This is one way the boy who *must* control his mother finds it possible to do so. Most mothers will interrupt almost anything they are doing if they feel that by doing so they can keep their son clean.

Some mothers have found that one way to solve the problem is to require the boy to wash out his own underpants. In some, this cleans up matters in a very short time.

Perhaps a kinder approach is one that we have long recommended. After checking with your pediatrician to rule out any physical reason for this delay, we suggest permitting the child to play in the bathroom, with his pants off, at about the time of day when you expect him to function. (If his functioning has not yet settled down to any particular time of day, you will just have to admit that you still have a long way to go.)

Put a newspaper on the floor in a corner of the room,

and tell the child that when he is ready he may use the paper. Often he is able to get this far in just a few days—a few weeks at most. Once he has succeeded with this, it is often just a small step to get him to use a potty—best in saddle potty form or a potty chair. From there to the adult-size toilet is usually fairly easy.

BATH AND DRESSING

The bath is now an easy routine, the child often being capable of washing himself fairly well as long as his mother suggests part by part what should be washed. Otherwise he is apt to get marooned on some one part of his body and wash that over and over.

Most can now let the water out of the tub and can wash out the tub (after a fashion). And can dry themselves (after a fashion). Most can also make the necessary wrist-and-hand motions to do a reasonably good job of brushing their teeth, combing their hair, and washing and drying their hands and face. Many can now wash their faces without soaking shirt or blouse.

Time of bath may now be shifted to before supper, if the family schedule permits, since the child is less tired at this time and can do a better job of washing himself. And oh, how he loves to play in the tub with all his bathroom toys!

The child of this age often dresses and undresses himself without too much help, though clothes may need to be laid out for him, each garment correctly oriented, since a few may still have trouble distinguishing front from back. If any special garment gives trouble and makes the child angry, you can plan ahead for the future as to just how he can manage that particular garment more successfully. (Or, ask yourself, Why is the garment so difficult? Is it really appropriate or necessary?)

Special difficulty may occur in relation to buttoning, though most now unbutton with ease. Fortunately, with modern zippers, less buttoning is demanded than formerly.

At Three-and-a-half, a good many children give much trouble about getting dressed. They resist and object. Four, as a rule, likes to dress himself, is proud of his increasing abilities, and may like to beat the clock or otherwise race to complete the process.

The majority can distinguish front from back, button some buttons, get shoes on the right feet and even lace them. (Some children consistently put their shoes on the wrong feet, and why this does not produce discomfort is hard to say.) Some can tie a knot in their shoestring but cannot yet manage a bow. Many boys, as well as girls, now *love* to dress up in adult clothes—hats, shoes, belts, scarves, skirts, pocketbooks—at playtime.

TENSIONAL OUTLETS

The Four-year-old seems much less tense than he was just earlier, at Three-and-a-half. There is less facial twitching, less stuttering, less blinking. There is even somewhat less thumb sucking, though many do still suck their thumbs, especially on going to sleep. Some have now given up their security blanket, though they likely still cling to their favorite stuffed toy. Some have replaced thumb sucking with nail biting and/or masturbating. Any of these behaviors may be expressed not only in private but even in public, as in nursery school at story time.

If tension is felt, it is more likely to be expressed in a large, gross-motor way, the child running, kicking, shouting. Tension may be experienced more in the genital region than in the facial region. Boys, in times of anxiety or excitement, may clutch their genitals.

Both boys and girls in social situations or at other times of excitement or strain are apt to have to go to the bathroom. This need is real and should, of course, be respected. Some may actually have toilet accidents in a demanding social situation if they do not get to the bathroom in time. A few may feel tension pains in their stomachs and may on occasion actually be sick to their stomachs with excitement.

However, when a Four-year-old feels tense and keyed up he may simply express this feeling in general overactivity, in running around and shouting or in talking too fast or behaving too wildly, rather than in the smaller and more specific ways (as thumb sucking or blanket fondling or nose or eye twitching) of just earlier.

Health in most is reasonably good, though a few seem to have one cold after another all winter. If these colds seem to be exaggerated by nursery school attendance, it may be best to keep the child at home for a while. At this age, if the child falls down (as he often does) he tends to fall on his face and may very possibly knock out a front tooth. (At later ages he seems more likely to break his collarbone or his arm when he falls.)

chapter seven

YOUR CHILD'S MIND, OR DON'T PUSH YOUR PRESCHOOLER

For all the talk we hear nowadays about the cognitive development, or the cognitive training, of preschoolers, it is most important that you not be self-conscious about all this. Without your doing very much about it, you will find that the normally endowed Four-year-old is a creature of tremendous curiosity, wild imagination, delightful creativity. You will want to answer his many "whys" and to encourage his imagination and creativity. But don't take too seriously the sometimes-proposed notion that it is all up to you to teach him to think.

Especially, *do not feel that you must teach your preschooler to read.* Hopefully you will read to him, and read to him some more. Hopefully he himself may enjoy looking at books. And if by chance he is somewhat advanced and is already asking what certain letters mean, or is trying to spell out words, give him the help and encouragement he seeks.

But do not push. It really doesn't make a bit of difference in the long run whether he begins reading at Three or Four or Five or Six or even Seven. If your child should show spontaneous interest in letters and numbers at an early age, fine for him but no special credit to him or to you. If, on his own, or through the stimulation of certain television programs, he should, fairly early, come to recite

the alphabet or to say some numbers, so be it. Let him enjoy this activity, but don't take it as a sign that he is ready for early entrance to kindergarten.

In fact, try not to worry too much about your child's so-called cognitive development. It is almost, of recent years, as if psychologists and educators had discovered the child's mind. They rather give the impression that one must *teach* the child to think, and that it is necessary to provide all sorts of techniques and materials by means of which his mind will develop. It just isn't so!

So, try not to feel that you as a parent "ought" to be

doing something special about your child's intellectual life. Dr. Arnold Gesell commented long ago, "Mind manifests itself." The child's mind is not something separate from the rest of him. It manifests itself in almost everything he does, except perhaps through such purely reflex actions as swallowing or breathing. It manifests itself when he runs and jumps and climbs, when he shouts and laughs and sings, when he plays with his real friends or with his purely imaginary companions. A child who paints a picture or throws a ball is giving expression of his mind in action.

In fact, virtually everything the young child does is an example of his mind in action. It is not necessary for him to learn letters and numbers before he goes to kindergarten to show you, and others, that his mind is in good working order. If your boy or girl has good potential, and if you provide a reasonably rich and lively environment and give your love and attention, the mind should take care of itself.

Whatever his age, you do not have to be specially concerned about teaching your preschooler to think. If you provide a usual environment that contains a reasonable number of friendly, interested, sharing people, a reasonable number of books and toys and creative materials, a usual number of games and jaunts and pleasant excursions—the usual attributes of comfortable family living—he will learn as naturally as he grows and breathes. *Let us all relax*!

And here let us give you a specially important warning. Young Four-year-olds will, in the normal course of development, very shortly be turning Five, and you will be thinking about school for them. They will very soon be taking that important step of starting kindergarten.

And here is where all too many parents make that fatal mistake, which, for many children, stands in the way of school success and more or less guarantees failure, or at least academic difficulty, in all the years to come. They start their child too soon.

Regardless of what the law may permit in your particular state, we prefer to start children in school, and to promote them subsequently, on the basis of their behavior age rather than their age in years or their intellectual level.

It is the age at which a child is behaving, not his birthday age, that should ideally determine the time of school entrance. Thus, your child might be Six years of age come September and might have a decidedly high intelligence quotient, but if in his behavior (which can be determined by simple behavior tests[5]) he is only at a Five-year-old level, he will be best suited in kindergarten, with others who are behaving at this same level, rather than in first grade.

If your own school system does not offer prekindergarten screening and you have no way of finding out about your own particular child's behavior level, then you will more or less have to go by his chronological age.

In that case, we urge all parents to be very sure that that boy or girl is on the older side before he starts school. And since boys, as a rule, develop more slowly than girls, it would be best if your daughter is fully Five years of age before she starts kindergarten in September. Your son will do best if he is fully Five-and-a-half.

Teachers and administrators from all over the country tell us that it is the "fall babies"—children who have their fifth birthday in the fall after they begin kindergarten—who have the most trouble. They often have trouble not only in kindergarten but in all the years to come.

So, though we do not think that the notion of developing or improving your child's mind should be a matter of great concern for you, many parents are understandably interested in the way any child's thinking develops.

Here, then, are a few clues as to the ways that in general children's concepts of time, space, and number do develop in the usual child; a few clues as to the level of thinking often attained by the Four-year-old in such basic areas as sense of time, sense of space, sense of number, and sense

of humor. Here, also, is information as to what one may expect in the way of creativity in the child of Four.

SENSE OF TIME

Four may still seem young compared to what comes after, but the ordinary Four-year-old is actually a rather sophisticated person when it comes to his sense of time.

The child of this age seems almost equally at home, verbally, in past, present, and future, and use of tenses is usually accurate. Such a common time word as "day" is used in many different inflections: "today," "this day," "every day," "another day," "once a day," "day after today."

Generalizations include such somewhat sophisticated words and phrases as "for a month," "once a day," "usually."

"Time" is included in many compound words: "lunchtime," "dinnertime," "every time," "sometimes," "one time," "almost time," "meantime," "for a long time," "Our time is over," "Is it time?" Even such broad generalizations as "springtime," "summertime," "wintertime" are now used quite glibly.

Or the seasons can correctly be put in their context: "next summer," "last summer," "this winter" are used correctly.

And so far as "minute" goes, not only can the child say, and mean, "in a minute," but also "in five minutes," "this minute," "a minute ago," "just a few more minutes."

"Week" and "month," too, are used effectively, such as in "next week," "some other week," "next month," "for a month," "in a month." "Night" and "morning" are comfortably used in many expressions, such as "late at night," "early in the morning."

Children are beginning to grasp the sense of seasons and activities related to seasons.

Most seem to have a reasonably good understanding of when events of the day occur in relation to each other.

Four-year-olds can, as a rule, tell not only what we do

at Christmas and Easter but also what we do at Halloween, though Thanksgiving is still beyond most. Most Four-year-olds still cannot tell correctly what time they go to bed, have supper, get up, go to school.

Though most girls can tell their age correctly by Three-and-a-half, most boys are Four before they can give this response correctly, most often by showing four fingers. Four-year-olds cannot, as a rule, tell when their birthday comes.

SENSE OF SPACE

The space world of the Four-year-old, like so many aspects of his living, is definitely expanding. Outstanding at this age is the use of expansive space words characteristic of the out-of-bounds, expansive tendencies of the Four-year-old. Some of these words have been used before, but are especially noteworthy as a group at this age. Typ-

ical are “on top of,” “far away,” “out in,” “down to,” “way up,” “way up there,” “way far,” “out,” “way off,” “way out,” “out in.”

“In,” “on,” “up in,” “at,” and “down” are space words perhaps most often used. As the child climbs on his Jungle Gym he is experiencing all these changes in space, and this may be why a Jungle Gym is such a favorite with Four-year-olds.

A new dimension is suggested in the frequent use of the word “behind.” The Four-year-old tends to be much concerned with the backs of things. He wants a book to have a back as well as a front. And if his book has a house on the front cover, he anticipates that the back of the house will be on the back of the book.

He is especially interested in his own back and hopes he can view it with special mirrors. As two Four-year-olds, enamored of David Brinkley on television, watched him but saw only his front, one of them was heard to say,

"My daddy says David Brinkley has a back, just the way we do."

And, finally, most Fours can now tell both on what street they live and in what city they live. They can put put a ball *on*, *under*, *in front of*, and *in back of a chair.*

SENSE OF NUMBER

The ordinary Four-year-old can count, with correct pointing, three objects. Many are reported to count to ten, though they may start their counting with a number higher than one. Verbal counting, that is, rote counting, without objects, definitely exceeds counting of objects.

Stimulated by television, some children nowadays can count by rote even higher than ten, but this does not in most instances constitute any real understanding of numbers or an ability to count real objects.

Their hands provide at least ten units. Let them use their fingers as they wish. This is the way children learn naturally.

And, Fours love double numbers like 44 or 66 or 77. They also love games that include numbers, as beanbag throwing.

SENSE OF HUMOR

The typical Four-year-old is gloriously humorous. From a loud guffaw to a subtle, sly wink, he runs the gamut of humorous expression.

Nobody will ever appreciate your own humor more—so enjoy yourself while this full appreciation lasts. Enjoy the child's humor and enjoy his enjoyment of your own!

Four loves silly language. He loves the ridiculous. He loves the imaginative. He loves the very fact that *you* have a sense of humor and are making a joke, even when he may not fully understand what the joke is about.

He especially appreciates it when *you* appreciate *him.*

Silly or funny books are among the things he appreciates most, and are among the things that you can enjoy together.

Four is not above the same kind of humorous appreciation one sees at Two and Three—anything that goes wrong: a shoe on the wrong foot, a sweater sleeve that sticks, a hat on backwards.

But he now has moved, also, into the somewhat subtler realms of humor. In his own spontaneous storytelling he demonstrates the kinds of things that seem funny to him. Thus, a Four-year-old child, in his stories, may think very funny something like:

> A car went the wrong way. It broke the ceiling. He ate up her door and her whole house. He ate up hisself. He ate the whole world.
>
> I had a silly dream about a talking tractor.
>
> The mother clowns came. They made funny faces. Boy found anudder monkey and then the monkey did laugh.

By Four-and-a-half, most humor has not proceeded too much farther in the direction of subtlety. In typical stories, children of this age tell us:

> David's mother pulled off my mother's nose. And then my mother pulled off David's mother's nose.
>
> Rabbit, he ran. He got caught in a trap. He couldn't get out of the trap. Ha! Ha!
>
> The girl shook when she took a look. And the tree shook. The whole world shook. A head shook.

The great thing about Four is that he can on occasion be really quite funny from the adult point of view, and even when he isn't, he so enjoys his own humor and is so ready and willing to share his enjoyment and his joke that his attempts at humor are amusing for you as well as for him.

CREATIVITY: SPONTANEOUS STORIES

The ordinary Four-year-old is a great one with language. He loves words—loves to hear them and loves to utter them. Rather surprisingly, then, it may be more difficult for you to get him to tell you a story than it was just a few months earlier. Now he may feel self-conscious about what a story is. Whereas when younger, with fewer words at his command, he might blithely proceed to "tell a story," now he may feel that this requirement is too hard for him.

A little persuasion usually suffices. And once embarked on a story, Four is fluent, glib, and often surprisingly violent. Three-quarters of both boys and girls express some kind of violence in their stories—accident, aggression, harm to objects or people. Falling down seems to be the leading type of violence for girls—boys stress things breaking or broken.

Not only do many bad things happen in Four-year-old stories, but for boys, at least, Four is the low point in the entire preschool range for kind or friendly themes.

Here, as earlier, there is a rather marked difference between the sexes in feelings expressed about parents. Though boys at this age see their mothers as entirely friendly (caring for, providing, sympathizing, protecting), girls seem to see their mothers as primarily disapproving, disciplining, punishing, or hurting them. They see their fathers as friendly. Boys in our group do not mention their father in stories.

Another clear-cut sex difference is that girls talk mostly about mothers or girls in their stories; boys talk about boys.

People who worry about the effect of violence on TV on preschoolers might be surprised to know that small children in their spontaneous storytelling (and this was true long before we even had TV) often rival or outdo the largest amount of violence one may see on the screen.

Girls at Four are more violent in their storytelling than at any other age, earlier or later. Their stories now stress death, killing, things eaten up, objects that crash or fall down or are burned up, children throwing things into the garbage or being spanked or broken to pieces.

Fantasy predominates, and stories have now moved from the home or immediate community and many are laid in unfamiliar or distant places. A typical girl story:

> A little ducky. He fell in the water and he drowned. His mother came along and she picked up her ducky and threw her in the garbage pail. Then a frog came along and swallowed her up. And then the frog was so big he ate up everything. You know what else he ate? He ate the whole world all at once. You know what else he did? He ate up her door and her whole house. And the next morning you know what else he ate? He ate hisself.
>
> Don't grab anything from toys when children have them. Balloons you blow up and sometimes they break. If the ants eat your house and break the stones and make holes in the stairs 'cause they want to live there you can't get into the house. If you eat food and throw the dishes they break and you get spanked. You throw them and cut yourself and you get spanked. You get a needle and punch it right down your arm and then you bleed. If you throw books you get spanked by somebody you don't know.

Boys, too, emphasize themes of violence. Things in their stories are burned up, broken, fall into the water. People are killed, go to the hospital, are kicked, fall, are eaten up, hurt, crash, or die. As with girls, stories are laid primarily in somewhat distant or unfamiliar places, and fantasy predominates over reality. A typical Four-year-old boy story:

> Boy got killed from a rocket. And then another boy came and he got killed from the rocket and then another boy came and he got killed. And then another boy came

and that missile killed him. And then another boy and the snowman came and a girl came. A snowman got on the rocket and went scuffing around and flying away. . . . The car broke. The motor crashed. It crashed into a truck.

CREATIVITY: IN GENERAL

Though some children are by nature much more creative than others, there is a very great deal you can do to encourage creativity in your enthusiastic, outgoing, spontaneous, though sometimes combustible Four-year-old.

Even by Two or Three years of age in some, and quite certainly by Four, you may have determined whether your own particular child is by nature primarily a hearer, a talker, a toucher, a mover; whether he or she is most affected by sounds, colors, words.

Some best show their creativity by combining words, some by combining shapes and colors, some by combining ideas, and some through their own physical movements.

Lise Liepmann, in her own highly creative book—*Your Child's Sensory World*, suggests the following creative opportunities that you might like to provide for these different kinds of children.

The child who primarily experiences through hearing may enjoy listening to music and (later on) creating his own musical sounds. Or, he will enjoy listening to books and stories and then telling his own stories, dictating to a tape recorder, or playing any and all word games.

The primarily visual child may be the one who most enjoys crayoning and painting, and working with paper—especially colored paper—and paste and scissors. And if he has good fine-motor coordination as well, he will enjoy stringing beads in creative design, in making (very simple) models, or playing with Tinkertoys or Lego blocks.

If your child is a toucher, right from the beginning clay and fingerpaint may be his favorite materials. And if he is a mover, dancing, running around, climbing, swinging, sliding, or simple acrobatics—each of which can include its own creative aspects—may provide his favorite forms of self-expression. Or, he may prefer fine-motor to gross-motor activities and may combine imagination with the movements of his hands in finger play or puppets.

These are, of course, just a few of the many things any preschooler may enjoy, and any child may very likely find pleasure in a combination of many different kinds of interests.

It is generally agreed, both by child specialists and by artists themselves, that children are best encouraged in their creativity if you permit much freedom of enterprise. Adults will do best by enjoying and permitting the child's own enjoyment of art works that are less than "perfect" and that do not necessarily resemble what the child set out to make.

Efforts to have them copy from models, and criticisms of less than perfect products, tend to stifle the child's own spontaneous creativity. That he work in any medium with enthusiasm and enjoyment is obviously more important than that he produce some special product.

The young child creates primarily to please himself, but he also likes to please those around him. Admiration and praise can hardly be applied too lavishly when the child is only Four. He loves the things he makes, and he loves to have you praise them.

We sometimes think of creativity in relation chiefly to paint and painting, but as Milton A. Young points out in his imaginative book *Buttons Are to Push*, the young child can create not only with almost any conceivable material or equipment, but he can create without any material or equipment other than his own often vivid imagination. Some children show perhaps their greatest creativity in their spontaneous play with their imaginary companions—human or animal—or in their own impersonation of an animal.

If you want to give your child what we *usually* think of as a good opportunity to develop his creativity, you will provide crayons and paper, fingerpaints and paper, or waterpaints and paper. By Four years of age, some of the products he will make with these will be pleasing to him and may even seem attractive to you, his parents. Modeling clay, too, provides a customary and gratifying medium for creative and artistic expression. Puppets please many.

But there are many other things you can do to encour-

age creativity in your preschooler. Here are some of the special activities that Young and others recommend. Most of you will also have your own favorites.

Go for a walk and talk about the things you see.

Suggest that your child look for shapes in the clouds.

Watch birds together and try to identify them. Build bird feeders, birdhouses.

Make a (simple) treasure map and then have the child follow the map to find a treasure.

Play hunting games with "hot" and "cold" for clues as to whether the child is getting nearer to or farther from the object sought.

Help your child keep a notebook. It could be a notebook of birds, of flowers, of cars. Or, it could be a notebook about the trips and excursions you take together. He could cut out and paste in pictures himself. The text or titles, he could dictate to you.

Ask your child to draw a picture of an animal that does not live on this planet, and to explain how it lives.

Or, put several common household objects in a bag and tell the child to feel them (without looking at them) and to identify each one. Then ask him to make up a story, including each one.

Play simple word games, asking your child to name all the things that can fly, all the things that are red or green or blue, things that rhyme with certain words.

Ask him to describe something without looking at it.

Ask him to be very quiet and then listen to the sounds he hears and tell you about them.

Start a two-line poem and ask the child to think of a final word to rhyme with the last word of the first line.

Present your child with a simple problem situation—what would he do if such-and-such a (simple) crisis should arise.

Actually you don't have to ask a Four-year-old to tell you a story, or even play word games or set up such specially stimulating situations as listed above. If you have an imaginative child (and most Fours seem to be highly imaginative) and have even an ounce of imagination yourself, just a plain conversation with a child of this age can be fun for you both. Four is so appreciative that he quite inspires an even halfway imaginative adult. Few people will ever be so appreciative as he of your slightest whimsy.

If he's telling you about all the magic things the Black Knight can do, ask him if he knows about the Green Knight. He'll be delighted if you tell him that the wicked Green Knight steals a little boy's shoes and his parents think that *he* has lost them.

Or, he will tell you, if indoctrinated by a religious grandparent, that if the Devil punches *him*, he will kill the Devil with his shining sword. He will listen with interest while you explain that, so far as you know, the Devil harms children not by punching them but by *tempting* them. A discussion of temptation can be long and fruitful.

You don't need toys or even books, you need only words —yours and his—to have a more than satisfactory playtime with a typically lively and imaginative Four-year-old. Each family may have its own special imaginative games. After swimming, one boy we knew liked to lie down on the sand, all covered up with towels, pretending he was a cocoon. When you touched the cocoon gently, you could see a butterfly emerging. It began by his lifting one arm and leg under the towel, stopped if you approached too quickly, and closed up again. This activity repeated itself until finally a beautiful butterfly was there in all its glory. (But you had to watch out, for it could turn into a poisonous insect if it chose. Anything can happen, with a Four-year old!)

Or, finally, though some may not go along with the idea, you could watch selected television programs together and then talk about *them*.

Whatever you choose, try not to formalize any of these creative activities. Keep the situation fluid and be very careful about your timing. When the child's interest fades, it's clearly time to stop.

chapter eight
INDIVIDUALITY

We have been describing ways the Four-year-old may be expected to behave. But this does not mean for a minute that all Four-year-olds will actually behave in these ways. *Every child is an individual and different from every other child*, even from others of his own age, sex, or background.

There are many different ways of looking at personality and of describing individual differences—some systematic, some hit-or-miss. Though in this chapter we shall lean mostly on the systematic classifications of constitutional psychology as offered by Dr. William H. Sheldon, in his book *Varieties of Temperament*, we would like to remind you of some of these special differences we mentioned in our earlier book on *Your Three-Year-Old*.

Some of you might like to check on your own boy or girl to see if he or she is one who could be described as having high drive and high energy, or low drive and limited energy. You could check to see if he is one who might be described as highly focal, tending to concentrate on a single activity, or, if of a more peripheral nature, he finds it hard to concentrate and settle down.

Is he a perseverator—one who goes on and on with some single activity—or is he one who tires easily of any one task or situation and flits quickly on to something else?

Is your child one who organizes from within, or is he

chiefly influenced by people and things around him? Is he one who starts himself, or do you have to wind him up and start him?

Is he one who is mostly influenced and controlled by his intellect, or does he work mostly through emotions? That is, can you appeal to him intellectually, or do you merely work on his feelings?

Is your son or daughter one who adapts very easily to the environment, or does the environment have to do the adapting?

Is he speedy or slow? Is she messy or spotless? Does he look forward or backward, do best if you warn in advance or if you spring things at the very last moment?

Is he a perfectionist, never satisfied unless everything is perfect? Or is he casual and careless, quite satisfied with a lick and a promise and then on to something else?

These are but a few of the dimensions of difference that you might like to identify, and then respect. You yourself can probably think of many other pairs of characteristics and then identify your own boy or girl as being like one or the other of the pair.

A more systematic approach to the fascinating area of individual or personality differences is that offered by Dr. Sheldon. His system of constitutional psychology proposes that behavior is a function of structure and that we can to quite an extent predict how any child will behave from an observation of what his body is like. Though no individual is *all* one thing or another, there are three main components that go to make up the human constitution, and in most people one or the other does predominate.

These three components are endomorphy, mesomorphy, and ectomorphy. The body of the endomorph is round and soft; that of the mesomorph hard and square; that of the ectomorph linear, fragile, and delicate.

In the *endomorph*, arms and legs are relatively short as compared with the trunk, with the upper part of the arm longer than the lower part. Hands and feet are small and plump. Fingers are short and tapering. In the *mesomorph*, extremities are large and massive, with upper arm and leg equal to lower arm and leg in length. Hands and wrists are large, fingers squarish. In the *ectomorph*, arms and legs are long compared with the body, the lower arm longer than the upper arm. Hands and feet are slender and fragile, with pointed fingertips.

Recognizing your own child's body type and knowing

how endomorphs or mesomorphs or ectomorphs customarily behave, or are thought to behave, may help you fit your own expectations closer to reality than might otherwise be the case. It is sometimes easier to understand and accept your child's behavior if you believe that he behaves as he does because of the way his body is built rather than if you think that sometimes less than ideal behavior is either your fault or his.

According to Sheldon, then, the endomorphic individual is one who attends and exercises *in order to eat.* Eating is his primary pleasure. The mesomorph attends and eats *in order to exercise.* What he likes best is athletic activity and competitive action. The ectomorph, on the other hand, exercises (as little as possible), and eats (with indifference) *in order to attend.* Watching, listening, thinking about things, and being aware are his most enjoyable activities.

Another clue to the differences among these three types is that when in trouble the endomorph seeks people, the mesomorph seeks activity, the ectomorph withdraws and prefers to be by himself.

Time orientation, too, is something that may vary with physical structure. Our experience has been that the endomorph tends to be most interested in the here-and-now. The mesomorph seems to be forward looking. The next thing or the new thing is what interests him. The ectomorph seems interested in past as well as future.

It may help you to identify and to know what to expect of your own boy or girl if we tell you something about the way children of each of these three kinds of personality behave in ordinary life situations. Even in things as basic as eating and sleeping and relating to others, we see big differences.

EATING

The typical *endomorph* loves food. He may almost be said to live to eat, and he will eat almost anything. Even when not eating, he likes to be doing something with his mouth like chewing gum, sucking a lollipop, or enjoying a nice soft drink. Mealtime is seldom a problem with such a child, except that he may tend to eat too much, too often.

The *mesomorphic* boy or girl is less enthusiastic about food but still tends to have a big appetite. If you do not, by your insistence on certain specially disliked foods, spoil things, the mesomorph, as a rule, does not give too much difficulty in the food department. He consumes large quantities of food and usually eats rapidly.

Not so with the *ectomorph.* Mealtimes for him may be the hardest time of day. Appetite tends to be very, very small, and even the mere sight of a plate heaped with food may turn off what little appetite he has. Color and texture of food may also turn him off. He may refuse to eat anything mushy, or lumpy, or of the wrong color, as, for instance, "Those little green balls [peas]."

The ectomorph can live and thrive on much less food than most parents think he needs; and five small snack-meals a day might suit him better than the customary three large ones. Don't push, and he will as a rule comfortably decide on his own nutritional needs.

SLEEPING

The *endomorph* not only loves to eat but as a rule he also loves to sleep. He snuggles down contentedly with his thumb or teddy bear, and enjoys nap or night sleep, lying limp and sprawled in almost any position.

The *mesomorph*, as a rule, is also a good sleeper. He drops off to sleep quickly and easily, sleeps soundly though often with much thrashing around. He often seems to need less sleep than do other children, and is one who wakes quickly and easily, jumps out of bed and then wakens you, cheerfully, at 6:00 A.M. or even earlier.

The *ectomorph* has trouble with sleeping, as with eating. He finds it hard to get to sleep but once asleep finds it hard in the morning to wake up and get going. He needs a great deal of sleep, but it is hard for him to fall asleep unless he is close to physical exhaustion. He sleeps lightly and dreams a great deal. That is, his relaxation, even in deepest sleep, is incomplete.

REACTION TO OTHER PEOPLE

The *endomorph* likes people, and people like him. He is warm and friendly with others, and they tend to feel relaxed and comfortable when they are with him. He does not, even as a young child, like to be alone.

The *mesomorph* likes people, too, but he is nowhere near as dependent on their company as is the endomorph. However, he usually has plenty of friends and is a natural-born leader, even in his preschool years. As a rule, other people have to adapt to *him*. He gets on best as a leader or as the one the others look up to. He likes others primarily because of the things they can do, because of the activities they can enjoy together.

The *ectomorph*, in contrast to the other two, has a strong need for privacy. He likes to be alone and dislikes to be socially involved. If he has a choice—which the young child does not always have—the ectomorph avoids being too much involved with other people. He tends to be distressed, uncomfortable, anxious, and shy in social relationships, as in nursery school, where he relates better to the teacher than to the other children.

EMOTIONS

In this respect as in others, unless we know our own child well and know what it is reasonable to expect of him and what his behavior really means, we are apt to misjudge him. It is important for parents to know that the typical *endomorph* expresses his emotions fully and freely. He may cry as if his heart will break, but then gets over it quickly. He is easily comforted with kisses and hugs. Loud howls do not necessarily mean that he is in great difficulty.

The *ectomorph,* even as a very young child, finds it much harder to express his emotions. He may suffer deeply without shedding a tear. Parents and teachers need to keep an eye on him, since it may be hard for him to show when he is in trouble. If he does break down and cry, especially in nursery school, it may embarrass him deeply. It is difficult to comfort him because it is hard for him to accept physical comforting.

He is the child who minds terribly if he does not get his "turn," but may find it extremely difficult to *ask* for a turn. He needs more help and support emotionally than do other children.

Things are quite different with the *mesomorph,* who may be characterized as one whose emotions are best expressed in his love of power. He loves to compete, to dominate, to command, to conquer. He has great push, drive, and energy. He is *not* sensitive to the feelings of others, and seems himself almost insensitive to pain. He is courageous and likes to lead. If angry or upset, he tends to take it out on somebody, usually his mother or a younger sibling.

PROBLEMS

Here are some of the things that cause parents the most anxiety about behaviors characteristic of children of different body types:

The *endomorph,* typically jolly, friendly, and well adjusted, does not, as a rule, pose any great problem to his parents. As a baby, such a child is often described as unusually "good." He eats well, sleeps well, and seems to love life. As he grows older, he gets on well with most everybody. He is a nice kind of child to have around.

If parents, too, are of this temperament, there is not much to worry about. But if parents are more ambitious, then they do tend to worry that their endomorphic child does not try hard enough, does not compete. They consider him lazy, and even in the preschool years his lack of drive may cause them (not him) anxiety. Try to accept the fact that great drive and extreme good nature seldom go hand in hand.

The *mesomorph*, on the other hand, especially in the preschool years before he learns to channel his great energy into acceptable lines, can be a great source of anxiety to his parents. He tends to be constantly active, into everything, highly destructive. His hands must touch everything he sees, and he seems to break nearly everything he touches. His mother is worn out just trying to keep up with him, and he easily earns the reputation of being "the worst child in the neighborhood." Though he usually gets on well with contemporaries (he bosses them around and is looked up to as a leader), he tends to lack sensitivity and thus may be hard to reach. One thing that makes him a lot of trouble to adults is that he is so very loud and noisy.

Though this has its good side as well as its bad, all things seem to suggest action to him. A stick is something to pound with, a flower is something to pick or smell. He may even activate his nouns and say, "It's winding outside." The onrush and speed of his thinking may make him go through periods of mumbling hesitancy, which is not the same as stuttering.

He loves action words: "crash," "bang," "boom." He early and accurately knows the position of things in space. Kinesthetically he feels the positions of on, under, and behind. But it is hard for him to stop and think, for he wants to translate everything into immediate action. He tends to be very speedy, shifts quickly and easily from one activity to another, and does not like to be required to slow down and repeat.

He needs much opportunity for active play, especially outdoor play. He needs somebody strong and tireless to play with him. He needs adults who enjoy rather than suffer from his displays of boundless energy.

The *ectomorph* causes anxiety for quite another reason. He is likely to suffer feeding disturbances and also often has sleeping problems. He may have more than his share of allergies. What worries parents most, however, is his oversensitivity, his social shyness, his immaturity, and the fact that he may not seem to need people. All these things combine to make it hard for him to make friends. Keep in mind that this kind of child needs time alone. He needs people who understand his quietness and shyness. He especially needs parents who will not push him into athletic and social activities for which he may be unsuited.

UNDERSTANDING YOUR CHILD FOR WHAT HE IS

If you have been blessed with an *endomorph*, try to enjoy his warmth and friendliness. Don't push him too hard. He may never be a real go-getter, but if you can accept him for what he is, you and he will both be happy.

With your energetic, trouble-prone *mesomorph*, since spanking and corporal punishment may have only momentary effect, concentrate more on supervision and on providing legitimate outlets for his boundless energy. Try not to "see" everything that happens. You cannot punish him for every "bad" thing he does—there will be too many. Praise him for the good things he does in order to encourage him to repeat them.

Try to keep your equilibrium, protect your property and your child from physical harm, and see that you have some relief every day (school or baby-sitter). Keep in mind that the mesomorphic drive that makes so much trouble now may in later life lead him to great success.

Get as many secure locks as possible to protect medicine and any other dangerous or fragile items in your house. Put other things as high as possible. Give this child a good supply of things to be messy with—clay, dough, paint, sand, water, soap. Also, provide as much equipment as possible for the outlet of gross motor energy—a Jungle Gym, bouncing board, doorway swing.

And now for the *ectomorph*. How can you best help him? One thing is to keep in mind that this boy or girl, though often quite bright, matures slowly. Don't worry about this or about his lack of social success. Later on he may catch up with, or even surpass, in some ways, those who got an earlier start. But most of all, and this is especially important for fathers, let this kind of child know that you like him and appreciate him even if he is not athletic and outgoing, even if he is diffident and shy, even if very small things that go wrong seem to bother him unduly.

A special warning about body types. In trying to figure out your own child's physical type, it is important for you to remember that people are not *all* one thing or another, but rather are a *mixture* of all three components described. It is just that unless a child is unusually well balanced, one component or the other (endomorphy, mesomorphy, or ectomorphy) tends to predominate and in all likelihood will have the most influence on what he will be like.

A further warning about the importance of appreciating the effects of the interaction between heredity (or, in this instance, basic body type) and environment is probably necessary. This is so because many people mistakenly interpret both the Sheldon and the Gesell points of view as ignoring the effect of the environment on the human organism.

Dr. Arnold Gesell first gave this warning back in 1940 when he stated explicitly:

> In appraising growth characteristics we must not ignore environmental influences—cultural milieu, siblings, parents, food, illness, trauma, education. But these must always be considered in relation to primary or constitutional factors, because the latter ultimately determine the degree, and even the mode of reaction to the environment. The organism always participates in the creation of its environment, and the growth char-

acteristics of the child are really the end-product expressions of an *interaction* between intrinsic and extrinsic determiners. Because the *interaction* is the crux, the distinction between these two sets of determiners should not be too heavily drawn.[6]

SENSE OF SELF

One extremely important part of any child's individuality, and one about which adults are becoming increasingly concerned, is his sense of self or the way he feels about himself. Parental emphasis is shifting, somewhat, from interest in the child's accomplishments—having him do the "right" thing—to his feelings about himself as a person.

Clearly, two of the best ways to make a child feel good about himself are to let him know that you like him—that he pleases you—and to help see to it that much of the time he encounters situations in which he can perform successfully.

The better you understand your child as a person, with all his strong points and his weak ones, the more effectively you can manage to see that much of the time he will be successful.

It is here that a good understanding of the child's physical body, and how that body may in general be expected to behave, can be so useful. If you have a fairly good understanding of what is and is not reasonable to expect of your child in the way of behavior, it will help you do a better job of letting him be his best self and not trying to twist him out of shape in an effort to have him accomplish the impossible. You can help him to be a good person of his own kind without trying to make him into something he can never be.

As you read our descriptions of the endomorph, mesomorph, and ectomorph you will perhaps appreciate the fruitlessness of trying to change an ectomorph into an endomorph, or an endomorph into mesomorph. And having understood your child *yourself* during his formative years, hopefully you may, when he grows older, help him to understand *himself*.

But a person's very physical structure will to some extent limit the extent to which he will, early or late, take an interest in his own individuality. The typical mesomorph acts—without too much introspection. The typical endomorph feels—without perhaps worrying too much about his own self or his own personality. It is the sensitive ectomorph who perhaps is most concerned about and most interested in his own individuality, in himself as a person. Even in this respect children vary, and every child is an individual.

chapter nine

STORIES FROM REAL LIFE

MOTHER CAN'T STAND HER FOUR-YEAR-OLD

Dear Doctors:

When I was a teenager I remember reading something about how wild Four-year-olds are. Little did I realize that in just a few years I would be the mother of one of these little monsters.

Our daughter Sandy is terribly fresh, rude, hard to manage. She seems to accept no limits. Sometimes she exasperates me to the point of active dislike. She is bright and affectionate with others and is no bother when visiting. But in our house I can't stand her positive manner and her insistence on always having her own way. She loves lipstick and dressing up in adult clothes. How I hate to hear her clumping around in those shoes!

For a while we sent her to nursery school because I couldn't cope with her. Fortunately she does get on well with her dad. I would appreciate any suggestions as she is really spoiling my life to the point of quiet desperation.

Your very best bet in calming down any Four-year-old's wilder ways is to ignore them as much as you possibly can. At least some of their wildness is to attract attention, and if nobody cares, what's the fun?

An opposite technique is that, if your daughter is being exaggerated and silly, you go even farther in exaggeration and silliness. She will love it, and you may both have fun.

You say that Sandy will accept no limits. Have you tried specific directions: "as far as the gate," "when the big hand on the clock is at the top," "It's the rule that you mustn't throw toys"? Many will accept such directions. Or, in a more positive vein, try going along with Four's love of newness and adventure. Take your daughter on trips, take her on excursions, especially since you say she is good when visiting.

Take advantage of the Four-year-old's love of praise. Find something to praise Sandy for, and praise her lavishly. Take advantage of the child's love of "tricks" and new ways of doing things to liven up your daily routines.

There are many little girls, like Sandy, whose lives, at Four, seem to be spent in dress-up dresses, walking around in high-heeled shoes, or wearing old lace curtains, wanting to wear fingernail polish and even lipstick. This kind of play is pretty tiresome to watch, but if it can be used in a dramatic way, it can be contained within rather specific time intervals; and if you can bring yourself to take part, it can be less wearing for you and more fun for her. Have a box of special clothes and a special time for dressing up.

Since Sandy gets on well with her father, try to persuade him to take her for occasional Saturday or Sunday excursions. Even short periods when you are completely free of her presence can do a lot toward giving you a better attitude toward your demanding daughter.

We don't blame any mother for feeling at least temporary dislike for some one of her children. But remember, *you are the only mother she has.* For her to feel that certain of her specific behaviors annoy you, and won't be permitted, is reasonable. But it would be pretty tragic for her if she believed that you really did not like her.

FOUR-YEAR-OLDS DON'T ALWAYS TELL THE TRUTH

Dear Doctors:

I am very much concerned about my Four-year-old son, our first and so far our only child. My wife and I are churchgoing people, and we have very strong standards of right and wrong. We have always impressed on Irwin the importance of telling the truth.

But the other day, when my wife caught him misbehaving, within the first five minutes of questioning he had five different lies about what had actually happened. Where and how did we go wrong? How can we impress on Irwin that he must tell the truth?

You can impress on Irwin that he must tell the truth by continuing as you have begun. Maintain your own firm standards of right and wrong, set a good example for him, and, when the occasion arises, emphasize to him the importance of truth.

And then you wait. The majority of Four-year-olds do not always tell the truth. Four is a time when children boast and brag and exaggerate, and, above all, lie. No matter how good your example or your teaching, most Fours are not ready to tell all of the truth all of the time.

Our guess is that both you and your wife perhaps need to know much more than you do about how normal children develop.

THERE'S NOTHING WRONG WITH HAVING AN IMAGINARY COMPANION

Dear Doctors:

My husband and I are the somewhat older parents of an only child, a Four-year-old boy named Jonathan. He has been a delight to us, and we try to be good parents, though sometimes we feel we don't know as much as we should about children.

Only one aspect of his behavior troubles us, and has

done so for the past eight months. Though Jonathan has plenty of friends to play with in the neighborhood, he devotes most of his time, and his interest, to a purely imaginary playmate named Tulipka. Tulipka not only takes up vast amounts of his time, but she rules our household.

If Tulipka won't go on a walk or auto ride, Jonathan won't go, either. If Tulipka doesn't like a certain food, Jonathan won't eat it, either. Etc. This goes on all day long, every day.

Our friends and our pediatrician give widely differing advice about this strange phenomenon. This varies as follows:

a) The behavior is normal,

b) It is a sign that Jonathan is emotionally disturbed since he can't distinguish reality from unreality,

c) Jonathan plays this way because he is an only child and thus lonely. Some feel we should permit the behavior, or even encourage it; others say we should stop it. Can you advise?

We vote for (a); that is, we believe the behavior is normal. It is by no means a sign that Jonathan is lonely, but rather suggests that he is a highly imaginative and probably intelligent youngster who is clinging, a bit long and hard, to an extremely typical Three-and-a-half-year-old kind of behavior. Some of the most superior boys and girls that we have known do enjoy their imaginary companions.

We can practically guarantee that the behavior will drop out, or most certainly diminish, within the next few months. In the meantime, take advantage of it while it lasts. If you want him to do something, tell him—quickly, before Tulipka has a chance to object—that Tulipka does this particular thing so nicely. Or, suggest that "You and Tulipka might like to come out for a nice walk." Use her as an ally, not an enemy. And don't worry.

BABY-SITTER, TIME WITH DAD, SUGGESTED AS SOLUTIONS TO WHINING PROBLEM

Dear Doctors:

My problem, in one word, is whining!

Jacob is Four and has whined on and off for the last several years. It was very bad at Three-and-a-half, dropped off a bit, and now is ten times as bad as ever.

We hoped nursery school would help. It does. But he goes only three mornings a week, and the days he is at home are brutal. If I stop my housework and spend time with him, he is fine for ten minutes. Then he says, "Go back to your ironing, Mommy." But then the whining starts again.

Unfortunately, I don't have a car, so can't take him with me shopping and visiting, which he loves. He has no other tensional outlet except whining.

Possibly whining has driven more mothers over the brink than anything else. Fortunately, it seems to come and go with Jacob. You can hope for an improvement by Five.

In the meantime, we think you'll have to plan your days, when he isn't in nursery school, with a little more time with Jacob and a little less with housework.

You say you haven't a car, but surely there are short excursions near home that you can arrange to satisfy him. A very small thing makes a big excursion for a little boy. Just to watch some excavation; a short trip to some neighborhood store; whatever your neighborhood offers.

You say he is sociable, and most Fours love to visit. Do you have any neighbors who would receive him for a short visit if you planned it with them?

Also, we think that Jacob would be less likely to whine with a baby-sitter than with you. Could you plan, say, two afternoons a week after his nap, to have somebody come and take him out for an hour or two?

Tired children tend to whine most at the end of the day when you are getting dinner. Possibly you could have the sitter come late instead of early. Or, perhaps you could arrange to feed Jacob early and get him to bed before that bad five-to-seven-o'clock hour when everybody in the family is likely to be at his worst.

All of this planning is not guaranteed to make your son less whiny. But he is *much less likely* to whine when he is rather fully occupied. On weekends we hope his father can take a turn. Most boys don't whine when they're out alone with their fathers.

FOUR-YEAR-OLD WON'T EAT

Dear Doctors:

I have three children, a girl of Six and two boys—a Four-year-old and one who is ten months old. The Four-year-old boy presents all my problems. He refuses to eat. Last year we brought him to a doctor for a check-up as he was always complaining of a stomachache at mealtimes. The doctor told us there was nothing wrong with him physically and suggested we ignore him and that he would eat when he got hungry.

Well, for several months we went along with the doctor's suggestion, ignoring his threats of "I'm not eating tonight." He ate just what he liked—salad and desserts. This method of ignoring him did not help. Really, he eats almost nothing! I believe it only shrank his stomach up. He still wouldn't eat the proper foods.

So, back to the old routine of forcing him, bribing, punishing.

Does every mother have to go through this? My girl never presented this problem. Please tell me what you suggest as we are getting so we dread mealtime with him around. He will eat when he visits his aunt and we're not there. We can't let him starve to death. Can you suggest some method we haven't tried?

We'd like to answer in the words of another mother who had your same problem. Here is what she suggests:

1. The hardest part is for the mother and dad to change

their attitude. I myself used to feel desperate, too. After you've checked with your doctor that your child is healthy even though he doesn't eat much, accept it.

2. Don't keep any sweets around. Exclude them entirely except for birthdays. We used to wait for our dessert and coffee until our three boys were in bed.

3. Unless it is much more convenient to serve him alone, feed your noneater with the family. I used to feel far worse when I had especially prepared something for the little darling and then he didn't eat it.

4. Give the small eater only a half teaspoon of everything and say nothing. Be prepared to scrape the plate into the garbage for quite a while.

5. Don't you two sit there eating and watching him. Plan your conversation ahead of time if you must so you can keep it going easily.

6. Excuse him with a smile even if he has only just arrived at the table, if he wants to get down.

7. We didn't let our boys help themselves because they think dishing up is great fun but usually can't eat as much as they take. This same thing often applies to choosing their own menus. It may work out to let them choose between two kinds of fruit or two kinds of vegetable. Complete freedom of choice often ends up with difficult or peculiar menus, which they may not eat even after they have chosen them.

8. Between-meal snacks seem to be an individual matter. Our boys ate just as much, or rather as little, for meals whether they had them or not, so we allowed nourishing snacks. Raisins, fruit juices, and crackers were favorites.

9. A few foods you may not have tried yet for snacks or part of the meal: one or two dried prunes or figs; a small amount of grated American cheese; an egg beaten up in orange juice, or in milk with vanilla and sugar. Serve only half a glassful, with a colored straw. Popcorn made at home is good, also quartered apples.

10. The most important thing is to realize what a very *small* appetite many children have.

GIRL PULLS COVERS OVER HEAD AT BEDTIME

Dear Doctors:

I have read your writings for several years and marvel at your solutions for people who seem to need them. I hope you can do the same for me.

I have what I think is a problem with my Four-and-a-half-year-old daughter Martha. It just started recently. When she goes to sleep at night she has to have her head covered up, no matter what the weather.

If she sleeps with someone else, or takes her nap in the daytime, she doesn't cover her head. Just at night if she is alone. I have talked with her, warned her that she may smother, even spanked her, but it does no good. She waits until she thinks everyone is asleep and then covers her head. I've asked her if she is afraid of something, but she says no.

Is this just a stage? If not, how can I stop her?

Martha's rather odd bedtime behavior is probably just a stage, though admittedly you don't want her to smother while she is going through this stage.

Actually your daughter is solving her Four-year-old problem rather nicely. She is just blotting out all visual stimuli. This is a stage when many children are very much aware of shadows or of moving lights. Even figured wallpaper may seem to move. Sometimes they are awakened when car lights suddenly flash through their window.

When a child has this trouble of adjusting to light and shadows, we are cautious about where her bed is placed in the room, so that she isn't looking into the window. Or, shades can keep out light stimuli. But then the darkness may be too intense, so that you may wish to relieve it by a baseboard low-voltage light that will not cast shadows. Or, leave the door ajar into the hall, where a light may be kept on.

You may be able to purchase one of those little phosphorescent figures or pictures that many children love.

These give off light and also give a feeling of companionship.

We have never heard of a child suffocating when she chose to keep the covers over her head, though parents may feel more comfortable if she uses one of the more porous blankets. But we would recommend trying to find out just why your daughter does this. The presence of another person seems to dispel her fears, which suggests that they are not too deep-seated.

REASSURANCE, STORYTELLING MAY HELP CHILD FRIGHTENED BY NIGHTMARES

Dear Doctors:

My Four-and-a-half-year-old daughter Andrea has been waking up about an hour after she gets to sleep, with nightmares. She cries, trembles, pulls at her bangs, and seems terribly nervous and upset. Her speech is incoherent, and she has difficulty telling me what's the matter.

Last night she was asking me, "Where is Andrea?" I explained to her that she was Andrea. I can usually quiet her, but often she just gets to sleep and then goes through the whole thing again. She thinks bugs are crawling in her bed.

Our doctor prescribed a nerve tonic, but it hasn't helped too much. During the day she is fine. She is devoted to her twin brother and plays well with him and with a younger sister, though she won't stand up for herself. Rather, in any quarrel, she throws herself on the floor and cries.

It may be that I'm making too much of this, but I would appreciate an opinion.

Nightmares are common to Four-year-olds. We doubt that anything is seriously wrong, but it is disquieting. Andrea may need to build up a little more stamina in playing with her siblings, but her nightmares are not unusual for a girl of this age. And they may continue for the next several years.

Her frightened, bewildered manner naturally frightens you. But about all you can do—aside from trying to see that her days are happy, well filled, and not too demanding or exciting—is what you have been doing. Comfort her, soothe her, talk to her, and then put her back to bed.

Some children are soothed at such times by a little food or drink, or by washing their faces with cold water. Taking them out of their bed and into other surroundings often helps.

As to the bugs and things in her room and bed, these, too, are quite common. Some parents do best by assuring the child that there aren't really any bugs. Others get best results by shooing wild beasts away, brushing the bugs out of the bed, either with their hand or with a whisk broom. Andrea might like and might benefit by hearing a very good bedtime book called *Bedtime for Frances*, by Russell Hoban.

Thus, from a practical point of view, about all you can do is continue what you have been doing. See that she has a nice, relaxed, cozy bedtime period, with reading from her favorite books, the usual kissing and goodnight wishes along with her prayers.

However, don't forget that all fear is not necessarily unpleasant to children. One little Three-and-a-half-year-old we know told us one day that he was afraid of everything, "even my own name." He added, "Major [his dog] scares me. Even dreams scare me." He reported with satisfaction that alligators sometimes bit him in his dreams.

At any rate, nightmares at Four are natural and probably harmless, even though possibly a little unsettling to all concerned.

MOTHER HAS FOUR WET CHILDREN

Dear Doctors:

Like the "bed-wetting family" you wrote about recently, I have four wet children. I resigned myself to letting them grow out of it, thinking it was common. But is it?

My biggest problem right now is my Four-year-old girl Tammy. She still wets at night, but like the others she at least would wear rubber pants, which kept the bed fairly dry. However, the other day she ran outdoors the first thing. A Five-year-old neighbor saw the rubber pants and taunted her, "Baby pants! Baby pants!" That did it.

Since then she won't wear rubber pants, just diapers. So, each night she wets right through her diaper and floods the bed. I had never thought too much about the whole thing before. But I began to wonder. So I conducted a neighborhood survey of thirty families with forty-one kids past Three years.

Here's what I found: Twenty-nine were dry at night as early as Three years of age; thirty-eight were dry by Three-and-a-half; forty of the forty-one were dry at night by Four years.

Yet, all the stores sell the Four-year-old size of rubber pants. Either my own children are unusual, or most parents are ashamed to admit the truth, even in this enlightened day. Can you tell me where to get accurate information about the percentage of Four-year-olds who are not yet dry?

We doubt that the percentages you ask for are available. However, a parent would be insecure indeed if she needed percentages to convince her of the simple and generally accepted fact that it is not unusual for a Four-year-old to be wet at night.

As to the figures you gathered, either the forty-one children in your neighborhood are unusual, or their mothers are less than truthful. It is not at all unusual for Three-year-olds, Four-year-olds, Five-year-olds, and even Six-year-olds to be wet at night. Rubber pants for Four-year-olds are available because they sell. We receive more letters asking how to dry up Four- and Five- and Six-year-olds than any other single question asked.

We assume that you do use a rubber sheet on Tammy's bed. Could you get her to go back to rubber pants by providing shortie nightgowns with matching pants but telling her that she can't have the matching pants unless she wears her rubber pants underneath? You may easily have a year or more to go, and that would be a lot of wet beds.

How old are your other three bed-wetting children? If they are younger, you have your hands full. If they are older, you'd better think of using one of the conditioning devices mentioned in the following letter.

CONDITIONING DEVICE MAY HELP OLDER BED WETTERS

Dear Doctors:

I read in the paper about a mother who made her Five-year-old son stay in his room and do without food because he wet his bed. I have a Four-year-old girl who also wet the bed until I found a product to help her.

I called in about an ad in the paper about bed wetting. Believe me, it was out of this world to rent ($300 a month, with a year's guarantee). In thirty days the child is supposed to have stopped. However, I was then told that one of the department stores had a similar device. I called and found out that they put one out for under $50. It is battery operated with two tinfoil sheets and a separating pad. A buzzer sounds as the child starts wetting. (The tinfoil sheets can be replaced very cheaply if necessary.)

More people should be informed about this. I used it on my daughter, and three weeks to the day she was broken of wetting her bed. I also showed this to my doctor, who had never heard of it. I now have ours stored in our cupboard, should we ever need it again.

I wish more people knew about this product. It would help lots of bed wetters because the buzzer rings until the person gets up and shuts it off.

We are glad to quote your letter because we believe that your experience may be helpful to many who face this problem of bedwetting and do not already know about the several excellent conditioning devices now on the market.

There has, unfortunately, been a school of psychological and medical thought that holds that bedwetting is a sign of emotional disturbance, and that since it is a symptom of trouble, if you clear up the symptom, you still have the trouble.

Now it is certainly possible that a child who is emotionally disturbed may, among other difficulties, be a bed wetter. But we know of no evidence to prove that all bed wetters are emotionally disturbed or that emotional disturbance necessarily has anything to do with bedwetting. It has been our experience that some children are just naturally late in attaining dryness, just as others talk late or walk late.

Age is generally the biggest problem solver when there is late wetness. Thus, we ourselves prefer to wait until a child is at least Six (preferably Seven) before stepping in with outside help, such as the kind of device that this mother mentions. By Six or Seven, however, many parents do find that even a week or two with one of these mechanical devices will bring about the desired dryness.

With a few children who are thus dried up, there may be a relapse, and the conditioning device must again be resorted to. With others, the dryness, once achieved, is permanent.

These conditioning devices come in all prices, so it is easy for any family to pick out one they can afford. It is best to use them under the guidance of your own pediatrician if you are fortunate enough to have one who approves of them. Among those which we like best are one called U-Trol, sold for $47.95 by J. G. Shuman Associates, Box 306, Scotch Plains, New Jersey 07076; and Dry-O-Matic, sold for $39.95 by the Dry-O-Matic Company, 10055 Nadine, Huntington Woods, Michigan 48070.

DIFFICULT TO STOP THUMB SUCKING IN EARLY YEARS

Dear Doctors:

My Four-year-old daughter Donna constantly sucks her thumb. My dentist recommends that she stop this habit now. Is there any advice you can give me about this problem? Or, better yet, do you know of any device I may use to help my child correct this habit?

Some dentists do indeed take a very dim view of thumb sucking. But most today seem to believe that if sucking of an intense nature stops before the second teeth come in, probably little harm will be done if Nature has lined the teeth up straight to begin with.

Our own preference is not to make too much of the whole thing, certainly in the years before Six or so. Most children realize that their parents do not especially favor this behavior. Many by Five or Six are old enough to accept the rule that if they want to suck their thumb, they must go into their own room to do it.

Earlier, how much effort you make to stop the sucking can best be determined by the extensity and intensity of the behavior. If you have a child who sucks much of the day and most of the night, chances are your efforts to terminate the behavior will not be effective. And if you talk too much about it too soon, the child will become deaf to the sound of your voice later on when you might otherwise have had a chance.

Yes, there are devices, rather horrible-looking little wire devices, which can be fastened to the roof of the child's mouth and which then scratch the thumb as the child sucks. We have never recommended these, but your doctor might provide one if you wish.

Our own feeling is that if the child needs the comfort of his thumb, perhaps he's lucky that nature provided this handy device for consoling oneself. Most children no longer suck much in the daytime after they start school.

If sucking does persist on into the school years, then

the child may be old enough to plan with you for ways that will help him give up his habit. Four is not, in our opinion, a very good age to make an issue, but it can be an age when a child often restricts sucking to going to sleep. This suggests it is on its way out.

Many mothers now call thumb sucking a *tensional outlet* rather than a *bad habit*, and are not hostile to it. And there is now available a very comforting little book called *Danny and His Thumb*, by Kathryn Ernst, which actually goes so far as to assure young thumb suckers that their behavior is all right and urges them not to worry about it.

HOW TO TELL BOY ABOUT NEW BABY

> Dear Doctors:
>
> Our Four-year-old son Kenny has been the only one so far. Now we are expecting a baby. Though I am already six months pregnant, Kenny hasn't seemed to notice anything different about me. I am wondering when I should tell him about the coming addition to the family and what I should tell him.

How to tell him? In as unembarrassed and straightforward and matter-of-fact a way as you can manage.

What to tell him? Well, you know the facts. His own questions, once you have brought up the subject, will give you clues as to just what kind of information he is ready for. Some Four-year-olds are ready to believe that the baby grows inside their mother, but others cling to their earlier notion that it is purchased. Tell Kenneth the truth, but don't belabor the issue, and if he doesn't want to believe, don't insist.

When to tell him? You have done well, especially since he hasn't asked any questions, to delay telling him as long as you have. Four-year-olds have a quite different time sense from our own, and when a mother gives this information at the very beginning of her pregnancy, any preschooler grows very tired of waiting for the blessed event.

Any one of the many good books now on the market can help Kenny understand what it is you are talking about. If it's not too frank for you, we strongly recommend *Where Did I Come From?*, by Peter Mayle. If you want something more conservative, try *The Baby House*, by Norma Simon, *Before You Were a Baby*, by Paul and Kay Showers, or *Making Babies*, by Sara Bonnett Stein.

FOUR-YEAR-OLD MASTURBATES

Dear Doctors:

Our little boy, who is just Four years old, has been masturbating since the age of seven months. His only sibling is an Eleven-year-old sister with whom relations are exceptionally good. But otherwise he is a lonesome little fellow. We live in a third-floor apartment, with the people under us objecting to noise. And I can't allow him to play in the street with other children, who are invariably unattended.

Ours is a reasonably happy and well-adjusted home, and both our children are loved and wanted. The masturbating has increased lately, and there doesn't seem to be anything we can do to restrain him. We tried additional expressions of love, we tried to divert his attention, and we tried spanking and even a "serious talk." Nothing helps because, as he insists tearfully, "I have to do it so I'll feel better." We would greatly appreciate advice.

When a child masturbates during the first year of life, the course of this behavior may be a fairly long one.

You have tried all sorts of diverting techniques, but the problem continues. In general, Four and Six years of age are periods when boys, especially, have increased genital sensations and often do grasp their genitals. Your son's tension sensations may be more marked than they will later on.

In the same way you'd handle thumb sucking, you can at least request that he go into his room to indulge in this behavior and not do it in the presence of other people. Unquestionably, better outlets, such as a good play group, nursery school, or time outdoors with you (going for walks and excursions) would help considerably.

The very fact that he knows what he is doing makes us feel it is not just an automatic release. He sounds like a boy who a little later will really try to stop.

Few if any child specialists know how to stop this behavior, and many think it may be best not to step in at all. Except for the hygienic aspect, many feel that masturbation does not harm children unless they do it excessively. Your son's behavior does seem a little excessive, and hopefully more outside interests will make it unnecessary for him to rely on himself quite so much. So, for the present, try to work up good play interests for your boy, with more attention from both you and his father.

Eventually, if the problem continues into school age and interferes with school adjustment, you may need to take him to a local child guidance clinic for professional help. In the meantime, *must* you continue to live in a third-floor apartment? If there is any way to make your home environment more relaxed it might be of great help to your son.

SEX PLAY

Dear Doctors:

My Four-year-old Jennie and her friend David, who is Five, play together a good deal. About two years ago they began undressing and going to the bathroom outside. David's mother and I tried to stop this by explanations to the youngsters, and by watching them more closely. Last year, more tricks were added to this fascinating game. Again, I spoke to David's mother, and I personally kept them under closer supervision. David delights in a closed door or a secret hiding place. To be honest, Jennie also seems to enjoy this sort of thing.

Last week I returned home to find Jennie and David in her bedroom behind a closed door, again with their pants at half mast. My husband was at home but paid little attention to them as long as they were playing quietly. He feels I'm making too much of this. David's mother, too, seems quite satisfied to leave them to their own devices. Am I right to worry?

Your problem is a common one, and opinions differ. Some child specialists do not think sex play is particularly harmful at the younger ages, and believe that too much suppression and scolding might harm a child more than the actual play itself.

Most mothers don't like it and do prefer to prevent it. (Fathers are more unpredictable. They tend either to get very angry or to be quite indifferent.) So far as we know, adequate supervision is about the only way to prevent it. Talking, scolding, and punishing don't do much good. If the interest is there, and the opportunity presents itself, sex play does take place. If David and Jennie are going to play together, you will just have to supervise very closely.

Sometimes it is hard to supervise directly. But try to have them play in clear and open areas. Avoid closed doors and small, isolated places and bedrooms. Then, if the behavior still continues, the children may have to be separated for a few weeks. This may get the message across.

We're glad you recognize that, enthusiastic as David may be about all this, Jennie is also enthusiastic. Sometimes the greatest harm that comes from neighborhood sex play is that all the mothers of children involved become angry at each other and blame each others' children. It is important for all mothers to appreciate that this kind of play goes on in "good" neighborhoods as well as in "bad"; among "nice" children as well as among "naughty" ones.

Here are a few general comments on the subject:

Circumstances have a lot to do with it. There are some children who might skip it altogether if they never got a chance to play alone without supervision, or were always extremely busy at more productive activity. It is much worse in some children than in others; worse at some ages than at others.

Probably the two main things to do about it are: First, be calm and casual. Give the child the impression that you don't favor (or won't permit) this kind of thing. But avoid being shocked, horrified, or overly upset. The harm you might do a child by your attitude that sex activity is wrong and awful and shameful might do much greater damage than the actual sex play itself.

Second, try to keep your child out of situations that will lead to sex play. Some playmates may seem to arouse this more than others. There may be periods when you will avoid having him or her play with just those children. Or, there will be times when your child, in certain combinations, just can't seem to play unsupervised without getting into such activity.

A rather extreme but workable solution is to get one-piece underwear and also one-piece playsuits except for dress-up. Mere inaccessibility *can* provide an answer.

Who is to *blame* isn't the important thing. The boy next door may start it this year; next year it may be your own child who makes the initiating moves. We don't say that sex play is universal, but it seems to be nearly so. The absence of any sex interest or questions may be more indicative of later difficulties than a too great early interest.

BOY SUDDENLY AFRAID OF DYING

Dear Doctors:

Our Four-and-a-half-year-old son Robby has all of a sudden become terrified at the idea of dying. He had a pet dog die about a year ago, and we thought he had a general notion of the whole thing.

But now, all of a sudden, he is so frightened. My

wife assured him that nobody in this family was going to die. I thought that was wrong because she couldn't guarantee it. So I told him about God and that if he or any of us did die, we would go to be with God, so we would be all right.

Now he seems more frightened than ever because he says he doesn't *want* to go to be with God. What do we do now? His worry seems to be specifically about himself, and that he himself will die.

There are ages when the thought of God *can* bring children comfort in certain situations. The thought of God as a Father who takes care of you can sometimes allay the fears of a Four-year-old. But a child of this age has a lot of trouble with himself about what is real and what is not.

As reality takes a stronger hold, Robby may be able to accept the fact that people die mostly when they are old. But most Four-year-olds have only a very limited notion of what death means. You may be amazed at your son's callousness by the time he is Five. Many Five-year-olds in their discussions of death are like little lawyers, investigating the circumstances of death and the position of the body and just what will happen.

Some at Four, and many at Five, tend to think of death as reversible.

But Four-and-a-half-year-olds tend to be great worriers. Even without the impact of a specific experience, anxieties, and especially anxieties about death, do crop up. Some can be helped to an acceptance of the reality of death by the death of a pet. This didn't seem to help with Robby.

The notion of God does help some Four-year-olds, but Robby would probably have been helped more by the notion that God—if you wish to bring in this concept—is protecting him and looking out for him here on earth so that he won't die, rather than that if he went to Heaven he would be with God. Perhaps you can backtrack a little.

What Robby wants right now is a strong assurance that

he himself and, if possible, all members of his immediate family are going to be all right. Even though life is at best uncertain, we do think you would be reasonably safe to give him the assurance he seeks. However, word it a little loosely, so that you can get out of it if disaster should strike somebody near or dear.

HOW DO YOU TELL A FOUR-YEAR-OLD ABOUT DIVORCE?

Dear Doctors:

I am very much concerned about something that is happening in our family and don't know how to handle it. My husband and I are getting a divorce, and so far we haven't broken this news to our Four-year-old son Jimmy. How can I tell him? How will he take it? Do you think the effects of divorce are always disastrous to a young child?

My husband and I have known for some time that our marriage was not working out. At first we hoped we could manage to stay together for Jimmy's sake. Now we know that isn't possible. Help!

We think you are right *not* to stay together "for the sake of your son." Child specialists have long felt that it is the emotional divorce that precedes the legal divorce that harms most.

Jimmy, obviously, will not welcome this news. Even a young child generally would prefer that his family, even though an unhappy one, remain intact. However, a very young child often recovers from divorce, and adapts to a new way of living, more easily than an older one.

Jimmy will be most influenced, perhaps, by the way you and your husband conduct yourselves. If both of you remain calm, and at least superficially friendly, and you yourself don't act as if the end of the world had come, chances are that Jimmy, like thousands of other children of divorce, will survive emotionally.

So, make every effort to convey to your son that what

is happening is not dreadful. Assure him that his father is not leaving because of anything that he, Jimmy, has done or has not done. Assure him that his father will still be his father and that his father still loves him. Tell him specifically that he will continue to see his father.

Do your very best to refrain from saying hostile or ugly things about your husband. Try to give the explanation of why he is leaving in as calm and matter-of-fact a way as you can, explaining that when people marry they hope it will last forever but that sometimes it just doesn't work out that way. This does not mean that either person is bad, or that either does not love the child.

Be sure to emphasize to Jimmy that though his father will no longer be your husband he still will be Jimmy's father and will not be lost to him.

And, from a practical point of view, because even a Four-year-old does have practical questions, tell him what is going to happen to him. Thus, tell him, if this is the case, that he will go right on living in his own house and that he will have a chance to visit with his father on weekends. Parents need to determine the most desirable frequency of visits. Often, once every three or four weeks works out better than the more customary every weekend.

Be aware, too, that with the very young boy or girl you may need to give the same information more than once.

SHOULD YOU TREAT TWINS ALIKE?

Dear Doctors:

My husband and I have Four-year-old girl twins, Jane and Samantha. They are darling little girls, and we have had a reasonably easy time of it so far. Our problem now concerns school this fall. The twins are very close to each other and, though we certainly haven't pushed it, like to do things together. Some of our friends say they should be separated when they go to school. We're afraid that would be extremely upsetting to them both. Should we, or shouldn't we, urge the school to keep them together in kindergarten? And, can you recommend a good book on twinning?

People nowadays seem to feel rather strongly that twins should not be dressed alike, named alike, or kept always together. Most seem to feel that each twin should be treated as much like an individual as possible, even though it is a temptation to make a lot of their twinship.

Thus, it is generally felt that it's best to separate them in school. Then if they want to stick closely together in out-of-school hours, that's up to them. Kindergarten can be an exception. If your girls are the kind who find it hard to accept and adapt to new experiences, you may feel that school in itself will be enough of a problem without facing them with the problem of separating from each other.

If in your judgment they can make it, it would probably be desirable to start them in separate classrooms. If not, you might prefer to have them together in kindergarten and then start the separation with first grade. However, it can make a difference whether twins are identical or fraternal. We tend to allow identical twins to stay together until they are ready to separate. This may not be until third or fourth grade or even considerably later. But the sooner you separate fraternal twins, possibly the better.

The best, in fact just about the only book that talks about twins much past infancy, is Herbert Collier's *The Psychology of Twins: A Practical Handbook.* We think you'll find it helpful.

WILL BOY BE BORED IN KINDERGARTEN IF HE GOES TO NURSERY SCHOOL FIRST?

Dear Doctors:

I would like to send my oldest son, now Four, to nursery school. But people tell me that if he goes to nursery school now, he will be bored next year in kindergarten, and even more bored in first grade because by then he will be tired of school. Do you think this is true? And can you explain to me, clearly, the differences between kindergarten and nursery school?

Kindergarten and nursery school are not different by some arbitrary ruling. To some extent even the same materials might be used in the two situations.

Rather, they are different because of the different ages and abilities of the children enrolled, which make necessary quite different curriculums. In fact, the daily schedule and type of experience are actually quite different within the nursery school itself for the different age groups.

Thus, all groups might well play with drawing and painting materials, clay, and blocks, but Two-, Three-, Four-, and Five-year-old groups each play with these materials in an entirely different way. The skilled teacher not only recognizes the different needs of children using the same materials but would be prompted to change or modify materials when this is necessary.

The most important aspects of a school are the teacher and the children. Almost any appropriate materials, with skilled guidance, can enable the child to experience the satisfactions of his age level, and can stimulate him to growth toward the age he is to become. In addition, one important aspect of either nursery school or kindergarten is the satisfaction of being with children of one's own age.

As to the danger of being bored, it would be most unlikely for a rich nursery school experience to cause a child to be bored in a following year with a kindergarten experience that would in many ways be entirely different—different not only because the situation is set up differently, but mostly because the child himself is different. In any event, being bored in school seldom occurs because a child is too smart for his grade or because he has had too much earlier school experience. It usually occurs because a child is noncreative in using opportunities that are almost always available in a well-conceived school situation.

SHOULD DONALD START KINDERGARTEN BEFORE HE TURNS FIVE?

Dear Doctors:

My problem is my oldest son, Donald, now Four. He will be Five on November 13. The cut-off date in our town is December 31, so Donnie is eligible to enter kindergarten when school starts in September. Parents are allowed to use their judgment about keeping a child out of school.

My husband, having started school too early himself, knows that school life can be miserable if you are not physically and emotionally ready to accept it. Friends and relatives, however, think we are being overconscientious and that a problem exists only in our minds.

Both my husband and I would rather that Donnie start next year, rather than start now, fail, and then have to be held back. Another factor which contributes to our confusion is that his two best friends will be sent to school according to schedule. We fear that he would be heartbroken, at first, if he were left behind.

Donnie seems to us like a very bright boy, but he is small and seems immature. Both my husband and I are thoroughly confused about this whole problem. It seems that the more we read, the more we find conflicting opinions.

True, there are conflicting opinions. Our own is that it is the very unusual November boy who is ready to start kindergarten in the September *before* he has had his fifth birthday. A December cut-off date is, in our eyes, inexcusable unless a young or Four-and-a-half-year-old kindergarten group is provided. The ideal cut-off date is September 1 or earlier.

You say that your husband knows from his own experience what a too-early start can do. He is right that it is better to start late, rather than to start early and then repeat.

True, Donnie may feel sad if his friends start school before he does. But it would be a very poor decision to put him into a situation where he may be unhappy and may do poorly for the next twelve years or more just to keep from hurting his feelings now.

EPILOGUE

Yes, Four is indeed wild and wonderful. We hope you will enjoy this age to its full because Five, if growth follows its usual course, is quite something else again.

Four is exuberant; Five is controlled. Four tests the limits; Five conforms. Four delights in seeing how far he can go; Five wants to do what you, his parents, want him to do.

When your boy or girl is only Four, visions of delinquency may dance before your eyes; when he is Five, you may wonder if he or she isn't perhaps a little *too* good.

The rhythm of growth seems at times almost as lawful as that of the tides. Equilibrium—disequilibrium. Expansion—contraction. If you can add respect for what is going on to your natural love and affection for your own preschooler, you will add immeasurably to *your* enjoyment of these early years as well as to his!

APPENDIXES

Good Toys for Four-Year-Olds

Animals, toy
Balls
Baskets and boxes
Blocks
Boards and sawhorse for seesaw
Boards for balancing and sliding
Board games, simple
Books
Bouncing board
Brushes for painting
Camera (toy)
Cash register (toy)
Chest of drawers, cupboard, doll-size
Clay
Climbing apparatus, as Jungle Gym, Tower Gym, ladders, boxes
Cooking equipment (toy)
Costume box, including pocketbooks, hats, gloves, scarves, jewelry, curtains, shoes
Crayons, large-size
Dishes and cooking utensils
Doctor and nurse kit
Doll bed, carriage, high chair
Dollhouse
Doll clothing with large buttons and buttonholes
Dolls
Doorway gym
Drawing and coloring materials
Easel
Easel paper
Fingerpaints
Fit-together construction toys and Tinkertoys or Lego
Flannel-surfaced boards and pieces of flannel or felt in different shapes and colors
Flashlight
Garden tools, small
Hammer with short handle and heavy head
Hand puppets
Hollow blocks
Housekeeping toys, including broom, vacuum cleaner, dust mop

Jigsaw puzzles
Jump rope
Kegs
Kites
Logs
Magnets
Miniature people or animals
Musical instruments, such as wrist bells, drum, tambourine, castanets, triangle
Nature specimens, such as fish, turtles, salamanders, rabbits, guinea pigs, or plants. (These of course are not really toys.)
Nests of boxes or cans
Packing boxes large and sturdy enough for child to climb on
Paints and easel
Phonograph and records
Pipes for blowing bubbles
Playhouse
Pregummed dots, squares, triangles of colored paper
Punching bag
Ring toss
Rocking horse
Roller skates
Rope and string
Sailboats (toy)
Sand toys, including spoon, sugar scoop, pail, cans, sifter
Sandbox
Sawhorse
Scissors
Scooter
Scrapbook
Screwing toys
Seesaw
Sled
Slide
Small airplanes, automobiles, trucks, boats, trains
Small boards for building, hauling
Stove
Suitcase
Swing, adjustable
Table and chair, child-size
Toy telephone
Train, dump truck, steam shovel large enough for child to ride on
Tricycle
Wagon
Water-play materials
Wheels of all kinds: cars, dump truck, bulldozer, tractors, wheelbarrow
Workbench and vise

Books for Four-Year-Olds

Allard, Harry. *The Tutti-Frutti Case.* Englewood Cliffs, N.J.: Prentice-Hall, 1975.

Benton, Robert. *Don't Ever Wish for a Seven-Foot Bear.* New York: Knopf, 1972.

Berger, Terry. *I Have Feelings.* New York: Behavioral Publications, 1971.

Boden, Alice, *The Field of Buttercups.* New York: Walck, 1974.

Bottner, Barbara. *Fun House.* Englewood Cliffs, N.J.: Prentice-Hall, 1975.

Brenner, Barbara. *Barto Takes the Subway.* New York: Knopf, 1961.

Brinckloe, Julie. *The Spider Web.* New York: Doubleday, 1975.

Brown, Margaret Wise. *The Indoor Noisy Book.* New York: Harper & Row, 1942.

———. *Shhh! Bang!* New York: Harper & Row, 1943.

———. *The Important Book.* New York: Harper & Row, 1949.

———. *Three Little Animals.* New York: Harper & Row, 1965.

Brownstone, Cecily. *All Kinds of Mothers.* New York: McKay, 1969.

Buckley, Helen. *Grandfather and I.* New York: Lothrop, Lee & Shepard, 1959.

———. *My Sister and I.* New York: Lothrop, Lee & Shepard, 1963.

———. *Grandmother and I.* New York: Lothrop, Lee & Shepard, 1965.

Clifton, Lucille. *Everett Anderson's Year*. New York: Holt, Rinehart, and Winston, 1974.
DePaolo, Tomie. *Michael Bird Boy*. Englewood Cliffs, N.J.: Prentice-Hall, 1975.
Duvoisin, Robert. *The Rain Puddle*. New York: Lothrop, Lee & Shepard, 1965.
———. *Jasmine*. New York: Knopf, 1973.
———. *Our Veronica Goes to Petunia Farm*. New York: Knopf/Pantheon, 1973.
———. *The Crocodile in the Tree*. New York: Knopf, 1973.
Emberly, Ed. *Klippity Klop*. Boston: Little, Brown, 1974.
Ernst, Kathryn. *Danny and His Thumb*. Englewood Cliffs, N.J.: Prentice-Hall, 1972.
Ets, Marie Hall. *Gilberto and the Wind*. New York: Viking, 1963.
———. *Just Me*. New York: Viking, 1965.
Fassler, Joan. *My Grandpa Died Today*. New York: Behavioral Publications, 1970.
———. *Don't Worry Dear*. New York: Behavioral Publications, 1971.
French, Viona. *King Tree*. New York: Walck, 1973.
Ga'ag, Wanda. *Millions of Cats*. New York: Coward-McCann, 1928.
Galdone, Paul. *The Frog Prince*. New York: McGraw-Hill, 1975.
Garland, Sarah. *The Joss Bird*. New York: Scribner, 1975.
Geis, Darlene. *Dinny, Big Little Dinosaur*. New York: Wonder Books, 1959.
Grollman, Earl. *Talking about Death*. Boston: Beacon, 1970.
Hample, Stoo. *The Silly Book*. New York: Harper & Row, 1950.
Heide, Florence, and Van Clief, Sylvia. *That's What Friends Are For*. New York: Scholastic Book Services, 1968.
Hoban, Russell. *Bedtime for Frances*. New York: Harper & Row, 1960.
———. *Bread and Jam for Frances*. New York: Harper & Row, 1964.
———, and Selig, Sylvia. *Ten What: A Mystery Counting Book*. New York: Scribner, 1975.
Jewett, Nancy. *Cheer Up Pig*. New York: Harper & Row, 1975.
Johnson, Crockett. *Harold and the Purple Crayon*. New York: Harper & Row, 1955.
Joslin, Sesyle. *What Do You Say, Dear?* New York: Young, Scott, 1958.

Keats, Ezra Jack. *The Snowy Day* (and others in this series). New York: Viking, 1962.

———. *Peter's Chair*. New York: Harper & Row, 1967.

Kent, Jack. *The Egg Book*. New York: Macmillan, 1975.

Kessler, Ethel. *Do Baby Bears Sit on Chairs?* Garden City, N.Y.: Doubleday, 1961.

———. *The Day Daddy Stayed Home*. Garden City, N.Y.: Doubleday, 1971.

———, and Kessler, Leonard. *The Big Red Bus*. Garden City, N.Y.: Doubleday, 1964.

Klein, Leonore. *Silly Sam*. New York: Scholastic Book Services, 1971.

Kraus, Ruth. *The Backward Day*. New York: Harper & Row, 1950.

———. *A Hole Is to Dig*. New York: Harper & Row, 1952.

———. *I Want to Paint My Bathroom Blue*. New York: Harper & Row, 1956.

———. *Somebody Else's Nut Tree*. New York: Harper & Row, 1958.

Kuskin, Karla. *All Sizes of Noises*. New York: Harper & Row, 1962.

———. *Near the Window Tree*. New York: Harper & Row, 1975.

Langstaff, Nancy. *A Tiny Baby for You*. New York: Harcourt, Brace Jovanovich, 1955.

Leaf, Munro. *Ferdinand*. New York: Viking, 1962.

Levine, Joan Goldman. *A Bedtime Story*. New York: Dutton, 1975.

Lionni, Leo. *Swimmy*. New York: Pantheon, 1963.

———. *The Biggest House in the World*. New York: Knopf/Pantheon, 1973.

———. *The Greentail Mouse*. New York: Pantheon, 1973.

———. *In the Rabbit Garden*. New York: Pantheon, 1975.

Lobel, Arnold. *A Zoo for Mister Muster*. New York: Harper & Row, 1962.

McGovern, Ann. *Too Much Noise*. Boston: Houghton Mifflin, 1967.

Mayle, Peter. *Where Did I Come From?* New York: Lyle Stuart, 1973.

Meredith, Judith C. *Now We Are a Family*. Boston: Beacon Press, 1971.

Merriam, Eve. *Boys and Girls: Girls and Boys.* New York: Holt, Rinehart and Winston, 1972.
Milne, A. A. *Now We Are Six.* New York: Dutton, 1961.
———. *When We Were Very Young.* New York: Dutton, 1964.
———. *The Christopher Robin Book of Verse.* New York: Dutton, 1967.
Minarik, Else. *Little Bear.* New York: Harper & Row, 1957.
Moffett, Martha. *A Flower Pot Is Not a Hat.* New York: Dutton, 1972.
Moore, Lilian. *Little Raccoon and the Outside World.* New York: McGraw-Hill, 1965.
Nôdset, Joan L. *Go Away Dog.* New York: Harper & Row, 1963.
———. *Who Took the Farmer's Hat?* New York: Harper & Row, 1963.
Parsons, Ellen. *Rainy Day Together.* New York: Harper, 1971.
Paterson, Diane. *Eat.* New York: Dial, 1975.
Petie, Harriet. *Billions of Bugs.* Englewood Cliffs, N.J.: Prentice-Hall, 1975.
Preston, Edna Mitchell. *The Temper Tantrum Book.* New York: Viking, 1969.
Ray, Wade. *A Train to Spain.* New York: Knopf, 1963.
Rey, H. A. *Curious George* (and others in this series). Boston: Houghton Mifflin, 1941.
Richelson, Geraldine. *What Is a Grownup?* New York: Crown, 1975.
Ringi, Kjell. *The Sun and the Cloud.* New York: Harper & Row, 1971.
Rodgers, Mary. *The Rotten Book.* New York: Harper & Row, 1969.
Schick, Eleanor. *A Surprise in the Forest.* New York: Harper & Row, 1964.
Schlein, Miriam. *Fast Is Not a Ladybug.* New York: William R. Scott, 1953.
———. *Heavy Is a Hippopotamus.* New York: William R. Scott, 1954.
Sendak, Maurice. *Where the Wild Things Are.* New York: Harper & Row, 1963.
Seuss, Dr. *The Cat in the Hat.* New York: Random House, 1957.
———. *Green Eggs and Ham.* New York: Random House, 1960.
———. *The Foot Book.* New York: Random House, 1968.
Showers, Paul. *Your Skin and Mine.* New York: Crowell, 1962.

———, and Sperry, Kay. *Before You Were a Baby* (New York: Crowell, 1968).
Silverstein, Shel. *The Giving Tree.* New York: Harper & Row, 1964.
Simon, Norma. *The Baby House.* New York: Lippincott, 1955.
Slepian, Jan, and Seidler, Ann. *Lester and the Sea Monster* (and others in this series). New York: Follett, 1964.
Stein, Sara Bonnett. *Making Babies.* New York: Walker, 1974.
———. *That New Baby.* New York: Walker, 1974.
Udry, Janice. *A Tree Is Nice.* New York: Harper & Row, 1956.
Ungerer, Tomi. *Crictor.* New York: Harper & Row, 1958.
———. *The Beast of Mr. Racine.* New York: Farrar, Straus & Giroux, 1971.
Watson, Jane, and others. *My Friend the Baby Sitter.* New York: Golden Press, 1971.
White, E. B. *Stuart Little.* New York: Harper & Row, 1945.
Williams, Babar. *Kevin's Grandma.* New York: Dutton, 1975.
Williams, Margery. *The Velveteen Rabbit.* Garden City, N.Y.: Doubleday, n.d.
Withers, Carl. *Painting the Moon.* New York: Dutton, 1970.
Wright, Ethel. *Saturday Walk.* New York: William R. Scott, 1954.
Zemach, Harve and Kathe. *The Princess and the Froggie.* New York: Farrar, Straus & Giroux, 1975.
Zindel, Paul. *I Love My Mother.* New York: Harper & Row, 1975.
Zion, Gene. *Harry the Dirty Dog.* New York: Harper & Row, 1954.
———. *No Roses for Harry.* New York: Harper & Row, 1958.
———. *The Plant Sitter.* New York: Harper & Row, 1959.
Zolotow, Charlotte. *Do You Know What I'll Do?* New York: Harper & Row, 1958.
———. *The Quarreling Book.* New York: Harper & Row, 1963.
———. *The Sky Was Blue.* New York: Harper & Row, 1963.
———. *Someday.* New York: Harper & Row, 1965.
———. *A Father Like That.* New York: Harper & Row, 1971.
———. *Hold My Hand.* New York: Harper & Row, 1973.
———. *William's Doll.* New York: Harper & Row, 1972.
———. *When the Wind Stops.* New York: Harper & Row, 1975.

Books for the Parents of Four-Year-Olds

Ames, Louise Bates. *Parents Ask.* A syndicated daily newspaper column. New Haven, Conn.: Gesell Institute, 1952–.

———. *Child Care and Development.* Philadelphia: Lippincott, 1970.

———, and Chase, Joan Ames. *Don't Push Your Preschooler.* New York: Harper & Row, 1974.

———, and Ilg, Frances L. *Your Two-Year-Old: Terrible or Tender.* New York: Delacorte, 1976.

———. *Your Three-Year-Old: Friend or Foe.* New York: Delacorte, 1976.

Braga, Laurie, and Braga, Joseph. *Learning and Growing: A Guide to Child Development.* Englewood Cliffs, N.J.: Prentice-Hall, 1975.

Brazelton, T. Berry. *Infants and Mothers.* New York: Delacorte, 1969.

———. *Toddlers and Parents.* New York: Delacorte, 1974.

Caplan, Frank, and Caplan, Theresa. *The Power of Play.* New York: Doubleday, 1973.

Cleveland, Anne. *Parents from Zero to Ten.* New York: Simon & Schuster, 1958.

Coffin, Patricia. *1, 2, 3, 4, 5, 6. How to Understand and Enjoy the Years That Count.* New York: Macmillan, 1972.

Colew, Colin. *How to Raise Your Child Without Threats or Violence.* New York: Exposition Press, 1975.

Collier, Herbert. *The Psychology of Twins: A Practical Handbook.* Phoenix, Ariz.: Twins, 4227 N. 32nd St., 1974.

Comer, James P., and Poussaint, Alvin F. *Black Child Care.* New York: Simon & Schuster, 1975.
Crook, William G. *Can Your Child Read? Is He Hyperactive?* Jackson, Tenn.: Pedicenter Press, 1975.
Dodson, Fitzhugh. *How to Parent.* Los Angeles: Nash, 1970.
———. *How to Father.* Los Angeles: Nash, 1974.
Feingold, Ben J. *Why Your Child Is Hyperactive.* New York: Random House, 1975.
Forer, Lucille K. *Birth Order and Life Roles.* Springfield, Ill.: C. C. Thomas, 1969.
Gardner, Richard A. *Understanding Children.* New York: Aronson, 1973.
Gesell, Arnold, et al. *The First Five Years of Life.* New York: Harper & Row, 1940.
Gesell, Arnold; Ilg, Frances L.; and Ames, Louise B. *Infant and Child in the Culture of Today.* New York: Harper & Row, rev. ed., 1974.
Grollman, Earl A. (Ed.) *Explaining Death to Children.* Boston: Beacon, 1967.
———. *Explaining Divorce to Children.* Boston: Beacon, 1969.
Harrison-Ross, Phyllis, and Wyden, Barbara. *The Black Child: A Parent's Guide.* New York: Peter Wyden, 1973.
Hartley, Ruth E., and Goldensen, Robert M. *The Complete Book of Children's Play.* New York: Crowell, 1970.
Holt, L. Emmett, Jr. *Good Housekeeping Book of Baby and Child Care.* New York: Appleton-Century-Crofts, 1957.
Ilg, Frances L., and Ames, Louise B. *Child Behavior.* New York: Harper & Row, 1957.
Ilg, Frances L.; Ames, Louise B.; Goodenough, Evelyn; and Andresen, Irene. *The Gesell Institute Party Book.* New York: Harper & Row, 1959.
Johnson, June. *Home Play for the Preschool Child.* New York: Harper & Row, 1957.
Kraskin, Robert A. *You* Can *Improve Your Vision.* New York: Doubleday, 1968.
LeShan, Eda. *How to Survive Parenthood.* New York: Random House, 1965.
Levinson, Boris M. *Pets and Human Development.* Springfield, Ill.: C. C. Thomas, 1972.
Liepmann, Lise. *Your Child's Sensory World.* New York: Dial, 1973.

McIntire, Roger W. *For Love of Children.* Del Mar, Calif.: CRM Books, 1970.
Maynard, Fredelle. *Guiding Your Child to a More Creative Life.* New York: Doubleday, 1973. (Contains excellent lists of books for parents on arts and crafts, drawing, painting, crayoning, clay, modeling, ceramics, fabrics and yarns, puppets, also children's records.)
Pitcher, Evelyn G., and Ames, Louise B. *The Guidance Nursery School.* New York: Harper & Row, rev. ed., 1975.
Sheldon, William H. *Varieties of Temperament.* New York: Hafner, 1970.
Slepian, Jan, and Seidler, Ann. *Mr. Sipple and the Naughty Princess, Magic Arthur and the Giant* (and others in this series). Chicago: Follett, 1964.
Smith, Lendon. *Improving Your Child's Behavior Chemistry.* Englewood Cliffs, N.J.: Prentice-Hall, 1976.
Toman, Walter. *Family Constellation: Its Effect on Personality and Social Behavior.* New York: Springer, 1969.
Wender, Paul H. *The Hyperactive Child: A Guide for Parents.* New York: Crown, 1973.
Wunderlich, Ray. *Allergy, Brains and Children Coping.* St. Petersburg, Fla.: Johnny Reads Press, 1973.
Young, Milton A. *Buttons Are to Push.* New York: Pitman, 1970.

NOTES

1. Information on visual behavior was furnished by Richard J. Apell, O.D., director of the Vision Department of the Gesell Institute of Child Development.
2. In order to make use of a controlled situation, our observations were made during the course of the Gesell Preschool Examination, as described in *The First Five Years of Life,* by Arnold Gesell et al. (New York: Harper & Row, 1940). This examination was given individually to boys and girls of each of the preschool ages.
3. Laurie Braga and Joseph Braga, *Learning and Growing: A Guide to Child Development* (Englewood Cliffs, N.J.: Prentice-Hall, 1975).
4. Among the physicians who have written helpful and informative books on the damaging effects that can come from a harmful diet are Drs. William Crook, Ben J. Feingold, Lendon Smith and Ray Wunderlich, whose books are listed on pages 144 to 146.
5. For a description of these tests see Frances L. Ilg and Louise B. Ames, *School Readiness* (New York: Harper & Row, 1965); and for a discussion of what they mean to the parent, see Louise B. Ames, *Is Your Child in the Wrong Grade*? (New York: Harper & Row, 1967).
6. Arnold Gesell, "Stability of Mental-Growth Careers," *Thirty-ninth Yearbook of the National Society for the Study of Education,* part 2 (Bloomington, Ind.: Public School Publishing Co., 1940).

INDEX

Photo Credits

CLARK BROADBENT, *pages* 11, 15, 16, 20, 26, 39, 43, 52, 68, 95, 99

MAURY ENGLANDER, *pages* 5, 45, 79, 82, 88

MARTIN IGER, *pages* 19, 40, 51, 71, 85

EARL SCOTT, *pages* 6, 87

Photos from "Playmates-Schoolmates," preschool children's television series, with permission by Group W (Westinghouse Broadcasting Company), *pages* 23, 55, 56

B-2

649.123 B2
A513
AMES, L
YOUR FOUR-YEAR-OLD

JAN 24 '77

RODMAN PUBLIC LIBRARY
215 East Broadway
Alliance, OH 44601